Carnival for the Dead

David Hewson

W F HOWES LTD

This large print edition published in 2012 by
W F Howes Ltd
Unit 4, Rearsby Business Park, Gaddesby Lane,
Rearsby, Leicester LE7 4YH

1 3 5 7 9 10 8 6 4 2

First published in the United Kingdom in 2012
by Macmillan

A CIP catalogue record for this book is available
from the British Library

ISBN 978 1 40749 545 3

Typeset by Palimpsest Book Production Limited,
Falkirk, Stirlingshire

Printed and bound in Great Britain
by TJ International Ltd, Padstow, Cornwall

A city of marble, did I say? Nay, rather a golden city . . . a wonderful piece of world. Rather, itself a world.

Modern Painters, John Ruskin

Millions of spiritual Creatures walk the Earth Unseen, both when we wake, and when we sleep.

Paradise Lost, Book IV, John Milton

A VENETIAN GLOSSARY

Bauta – a full-faced carnival mask with a square jaw tilted upwards.

Baccalà – a popular cicchetti dish made from salt cod.

Calle – a street or alley.

Campanile – a bell tower.

Campiello – a small square.

Campo – a large open space, normally at the centre of a Venetian parish.

Cicchetti – Venetian snacks served with drinks, similar to Spanish tapas.

Colombina – a female carnival mask based upon a comic servant from the Commedia dell'Arte.

Fermata – the 'stop' for a vaporetto (or bus elsewhere).

Fondamenta – a waterside street or quay.

Forcola – the complex wooden rowlock on a gondola which holds the gondolier's oar.

Frittelle – sweets, like doughnuts, made specifically for the carnival.

Larva (Volto) – a ghostlike white carnival mask

normally worn with a black costume and black tricorn, similar to the bauta.

Medico della Peste (The Plague Doctor) – one of the most striking carnival costumes, based on the uniform recommended by the sixteenth-century French physician Charles de Lorme for 'safely' treating plague victims.

Moretta – an oval mask for women, originally used when visiting convents.

Ombra – a small glass of wine.

Pasticceria – a pastry shop.

Piscina – an open space or street that was once water.

Quatrefoil – a common architectural feature based around four petals or leaves arranged in a symmetrical pattern.

Remo – the gondolier's oar.

Rio – a small canal.

Rio terà – a former canal that has been filled in to form a street.

Riva – a street along a canalside quay.

Salizada – an ancient name for a paved street (though not all paved streets are called a salizada).

Sarde en saor – a Venetian speciality of pickled fish, a common cicchetti dish.

Scuola – literally 'school' but in Venice from the thirteenth century on the meeting place for a religious and charitable confraternity. The scuole were divided between the grandi (great) institutions and the piccole (smaller), less important bodies. The Accademia and the entrance to the civil hospital of Giovanni e Paolo are both former scuole grandi.

Sestiere – a city district. Venice is divided into six, as the name suggests: Cannaregio, Castello, San Marco, Dorsoduro, Santa Croce and San Polo.

Sotoportego – a public passageway running beneath a building.

Spritz – a popular drink in Venice, usually made of a bitter such as Campari or Aperol with prosecco, sparkling water, a slice of lemon and an olive.

Zattere – the southern shore of Dorsoduro, so called because it was once the place where zattere (rafts) were moored.

DORSODURO

The man on the Zattere vaporetto jetty wore a grotesque white mask, a black flowing cloak and a broad-brimmed hat with a silver clasp. A shiny silk ruff stood in a stiff circle from his throat around the edge of his broad shoulders. At the front a long ivory beak extended to his chest, like that of a monstrous giant bird, curving downwards with a cruel sneer. In place of the creature's eyes were spectacles covered in deep blue crystals, opaque and sinister. He was tall and seemed strong and familiar with the process of helping travellers clamber onto the shore in difficult conditions.

'Come, come,' he called as the narrow vaporetto bobbed awkwardly on the heavy swell of the Giudecca canal.

It was the first week of February and carnival had begun, in the coldest, brightest weather Teresa Lupo had ever known in Venice. Conditions that seemed appropriate for this strange and unexpected visit.

'Mother,' she said, placing her frozen fingers on the brown fox-fur coat of the woman next to her.

'I'm not an invalid,' Chiara Bianchi declared, tugging at her small wheeled suitcase. 'I can manage.'

Then she grasped the hand of the masked man and took one step forward, placing a firm, stiletto-heeled foot on the slippery planks.

Teresa watched as he guided her to an area where the ice and remnants of compressed snow had been swept clear. After that she swung her own battered rucksack over her shoulder, trying to peer into the mask, to see behind the eyes. It was impossible.

'Very good,' he said, taking her hand with a firm, determined grip. 'Now . . .'

She found herself half-pulled out of the boat then firmly planted on the secure part of the jetty.

'What are you?' she asked and then remembered to thank him. '*Il Medico della Peste*,' her mother interrupted in a sharp, cutting tone, as if only a fool would have been ignorant of this fact.

'Exactly. The Plague Doctor,' the man said, bowing, doffing his broad black hat and sweeping it before them.

The pale, majestic shape of Redentore, the basilica across the water, caught her eye, its form reflected in the glittering ripples of the canal. A spear of winter sunlight shot across the waves, from Giudecca to Dorsoduro, like a pattern along the scaly side of some gigantic fish.

'Long time since there was plague in Venice,' Teresa muttered.

He popped the hat back on his head, tapped his long beaked nose and said, 'See what a good and careful job I do. *Buona giornata* . . .'

They watched the vaporetto bob sideways into the choppy expanse of lagoon then head out into the lively waters.

'Why did she have to come here?' Chiara moaned. 'It's cold and damp and miserable. What's wrong with Rome?'

Teresa took her mother's arm, envying with more than a little guilt the warmth of the thick fur. She could remember stroking this same coat as a curious child. The vast, enveloping garment was so old it must have been in and out of fashion four or five times over the decades.

Warily, taking care for both of them, Teresa led her onto the broad, icy cobblestones of the Zattere promenade. The wheels of the little suitcase squealed in protest at the cold. The air was sharp and salty, so bitter and dry it made Teresa's head ache. The day seemed to have emerged from the imagination of that English painter Turner, the one she'd adored since the moment she'd seen his tantalizing panoramas of *calli* and *campi* and *canali*. Above them the sky ran everywhere, a glassy blue coverlet over the lagoon, an artist's colour, reticent yet firm in its subtlety, imaginative and challenging. Beyond the line of the island opposite the sun hung low and sullen over the Adriatic. Even without the curious appearance of the *Medico della Peste*, Teresa Lupo felt as she always did in Venice: a stranger who had stumbled into a continuous and impenetrable drama, one that had begun centuries before and seemed fated never to reach its conclusion.

'Sofia's what . . . forty-six years old,' she pointed out as they struggled across the slippery stonework. 'Only ten years older than me. She can go wherever she wants.'

'A child!' The look was familiar and caustic. Chiara was never one to let what she saw as an error pass without mention. 'More than you ever were.'

'Sorry,' Teresa said quietly, trying to concentrate on staying upright.

According to the map the apartment was several hundred metres to the east, beyond the Ponte agli Incurabili, presumably an area once given over to a hospice. She'd visited the city many times but had never strayed much into this area behind the great basilica of Salute, close to the point where the tip of Dorsoduro narrowed until it formed the Punta della Dogana, the needle-like platform that protruded into the Basin of St Mark. As they strayed further from the busy vaporetto stop the condition of the terrace worsened. It was just past midday and there was scarcely a soul to be seen. This seemed hard to countenance. The station had been teeming with people arriving for the carnival, some in costume already. Yet not a soul had found this quiet, open stretch of promenade alongside the Giudecca canal, and so the massive paving stones became ever more treacherous with glassy ice. The papers said the weather had not risen above freezing in days, and would stay bitterly cold for a week or more. More snow was threatened. Winter had dug its teeth deep into Venice and seemed determined never to make way for spring.

Struggling with the heavy bag over her shoulder Teresa navigated them into the centre of the pavement and tried to stay upright, amused that her mother, in old-fashioned stilettos and with the suitcase to steady her, seemed to find this somewhat easier.

'You always wear flat heels,' Chiara Bianchi chided her, reading the expression in Teresa's face the way a parent always did. 'Why? Sofia *never* does.'

'We're different people,' she said simply, still focusing on the ice. 'Sofia has a mind of her own.'

'Half a mind. A weak one. Gallivanting over the globe . . .'

Growing up, Teresa was secretly jealous of her aunt. Sofia was beautiful in a way that she, as a plain, awkward and tongue-tied child, could never hope to emulate. Tall and elegant, curly and wayward hair dyed blonde, forever smiling, always ready with a witty, amusing and, the older Teresa soon appreciated, coquettish remark. The kind of woman that men liked, yet a good aunt, one who never forgot her niece. To the young, confused and occasionally deeply miserable Teresa she had been a confidante, a friend, a not-so-secret ally in the battle a difficult child turning into a yet more difficult teenager wished to wage against the world.

'I envied her,' she murmured, knowing this would infuriate her mother, but aware that it had to be said.

'What? Twice married, once widowed, once divorced. Traipsing through New York and London and God knows where else like some gypsy? Forever falling in love, out of love. Impoverished, with no career . . .'

Sofia wanted to paint. And write. She craved freedom, a different challenge with every new day. She was everything a plain young studious girl ached to be. But as she watched her aunt embrace horizons that stood further away from Rome with each passing year, Teresa had come to understand that she lacked both the talent and the courage. Teenage rebellion gave way to learning, duty and, as much to her surprise as that of her mother, a calling. First medicine then a career as a pathologist with the Roman police. A decade and a half disappeared so quickly she never saw it go. As Sofia stumbled from man to man, city to city, never quite selling a painting, never getting round to finishing the book she'd been promising the world since she was nineteen, her niece emerged from the awkward chrysalis of childhood and metamorphosed into a respectable, reliable civil servant, a woman of duty, happily tied to a loving relationship with an older police officer she adored.

There were no regrets really, nor after all these years any envy. Men and women were what they were. What remained were the memories and these she still held dear: Sofia's headstrong emotions and unstoppable enthusiasms, her love for those around her, and the energy she brought to every incomplete task that occupied her until another came along to take its place, and was duly embraced with such overwhelming passion that the memory of its predecessor was erased in an instant.

In time Teresa had come to feel as her mother did, responsible. That made the present situation worse. They had, perhaps, failed Sofia, in ways they could not yet understand.

It took ten minutes to stumble and skate their way along the ice. Across the water Palladio's Redentore church stood serene and timeless on the island of Giudecca.

Redentore. The Redeemer. As a student Teresa had come to Venice for the feast of the same name in July, a celebration of the end of the sixteenth-century plague that had taken the lives of thousands, among them the painter the English called Titian and the Italians Tiziano. The basilica was a companion, a sister almost, for the other great church of Salute, which stood no more than a few hundred metres from where they now laboured on the unsure cobblestones of the Zattere promenade.

She could still picture the fireworks over St Mark's Basin and the illuminated boats upon which the Doge himself had once walked across the lagoon, to give homage to God in the church Palladio had built as a plea for the return of health and sanity to the city.

As a Roman, Teresa Lupo was familiar with the idea that one never quite escaped the past. The insidious hold the dead maintained on the living was, however, different in Venice. In her native city history stood out boldly in the midst of the modern world, proud of its heritage, always keen to tap the shoulder of any passing stranger and whisper, 'Listen to me.'

In Venice the past was more reticent. Beyond the tourist sights, San Marco and the Rialto, it lurked in the shadows, seeping out of the cracked stones like blood from ancient wounds, as if death itself was one more sly performance captured beneath the bright, allseeing light of the lagoon.

A sudden chilly breeze caught around them and its arid freezing power stole away her breath. She remembered the painter Turner again. There was no real horizon to this place, nothing to define their position here but the sky and the sea. Venice was a world of its own, aloof, separate, impenetrable.

One that cared little for anything but itself. For where else was so beautiful, so unique?

Teresa Lupo checked the address. They were almost at what was once the salt warehouse at the point of Dorsoduro, by the last few houses before the open space at the tip. There was a green iron gate with bells and nameplates. Beyond lay a narrow footpath leading to a ramshackle building that seemed to lean a little drunkenly a good forty metres back from the pavement.

To their right a large wooden platform extended out over the lagoon pointing directly at Palladio's masterpiece on the island opposite.

'Look!' she said, turning on her mother. 'We could have taken a water taxi from the station and saved ourselves all that trouble!'

A sour, knowing look spread over Chiara's features.

'I've better things to do than haggle with Venetian thieves,' her mother responded. 'Everyone in this city wishes to steal from the Romans. Well, not this one, thank you.'

'Oh, Mother,' Teresa grumbled, and opened the gate with the key Sofia had sent her the week before.

The ice had been cleared from the meandering path. They passed two bare orange trees in a little patch of grass covered with pristine snow.

As they reached the front door the paving stones beneath them began to shake. Teresa Lupo stood there, wondering. An earthquake in Venice was

9

impossible. Yet the ground trembled so much that her mother took her arm for safety.

They both looked back at the way they came. A vast and impossibly tall cruise ship was moving steadily along the Giudecca canal, a vessel so high and long it seemed a city in itself, blocking out the island opposite entirely, sending its power shuddering through the grey lagoon waters into the mud and timber and stone that formed the uncertain bedrock of Dorsoduro, as it did for the rest of Venice. They could see tourists swarming at the windows of the upper deck, so small they seemed like insects.

'How could she come here?' Chiara asked, and there were tears in her eyes.

This was rare. Almost unknown.

Sofia's block was squeezed between two taller, newer and smarter buildings that reclined against it like thugs picking on a skinny pauper. The nameplates indicated the place had four storeys. There was no lift, only a stone staircase winding round an open space that rose vertiginously to a sunny skylight at the summit of the building. The place seemed so narrow there was room for just a single apartment on each floor. A red door at ground level, a livid purple on the first. Then green again on the penultimate floor, Sofia's. The paint there was cracked and old. A small, simple watercolour of the view from the front gate, across the canal to Redentore, was attached to the wood with drawing pins. Sofia's work, it had to be. Bright with colour, naive, childlike.

Teresa was pleased to see that her mother took the steps quickly, almost eagerly, not pausing for breath despite her sixty years.

Together they stood and stared at the painting. Next to it was a smaller picture, an upright depiction of Capricorn, the sea goat. Sofia's birth sign. She seemed to have something personal like this on the door of every apartment she'd ever rented.

Neither knew what to expect inside. All they had was the mysterious envelope Teresa had received in Rome with the keys and a short note that read, 'I'm sorry to be a pest, but I seem to have a few problems in my new home in Venice. If by any chance I fail to answer my mobile in the days to come . . .' And at this point she passed on a mobile number which was completely new to them. '. . . please look after my place if you can. It's very sweet and not quite finished and I'm sure I won't be gone long. Your ever-loving friend who happens to be your aunt, Sofia.'

Teresa had called the number and got no answer, not even voicemail. Then she drove round to her parents' retirement home in Frascati, in the Alban hills south-east of Rome, and showed it to them. Her father had shrugged and said simply, 'Sofia.' After that he walked down the hill to his part-time job in one of the local wine makers. Her mother, clearly offended that the letter had gone to Teresa, not her, tried the number with no success. Given Sofia's penchant to move cities, countries even, at whim, Chiara seemed unusually concerned.

They took turns calling in the intervening days. Teresa skipped work on a rather clumsy pretext, trying to track down Sofia while keeping the peace in Frascati. The previous evening she contacted the Venice Questura. The duty officer was curt and unhelpful. He knew nothing about a woman called Sofia Bianchi and had not the slightest intention of checking the apartment to see if anything was amiss. Sofia's name had yet to be entered into whatever system the Questura possessed. At the end of this terse conversation Teresa called her deputy in Rome and told him she had pressing personal business to deal with which meant she had to extend her absence by a day or two. Ignoring his protests she then bought a ticket for the first fast train from Rome to Venice. To her surprise, and perhaps disappointment, her mother had decided to join her. There was, Teresa tried to convince herself, no need for alarm. Sofia was a grown woman, one with bohemian ways. This was not the first time she had taken herself off at short notice. Usually the spur turned out to be a man, one who didn't stick around for long.

It was not a good time to take leave from her job as head of the forensic department with the state police in the *centro storicor*. February was a busy spell for much-hated paperwork: reviews, reports, not real work at all in her opinion. They would have to wait. Nor were there family ties. Her partner and colleague Gianni Peroni was in Sicily with his boss, the inspector Leo Falcone, and his *sovrintendente* Nic Costa, seemingly chasing mobsters on an assignment they couldn't talk about with anyone, even her.

All that stood between her and the Venetian lagoon at that moment was a flood of pointless documents and tedious meetings to do with ephemeral issues such as strategies and budgets. They would be furious with her for abandoning them. They could live with it.

'Well,' Chiara said, prodding the door with a gloved finger. 'Open it. Let's see.'

Her mother, normally indomitable to the point of insensitivity, seemed strangely nervous.

'Is there something you've never told me?' Teresa asked, taking out the keys.

'Millions of things,' her mother replied mournfully. 'We're a family. Confessions are for priests.'

Teresa sighed and fumbled with the lock.

'I meant about Sofia,' she said. 'You didn't need to come. You make me nervous. We both know she's probably gone off skiing with a man.'

Chiara blinked. There were tears beginning to form in her eyes.

'Open the door, will you? Let's get this over with.'

Her voice seemed to be breaking.

It was a heavy, old-fashioned lock that required

several turns. After four attempts, Teresa managed to prise the thing open though the door was still sufficiently stiff to require a hefty push from her shoulder before it would move.

The green cracked paint shifted under her weight half a step then stopped again. Something heavy and solid behind stood in the way.

Teresa Lupo's profession revolved around death. Suicides and worse. So many over the years. It was understandable, given her mother's strangely depressed mood, that those memories should wish to flood her head, even if there was no rational reason for them, no cause to believe anything was truly wrong.

'Wait a moment,' she told her mother, who was now shivering beneath her ancient fur coat.

Teresa pushed harder until the object on the other side moved again, resisting still, unseen, silent.

A damp and musty smell emerged from behind the door. Her brief glimpse of the room beyond showed that it was dark. The bright, naked bulb in the hall did little to illuminate what lay there.

She was not a small woman, though a little slimmer than she had been before Peroni came into her life. One more heave and there was the sound of something shifting behind the door. The wood moved swiftly, falling back as whatever blocked it was forced out of the way.

She couldn't stop herself tumbling forward,

half-falling into the apartment, shoving the door wide open so that what lay beyond tipped over sideways and became visible in the light from the stairwell.

Her mother was screaming, a high, sharp howl, one that Teresa Lupo had never heard before. It hadn't occurred to her to associate fear with either of her parents. They seemed above such emotions. Stoic, resolute, never brave, because that would have required a conscious attitude on their part, not a simple acceptance of fate, of the passing of time, of age and all that it brought.

One brisk step forward prevented Teresa's fall. Fumbling anxiously at the wall she found an old-fashioned light switch, circular Bakelite, a simple up-and-down, on-off device with a lever that fell easily beneath her fingers.

What looked like a large and dusty Murano chandelier came slowly to life ahead of them. Her mother cast a frightened glance at the shape on the floor and screamed again, kept screaming until Teresa turned, took her bulky form in her arms, gripped the warm fox-fur coat, kissed her once on the cheek and held her, saying nothing, simply guiding her, letting her see, begin to comprehend enough for the terror to abate.

'It's not Sofia,' she said quietly, taking them further into the room. 'It's not anyone.'

Chiara removed her hand from her face and looked first at the figure on the threadbare Persian carpet, then at the gloomy interior in front of them.

Fear turned to outrage. She stormed across to the windows and threw open the heavy velour curtains.

The radiant light of the lagoon day streamed through the glass. The apartment was a mess, a jumble of paper and clothes and belongings scattered around the floor, the sideboard, over the rickety furniture, the misshapen cushions of a well-worn sofa. On a large shiny dining table, next to a dusty glass vase containing plastic flowers, stood a battered old laptop and next to it a copy of *Il Gazzettino*, the Venice daily. Teresa walked over and picked up the paper. It was six days old and looked as if it had never been read. Clothes, paper, paintings and magazines were strewn everywhere. A pack of tarot cards and a crystal ball – fortune-telling was another of Sofia's idiosyncratic pastimes – stood in a little pile to one side near the computer. A small hand-operated sewing machine stood on the sideboard next to a crystal carafe and some unfashionable goblet glasses. By the window a cabinet full of old pottery teetered against the wall: cups and plates, too fragile, too ancient to be used. On the top was a large case containing a stuffed golden pheasant, trapped in a pose of outraged fear amidst dry, brittle grass with a badly painted view of the lagoon behind. The place reminded her of a wayward child's bedroom, one that hadn't been disturbed in fifty years.

It was much too warm.

'Sofia!' Chiara declared, as if she were scolding her younger sister directly. Then, more quietly, 'This is her.' And after a moment, 'This *was* her.'

'Oh please,' Teresa said softly. 'Stop being so . . . so very . . .'

What? Her mother knew something, something she had concealed.

Teresa went back and looked at the object that had been blocking the door then set it upright. The thing was a tailor's mannequin clothed in an elegant costume, unfinished, judging by the needles and thread that lay over the fabric. Stitch-work and embroidery? Were these two more of Sofia's diverse and unfocused talents? She couldn't recall. Over the dummy's shoulders hung a long gown of sky-blue silk, a shade that seemed old, primitive even. The dress was ankle-length, she guessed, though the hem had yet to be fixed by stitching. Rich gold brocade patterned the slashed halter neck and the waist. A generous scarlet cloak, again in silk, was cast around its shoulders, loosely pinned. A slender circlet crown of gold and pearls was attached to the head with tape. The costume looked as if it belonged on the stage or in some historical pageant.

Carnival, Teresa thought as she pulled the whole thing upright onto its three curved wooden legs.

She crossed to the corridor that led off from

17

the living area. There was a bathroom that looked as if it hadn't been painted in decades. The ancient tub was cracked and the gas water heater above it grumbled like a tin beast afflicted with indigestion. Two bedrooms followed, one full of junk, the other with a double bed, unmade, with clothes, everyday ones, scattered everywhere. Beyond was a kitchen and the oldest stove she'd ever seen. Packets of tea – oriental and American brands, nothing Italian – stood next to it.

There was an old tin kettle, distinctly worse for wear. She filled it with water and set it to boil. Small, routine activities, mindless but comforting somehow. Then she went to the window. It stood directly over the narrow alley at the front of the building. She could see the Giudecca canal again and, in the clear, bright distance, the coast.

Terraferma to the Venetians. Solid land, not mud and tree trunks dug into the lagoon bed. Another country. Another world.

As she stood there trying to gather her thoughts the vast shape of a second cruise ship hove into view. The floor began to tremble. Cups and plates in the small kitchen cabinet next to the window rattled in concert to the thrumming of the distant vessel's engines.

A small central-heating boiler, relatively modern, was set on the wall. Teresa examined the thermostat and the timer. The former had been set to twenty degrees. The timer was disengaged.

The gas had been running nonstop since the last person touched these controls. For days perhaps. A week even.

'Where in God's name are you?' she muttered then set about making some very strange tea.

She was comfortable throwing awkward questions at strangers. Trying to ask them of her own mother was difficult. *Wrong* somehow. So they tidied away Sofia's mountain of strewn papers and sat on the lumpy, patched armchairs, struggling in vain for the right words. When the fractured, meandering conversation became more than she could bear Teresa got up and sorted through the documents on the table. Bills mainly, unopened. And a diary, a local one with a picture of carnival costumes on the cover, the days in the strange language she recognized as Veneto.

There had been no entry since the turn of the month. January had a few in the early weeks, perhaps engagements with tourists since they all seemed to begin at familiar haunts in the city, the Rialto, the Accademia, the Piazza San Marco.

On the last four days for which there were entries she saw only one single line.

It read: *Il Gobbo*!

Someone called Gobbo? But then why was it *Il* Gobbo? The hunchback or the goblin, a figure from myth, whose hump a child might stroke hoping for good luck. It could mean anything. A person. Some unfathomable reminder that only Sofia might understand.

Since then . . . nothing.

Teresa turned on the laptop. It was so old she could barely remember how to operate the thing. There was no wireless connection, no Internet. Nothing but a word processor as far as she could see, and a folder with ten or so documents.

'She thought she'd write a book one day,' her mother said, as if writing was the province of fools.

'I know.'

Teresa pulled up the dates on the files. The newest was a few weeks old and appeared to be some notes on various tourist destinations. Everything else dated back to the early part of the previous year. Sofia hadn't arrived in Venice, from England it seemed, until the beginning of November. She'd written nothing much of any substance since she came here. Not on this machine anyway.

Her mother got up and peered at a watercolour on an easel near the window.

'She thought she could paint too,' she said.

It was a view of the canal near the Zattere vaporetto stop. A pretty picture, with bright colours and a radiant sun. Sofia must have worked on it from a photograph or her imagination. The light here was so local, so particular. It varied from one hour of the morning to the next. This was not winter.

'Did Sofia live here once before? In Venice, I mean?' Teresa asked.

Her mother closed her eyes for a moment then stared at the picture again.

'She used to sell these things when she needed money. In London. In Rome. In Paris when she lived there.'

'I didn't know she lived in Paris.'

'She'd approach anyone.' A bitter pang of self-reproach crossed her face and Teresa felt her own heart begin to ache. 'Any stranger. The idea that trust was to be earned, to be tested, never occurred to her.'

'So she lived in Paris once? In Venice too? And I never knew?'

'You were at university! You looked ready to find a life of your own! At least. After all the trouble . . .'

'This is about Sofia. Not me.'

'You asked why I never told you! Because I was too frightened. You two were so close. If you knew what was going on . . .' Chiara's eyes turned to the glistening waters of the canal beyond the window. 'I saw it all in my own head as clearly as if it was real. You'd give up medicine. You'd run to her.'

'Did she need me then?'

Chiara placed a hand on the painting, traced the outline of the canal with her fingers. It was the kind of work a tourist would buy, Teresa thought. Simple, pretty, lacking in wit and observation. A photograph reduced to paint, just to raise a little

money. Sofia could do better than that if she wanted.

Her mother left the window, came and took both of Teresa's hands quickly, held them, two quick squeezes. Familiarity, as much as it ever happened.

'Sit down,' she said. 'This tea is almost cold. And I quite like it. I never knew where Sofia got her ideas from. Her friends.'

Chiara stared at her daughter and smiled for a moment.

'More of a child to me than you. More of a sister to you than me. That's what your father always said.'

'Not when I was around,' Teresa complained.

'Oh no. Neither of us would dare do *that*.'

It was clear. Whatever it was that Teresa Lupo was about to hear was a burden that had hung heavily on her mother for many years. A constant weight she'd borne, uncomplaining. She would be glad to be rid of it.

Teresa took the cups into the kitchen and made more tea. It tasted of fennel and strange herbs.

Then she came back and sat opposite her mother, amidst the newspapers and the unopened bills, the scraps of paper with pencil sketches on them, the detritus of the missing Sofia Bianchi scattered across the living room of this strange apartment beneath the glassy gaze of the long-dead pheasant.

'A nightmare must end before you try to make

sense of it,' Chiara said. She shrugged. 'Even then that's all you do. *Try*. Forgive me.'

Teresa could still recall that summer, sixteen years before. Her own life hung in the balance too. It was the time of crucial exams at college, the pivotal point on which her future turned, would either allow her entrance into the wide, beckoning world of medicine or damn her with failure to a lost fate she couldn't imagine.

Nothing had mattered during those few hectic months except study, revision and success. She was living in a cheap, run-down student house in San Giovanni, working from eight in the morning till midnight trying to catch up on every scrap of learning she might have missed. Later she would discover that she had won the highest marks of any of her peers, an event that would lead to a riotous night in the Campo dei Fiori, a triumphant laurel wreath around her neck. Until the moment she saw the results on the college noticeboard she had been convinced she would be lucky to scrape through, to avoid the embarrassment of being sent down for a year or ejected from college altogether.

From this distance she could so easily understand why her mother never told her what had happened to Sofia. In her heart she knew she ought to be grateful. Had the news reached her nothing would have stopped Teresa abandoning Rome for Venice immediately, regardless of the consequences and any personal cost.

It was an interminable few months throughout Italy, a time of drought and lethargy. Sofia's first husband, an American banker named Bardin, had died in a car accident near their home in New Jersey four years before. A variety of men, of different addresses around Europe, had followed. By the time Teresa was in touch with her again Sofia was in London, briefly married once more to a British artist who treated her so despicably that she had walked out after a year and returned to Rome to teach in a language school for a while. Then, within twelve months, she was gone again, this time travelling in Asia.

Thinking back Teresa could pinpoint the lacunae in her aunt's life around that time. With the revealing yet ultimately hollow benefit of hindsight they stood out like underexposed blemishes on a photograph, a patch of emptiness in the midst of a life so apparently glittering the darker parts were never cast into relief.

She listened very carefully to what her mother said then asked, 'You seriously believe Sofia tried to kill herself?'

It seemed impossible.

Chiara clasped her own hands tightly, as if seeking reassurance.

'You weren't there. I was. Sitting in that hospital by the water, the one near Fondamenta Nove. Opposite that strange island where they bury people. Listening to the doctors. Sofia barely willing to speak, as pale as a ghost.'

She put a hand to her mouth and shook her head. The tears were there again, more real than ever.

'They didn't think she'd live at first. She didn't want to. The drugs . . .'

'What drugs?'

'I'm not a doctor.'

'Please.'

'Sleeping pills. Barbiturates or something.'

'From where? Was Sofia prescribed them? Was she suffering from insomnia?'

'I don't know!'

Sixteen years. The records would probably be gone by now, not that Teresa had the slightest right to see them.

'Had she ever tried to harm herself before?'

Chiara frowned and said, 'Not that I'm aware. She's spent more of her life outside Rome, outside Italy, than here. How would any of us know?'

We would, Teresa thought to herself. Somehow.

'What did she say? When she wanted to speak?'

'Nothing. Except that she wanted to go back to Rome. She said she had no recollection of what had happened.'

'And?'

'And what? That was it! A lie. A concoction. I could see it in her eyes. She didn't want me to know the truth.'

'Had she been hurt? Physically?'

'No one mentioned such a thing to me.'

It had to be asked. Date rape had become only too common in the Nineties.

'Had she been . . . molested?'

'No! How do I know? Please . . .' This conversation was painful, for both of them, not that her mother seemed much aware of that fact. 'Sofia was living here on her own. She had no money. No future. No idea where she was going. I took her home for two months until she felt better. After that she went to Paris. She seemed to think she'd recovered.'

'Home?' Teresa Lupo tried hard to staunch the anger and disbelief. 'I must have come back around then. Are you telling me she was there?'

A guilty look, a frown.

'She didn't want you to know. She went out when I said you were coming. No one wanted to disturb you. There were still exams. We knew what that might mean.'

'Thank you!'

Chiara Bianchi's eyes roamed around the dilapidated living room, cast an exasperated glance at the mess on the floor and the furniture, the childlike painting on the easel, the half-finished costume on the dummy by the door.

'Sofia did the right thing. She suggested it, before I could. I had to take her back. She was alone. Just as she was when she came back here last year.'

'Except now we don't know where she is,' Teresa said firmly.

'I imagine it's the role of police officers to state the obvious.'

'I'm not a police officer and you're missing my point. Everything seems to indicate Sofia hasn't been in this apartment for six days. If something dreadful had happened someone surely would have noticed. I've called the police, the hospitals. Only this morning. From the train. You heard me. No one has any record of her.'

Her mother's eyes went to the window and the grey lagoon beyond.

'Venice,' she hissed. 'Anyone could die in this place and never be noticed. The water . . .'

This was going to take days. Weeks perhaps. The idea that her mother might be around, in this despairing, mournful mood, was unimaginable. There was work to be done.

'I don't believe for one moment she's dead,' Teresa Lupo declared, and found that the words heartened her already. 'If this case came to me as a professional I would find no evidence to support such an idea. Certainly not some unexplained incident from sixteen years ago . . .'

'She tried to kill herself! In this very city! I asked her not to come back. I *begged* her. It was useless.'

'You said yourself, you don't know what happened. I'm not a child and I'm not a fool. Until I see some proof to the contrary I will continue to believe that Sofia is alive and out there . . .' Her own gaze went to the glass and the icy blue sky beyond. 'Somewhere.'

Chiara was shaking her head and this made her daughter's decision, already half-confirmed in her head, even more certain.

'I'll find her,' Teresa said. 'I promise.'

'Ever the optimist,' Chiara murmured, reaching for her little suitcase. 'There are two bedrooms? Or one and we must share?'

'There are two bedrooms but you needn't unpack.'

Her mother's face creased in puzzlement.

'I think you should go back to Frascati,' Teresa said. 'You're more use to me there.'

'I beg your—!'

'No. I won't hear any arguments. I may need to deal with the Questura back in Rome. They won't be happy I'm here. You can smooth things for me. Explain to them. Be my contact.' This was a lie, and she suspected they both understood it. 'There are people in Venice I know. Officials who may help. You can't be a part of that. It's impossible.'

Chiara listened, nodded, then said, 'You don't want me here, do you?'

'If I thought it would achieve anything . . .'

She got up, crossed the room, knelt in front of her mother, took her cold, wrinkled hands. In all the years, the long and difficult decades, there had been few moments like this.

'I promise,' Teresa said, 'I'll get to the bottom of it. But I can't be answerable to you. I have to do things my way.'

'Is there any other?'

'No,' Teresa said simply.

She put her arms around the woman who sat there stiff and miserable inside the ancient fox-fur coat.

'Do you have anything else to tell me?' she whispered into her mother's ear.

Two dry lips briefly brushed against her cheek and mouthed a single word, 'Nothing.'

Then this brief intimacy was over. The two parted, stood up. The handle of the little suitcase was in her mother's hand. Teresa was surprised she had given in so easily. This was clearly that rare kind of battle, one she was happy to lose.

'You know what I know,' Chiara said. 'The doctors told me they assumed she tried to kill herself. Sofia claimed she had no memory of this and seemed too embarrassed to discuss what might have happened. When she was well enough to leave she came home with me to Rome. After that she went to Paris. Then London.' A pause. 'The circus . . . the carnival resumed.'

Fifteen minutes later they stood on the wooden jetty near the Ponte agli Incurabili, waiting for the water taxi Teresa Lupo had insisted on calling.

Her mother turned as she was about to step onto the gleaming launch with its white hull and polished walnut decking.

'There was a man,' she said in a matter-of-fact tone. 'I'm sure of that. I asked Sofia at the time if there was anyone in Venice I should talk to. About her being in hospital. She said no one. Said it in that way I recognized. It was a lie. You'd never have seen that. You knew her differently.'

Chiara gazed at the grand form of Redentore across the Giudecca canal. The day was dying in a glorious smear of colours: cerise and blue, copper and gold, their reflections drowning in the dappled surface of the lagoon.

'There was always a man, wasn't there?' Teresa asked as the boatman guided her mother into the vessel.

'Something happened here,' Chiara told her. 'Something special. Something bad.'

'In Venice?' the boatman interjected. 'Bad? No, signora. This is the quietest, most peaceful city on earth.'

He tapped the side of his long nose and glanced at them both.

'Want to know a secret? Most of us are dead already. This is a city of ghosts.'

'You won't have need of a tip then,' Chiara said and clambered onto the red leather seats in the rear.

The archaic laptop contained no new information. The papers proved to be either bills, advertising flyers or notes Sofia appeared to use as background for her work as a freelance guide. After an hour of sifting through the material scattered around the place like confetti Teresa accepted that the ramshackle apartment had nothing to tell her that she didn't know already. Sofia had been gone for almost a week and seemed to have left unexpectedly. On the days before she disappeared it looked as if she was keen to meet someone she dubbed Il Gobbo, the hunchback. That was it.

She bundled the mess from the living room into five black rubbish bags then stored them in the spare bedroom in case they were needed again. After that she cleared out the smelly remains of some cheese, milk, yoghurt and prosciutto crudo from the refrigerator, put on her jacket and woolly hat and walked down to deposit the rubbish in a bin by the bridge.

It was almost eight o'clock and bitterly cold, the air sharp with the salt bite of the ocean. The lights of the island of Giudecca opposite glittered on the canal alongside the dark, sparkling shapes of vessels moving across the lagoon. Large and small they came: fast, sleek public vaporetti, slow ferries heading for the Lido, private craft still delivering goods even at this hour. Venice seemed more alive on the water than on the land sometimes.

As she stood there, reluctantly transfixed by the beauty of the view, a small, luxurious-looking cruiser edged past. A good dozen or so carnival figures were gathered in the brightly lit stern determined to be visible, buoyed by loud music, chinking glasses, gossiping and laughing. She took in the masks and the gaudy costumes, some bright

31

gleaming silk like Sofia's unfinished gown upstairs, some, the men's mainly, in velvet the colour of the night sky. She'd worn a mask here once during a student weekend. They all had different names, different styles. The *bauta*, with its jutting jawline. The pale, eerie *larva*, named, she seemed to recall, after the Latin word for ghost. There was someone in the popular Plague Doctor costume she'd seen earlier, the one with the long ivory nose and round, dark spectacles for eyes. Five or six beautiful young women stood together in a group. They looked as if they'd walked out of a painting by Tiepolo, with radiant, artificial hair and half-masks that let them drink and eat and smile coyly at the men.

Another world, Teresa thought, one she would never quite comprehend. Her career had taken her to strange places at times. That student weekend apart, there were none where she had felt a need for the frisson of a hidden identity, the quick, frantic stab for the affections of someone who might, or might not, be a complete stranger.

Sofia, though . . .

Her mother's story continued to puzzle her. How well did she really know her aunt? Was the face Sofia had shown her over the years manufactured to fit the needs of a troubled and awkward young woman in awe of someone older? One more mask, like those of the figures on the passing cruiser? And if so, what lay beneath? Depression and doubt? Then some unknown, unexplained moment of despair in which she sought to take her own life?

All things are possible. Her work in Rome and beyond had taught her that. But likely? She still doubted it.

The carnival figures on the pleasure craft floated past towards the Punta della Dogana and St Mark's Basin, their vessel starting to cut a sharp silhouette against the basilica of San Giorgio Maggiore and its towering campanile across the water.

Teresa Lupo became aware that she was ravenous. Carefully, wrapping herself more tightly in her plain and practical winter jacket, she picked her way in the flat-soled shoes her mother hated along the ice and compressed snow of the Zattere waterfront, crossing three low, pretty bridges until she was back near the vaporetto stop. Some residual memory told her the carnival occurred elsewhere, principally around San Marco, a fifteen-minute walk away across the bridge by the Accademia, and around the Rialto, a similar distance in the opposite direction. The festivities had not reached this area of Dorsoduro. A single restaurant was open, deserted apart from a silent couple: a surly middle-aged man in a grey suit and someone who might be his daughter or mistress, an elegant blonde with Asiatic features, foreign perhaps. Teresa took a table at the opposite end of the room by the window and ordered a *quattro formaggi* pizza and a small carafe of the local red Refosco from the Colli Orientali in Friuli. Both were excellent and, with the view and some idle chatter from a polite and interesting waiter, welcome.

As she sat there watching the lights on the canal her conviction that Sofia Bianchi was alive continued to grow. Perhaps it was the wine or the pleasant atmosphere. There was, she knew, no reason for this belief, and reason was, in Rome, her watchword, the guiding light of her professional life. Nevertheless she felt as she sat there, picking at the remains of the pizza, that her aunt was somewhere in the Veneto region; if not in Venice itself, perhaps in the Dolomiti mountains she loved so much for the wild bleak peaks and the skiing. There was a reason for her absence and the mysterious message she had sent. What mystery lay behind her disappearance lurked here somewhere, in this city, waiting to be found. That was one benefit of an island. It was hard for anything to escape completely. Hard to escape it oneself, too.

Ever since she first visited Venice as a child Teresa had felt that a part of the place stayed with her always, a stain on the memory, a perpetual scar, ready to be brought back to a life by a random event or experience: a glimpse of the reflection of an ancient palazzo flickering in the dappled dark waters of a canal, the endless, over-whelming sky, the smell of the water, the steady rhythm of the vaporetti, even the taste of the food, cold sharp fish, *sarde en saor* and creamy *baccalà*, local dishes she'd loved from the moment she first tasted them.

One never quite left behind these aspects of the city. There were traces of Sofia here somewhere too. If her aunt did not simply re-emerge from the night, smiling innocently as if nothing had happened – this had occurred before – these signs had to be found.

She finished her meal and returned to the apartment, checked the other rooms more thoroughly, found nothing.

Then she went into the bedroom and looked more closely at the object she'd seen earlier, when her mother was still around, and quite deliberately failed to mention.

The photograph was almost thirty years old, in a frame by the bed. A picture that must have followed Sofia around the world, through two marriages, innumerable failed affairs, from America back to Europe and then the years she had spent in Asia. The colours were a little faded now and Teresa could not place the exact date, only the location. She was ten or so, with Sofia and her mother standing in the portico of the church of Santa Maria in Cosmedin in Rome, next to the famous Bocca della Verità, a bearded god's head carved in marble, jaws open. The 'Mouth of Truth'.

As a child the budding scientist in her had soon discovered this was some kind of Imperial-era drain cover, rejecting the popular notion that the stone creature would bite off the hand of anyone who inserted his or her fingers into his mouth and spoke a lie. But it was a fetching legend, and one that brought a stream of visitors to the little church near the Tiber.

Sofia had her wrist in the Bocca della Verità at that moment and was smiling at the camera, her hair long and beautiful, her face innocent, a little puzzled perhaps. Chiara was gazing at her severely with the concerned intent of an elder sister. Teresa merely stood there, a lost and surly child, expressionless, plain and moody, hating, as always, the sight of the camera.

She vaguely remembered seeing this photograph years before but had never really looked at it closely. A kind of inverse vanity was the reason. She didn't hate her own forgettable if pleasant looks, her sturdy body, the way she slouched. She just didn't want to be reminded of her physical ordinariness. Why? She knew she was just one more face in the crowd.

Now she did peer closely at the picture and she saw something in the face of her mother, some half-resented sense of care, the kind a parent would show to a wayward child. It was directed at Sofia, not at her.

Teresa reached over for her bag, took out her phone and called Frascati. It was now past ten o'clock. Chiara had just arrived. There was a brief and polite conversation about the journey and the lack of any further information in Venice. Then she asked, 'Were some of Sofia's stories untrue? Please, tell me.'

Chiara Bianchi sighed and her daughter wondered how many times she'd heard that careworn sound.

'What stories?'

'The ones that weren't obvious. The ones where you had to take her on trust.'

'I never knew what to believe,' Chiara said eventually. 'The marriages, yes. I met both those men. Everything else. The life in London. In Paris. Asia. The dreams . . .'

'She went to those places?'

'She went to some of them,' her mother replied. 'Asia . . . I don't know. When she was supposed to be there someone told me she'd seen her working in some ski resort outside Turin. A cabin girl. Cleaning, cooking, fetching. I don't know what to believe. I never did after a while.'

Teresa closed her eyes and fought for some self-control.

'You could have asked.'

'And punctured what little confidence and self-respect she had?'

'Has. People who are about to commit suicide don't send their niece their keys and a note saying they might have some small problem on their mind. Not in my experience.'

There was some hesitation on the line then Chiara said, not unkindly, 'Difficult as you may find this to believe, there are still matters outside your experience. You have a very strict and defined view of humanity. I imagine your job demands that. Your character too. Don't imagine it encompasses everything.'

This strange, stark criticism astonished her.

'I've no idea what that means.'

'I'm sure you don't. I did my best with Sofia, believe me. She was my sister. I still remember holding her in my arms when she was a baby, feeling so proud. Looking forward to all the time we'd spend together. But it never happened. We were sisters, never friends, not really.'

'Mother . . .'

'Listen to me, please. We don't possess other people. We can only offer our help and then, when it's rejected or ignored, offer it again a little later.' Her mother's voice was beginning to crack. 'I never stopped trying, believe me. You were right that I should leave. It's time to try your kind of talent. Mine, such as it may be, always seemed squandered somehow. My fault, not hers.'

'I'm sure you did everything you could.'

'If it was a waste what was the point?'

'The point is you tried. You're a good sister and a good mother and I love you very much,' Teresa said, aware that she could never have uttered those words face to face, aware too that her eyes were beginning to cloud over with tears.

Nothing that had occurred between them these last thirty or more years came close to this moment and they both knew it. There was only space after that for a brief and clumsy goodbye.

A few minutes later, as she was beginning to accept that there was nothing left to do but change the old, crumpled sheets on Sofia's bed and try to sleep, the doorbell went, followed by several rapid knocks and a voice calling loudly, 'Sofia! *Sofia*!'

A young woman stood there, pretty, with long dark hair and a very pale, almost bloodless face. She wore the most extraordinary costume: a grey hooped floor-length skirt, a white lace cotton apron and neckpiece and a bright scarlet jacket trimmed with crumpled velour. A red-and-white lace bonnet sat above her forehead, tied beneath her chin. In her right hand was a large manila envelope, in her left an expensive-looking bouquet of roses.

She laughed self-consciously, a warm and pleasant sound, clearly expecting to see someone else.

'I'm so sorry,' she said, in an accent that had a foreign tone to it, 'I heard noises. I thought it must be Sofia.'

Teresa explained herself and told what little she knew. She waited. The young woman, who could have been no more than twenty she imagined, listened and shook her head.

'This is very strange,' she said. 'I haven't seen her in a week. She never said she was going away. Nothing. To you?'

'Only that she had some kind of problem.'

'What kind?'

'I don't know,' Teresa confessed.

'Camilla Dushku.' The young woman held out a white-gloved hand. 'I live in the apartment downstairs. We should talk in the morning. I'm sorry. I have to go to work now.' A sigh. 'Handing out overpriced champagne to the multiple mistresses of Russian businessmen. Welcome to *Carnevale*. Here. Now at least something makes sense.'

She held out the flowers and the envelope.

'They're addressed to you, not Sofia. Both of them. In this apartment,' Camilla explained. 'The post came yesterday. The flowers this evening. No one answered the bell so I signed for them. I thought Sofia must have missed the envelope when she came in.'

'No one knew I was here,' Teresa told her.

The young woman grinned apologetically.

'Someone did. Look. Your name. This apartment.'

Teresa Lupo took them then watched her go. She checked the tag on the bouquet and the address. Camilla Dushku was right. Then she realized there was a logical explanation for the flowers at least. She'd left a voicemail message for Peroni through the Questura in Rome, with the address in Venice and a note about her visit. She'd mentioned an unspecified problem with Sofia too, no more than that since she didn't want to worry him. It was typical of the man that he would find time on assignment in Sicily to remember her.

Typical too, she thought, checking the rest of the card, that he forgot to add his name or the simplest of messages.

She went back into the apartment, tearing open the manila envelope. Inside was nothing but a sheaf of loose sheets, perhaps thirty pages of text in an old-fashioned typewriter font, double-spaced, like a book manuscript, but printed on a curious thick paper the colour of mustard.

One thing at a time.

Questura rules said she wasn't supposed to contact Peroni. That didn't mean she couldn't send a quick text saying she was fine and thanking him for the generous bouquet. It went off in an instant and she wondered what he was doing at that moment, with Nic Costa and Falcone, in Palermo perhaps or one of the mob towns in the interior.

There was no point in speculation. He wouldn't even turn on his private phone until he was off duty, back in the hotel or whatever police house the Sicilian authorities had found for them.

She took the manuscript with her into the bedroom, got undressed and lay beneath the sheets, reading by the weak light of the lamp set in the headboard. The work appeared to be a short story with the title *Carpaccio's Dog*. The typeface was deceptive. It was clearly the product of a modern laser or inkjet printer though the strangely heavy paper stock continued to puzzle her.

She flicked through the sheets. This seemed a

professional document, with the title on the top of each and a running page and word count. Yet nowhere was there any name for the author.

One page, she thought. Perhaps two.

Fifteen minutes later she realized it was impossible to stop, even when there was a distant beep from her phone in the living room.

So Teresa Lupo failed to see that Peroni had texted back from distant Sicily with a brief message.

What flowers?

CARPACCIO'S DOG

Jerome Aitchison, a tall and solitary Englishman of fifty-three years, stood in the narrow Castello street transfixed by the creature before him. The dog was small, less than a foot high, with a clean spiky coat the colour of bleached bone. It possessed keen black eyes and sharp, triangular ears pricked and alert over a compact head little larger than a grapefruit. The animal's damp and shiny nose was held high pointing, like its gaze, directly at Aitchison. No more than a single stride separated them in the narrow, dark alley where they had encountered one another.

The dog had been waiting for him. He felt sure of it.

There was a sense of immediate recognition, on both sides a part of him seemed to say. One hour before he had met this same small bundle of fur, determinedly rigid in a posture identical to the one it held now: taut on its haunches, which were very much like those of a chicken, back feet aligned geometrically behind its front paws, as if posing for a photograph.

The attentive, engaged expression on its tiny foxlike face was unchanged and, just as then, he found himself struggling, through inexperience, bafflement, and a muggy, befuddling cloud of recent alcohol, to make sense of its meaning. Expectation of a ball or toy thrown in play? A word of praise? Some gesture of encouragement?

There had never been a dog in his life, not as an introspective only child nor later when he moved into college rooms and fell, easily he had to admit, into the lonely though consuming round of a bachelor existence. He had no idea how to address the thing, let alone amuse it. There was, moreover, a more subtle problem. When he last saw the diminutive beast it was not in the least sense alive. The creature existed as paint on a canvas that was, if he recalled correctly, more than five hundred years old. A small and perhaps insignificant detail of a compelling and impenetrable work he'd stumbled upon after a long and rather over-indulgent lunch in a tourist-trap restaurant along the Via Garibaldi in Castello.

Staring at the minuscule creature in front of him, which seemed too independent to be anyone's pet, he wished someone would join them in the cramped, dank alley, puncturing this strange, dreamlike interlude, bringing him down to earth. It was just after seven o'clock on a chill January evening and Venice, this part at least, seemed quite deserted. There was not the slightest noise from any of the grimy, ramshackle terraced homes around him, not a light behind the windows. It was as if nothing existed in the city save the two of them: a middle-aged academic distracted from an endless, circular rumination on the destruction of his career and a tiny, seemingly lively animal, intent on monopolizing his attention and posing a question he could not possibly begin to understand.

He bent forward and, with an unsteady hand, cut through the air in front of him, uttering the one appropriate word that came into his head.

'Shoo!' Aitchison declared, sweeping away the inky night with his arm.

The dog continued to sit directly in the centre of the squalid lane, blocking his way.

'Shoo, damn you,' he repeated.

The tiny white head gazed up at him in the light of a waxing moon just visible through a herringbone sky that spoke of snow. The animal remained as motionless as it had been on the wall of the place, very like a church, where he had first seen it.

He checked himself. Drink had been taken. Even so it seemed ridiculous to be talking to what was either a phantasm from a brief waking dream or a neighbourhood stray which, through nothing more than centuries of breeding, bore an extraordinary resemblance to a long-dead Castello mongrel.

Aitchison ran the sleeve of his coat across his face, rubbing musty bachelor gabardine against whiskery bachelor cheeks. What *was* that look on the tiny animal's face? It appeared identical to when he first witnessed it on canvas. Longing? An eager adulation? Or was there even, and this last thought would once have amused him, some impudent hint of condescension in the creature's bright, black eyes?

Condescension . . . God knew he'd seen enough of that of late.

'Shoo, you bloody little beast . . .'

The dog stayed as rigid and motionless as one of the stone lions by the Arsenale gates which he had passed not long before.

'Get lost! Bugger off!'

It occurred to him that this was stupid in the extreme. The animal, if it knew any language at all, would be familiar with Italian. Or the local Veneto, even. Not angry vernacular English.

The red rage of ire, stoked by cheap alcohol, self-disgust and recent resentment, filled his head. A stream of vile invective rose in the night. Aitchison stepped forward and aimed a tipsy kick at the creature on the cobblestones, missed, slipped on a puddle that was minded to turn to ice, lost his footing and fell backwards, landing hard on his backside, squawking with pain.

There was the briefest of yelps from somewhere ahead of him, a high-pitched sound that seemed to contain an audible note of triumph. After a few brief seconds of mournful contemplation he looked around and was relieved to see he was once again alone. The way ahead – the direction, roughly, in which he had come from his inexpensive lodgings – appeared clear as he'd hoped, though the narrow alley of black cobblestones was now gleaming with the incipient arrival of what could only be frost, icy white beneath the dim light of a small and inadequate street lamp.

Aitchison got up, cleaned the dirt and moss from his clothes as best he could, then stumbled forward, peering round the next corner, fearful that he might see the same white shape sitting boldly out in the middle of the path, waiting. There was nothing. Carefully he felt his arms and legs. No broken bones. A bruise perhaps. A graze. He was shivering though and he wondered if this was only because of the sudden bitter cold that had closed in not long before he saw the damned dog.

Reassured to be alone once more he crossed the low stone bridge that soon rose to meet him and walked very briskly in the direction he felt sure would, at some stage, fetch up close to the broad piazza of Giovanni e Paolo – which the locals, he noted, invariably called Zanipolo for some reason – and home.

It took only three wrong turnings, two of them ending in the dead black water of a narrow canal, before he found his bearings. This was an improvement on any of the previous six nights in the city. Then he rounded a half-familiar corner and saw the crooked iron railing along the canalside path that led towards his lodgings.

The tiny café on the corner was about to close

in spite of the early hour. It was damnably hard to stay drunk in this city.

He strode in with a determination that told the owner he would be served, whatever.

The thickset Venetian behind the counter recognized him. His expression was as impenetrable as that of the dog in the night.

'I saw . . .' the Englishman began, then stopped as he watched the man reach for the grappa bottle without even asking. Aitchison didn't wish to appear foolish. Besides, this was his last opportunity for a drink. If he were thrown out . . .

'Saw what, signore?' the barman asked in good English.

'Nothing.'

The man poured a generous glass then glanced at his watch.

'Just a dog . . .' Aitchison murmured before taking a sip of something that tasted distinctly chemical, as if it bore a faint relationship to petroleum.

'That is all you see in Venice?' the barman asked. 'A dog?'

Aitchison slunk to a table in the corner. By eight thirty, after much vacillation, and a failed attempt to extract one more drink, he was out in the street again staring at the sky. The feathers of cloud now had the texture of swans' wings. They made him think of the Cam in summer, lazy days of beer and books, with the odd sly eye cast towards the pretty girls giggling in the procession of punts zigzagging up and down the still green water.

Another lifetime. One to which he would never return.

Nights were never easy since the unpleasantness and the allegations – shocking, untrue, though not entirely without some flimsy basis – made by the young girl student towards whom he had once felt great warmth and admiration.

When he decided to flee Cambridge in the dead week between Christmas and New Year, Aitchison had searched the college computer system seeking ideas. There he'd found the lodgings in Castello, recommended on a noticeboard by a student who had used them while backpacking around Italy. Aitchison hadn't dared contact the person responsible to inquire about their suitability. He was a pariah already by that time. The rumours were beginning to fly, in dining rooms, in pubs, whispered, he imagined, at college parties during the darkening days of December as his downfall seemed to gain more salacious detail with every passing day. St Jerome – he knew the nickname they gave him, and that it dated back decades – had fallen from on high. All his achievements, his years of work, counted for nothing. A pious man had been revealed as a hypocrite, or so they thought. It was the kind of small, personal tragedy that the enclosed world of a Cambridge college adored.

There was no time to plan, which was, in itself, deeply disturbing. He was a senior lecturer in actuarial science, a solid faculty member with a well-proven record, respected in every way. Perhaps a little too individual, too different to gain what he had once dreamed of, a professorship. Nevertheless he had won some esteem through a combination of talent, hard work and routine. Planning seemed, to Jerome Aitchison, an intrinsic and necessary part of daily life, like breathing or going to the toilet. That was why he chose actuarial science as his field of study. He was a good teacher too and had watched many of his students go on to make great fortunes in the City of London through the subtle arithmetical skills he had taught them, all with one aim: to predict the span of life itself.

Over the previous three decades he had given so many lectures on the subject he felt it was a part of him, an invisible limb. The talks he enjoyed most were for lay audiences, Women's Institutes and library groups, people he could amuse with history and obscure facts. Had they any idea the first actuarial calculation – an attempt to link compound interest with various mortality rates – was performed by none other than the seventeenth-century Prime Minister of the Netherlands, Johan de Witt? That de Witt's *The Worth of Life Annuities Compared to Redemption Bonds* represented the first real effort to analyse probability and chance, to pull hard fact from the superstitious ether of fancy, substituting blind faith with science?

Of course they hadn't. Everyone died, but no one wanted to contemplate their own end. Nor had the Dutchman's insights done the unfortunate man any personal good. While de Witt had begun to formulate actuarial skills that would one day enrich the insurance and pensions industries, keen to place the very best-informed bets on the life spans of those whose policies they held, the Netherlands remained steadfastly unimpressed. During a small and uninteresting war the mob rose up and entrapped the hapless politician and his brother in The Hague, promptly disembowelling and decapitating them, carving out their hearts and hanging their broken bodies from a scaffold.

Two years before Aitchison had visited Amsterdam for an international conference on the future of actuary. There he had found himself wandering into the Rijksmuseum. Almost immediately he had been confronted by a haunting and exceedingly gory canvas depicting the miserable, bloody demise of the de Witt brothers, hung upside down from the gibbet, corpses slashed and torn. He had, up to this point, regarded the Dutch as the mildest of men.

On hearing his recounting of this story Ursula Downing, the young woman whose bright, intelligent, smiling face had brought Jerome Aitchison to his present predicament, jokingly asked why such a clever man as Johan de Witt could not concoct a mathematical formula that predicted the end of his own life.

'Don't forget chance,' Aitchison had told her earnestly. 'Never mistake probability for certainty.'

'Or mess with politics,' she'd added, staring at him wide-eyed, as beautiful as Raphael's *La Fornarina*.

Ursula was angling for a first and would get it. Aitchison had no doubt about that. The dreadful, calamitous letter she had left behind when Michaelmas term ended would hinder her progress not one whit. Accusations of sexual impropriety and vague threats of legal action sent a chill through the flimsy spines of college administrators, none of whom weighed Aitchison's two and a half decades of loyal service against the unproven and unprovable accusations of a child. No arithmetical conceit could have predicted his downfall, nor the empty aching chasm in his heart that her absence caused: one aggravated by her treachery, not attenuated as a mathematician might have expected.

As he lay on the hard, cold single bed in the first-floor room of the simple hostel in a back street of Castello, the sole guest as far as he could gather, he found his fuddled head filling with thoughts and memories, images and half-formed fantasies. Questions too.

Why did he wander into art galleries so easily? Was it simply because those dead faces on the wall never objected to his avid and curious stares the way the living did? He'd had no need to visit the Rijksmuseum and find himself confronted by the ghastly end of a man who, in the confined reality of ink on paper, trapped within the words and pages of a book, was nothing less than a hero to actuaries around the world. Nor had he consciously decided to enter the building that contained the painting with the curious dog, thus bringing about the strange waking dream – it could be nothing else, surely? – that had afflicted him on the way home.

'You're a fool, Jerome,' he murmured to himself.

His return ticket on the budget airline could not be taken for another four days. It was important to conserve money. He'd little expectation that he could resume his position. There were even furtive whispers that his pension might be affected which, for reasons none in the bursar's office appeared to appreciate, he found utterly unimaginable, a horror tantamount to the bloody end wrought by the Dutch mob on de Witt himself.

For the next few days there was nothing else to do but wander the desolate streets of Venice.

'A fool . . .' he whispered, and closed his eyes, willing himself to sleep.

There were noises outside the single small, dingy window that gave onto the cobbled street. Voices from time to time, of drinkers and diners making their happy way home from some establishment that served the Venetians till the early hours, keeping out the foreigners, condemning them to cold damp bedrooms.

The distant waters of the lagoon offered the occasional blast of a vaporetto horn. From the city came the hourly metallic boom of a church bell.

Infrequently, though audible and unmistakable, the night was punctuated too by the distant rhythmic yapping of a dog.

So disturbed was Aitchison's sleep that he failed to wake until almost one in the afternoon and was only then roused by the hammering of the cleaning woman on the door. The middle-aged harridan who ran the boarding house declared that breakfast was absolutely no longer '*disponibile*'.

By various twists and turns, and many dead ends finishing in the black water of a canal, he found his way to the waterfront. The day remained dark and close to freezing. Puddles of icy water were congealing into treacherous black mirrors on the paving stones. He recalled the night before and avoided them carefully. Venice seemed full of dangers he had never, for one moment, anticipated.

The lagoon barely moved beneath a sky so heavy it made his headache worse. The shimmering horizon was vague and unreal, like a mirage, a *Fata Morgana* that was neither near nor distant. A vast ocean liner occupied much of the quayside, blocking the view to what he knew, from his book, to be San Giorgio Maggiore across the basin. There seemed to be even fewer real people around than the previous day, here at least, beyond the tourist magnet of San Marco.

The thought of that place drove him further east to the very tip of the city, the island of Sant' Elena, reached by a bridge from the desolate empty gardens of the Biennale exhibition with their sad little rough-hewn pavilions.

In spite of the chill he sat outside a solitary restaurant, huddled beneath a gas heater posing as a standard lamp. Aitchison was disturbed to see that it was impossible for any of the island dogs to pass him without taking notice. A look. A pause. A backward stare.

'Bugger off,' he growled in a low, harsh voice to one, as luck would have it, just as the waiter was returning with a second coffee and another glass of the biting white spirit he was finally, after some effort, beginning to appreciate.

'They hurt no one,' the man said. 'Just dogs.'

'In-bred stupid mutts,' Aitchison muttered to himself as the waiter departed. They did seem to come from a limited, near-identical gene pool. Colouring varied wildly, as did the shape of the head. But the size – corgi-like, with a low, rounded belly – and the tail – bowed, very upright and bushy – were too common to be random. His statistician's mind told him there would be a rational explanation for this. Darwin ruled even here. In a restricted gene pool physical characteristics would come to be dominated by a limited set of possibilities. The same might have applied to the men of Venice had they not been seafarers, possessing the morals and sexual curiosity that went with such a profession.

He downed the last of the drink and knew there

was an exception. The dog in the alley, a tiny white pyramid of fur, was nothing like the common mongrels wandering the empty streets of Sant'Elena. That thing was different, entirely so.

Head hurting a little, full of cheap booze and plentiful *bigoli* pasta, he stumbled back towards the city, across the bridge, by the bare pavilions, into the broad thoroughfare of the Via Garibaldi and on to the walls of the Arsenale, past the judgemental gaze of its stiff mute lions by the clock tower and the gates to the old dockyard.

Sometimes thoughts refused to die. They needed to be buried, with a conscious, deliberate act.

Even using the simple map he'd picked up for free in the restaurant it took three efforts, long annoying sorties into the warren of alleys and lanes that ran higgledy-piggledy inwards from the point at which the great liner was berthed.

Finally, at the end of the afternoon, with the light starting to fade so quickly it seemed night was falling from the sky like rain, he found the place and entered the gloomy, dusty interior.

It smelled of old people and mouldering books.

The Scuola di San Giorgio degli Schiavoni was a modest white Palladian building next to an attractive brown tiered bridge. Not quite a church, more some kind of religious guild house, or so he gathered from reading the pamphlet the man at the door handed over when, once again, he paid the entrance fee.

The painting was where he remembered it on

the right-hand wall. Jerome Aitchison made a point of ignoring the thing and instead wandered upstairs, finding himself in an old, timbered meeting room filled with heavy worn benches and tables blackened by time. Ahead of him lay an ornate altar and some shadowy paintings of obscure men in obscure situations. There was a tall, attractive woman, not young but not old, gazing at a canvas on a stand. She was about his own height with an intelligent and very pretty face and a physique that would once have been described as statuesque. She wore an old-fashioned black coat, half-open to reveal a plain red dress beneath, both somewhat shabby. An old, battered leather satchel hung over her right shoulder which, to Aitchison, made her resemble an impoverished post-grad student forever trapped in an endless cycle of study. Her calm grey eyes dominated a tanned, smiling face framed by ill-disciplined blonde curls that fell to her shoulders then tumbled down her back. Those eyes followed him carefully as he walked in, as if performing a calculation. She said hello in English with an accent that was hard to place, Italian yet American too. He grumbled a response then, deciding there was little to interest him in what seemed to be some kind of long-dead gentleman's club, returned to the ground floor, still keeping well away from the canvas with the dog.

The previous day he'd ignored the sheet of paper the same warden had handed to every visitor as they entered. Now Aitchison studied it carefully.

Everything on this level was by the same hand, that of the painter Vittore Carpaccio, and dated from the early sixteenth century. This was needless information. Aitchison was sufficiently familiar with Italian works of art to recognize the uniformity of style and approach in the paintings around him, and the rough period. The works were principally commissioned to record the lives of three Balkan saints, Schiavoni being a Venetian term for the Slavs who once formed an immigrant seafaring class within the city. The subjects held little interest for a mathematician. He preferred to see images that contained life and flesh, female preferably, Titian above all others, that Raphael of *La Fornarina* apart.

There was nothing so enticing here. For the most part he was surrounded by dour grey men in long medieval costumes, frozen in the performance of some everyday act, a conversation usually, in a pose meant to contain religious or philosophical significance. When he looked more closely, however, there were some oddities. A canvas labelled *The Daughter of Emperor Gordian is Exorcised by St Tryphon* depicted a young girl sporting a halo and accompanied by an extraordinarily nasty pint-sized monster, half horned donkey, half winged lizard. The city behind this bizarre scene looked much like the Venice beyond the door. Close by was a gruesome depiction of St George, another Slav hero it seemed, slaying a scaly dragon surrounded by maimed and half-eaten corpses, watched all the while by a virginal maiden who looked, it occurred to Aitchison, a little bored by the spectacle.

'Do you like Carpaccio?' asked the woman, who had quietly slunk behind him without warning, and spoke with such loud confidence it made Aitchison jump out of his skin.

'Raw meat?' he muttered without thinking.

She laughed and he found he was unable to take his eyes off her.

'No. The painter. Vittore.' She hesitated for a moment then added, 'Though the two are related.'

'I'm sorry?'

'Raw meat. And him.' She spoke easily, knowledgeably. 'It's not an old recipe, you know. A fake really, unlike the paintings. Giuseppe Cipriani invented it in 1950, on the spot in Harry's Bar. The Contessa Amalia Nani Mocenigo, one of his regulars, told him her doctor had demanded she follow a diet that forbade cooked meat. Cipriani went into the kitchen and returned with a plate of raw thinly sliced fillet of beef and a light sauce. When the Contessa asked its name . . .'

The woman watched, to make sure he was listening.

'There was a Carpaccio exhibition in Venice at the time. It was the first thing that came into his head. They're sly here, you see, particularly when it comes to commerce.'

Aitchison had seen the dish everywhere – with

beef, fish, crustaceans. Sometimes carpaccio even found its way into the college dining room.

'Is that true?' he asked.

'Absolutely. Venice is a city of invention. If something doesn't exist, one simply makes it up. Be warned, though. Reality here is entirely subjective. Remove one of these fabrications from its natural home in the lagoon and it'll crumble to dust in your fingers the moment you set foot on *terraferma*.' She held out a pale, strong hand and it gripped his before he even realized. 'Sofia Bianchi. Bad writer, mediocre artist, pathetically inaccurate fortune-teller, though competent and knowledgeable tour guide for those of an aesthetic persuasion. I don't suppose you need any help, do you? If you like Carpaccio you must see the Ursula cycle in the Accademia. Cecil B. DeMille before they invented movies. I can talk you through every scene, only twenty euros an hour, negotiable for a half day or more.'

Aitchison shivered at the name and the memories it stirred.

Ursula.

'I don't think so.'

'I also do Vivaldi and Casanova among others. Or we could go straight to every worthwhile grave in San Michele if you're feeling morbidly curious, which most visitors are for some reason. Death in Venice. It had a ring to it long before Thomas Mann.'

'No, no . . .'

He hated being approached by people wanting money. It was so impertinent, all the more from one so fetching that her presence left him a little tongue-tied.

'I'm s-sorry,' Aitchison stuttered.

She watched him, unabashed, coyly aware of his shy interest.

'I like to be on my own,' he added, unsure whether that was a lie too.

Sofia Bianchi took rejection well. Perhaps she was used to it, though he wondered why. She was a very attractive woman, blessed with striking, sophisticated features that grated with her apparent impoverishment. Her face was that of a model or a rich man's wife, not some down-at-heel tour guide trying to drum up custom in a deserted Venetian scuola.

'Oh well. I thought you looked at a loose end. I apologize for being forward. It's just that . . .' She held up her head and her fine nose flared, as if sniffing the air. 'It's so very deserted out there, apart from the poor sad sticks from the cruise ships and they're spoken for. This is a curious time in Venice. Beautiful but strange. So few people. And the light. On a good day anyway . . . Makes me wish I could paint properly. What I see in my head. I don't suppose you might be interested in a little local art for your wall back home?' She waited for a second then shrugged at his silence and said, 'It's like being in a dream really. One in which there's nothing for a hungry mouth like me to do but hunt, if you'll pardon the expression.'

'Quiet apart from the dogs . . .' he mumbled.

'Dogs? Oh! You like dogs? Join the club. So much sweeter than human beings, don't you think? I intend to adopt one soon, when I have the time.' She paused then smiled. 'And the money.'

She took his arm, simultaneously turning and dragging him across the room to the painting that had drawn him here, though he had yet to find the courage to face it.

'Now here's a riddle,' the woman said. 'Prove yourself. Name the breed, please.'

He gazed at the white bundle of fur seated on the floor of the study of some bearded saint working away, distracted, at his desk. St Augustine, the pamphlet said. This ancient ascetic was perched on a dais by the window in a room made for an academic, one Aitchison envied the moment he examined it. Books were everywhere, on the floor, on shelves along the walls, with an early astronomical instrument – an astrolabe? – and, at the rear, an alcove bearing the diminutive statue of what appeared to be a religious figure. Candlesticks lined the walls to afford light when it was needed. Nothing denoted the slightest sense of motion, not even the dog. It was a solitary place for quiet work and meditation, exquisitely painted, an entire universe of obscure frozen detail.

He couldn't take his eyes off the animal. Surrounded by a panoply of icons about learning, next to a famous figure even an atheist like Aitchison had heard of, the creature drew the viewer's attention from everything as it stared intently at the man at the desk.

'A Maltese?' he guessed.

It was the only small breed of dog he could think of.

The man at the door came over and looked at him as if he were mad. Aitchison had assumed he was a pensioner eking out the day. But now he looked the fellow seemed younger, more Aitchison's own age, with sharp, intelligent eyes behind thick horn-rimmed spectacles.

'A Maltese? Do you know how often I have to listen to this nonsense?' he asked. 'Every huckster, every amateur tour guide comes in here and says that. A Maltese? Listen to Signora Bianchi. She's an educated Italian lady. She knows.'

The woman beamed at hearing this praise. Aitchison was surprised to discover she was Italian. Her English, though tainted by an American accent, seemed so fluent.

'The dog is a volpino,' she declared. 'Unknown outside Italy until a few brave breeders started taking them abroad. Even now most people have never heard of the dears. *Volpino*. It means "little fox". One of the oldest established breeds of dog there is. Aristocratic Romans used to treat them as members of the family and dress them up with jewels and fine jackets. Here . . .'

She reached into her battered bag then thrust a

sheet of paper from a computer printer into his hands. Aitchison shoved it into his coat pocket without a second glance.

'These are some notes of my own on this painting. You can have them. A freebie for a fellow dog-lover.'

He couldn't drag his attention away from the shape on the canvas. It seemed alive.

'The volpino. Is it common?' he asked.

The warden and Sofia Bianchi glanced at each other and sighed.

'No, sir,' the Venetian replied. 'Most of us have never seen one, except . . .' His hand extended towards the wall. 'Here.'

'Worldwide,' the woman added, 'there are perhaps a couple of thousand at the most. So few that many dog clubs refuse even to recognize them as a breed. Exclusive, you see.'

Aitchison pointed to the door.

'I saw one. Outside.'

This very one, he thought.

The warden blinked and seemed to turn a little pale.

'There are no *volpini* in Venice, sir. You must have seen something else. We have many dogs . . .'

'But not like *this*.'

His comment appeared to make the man extremely uncomfortable.

'It's impossible, signore.' His keen narrow eyes stayed fixed on Aitchison. 'But if one were to meet a volpino, one would treat it with kindness and respect, I trust.'

'Same with all dogs,' the woman told him. 'They're just dumb little animals. We shouldn't take out our misery on them. No good and evil in their world, not unless we introduce it.'

'*All* dogs,' the warden agreed. 'Especially the volpino.'

Aitchison recalled the kick he'd aimed at the obstinate creature that had stood in his way in the narrow alley in the labyrinth of Castello the night before. It was poorly aimed but deliberate. He had wanted to hurt the thing and that was, he knew, because its mute, keen, expectant gaze seemed to mirror the expression he'd seen everywhere in Cambridge after his fall from a solitary form of grace. In kicking out at the volpino he had aimed his fury at the world, with all its uncaring, sneering cruelty, or so his drunken mind had told him. And he'd missed.

Their remarks went unanswered. Something else had caught his eye. Beneath the dog on the canvas, to one side, the artist had contrived to paint a small written note. It looked like a scrap of paper left idly on the floor.

He still had Latin in his head from public school. Both the rigours of the language, and the logic that it drummed into him, had never quite disappeared.

The paper read '*Victor Carpathius Fingebat*'.

It was a short, if artificial, step from the Italian 'Vittore Carpaccio' to the Latinized 'Victor Carpathius'. Jerome Aitchison had, however, always been proud of his ability to master the intricate detail of conjugating verbs, an exercise which was not so far from his beloved algebra and calculus. '*Fingebat*' came from '*fingere*', which might be translated as 'to form, create, devise or conjure'. It was by no means uncommon to omit the object – namely the canvas – from such a simple sentence, even though this was a transitive verb. Nevertheless, one would have expected the artist to have adopted the perfect tense – '*fingit*' – which would have rendered the signature as, 'Vittore Carpaccio devised this'. Or – as he had surely seen in other works of this era – to have used the more appropriate and common verb '*facere*', to make, as in '*Victor Carpathius me fecit*', indicating that the canvas itself was announcing the identity of its creator.

The import of the inscription beneath the dog was maddeningly unclear.

'The odd thing is,' Sofia Bianchi declared, interrupting his train of thought, 'it was never meant to be a dog in the first place. There's a preliminary sketch Carpaccio made in the British Museum. In that the animal on the floor is an ermine, representing purity. Somewhere along the way he changed it to a dog, for fidelity one imagines.'

The Venetian warden looked out of sorts and made noises about closing soon. Then he went back to his seat by the entrance and sat there, staring at the worn stone floor.

The smell of damp seemed to be getting more

marked. Through the open door Aitchison could see that it was beginning to rain. The light from the porch made the forceful shower resemble rods of glistening ice falling to earth.

'The inscription—' he began.

'It's known as a "cartellino",' she interrupted. 'The placing of a note within the painting to allow the work itself to declare its provenance. It means Vittore Carpaccio created this.'

'No!'

He was aware that his voice had risen in volume somewhat and now echoed round the empty hall of the Scuola di San Giorgio degli Schiavoni with an unintentional and brusque volume.

She eyed him, interested, waiting.

'It doesn't mean that,' Aitchison went on. '*Fingebat* is the third person imperfect. Not the perfect tense, which is how you said it. This note means Carpaccio was creating, or conceiving, or conjuring this. It implies an unfinished, incomplete action. He was devising this picture, and then . . .'

His eyes fell on the dog. Once again he had the feeling it was asking an impenetrable question.

The woman scribbled something on a small, cheap notepad and announced, 'Clearly there was some unfinished business, I imagine. I'll look into that idea. Enjoy Venice if you can.'

She turned without another word and left. Aitchison immediately regretted his rudeness. Sofia Bianchi was friendly, engaging, interesting. Not so far off his own age and unattached, perhaps. He didn't meet many women like that. Only ingenuous young students, devoid of interest and opinion, angling, on occasion, for nothing more than a better mark. Now he was alone in front of the canvas: an ancient saint staring out of a window, as if listening to some distant voice, not that it made sense to allude to sound in paintings at all. The thing was there to enrage him, just like the dog.

He walked to the doorway. The warden was counting his money: a handful of notes and coins.

'If you see a volpino, signore,' the man said without looking up, 'remember. A little kindness never goes amiss.'

'I was never much fond of animals,' Aitchison replied.

He'd scarcely crossed the little bridge by the *scuola* of the Slavs when the shower turned into a storm of hard, cold rain lashing from the black sky above. Aitchison had no umbrella, no hat. There was only one thing to do and that was to head into the first dark alley he could find, hoping that the buildings on both sides would keep off a little of the downpour on this biting winter evening.

Aitchison had no idea where he was headed, or how once again to find his way back to the waterfront and St Mark's Basin, the only geographical reference point he knew nearby that might guide him home.

The darkness seemed to seep from the sky,

consuming the streets, the stones, the ragged walls around him. After a few minutes he entered a lane that eventually broadened so that he could walk upright, free of the bitter rain.

Finally there was a light. At the end of another dingy passageway stood a tiny bridge over a canal so slender a younger man might be tempted to leap it. When he crossed to the other side he found himself standing beneath a large lampshade bearing a Nastro Azzurro logo. It stood over the door of what looked like a house with opaque windows, next to a sign with a long and curious name – Cason dei Sette Morti – etched in fading red letters. The House of the Seven Dead Men. He was surprised to realize that his Italian had come along a little simply through the process of listening and guesswork.

The place was a bar. Had to be. Jerome Aitchison pushed open the door and walked in, ordering without thinking the drink he'd seen them all consuming, every local, in the many places where he'd encountered them. Spritz, they called it, not an Italian name, he thought, an Austrian one, bequeathed to Venice by history.

The liquid in the glass was a livid shade of red and stank of Campari and prosecco. A fat green olive was plunged deep into the glass, on a wooden skewer. Aitchison gulped at it, not caring about the taste.

There was fried fish on the bar, plate after plate of it, small crisp bodies like whitebait, larger ones, mackerel perhaps, and chunks of unidentifiable fillet. They looked cold but fresh. He was ravenous and quite alone apart from the portly, ancient woman, in a stained apron and old black cotton dress, who stood behind the counter, arms folded.

'Food,' Aitchison said.

She looked at him blankly.

'Mangia.'

Pointing at the plates of fish, he made an eating gesture, one so crude and animal he immediately felt ashamed of it.

This place was turning him into a beast. He would never have behaved so badly in Cambridge. It was the fault of Venice. Of the damned dog somehow.

Outside the wind caught and sent sheets of rain lashing against the grubby narrow windows. The woman looked at her watch. She was going to close the place on him. He just knew it.

'This,' Aitchison repeated, pointing at some unidentifiable carcasses on the plates behind the counter, taking out his last fifty-euro note.

He picked up the glass, which was now reduced to stained ice and the half-eaten olive.

'And this.'

Dogs, he thought.

After a little while, seated at a bare, low table by the window, he could hear them beyond the opaque, dusty glass, yapping and snarling out in the night. Not howling, not sounding desperate or frightened. More like animals in conversation which was, he knew, ridiculous, though the bittersweet strength of the spritz damaged his conviction on this and other matters, not least his whereabouts within the entwined tangle of lanes that was Castello.

A hand appeared from nowhere. It was the woman reaching for his glass. She tapped her watch. It was five minutes past eight. The dead of night in Venice in January. An entire day had passed somehow, disappeared between his fingers like sand trickling from a broken hourglass. The money was running out. It seemed inconceivable that he could ever return to Cambridge. The future looked like the Venetian night: black and impenetrable.

He grabbed the spritz and finished it. By then her fingers were on the plate. Jerome Aitchison snatched at the last remaining piece of fish there – something like a headless sardine, skin and bone and all – and shovelled it into his mouth. He'd paid for all this, not much, but it was his money, and he would have what it was worth.

'*Arrivederci*,' the old woman said without a smile.

Goodbye. Or, more accurately, he recalled from the guidebook, *Until we meet again*.

Not bloody likely, Aitchison thought. He muttered something obscene, his mouth still full of the fish he'd grabbed off the plate, then shambled to the door and stomped outside.

Finally the rain had ceased. The sky had cleared.

71

A stiff and bone-chilling wind was weaving through Castello, howling a little as it wound its way down the narrow, bleak lanes and across the channels of black water. Above him he could see a bright moon, one so large it seemed to turn the slimy walls of the alley leading to the little bridge a strange shade of silver.

'Damn this place,' cursed Aitchison. One moment ugly as hell. The next quite bewitching, like a painting itself, daring the visitor to interpret what he saw in front of his own eyes.

Or was seeing.

Tenses. The perfect against the imperfect. The complete versus the unfinished. In his hunger and thirst he had quite forgotten the baffling inscription on the cartellino. What had the woman called Sofia Bianchi said? That she'd studied the work, had written notes on it.

Aitchison leaned against the wall of the Cason dei Sette Morti and fumbled in his pocket to find the sheet of paper. The woman's phone number was on the bottom. He tried not to think about that. He could dream of calling her all he liked. He lacked the words, the wit, the courage.

The page was crumpled, a little stained from the rain that had seeped into his coat. By the dim light of the window, as the old crone inside cleaned up to the sound of a tinny radio, he was, however, able to read the words.

'Nonsense,' Aitchison spluttered, aware that a bony piece of fish leapt out of his mouth with the venom of his reaction. 'Stuff and nonsense. Quite impossible. Utter . . .'

The dog was on the bridge ahead, seated, the same tight, pale bundle of fur that he'd seen that afternoon, and the day before, on the wall of the *scuola* of the Slavs, and alive out in the street. Its head was up, alert and bright-eyed. Staring at him eagerly, as if in anticipation.

An involuntary spasm gripped his chest. A cough half-formed at the back of his throat and held there, stiff and awkward.

His left hand went to his neck. Then the right, letting go of Sofia Bianchi's notes on *St Augustine in his Study* which fluttered towards the ground, before being picked up by the wind, propelled over the canal, and out towards the Basin of St Mark.

As Jerome Aitchison, a retiring bachelor from Cambridge, stumbled to his knees in the back lanes of Castello her observations on the Carpaccio canvas flew high into the night sky, over the chimneys and rooftops of Venice before falling, seemingly at random, into the face of a recently arrived female Roman pathologist perched on a seat by the lagoon, tears in her eyes, remembering a lost friend, one who had once shared this view of San Giorgio Maggiore, newly revealed by the welcome departure of the cruise liner which had previously concealed it.

Glad of the distraction, the woman put aside her grief and then her reading matter, a prolix academic report of a symposium in the city to which she had been invited the following May, and snatched the damp paper from her cheek. The sheet was so wet it tore in two. Curiosity – she was a singularly inquisitive woman – meant that she had to read the fragment in her fingers. It was in English, under the heading, 'Carpaccio's Dog'.

'The style of the painting clearly owes much to the influence of fifteenth-century works from the Netherlands, though the subject is entirely Carpaccio's own. It stems from his commission to mark the lives of the three Slav saints commemorated in the *scuola*. The incident recorded in this work is an apocryphal story from church lore of the time. St Augustine is at his desk, writing a letter to his beloved and saintly friend, seeking advice for a treatise he wishes to produce discussing the joy of the blessed. Unknown to him, his correspondent has, at that very moment, died. Miraculously, St Augustine hears his voice quite clearly as he puts pen to paper, and listens as his friend asks, from beyond the grave, why such a question is necessary, since the answer can only be given once life, this life, is over.'

Intrigued by the tale the pathologist continued.

'The role of the charming little dog is open to interpretation, though doubtless symbolic, like many of the other details contained in this cryptic and compelling work. Is he there to remind Augustine to return to the world of the present and concentrate on the fleeting opportunities to seek grace within his own life while there is still time? Or, more darkly, as some direct reminder of the saint's own mortality, a hint that he should perhaps be looking forward to death in order to discover the answer to a question which Augustine clearly feels pressing, and worthy of discussion? The breed – the volpino – is a rare and curious one, believed by some in the Veneto to possess uncanny powers of divination, a canine clairvoyant if you like. It also carries the reputation of being a harbinger of change. A portent of death, or some other momentous event. Though perhaps, more likely, it is simply a loving pet, transfixed by his master's astonishment and impending grief at the loss of a dear and close friend, yet . . .'

Here, tantalizingly, the torn piece of paper ended. She scrabbled around for the rest, determined to find out whose unexpected death, announced in such an unlikely fashion, was the source of the work.

The errant sheet was sticking to the iron arm of the bench seat. She managed to snatch it just as the wind threatened to steal the torn scrap of damp paper for the lagoon.

'St Jerome,' she said out loud as she read the words there. The woman thought for a moment then read the rest.

'The patron saint of Dalmatia.' She racked her brain for a connection. There was none.

'Never heard of him,' she muttered and let go of the scraps of print. They disappeared on the breeze, out over the black water.

In the back alleys behind, a middle-aged British lecturer scrabbled on the damp, grubby ground, choking, gagging on the hard dry fish bone that had stuck like a thorn in his throat.

A life imperfect. Yet – and he wished to scream this but couldn't – continuing. Unfinished.

Jerome Aitchison's eyes were on the pale white creature in front of him. It hadn't moved an inch and its bright little teeth, sharp as needles, animated by the faintest and lowest of growls, shone bare and menacing in the moonlight.

THE FLIGHT OF THE ANGEL

She was woken by the sonorous tones of Salute's bells, so loud, so close it felt as if they shook the building as much as the tremors of the passing cruise liners. When the peals began to die she heard her mobile trilling from the living room. The pages of the short story lay scattered across the bed. Strange dreams, of dogs and dragons and paintings, still scurried around the back of her head. The bedroom curtains were open, allowing through the harsh clear light of the winter morning. The horn of a distant boat sounded, hollow and reedy in the thin lagoon air. It was that which finally reminded Teresa Lupo where she was and why.

With a conscious effort she dragged herself out of bed and got to the phone.

'Doctor! Doctor!' said an excited voice. 'It is I! Tosi! You remember me?'

'Tosi?'

The name brought a face to mind: a careful old man holding sway over an antiquated morgue somewhere near Venice's Piazzale Roma bus station.

'Alberto Tosi,' he said slowly. 'That awful case in Murano which you and your friends solved so cleverly. You recall?'

Murano. A glass furnace and mysterious ashes. Leo Falcone shot, almost killed. A strange and disturbing interlude that should have been a happy holiday.[1]

'How could I forget?' she muttered.

'And now you're back! This is fortuitous. I cannot believe my luck!'

More of the bizarre story from the night before was returning, and with it her puzzlement. Whoever wrote that knew she was in Venice, and of her background. The comment about a dead friend could only refer to Nic Costa's late wife. During the difficult investigation which introduced her to Alberto Tosi she and Emily had grown close. It was only a matter of time until Teresa happened upon one of the places they used to visit and found, as the odd tale predicted, the recollections of her dead friend sharp and painful.

Tosi was aware of her presence too.

'I'm sorry,' she said. 'How did you know I was here?'

'I thought you didn't see me. I waved. You were on the vaporetto with a lady in a fur coat. Yesterday afternoon.'

'My mother.'

[1] See *The Lizard's Bite*.

'An elegant woman. Beautiful.'

'Alberto . . .'

There was no need to lay it on quite so thickly.

'I phoned the Rome Questura and spoke to that young deputy of yours. He seemed very keen to provide your number.'

Thank you, Silvio, she thought. I know I shouldn't be bunking off like this too.

'You and your mother shall be my guests for the carnival,' Tosi went on. 'Today, at lunchtime. We begin with the Flight of the Angel. After that, anything you wish. And then . . .'

She did not recall such fulsome enthusiasm when she was in Venice before. In fact there had been some distinct tension between the Romans and the local police on that occasion, and no small amount of unpleasantness in the end.

It was important to clarify the position from the beginning. Teresa was not blind to Tosi's advantageous position within the city. His family, if she recalled correctly, had held official positions in the police for generations. The old man ought to be able to open doors which would otherwise have remained closed to a mere visiting Roman.

So she told him as much as she could about Sofia and the mystery of her disappearance. Nothing more. Certainly nothing about a strange story concerning a lost and damaged Englishman wandering into a *scuola* in Castello which, she felt sure, was no invention on the part of the unknown author who had set down the narrative delivered the previous evening in a manila envelope bearing her name.

'Oh my goodness,' Tosi declared the moment she'd finished. 'What must you think of me? Here you are on a mission of some urgency and delicacy. And an old man who's a virtual stranger pesters you for his own selfish purposes. Please . . .'

'You weren't to know.'

'I must help. May we meet?'

She glanced at the clock on the wall. It was just after eight.

They arranged a rendezvous by the Ponte agli Incurabili at ten thirty. After that, if she agreed, he would take her to see the Flight of the Angel, whatever that was. An essential sight, he insisted, and on the way to the Castello Questura where he would introduce her to a police officer more amenable than any to be found in the main Questura near the Piazzale Roma.

This seemed to make excellent sense.

'What purpose of yours?' she asked out of interest.

'I won't waste your time with it now,' the old man replied. 'Let me do what I can to assist in regard to your aunt. I am retired, I regret. Times have changed. Rationalization . . .' He spoke the word with a bitterness that seemed uncharacteristic. 'Nothing matters any more except money. But I can still open a few doors.'

When he'd rung off she checked the kitchen. She should have realized the night before that there was nothing for breakfast. Nowhere in her brief wanderings nearby had she found a shop.

Hunting for food was not the way she wanted to start the day, but in the circumstances there was no choice. In Rome it had seemed obvious that she needed to be here. Thanks to the tension with her mother, she had never thought through why or how she would proceed once they arrived. At that moment she felt lost for a way forward. She was a pathologist, not a cop. She had no official standing, no way of forcing either the police or the Carabinieri to do her bidding. Even if she had some kind of lead – and the peculiar tale from the previous night scarcely fitted that description – she doubted it would do much good. A woman with a bohemian history, someone who had seemingly tried to kill herself in Venice sixteen years before, had gone missing without trace. Teresa Lupo understood what kind of response a stranger arriving from Rome with such a story would receive, even one who came with the blessing of a retired Venetian pathologist. Sympathy, a careful, polite audience, then a shrug.

What could they do? People went missing all the time. Usually they turned up unhurt and a little shame-faced.

'Not women who are forty-six years old,' she told herself, staring at the jumbled array of objects on the table, the computer, papers, bills, letters, a raffia box with needles and thread, a couple of paintbrushes that needed cleaning, and the vase containing the bouquet from the night before.

The mannequin in its expensive silk dress gazed at her from the doorway. Sofia was broke. Why spend money on something like that?

Somewhere at the back of her head lurked an unwanted stub of knowledge, a statistic that had fallen out of an official report. One that correlated the age of those who went missing with the eventual outcome of the case. The older they were, the bleaker the possibilities. Was that true? Perhaps her memory was playing tricks.

She needed food. She needed coffee. More than anything she needed hard information, not strange, anonymous fairy tales posted to her by name.

Teresa Lupo checked herself. She had only the word of the young woman downstairs for that. She was in an unfamiliar city, surrounded by people she didn't know. It made sense to question everything.

The phone beeped. It was a message from Tosi confirming the appointment. Automatically, out of habit, she deleted the text and, without thinking, the message before it, from Peroni, not seeing its content as her fingers flew across the phone.

Then, without much care, she got dressed and went downstairs one floor, stopping outside the bright purple door, wondering what she wanted to say, to ask. There was a drawing of a star sign there, Virgo. A starry-eyed woman out of Botticelli, with a crown of flowers.

She was still thinking when Camilla Dushku answered, wearing a heavy cashmere jumper the same colour as the woodwork and floppy, old-fashioned jeans. She was smiling. Her long dark hair was shiny and well managed in a way that Teresa Lupo always found difficult to compre-hend. The young woman's complexion was perfect though remarkably pale. She was already beck-oning Teresa into the room with an amiable, frank cheerfulness.

There was the enticing smell of coffee and fresh pastries.

'I heard your door close,' Camilla Dushku said, waving her in. 'You don't miss a thing in this funny old place. You want breakfast?'

Teresa was still staring at the painting.

'Sofia did that,' Camilla told her. 'She did one for all of us. A gift. Horoscopes. And painting. Talents of hers, I think.'

The living room of the young woman's apartment lay directly below that of Sofia's. It was precisely the same size and shape, with a similar, if slightly lower, aspect onto the Giudecca canal from the windows at the front. But this room was both modern and organized, so rigidly laid out that it might have been some kind of store or workshop. All with a single purpose: the production of masks, hundreds of them, rank upon rank of blank faces, every set of empty eyes staring blindly into space.

White and gold, black and scarlet, shiny, dull, simple and ornate, the masks were everywhere, on the walls, on the large work table at the centre of the room, hanging to dry on frames lined up in a row in the corridor to the kitchen.

'Carnival,' Camilla said simply, noting Teresa's interest.

'People say that as if it explains everything.'

'It explains a lot. I made more money last night than I do in a month usually.' She made a grasping gesture with her hands. 'Men with masks tip more handsomely for some reason. And when it's *not* carnival then . . .'

She pointed to a couple of large industrial plastic buckets by the window. On one side stood pots of powder and shredded paper; on the other what looked like masks-in-the-making, plain simple faces waiting to be painted and varnished.

Papier-mâché, Teresa realized.

'This is what you do?' she asked.

'It is now. Beats painting pretty views for tourists.' Camilla smiled. 'I think Sofia was beginning to work that out too. I was going to show her how to make masks one day.'

Past and present. Perfect and imperfect, continuous, unfinished. 'I am going to' is not the same as 'I was going to'. Tenses mattered to the fictional Englishman in that story the night before. They were important in real life too.

'Perhaps you still can,' Teresa said.

'I hope so. Is she coming back?'

'I can't answer that. I don't know where she is. Why she left. I don't know anything. That's why I'm here.'

Camilla shook her head, went into the kitchen for a moment and came back with two cups of strong coffee and some fresh and fragrant pastries, like round doughnuts with nuts and fruit in them.

Teresa tried one and nodded.

'*Frittelle*,' Camilla told her. 'Only in carnival. Unless you're a tourist.'

'Nice,' she said, and meant it. There was nothing quite like this – sweet, spicy and seemingly proud of its simplicity – in Rome.

Camilla held out her pale fine hands and smiled.

'Sofia told me my fortune once. With those cards of hers. She said I had a long and happy life ahead of me. With children!'

The cards, the crystal ball, the signs of the zodiac. Teresa remembered those from when she was a kid. They were one of the few points of disagreement between her and her aunt. The rational, level-headed child never understood why an intelligent, popular adult should resort to such superstition. They'd agreed not to talk about the subject. It surprised her that even now, thirty years on, her aunt still clung to those habits. A fortune-teller couldn't foresee her own future. Sofia had been adamant about that. It was one of the many reasons Teresa had found the idea so ridiculous.

'We have breakfast then I take you downstairs to

meet Filippo. He's as anxious as I am to know where Sofia is. As you are too,' Camilla emphasized. 'This is so strange.'

'It is,' Teresa agreed. 'Who's Filippo?'

The young woman gestured around the room with her right arm.

'The man downstairs. He taught me how to make all these for his shop. You'll like him. Everyone does.'

Filippo Strozzi's door, the red one at ground level, was ajar when they walked down the stone stairs. There was a small picture of Taurus the bull, in Sofia's hand. Piano music, the dazzling sound of waves of cascading arpeggios, flooded the hallway. With the light from the windows about the entrance this glorious burst of sound lent the old palazzo a fetching, human appearance. For the first time Teresa found she could imagine Sofia here, wandering from floor to floor, eating *frittelle*, drinking coffee, chatting. It felt at that moment like a student house and Sofia, in some ways, seemed to resemble a perpetual undergraduate, an individual always on the cusp of knowledge, never quite attaining it.

Camilla pushed open the door and they walked in. The music continued and Teresa realized to her astonishment that it was not the product of a sound system but live, coming from a large bearded man perched behind a battered grand piano set in the window, occupying most of the space there. He was clearly determined to finish, and she was glad of that. He played beautifully, fluently, his arms moving with the determined power and confidence of a performer.

Only once did he look up and, briefly, smile. He was a massive man, more than burly, fat and muscle in a frame that filled a ragged grey sack-like sweater. Perhaps fifty, Teresa thought, with a serious Mediterranean face, heavy jowls covered with a grizzled beard that looked as if it didn't get much attention. His hair was shoulder-length, grey and black, moving as he bent to the pulsing cadence of the testing piece that occupied him. He wore unfashionable round wire-rimmed spectacles. Behind them gleamed two rather prominent and intelligent eyes. There was no music on the piano, no notation anywhere that she could see. He was playing this complex and challenging piece entirely from memory, for pleasure, she imagined, not practice, since his face appeared relaxed, not taut with concentration.

Years before, as a student herself, Teresa had had a boyfriend who was determined to become a concert pianist. For a while she'd listened to him practise, fascinated by his technique and approach to the work. This piece was familiar from that time, one of the most difficult Chopin études of all: Opus 10 No. 1, the 'Waterfall', a pyrotechnic display of technical proficiency that was, she seemed to recall, designed as much to strengthen and flex the player's fingers as to demonstrate his or her mastery over arpeggios and stretch.

She closed her eyes. It was brief, two minutes at the most, and part way through when she came in. He performed the piece with an uncommon and fluent skill save for one detail that she still remembered from those years before, seated at the feet of a man who was now a teacher in Perugia, not the concert pianist he'd once hoped.

When the music came to a fiery end it sounded different somehow, not in the notes themselves but in the tonal quality. Then it came back to her.

'Pedal,' Teresa said without thinking. She opened her eyes and looked at Filippo Strozzi, her spirits cheered already by his presence, the bright and obvious talent and enthusiasm he had displayed at the piano. 'I had a friend who played that. He always used pedal at the end. Practised for hours. Said it was essential. Personal taste I imagine . . .'

The room was dreadfully cold. The temperature seemed to descend a couple of degrees further at that moment. She fell silent.

Camilla looked briefly aghast. The man at the keyboard thought for a moment, smiled and then reached down for something and began to retreat from the instrument. Teresa realized that he was seated in a shiny modern wheelchair, one with a battery mechanism that propelled him round and then out from the piano.

'Pedals are rather beyond me I'm afraid,' Filippo Strozzi said wryly.

He folded his arms and stared at her. Grey sweater, black shirt peeking above it, dark heavy workman's oversized jeans, John Lennon spectacles. The costume of a musician. But his legs had the stiff, flabby stillness of the invalid.

'I don't know what to say,' Teresa groaned. Her face was glowing in spite of the cold. She was blushing like an embarrassed child. 'I'm so sorry. So . . .'

The wheelchair buzzed over. He extended a hand. She took it, liking the firmness and warmth of his touch, unexpected in such a chilly room.

'Nonsense,' he said. 'How were you to know? What does it matter? I'm Filippo. And you are Sofia's niece, Teresa. The police officer from Rome. She told me about you. Camilla too.'

'Pathologist,' she corrected him. 'I only work with the police.'

'On investigations?'

'Yes, but I'm a forensic officer. Not an investigative one. Not in the real sense.'

He nodded then ran himself over to the small dining table set beneath what looked like a Modigliani print, and indicated two chairs there.

Money, she thought.

There was none in this room either. The temperature, the threadbare carpet, even the battered piano showed that Strozzi, like Sofia, was leading a pauper's life, struggling to get by.

She and Camilla took a seat.

'Who lives on the top floor?' she asked.

'Why?'

Strozzi seemed a man who didn't waste words.

'I'm trying to imagine Sofia's life here. I've met you both now. The top floor—'

'That belongs to Signor Ruskin,' Camilla interrupted. 'This is his property. He's English. His mother was a friend of Peggy Guggenheim all those years ago, or so they say. You know the gallery around the corner?'

Teresa nodded, recalling the modern, half-built palazzo on the Grand Canal where the grande dame of American art had lived and partied wildly several decades before.

'Michael . . . Signor Ruskin,' Strozzi added, 'is back in London now and has been for several weeks. We see him rarely. He has other properties in Venice, beside this one. Usually it's just us here. Three. Two now.'

He frowned and said, 'Sofia never mentioned going away. Where do you think she is?'

'That's what I'm here to find out.'

Teresa outlined the known facts as she understood them, though kept the detail of the story once more to herself. Both listened carefully. They seemed to know a good deal about Sofia's past, the marriages, the travel, the dreams.

'She painted here,' Strozzi told her. 'Tried to sell a few things to the tourists. To work as a tour guide when she could.' He sighed. 'It's not easy making a living this way. Venice was once the richest city in the Adriatic. A place for princes. But then we had banking and commerce and trade. And war. With all these things comes money. Now . . .' He was staring directly at her, perhaps trying to say more than he was willing to put into words. 'Fishing is the only industry left. Fishing for men. The tourists who trek endlessly to our door, to look, to wonder. Hopefully to buy.'

He drove the wheelchair forward and removed a mask from the wall. It was a woman's, a sad, pale face, mouth downturned, tears painted beneath the eyes.

'I came here to be a musician,' Strozzi said. 'What finer home could I have? Then one day . . .' Another long, resigned sigh. 'I am riding through Switzerland on my fine BMW motorbike. Only two hundred kilometres an hour, you understand. I was not in a hurry . . .'

'Filippo,' Camilla scolded him. 'How can you joke about such things?'

'What else is there to do after all these years? I crash, my legs are gone, and let me be frank. I am not so good a pianist that my disability may become a selling point. It's expensive ferrying around a man in my condition. So I must get by as I can. I play at weddings and social events. Peanuts mostly. I've got a small mask shop around the corner. I teach people, talented artists like Camilla, how to make them. Not cheap. Real masks. The *bauta*, the *Moretta*, the *Colombina*. And this . . .'

He reversed and Teresa knew what he would pick up.

'The *Medico della Peste*.'

Strozzi put it on and was transformed. Both anonymous and threatening.

'The Plague Doctor,' Camilla said. 'He's my favourite.'

Teresa Lupo met those bleak, crystal eyes and remembered the man in the black cloak and buckled hat who had helped them off the boat at Zattere the afternoon before. It was ridiculous, she knew, but she couldn't help but wonder if he'd been waiting for their arrival.

Strozzi removed the mask and placed it on the table.

'Sofia thought it would be easy to make a living in a place so full of foreigners. But nothing's so simple. We have a strange relationship, visitors and those of us who live off them. You'd think it would be close. Symbiotic. That they would appreciate us for our knowledge, and we them for their money. In truth there's resentment on both sides. They detest us for what they see as our avarice. We despise them because we know that without their custom we could not survive. Dependence breeds neither cordiality nor respect.'

He reached for the mask and briefly placed it over his face again.

'See. Making masks is the most honest, most

open way for any of us to get by. Sofia has yet to learn that, I think. It's hard for her. She's so truthful and decent.'

Strozzi stared at her again and she was struck by how earnest he seemed.

'Do you really have no idea where she's gone?' he asked.

'None.'

'She has a habit of disappearing like this?'

Too close.

'Sofia told you that?' Teresa asked.

Camilla was shaking her head as if this was news to her.

'No,' Strozzi said. 'I guessed. She and I were born in the same year. I am three months older than her. In all that time I have lived in five places in Italy, the last two decades here in Venice. Sofia seemed to have visited everywhere, and always found it lacking somehow.'

'But she had friends here, surely? She lived in Venice before. Sixteen years ago. Didn't she tell you that?'

'She didn't mention it to me,' Camilla said.

Strozzi shrugged and said nothing.

'She came out with us sometimes,' the young woman continued. 'There's a place in Campo Santa Margherita. A pizzeria. We would have dinner there. And we talked during the day, of course. But in the evening . . .'

'She went out on her own?' Teresa persisted.

'Most nights I heard the door go around seven,'

Strozzi said. 'When she came back . . . I don't know. I sleep early. Ten, ten thirty at the latest. I'm a true Venetian these days. I'm sorry.'

'She knew someone called Gobbo,' she said, watching for their reaction. The name clearly meant nothing. Then she recalled the precise entry in the diary upstairs. 'No. It was written *Il* Gobbo. As if it was a nickname or something.'

They looked at each other, clearly lost for any connection.

'She must have been seeing someone,' Camilla said. 'I heard her leave too, and get back sometimes. It was late. After midnight.'

'Alone?'

'I think so.' She hesitated then added, 'I didn't want to spy on anyone. We all have our own lives here.'

But I don't know what Sofia's was, Teresa thought. I believed I did and I was wrong.

'She was making a costume,' she told them. 'For the carnival I imagine.'

'No,' Camilla said immediately. 'You mean that thing on the dummy behind the door? I never saw that before last night. I didn't know Sofia could even sew.'

'A costume?' Strozzi asked.

'I've never seen a true carnival costume that looks like that,' Camilla insisted. 'They're as specific as the masks. You're allowed a little improvisation. But the styles, the characters are fixed. That wasn't one of them.'

Strozzi reached for the table and picked up his mobile phone.

'Take a photo, please,' he said, giving it to Teresa. 'I would like to see this.'

A nickname. An odd costume. A crazy story written by whom? Sofia herself? If so why deny authorship? Or the work of someone else? Someone who knew where she was and wanted to help? Even – this had to be faced – an abductor playing some cruel and intricate game? These were all threads without attachments, pointless without context or meaning.

'Have you heard of an Englishman called Aitchison?' she asked, clutching at straws.

They both shook their heads. There was no more time for this. She had to meet Alberto Tosi and then go with him to the Castello Questura.

'Bring me the photo,' Strozzi repeated. 'Let me think about this. Perhaps Sofia said something I've forgotten.'

Camilla followed her and took several shots of the gown and the dummy. Now Teresa looked at it again the thing seemed wrong for the carnival. The fabric was too rich, the small crown fetching rather than showy. The style seemed old, not eighteenth- or seventeenth-century, but something more ancient: the kind of dress seen in a painting from Caravaggio or earlier. It was light too, and thin. Most of the carnival costumes she'd seen were heavy and designed for outdoors in the bitter

95

Venetian winter. No one could wear this on a freezing February day.

'Where did this man Aitchison come from?' Camilla asked.

'You wouldn't believe me,' Teresa muttered.

'I could try.'

The acerbic comment seemed to have offended her. She was a bright young woman, a little ingenuous at first sight. Not Italian either. On the walk up the stairs she'd told how she came here two years before from her native Dubrovnik, looking to find a better living than could be made in Croatia.

'All right,' Teresa said and led her into the bedroom.

The yellow pages of the short story lay scattered on the crumpled bed. She didn't remember turning over every single one so that the typed side was face down on the duvet.

Teresa flipped over the nearest. The other side was blank too. The same for the next one. Growing ever more furious she dashed her fingers through the pile of sheets.

There wasn't a word on any of them. The story from the previous night, *Carpaccio's Dog*, was gone entirely, disappeared from this strange mustard-coloured paper as if by magic.

Camilla waited, embarrassed.

'Forget it,' Teresa said, then asked her to take the photographs to Filippo Strozzi.

When the girl had gone she lay down on the

bed in the midst of the blank sheets of paper, fighting back the tears, stamping her fists angrily into the mattress, furious in the sea of yellow that flew around her like gigantic confetti.

When she finally managed to recover some of her composure she glanced at her watch. The appointment with Tosi was only twenty minutes away. She sat upright on the bed, wiped her face, tried to think.

Everything had an explanation if only you could find it. That simple truth was central to her view of the world, of life. A tenet of faith almost.

She picked up one of the sheets of paper and rubbed it between her fingers. The colour, the thickness, the texture . . . all these were unusual. She wasn't insane, not imagining the eerie narrative of an English character named Jerome Aitchison and some dark, unresolved encounter in the back streets of Castello. It had been set out on these very pages then somehow made to disappear once she had read it. Offering up evidence then removing proof of its existence, shifting any blame, and perhaps even suspicion, on to her.

Back in the living room she looked at the manila envelope in which the short story had arrived. It had a strange and very firm adhesive seal and a lined plastic interior. The thing was airtight. Some chemical process must have been involved, one which began the degradation of the ink once it was exposed to air.

She placed a sheet of the yellow paper in an envelope then, on the way out, begged a postage stamp from Camilla, discovering as she did so that there was no Internet access in the building. Nor had she a modern laptop she could use. These matters would be rectified the following morning, regardless of the expense, if Sofia was still missing by then.

On the way to the bridge she posted the paper sample to her assistant, Silvio Di Capua, in Rome. It would not arrive till Tuesday. She'd no idea how long it would take him to come up with an answer. Di Capua was a talented man with a wide range of forensic interests. Perhaps not long.

Tosi stood where she expected him, a tall, lean man in his early seventies. He was resting on a black walking stick and wore an anklelength black over-coat and a moleskin trilby hat. She felt better for seeing him, better too for knowing that she was, finally, in possession of a scrap of evidence, proof of something strange pertaining to Sofia's disappearance. Even if it no longer contained a single word.

'Doctor! Teresa!' Tosi said when she reached him.

They exchanged kisses, cold lips against cold cheeks.

Then, smiling, the old man declared, 'And you look so at home in Venice already! Like a native!'

'Why do you say that?'

'The dog,' he said. 'The little white dog with you . . . I . . .'

He peered round her, back at the promenade

beyond the Ponte agli Incurabili. Teresa followed the line of his gaze. The rear quarters of a small white animal were disappearing down an alley beyond the bridge. Its head was out of view and the animal was trotting at quite a pace.

'I thought it was yours,' Tosi said. 'So many dogs in Venice. We love the little creatures, which is why you must always tread carefully, even when the weather isn't arctic.'

The vaporetto was making its way across the canal already, moving steadily towards the *fermata*, cutting through the dappled water that shone silver under the low winter sun.

'I don't have a dog,' she said. 'Can we go to the police station now?'

It was one of the smaller, faster boats that worked the outside of the islands and sped across the Basin of St Mark packed to the gills. Young and old, families, locals, tourists, either wrapped up well in winter coats or trapped inside incongruous carnival costumes, faces hidden behind masks ancient and modern, traditional and bizarre.

The light was so pale and weak there seemed no dividing line between lagoon and sky. The biting air made her throat ache. As they docked a pair of bright-eyed crested grebes watched from the water, heads bobbing with interest as if amazed by the sight.

There were so many passengers it took a good

five minutes to disembark then make their way through the crowds admiring the Bridge of Sighs.

'I know a quick way,' Alberto Tosi declared then led her by the arm and entered the shady loggia by the side of the Doge's Palace. The piazza seemed impossibly full. Men and women in feathers and masks, cloaks and billowing hooped dresses, grand aristocratic jackets and gowns. Children threaded their way through the forest of bodies as miniature lords and ladies, spacemen, cartoon characters, cowboys, beasts and insects.

Ahead of her a man in the full-length gown of a Benedictine monk with the mask of a demon on his face walked quickly into the crowd. He was smoking a cigar and carrying, inexplicably, a base-ball bat. Tosi scurried into the shadow of the palace, tugging her along. Then they ran into a solid wall of bodies. She knew this place. There was no easy exit route until they managed to get past the façade of the basilica then find the back lanes into Castello and the local Questura. He'd led her here deliberately; had they turned right when leaving the boat they could have escaped the crush entirely.

An army of gaily coloured bodies blocked their path. As they were forced to stop she heard the sound of trumpets, a fanfare voluntary, bright and military. Ahead, out of the side arch of the palace, came a procession of dignitaries, men and women grandly arrayed, one in the guise of the Doge himself, a beautiful creature by his side bedecked in jewels as the Dogaressa, his duchess.

They came to a halt and Tosi scratched his head.

'This is so *not* my kind of thing,' Teresa muttered through gritted teeth.

'I may have made a wrong decision back there,' he confessed.

Tosi turned round. The return route to the waterfront was blocked by a new influx of spectators. They were trapped for as long as the ceremony would take.

'You were determined I should see this, weren't you?' she said.

'No!' He looked offended. She felt guilty. 'It's not easy getting anywhere in carnival. The first day particularly.' His eyes rose to the upright brick column of the campanile rising above the piazza, and then the ornate windows and pinnacle at its summit. 'Especially when the angel is about to exercise her wings.'

'What?' she demanded.

'The angel. She comes down from the campanile into the square. On a wire.' Tosi thought about whether to say what was on his mind. 'In the old days we used to call it the Flight of the Turk and make one of *them* walk down the wire. Now it's some pretty actress usually. In a gown. Hooked to the wire. This year that girl from the television. Luisa Cammarota. The one from the papers.'

The name rang a bell. One more Italian starlet,

forever in and out of the magazines for her colourful private life. Blonde hair and the kind of figure Italian men of a certain age liked to ogle.

Teresa could not believe this was delaying their visit to the police and told him so.

'Sorry,' the old Venetian said with a shrug. 'I appreciate the urgency. But look around you. With so many people here no one will get anywhere very easily. Besides the police will be very occupied too. You wouldn't have seen an officer until after the angel had flown anyway. And it is quite a sight.'

'You did this on purpose, Alberto!'

Tosi grinned and put an apologetic finger briefly to his lips, like a child.

'Carnival is the busiest time of the year,' he replied. 'Nothing happens quickly.'

'Nothing ever happens quickly in Venice.'

'Thank you!' he said, beaming, then took her arm and propelled them forward until they were closer to the basilica. Something was happening. The steady beat of a military drum preceded a long line of men and women in ornate ancient costumes, soldiers and courtly ladies then a man in red with the horned hat she recognized. The Doge for the day emerged again and this time she could see him clearly. He was grinning, embarrassed, unduly proud, some local elevated for the procession more than two hundred years after the last real ruler of Venice had handed over the keys to the city to Napoleon.

It took ten minutes for this supposedly noble party to work their way through the crowds and cameras then proceed to the platform at the far end of the piazza, near the Museo Correr, with a speed that would certainly be denied to ordinary bystanders trapped in the general melee.

With the Venetian skill for pushing others out of the way, Tosi yelled '*Permesso! Permesso!*' and barged forward, both elbows working, creating a little room for them near a rubbish bin. Once there he smiled broadly, reached into his coat and retrieved two tiny pocket telescopes, handing one to her.

'I always come prepared,' he said. 'Look . . .'

The loudspeaker had started the announcements, in alternate Italian and English, a breathless commentator describing the illustrious history of the carnival, the importance of the coming angel's flight, and the beauty of the 'famous actress' Luisa Cammarota, who would soon descend to earth among them.

'Ridiculous,' Teresa grumbled, and placed the tiny telescope to her right eye then attempted to focus on the top of the campanile.

It wasn't easy. The feeble winter sun had risen a little over the lagoon now. After some fiddling and squinting she found the pinnacle of the bell tower and scanned the line of open stone arches near the top, seeing nothing out of the ordinary.

Tosi nudged her finger upwards. The focus of the scope travelled beyond the obvious to the ledge above the open windows, a narrow sliver of marble set against the flat brickwork beneath the green peak of the spire a hundred metres or so above the hard piazza pavement.

There was a roar of delight from the crowd around her. As she watched, two figures appeared, a man walking freely, without fear, at the very edge of the tower and a woman in a long, flowing feathery dress. She was attached to twin wires which ran directly from the spire across the piazza to the stage at the end of the square. Her young and beautiful face was rigid and expressionless, with fear or cold or possibly both. Teresa did remember her now, a glamorous showgirl-cum-actress.

She took away the scope. Heights didn't bother her normally. But this seemed so bizarre, so *unnecessary*. And the man supervising the angel's descent was walking around quite normally, unperturbed by the idea that one step too far would send him plummeting to the ground.

'Watch please,' Tosi insisted, pushing at her little telescope. 'Even Romans don't see a spectacle like this every day.'

This was true.

When her attention returned to the spire the woman was in the air, starting her descent to the piazza. This wasn't a fairground ride. It was slow and stately, which seemed to make the tension all the worse.

Teresa's attention wandered. She checked the

man on the ledge again, who seemed so pleased with his work that she expected him to sit down on the edge of the narrow parapet and dangle his legs over the edge like a happy child.

This thought made her feel a little giddy, so she roamed a little with the telescope, admiring the detail of the tower, so ornate and beautiful, with crests and shields and gold features one would never appreciate with the naked eye. As she scanned the white marble section beneath, a face appeared at one of the open arches.

The starlet who was the angel came from the Veneto region and had some part in one of the nightly quiz shows. The crowd loved her. It was obvious from the way they screamed her name as she came closer.

Photographers, Teresa thought. They had to have them in the tower to capture an occasion such as this. And wasn't that a camera the man had in his hand? A small dark one, with a long barrel-like lens.

She tried to fiddle with the focus ring to get the image sharper.

The figure was now clearer for the simple reason that he had walked out to stand boldly on the marble ledge beyond the arches, paralleling the wire supervisor above him, who was surely unaware of what was happening beneath his feet.

The man wore a costume she was coming to recognize: the Plague Doctor. A long black cloak, a broad felt hat with a buckle, a dark ruff at the neck. And that sinister, expressionless mask with the long, nightmare nose that bent down pointing towards the piazza pavement so far below.

The thing in his hand wasn't a camera. It was a gun.

'Alberto!' she cried, but the old man wasn't listening. His attention was with that of the crowd around them, focused on the figure of the angel descending slowly to the ground, her long feathery gown extending so far below her she seemed of an extraordinary height as she waved and smiled and blew kisses to the massed thousands gathered in the piazza.

Over the roars and shouts and catcalls there was a single explosive crack. Teresa's eyes dashed back to the Plague Doctor. His arm was extended, the gun rigid in his fingers. The woman on the wire was perhaps twenty metres away, moving further from him all the time. Not an easy shot.

One bullet gone already, target missed, and no one, it seemed, had noticed but her.

'Get the damned police,' she screamed, tugging at the old man's arm, pointing at the campanile, the last place anyone in the piazza was looking at that moment. 'Look up there!'

Finally he did as he was told, turning the scope to the tower, scanning it.

'Oh my goodness,' Tosi murmured.

He began to wave around him, bellowing in a hoarse Venetian accent. There was no one in a uniform anywhere near. Only this noisy, gleeful crowd that saw nothing but a grand and glorious spectacle, a beautiful angel descending into their midst, waving to each and every one of them.

Teresa looked at the tower again. The black figure was aiming. One more crack. This time the crowd fell silent, puzzled by something. She spun the telescope round to the wire in the middle of the piazza. The starlet was writhing around inside her harness, clearly terrified, uncomprehending. There was what looked like blood on her right thigh, staining the pure white feathered gown all the way down to its distant hem.

As Teresa watched she heard the loud retort of another shot. Sparks flew from the metal wire no more than an arm's length from the angel's head. The poor girl folded in on herself, in fear and bewilderment, Teresa thought, not pain. There was no more blood. That shot had missed too. One in three, and she was getting further away from him all the time. It would surely take a serious marksman to kill someone with a pistol in such a situation, halfway across the piazza of San Marco.

She turned the scope back to the tower. The supervisor on the roof was aware something was wrong. Arms waving, shouting words no one could hear, he was managing to force the wire mechanism to move more quickly. After a few long seconds the angel arrived on the platform, into the arms of the costumed figures there, and two or three baffled police officers.

Safe. With what appeared, from a distance, to be a minor gunshot wound.

She took Tosi's scope from her face and squinted into the sun, trying to make sense of what was going on at the summit of the campanile. The Plague Doctor was still there, the gun by his side, a black figure motionless and silent on the ledge, staring down into the crowd. The mass of people had forgotten the wounded angel now. Every face in the Piazza San Marco was turned to him, every throat silent. The pregnant stillness joined them all in anticipation, like an audience waiting for the climax of a performance.

She knew what was coming somehow. All the same she shivered and felt strangely distant as the figure in the dark flowing costume let go of the weapon, watched it tumble slowly out of his fingers, over the edge of the white marble ledge, turning and turning as it fell to the crowd below.

Head bent forward, the man watched and waited for it to disappear. Then he made a long theatrical bow, deathly white mask rigid, bent downwards, right hand waving below him, into the empty space beyond the campanile ledge, as if in thanks to those who had followed his act. After that, fearless, determined, he simply allowed himself to sink forwards over the ledge, hands by his side, plunging head first down towards the sea of bodies beneath him.

Romans can push and shove too, Teresa thought as she yelled 'Police' and 'Doctor' and anything else she could think of, fighting her way towards the area where he must have fallen. The press of bodies was against her, pushing and screaming to get away from whatever had happened in the shadows of the Procuratie near the famous café of Florian.

When she got there a single state police officer was standing over the bloody mess, wondering what to do. She flashed her ID and told him to stand back. Three bodies lay on the ornate patterned pavement. A woman in an elaborate carnival costume of purple silk and gold was sobbing, her mask by her side, what looked like a badly broken arm outstretched on the cold cobbles. An elderly man in the guise of an aristocratic eighteenth-century count, the husband perhaps judging by the way she reached out for him, groaned next to her, clutching his stomach.

You two will live, Teresa thought, aware as always that this was a time for swift clinical judgement, not sympathy.

The Plague Doctor was different. The man in the black costume was a broken mess on the ground, twisted, bloodied, torn. She got down and carefully removed the white mask, lifting it up by the long shiny nose with her right hand, freeing the fastening at the back of his head with her left. It was a coarse middle-aged face, light in colour, clean-shaven, mouth locked in an expression that would, in a living human being, be counted as a sardonic smile.

'Stand back. Police,' snapped a voice from behind.

'I'm a doctor,' she said, without looking. 'And police too.'

Teresa Lupo didn't budge. Death always moved her, all the more so when it seemed so inexplicable, so pointless. Was this a serious attempt at murder at all? Or madness? A theatrical form of suicide, in front of the largest audience anyone with a death wish could ever muster in Venice?

The ruff had ridden up under the force of the fall. She could see pale skin, grey chest hair, and something else too. Taking a tissue from her bag she retrieved the familiar object. It was a European Union passport with a maroon cover.

Then she got to her feet and turned round. Tosi was there next to a couple of uniformed cops, making excuses for her behaviour, trying to reassure them.

'Sorry,' Teresa said to the first cop, a surly-looking man in an ill-fitting blue uniform. 'Old habits die hard.' She held out the passport. 'Here. For what it's worth this man came here to die. You don't carry your passport underneath a costume like that for no good reason. He was trying to save you some work.'

She flicked open the back pages.

'He being . . .'

The name stared up at her, and a picture of the

man beneath the mask, looking severe and serious, academic even.

Someone, the passport said, called Jerome Aitchison.

Six hours later she was still in the Castello Questura. Alberto Tosi had done his best to help though no one seemed to pay him much attention. She had, at least, been assigned an officer to talk to about her missing aunt, a friendly young female *sovrintendente* from Chioggia at the tip of the lagoon, Paola Boscolo. She looked just turned thirty and readily admitted she dealt chiefly with domestic abuse cases. Like every police officer in Venice that day she had been assigned to carnival duties and would remain attached to them for as long as was necessary.

This large, cheery woman with a permanent smile had very little to say that wasn't blithely encouraging. Teresa felt sure she would have some happy aphorism to pass on to the late Jerome Aitchison's relatives if only they could be found. It seemed the man had none. From what they had gathered in calls to England over the previous few hours he was a solitary academic, in precisely the uncertain and unhappy position over his employment that the mysterious, and now disappeared, story had suggested.

'What are you going to do?' Teresa asked for the umpteenth time.

The interview had begun two hours after the

incident in the piazza, and followed at sporadic intervals as Paola Boscolo received further information. The starlet, Luisa Cammarota, was, as Teresa suspected, only slightly wounded, though deeply traumatized. The two spectators who were hit by the falling body of the Englishman had suffered minor injuries which would require no more than a night's stay in hospital. The feeling in the Questura was that the city had got off lightly. Teresa wasn't quite so sure. Had Aitchison intended serious harm to anyone but himself he would surely have chosen a more direct and efficient means of attack.

'As I've said, Teresa . . .' The woman seemed to be on immediate first-name terms with everyone she met. 'We've logged your aunt's name on the missing-person list. When you provide us with an up-to-date photograph . . .'

'This is the best I have,' Teresa said, showing the woman the picture she'd brought from Rome. It was at least ten years old: Sofia by the seaside at Ostia when they'd gone there one weekend.

'Does she look like this now?' Paola Boscolo asked.

She does to me, Teresa thought, and could hear in her head the sad, desperate voice of so many of the relatives she'd met in these circumstances as part of her work.

'Yes,' she said simply, and then insisted the policewoman copy the photo and give her back the original. She needed something for herself.

The only photo in the apartment was even older. There wasn't even an ID card, which proved, Teresa felt, that Sofia had left the place voluntarily with a purpose in mind.

'I'll make sure it's distributed,' the woman said when she came back after copying the picture. 'We have a national system—'

'I *know* about the system. I work in the Questura in Rome, remember.'

The uniformed officer smiled beatifically.

'Rome's a long way from Venice,' she said. 'We will look at your aunt's case exactly as we would any other.'

'That's what I'm worried about,' Teresa blurted out, and immediately regretted it.

'If you know about missing-person cases,' Boscolo said carefully, 'you know too how powerless we can be. We have very few options without some hard information, which is sadly lacking here. People disappear for a variety of reasons. Money. Love. Depression. From what you say of your aunt it could be any or all of the three.'

Teresa's temper was at breaking point.

'You're not listening to me.'

'You said yourself she tried to harm herself here sixteen years ago.'

'No! I said something happened here then. I don't know the details.'

'Most missing people turn up after a while. Safe and sound,' the officer insisted. 'We'll do what we can. But you must realize . . . usually there is some contact within the family. Someone will know, even if they're not telling right now.'

'The Englishman . . . The story I was sent.'

To Teresa's astonishment Paola Boscolo held up a large, matronly hand and attempted to wave her into silence.

'Enough,' the woman said. 'Please. You have told me this . . . thing a million times.' She shrugged her big shoulders. 'Where is it?'

'I've already said . . .'

'Disappearing ink?'

The woman had very large manly eyebrows and they were raised all the way.

'It does exist,' Teresa told her. 'My forensic people in Rome can look at that paper and confirm it's been treated in some way.'

'Your forensic people in Rome aren't involved in this case.'

'Are you?' Teresa asked.

'Yes.' She shuffled the documents in front of her, a sign that this was, perhaps, the last formal interview Teresa was to be allowed. 'I will do what I can, what I would do for anyone in such circumstances.'

'Listen to me. Jerome Aitchison taught actuarial science at Cambridge. He was suspended for an alleged sexual assault on a student. He came here trying to make sense of his life and, if that story is correct, *met my aunt*. After which, for reasons that seem a mystery to you, he appears to have formed some kind of fixation with the unfortunate starlet chosen for that circus act today. With the consequences we've all seen. How would I know all that if I didn't see that story?'

Paola Boscolo's pale flabby face remained fixed in a smile. For one brief moment Teresa thought, she suspects me for some reason. It was ridiculous.

'Isn't the answer obvious?' the policewoman said. 'Your aunt left you this information, in this curious form. She wishes you to know something but not so much.'

'It was hardly reassuring.'

'Perhaps she meant it that way. When people are disturbed they do odd things. Maybe she met this Englishman . . . I don't know. Give us the paper. We'll work on it. But if you think it makes much of a difference to what we can do at the moment . . . I'm sorry. How?'

It was a reasonable point, not that Teresa was going to allow that.

'Give me an officer to work with and I'll find out,' she said quickly.

The woman's eyes opened wide in amazement.

'That's what they'd do in Rome,' Teresa added, not very convincingly.

'Then Rome is even further from here than I realized. Do you have any idea how many people there are in Venice right now? For the carnival?'

'Not a clue.'

'Me neither. We don't have the time or the

resources to start chasing strange fairy stories. What with the drunks and the pick-pockets, and now this terrible attack on the actress. Please, as a fellow officer. You must understand.'

'I understand my aunt's missing and may be in danger. And that one way or another something links her to Jerome Aitchison.'

Paolo Boscolo cleared her throat and stood up.

'The first is undeniable. I suggest you talk to her friends and relatives. Find out the places she liked to go when she felt down.' She hesitated then added, 'And pray for her. I will.'

'I have to say that when a serving police officer suggests the best thing I can do is say a prayer then I really start to worry.'

'A little faith never hurt anyone.'

Teresa Lupo bit her tongue. The obvious remark – that Paola Boscolo clearly had no grasp of history – would scarcely have been helpful.

The woman passed over her card.

'My mobile number and email address. Use them. Any time. Night or day. If you have something concrete for me, I promise I'll do what I can to help.'

From beyond the office came the sound of a couple of belligerent drunks being hauled into interview. The woman threw open the door. Teresa saw them: red-faced, in dishevelled medieval costumes, masks around their necks on elastic bands. One had thrown up on his flowery waistcoat. The other looked as if he couldn't decide whether to pass out or start a fight.

Paola Boscolo's eyebrows rose again and she said, 'When the opportunity arises. Thank you. Is the old gentleman, your friend, still here?'

'You mean Alberto Tosi, who was until recently the city pathologist of Venice?'

The woman smiled and said, 'I think I remember the name. He retired, I believe.'

'No. He had to go home.'

'Then I assume you can make your own way. Goodnight.'

It was almost seven when she finally left the Questura. The night was black as ink and icy cold, well below freezing. The clear starlit sky suggested there was little change in the weather in the days to come. People in bizarre costumes wandered the streets shivering happily. Carnival, in its original form at least, was about a brief burst of gaiety before the enforced fasting and self-denial of Lent. Not that anyone fasted any more, or denied themselves much if they could afford it. Judging by the voices of the revellers – French, American, Japanese, Chinese, more than Italian – the world had moved beyond such seemingly simplistic ideas. Venice during carnival was an endless procession of masked men and women, eager for pleasure in the processions, the private parties, and the concerts, relishing the anonymity their disguises brought them, the chance to escape for a few brief days the cares and constrictions of the real world, *terraferma*.

She walked to the waterfront near La Pietà, 'Vivaldi's church', the guide books said, though they lied. She and Emily Deacon had learned that as they wandered this area together during that earlier case. The marble Palladian façade was early nineteenth-century, the interior a reconstruction from two decades after the composer's death, one he would never have recognized. Venice was built on myths and fabrications, ones so tantalizing and beautiful they were usually forgiven the moment they were revealed.

A sudden harsh memory struck her, so forcefully she had to sit on a bench outside the church to recover. The story from the night before had been perceptive. At that moment she recalled standing here with Emily discussing music and art, slowly getting to know the woman who would briefly be married to Nic Costa. It was somewhere nearby that she'd come to realize how much she liked and admired this resolute, tough American woman. That reminiscence was painful, as the unknown author of the lost short story had predicted.

Paola Boscolo had a point. Such knowledge could surely only have come from Sofia in the first place. The two of them had spoken about Venice a few years before when Sofia was home. Her aunt had never mentioned spending any time here. Teresa had probably talked too much. It wasn't long after Emily's murder. There was much to say, a lot to get off her chest.

She watched the slow swell of the lagoon. Beneath the moon-light it looked like semi-molten lead. She wished she could call Peroni. Introduce them all into this mystery, him, Falcone, Costa, her assistant Silvio Di Capua too. Together their array of quirks and talents could uncover answers hidden inside the most cryptic and difficult of puzzles. They'd want to help without a second thought. There was more than friendship at stake here. Over the years, watching the institutions that were meant to matter crumble and fall apart, the state, the police themselves after a fashion, something had emerged between them, a kind of love that was a bulwark against the harsh cruelty of the world. The sort of mutual protection an ordinary Italian like her would once have sought in faith or politics or trust in the goodness of society, before such intangible elements seemed to fade beyond reach.

But the cops were somewhere in Sicily on a covert mission that demanded operational silence. She couldn't call them. They couldn't respond to her. In Rome Di Capua would be facing the fury of the departmental officers over her unauthorized absence, the unfinished budget, the quarterly reports. She hadn't done him any favours there, and that omission, uncharacteristic and thoughtless, made her feel a little guilty. It was a rotten time to leave the unit in the lurch, however pressing her personal problems.

Who did she have to take their place? Alberto Tosi, a retired pathologist, well-meaning but out of the investigative loop for a good few years, with no real influence over the present-day Questura. That had been obvious from the moment she'd been assigned a domestic officer to investigate a case that was at best curious and possibly down-right sinister.

Not to forget, she reminded herself, a charming if somewhat naive young Croatian woman and a crippled pianist trapped in a wheelchair. They all wanted to help. She felt sure of that. But how?

A group of men in dark cloaks, with tricorn hats and ghostly white masks, went past without a word, marching like soldiers, desperate to keep warm. At least, she comforted herself, her own clothes, an unglamorous baggy winter anorak and heavy winter trousers, saved her from the worst of the freezing weather.

As they stumbled into a shady *sotoportego* three or four feathery swirls of light snow appeared out of the black mouth of a nearby *rio*, whirling like ghostly dervishes.

The flat shoes, mind, were still sliding on the icy cobbles . . .

That prompted a guilty thought. She called Frascati. As she expected, the incident in the piazza was the lead story in the news, one that her mother mentioned instantly.

'I don't know anything about that,' Teresa lied.

'I've been to see the police in person. They've logged Sofia as a missing person. Things are moving, and I'll make very sure they move a little faster tomorrow.'

Did her mother know this was less than the full truth? Was there some maternal instinct that enabled her to detect when her daughter was being disingenuous? Perhaps, Teresa thought. But if that were true they knew each other well enough by now not to mention it. Their last mindless screaming argument had occurred a good decade or so before, the spark some insignificant subject Teresa could no longer recall. With age came a kind of peace between them, the sort that existed between two neighbouring states that had come to acknowledge their mutual differences and given up trying to resolve them. Her mother was stolid, serious, doggedly middle-class and conventional. All traits Teresa Lupo could admire even if she did not wish to share them.

Different kinds of people. As was Sofia too, not that she'd realized quite how different until recently.

'Does anyone know *anything*?' Chiara asked.

'The people in the apartment block say Sofia was happy there. She had plans. To make money, to get some kind of job.'

'What kind?'

'Making masks,' Teresa said without thinking.

There was a long pause. Then her mother said,

'Don't feel you have to call me unless you have something to say.'

Fifteen minutes later in a back lane leading towards the Accademia bridge Teresa's phone rang.

'Good evening!' Tosi declared with boundless enthusiasm. 'Did the police help?'

'Not a lot.'

'Buffoons! All they think about are tourists and their blasted stolen handbags. We have no need of them. We have ourselves . . .'

'Alberto . . .' She found herself smiling at the idea that this kindly old man could so take to heart the disappearance of a relative of someone he barely knew. 'There's no need—'

'I've found your Gobbo,' Tosi broke in. 'Take a boat to the Rialto immediately. Meet me in the market. In front of the church of San Giacomo. On the San Polo side, as you come off the bridge.'

'He's there now?' she asked, amazed.

'I guarantee it.'

'Do you want me to call the police? We don't want him to leave.'

She heard laughter down the line.

'I don't think we need worry about that,' Tosi said cheerily. 'To the Rialto please. And best bring some ear plugs if you have them.'

She thought she knew this part of Venice well, but that was during the morning, in the daylight. Then the piazzas and arcades near the Grand

Canal thronged with fish and fruit and vegetable stalls as they had done for centuries, while those close to the Rialto bridge were given over to hordes of tourists buying masks and souvenirs and other trivia.

The market closed well before one o'clock leaving the afternoon to straggling lines of visitors. At night the Rialto changed once more. She had never come to this area much before after dark, except to visit one of the popular restaurants by the waterfront on the Riva del Vin. As she crossed the bridge she found herself walking beneath lines of bright blue snowflake lights strung above the pavement, descending past the souvenir stalls, most of them closed, their wares being carted away by intent, muscular men heaving trolleys up and down steps, the porters who kept this strange city moving, lugging goods everywhere, regardless of bridges and the hordes of pedestrians ahead of them.

Some kind of festive event had clearly taken place earlier. Musicians in garish costumes carrying a variety of instruments – horns, drums, a glockenspiel – wandered back towards the vaporetto jetty. Crowds of costumed carnival-goers meandered through the arcades as if lost for where to wander next.

Teresa followed Tosi's instructions and bore right, away from the lights and the people, into the pools of darkness and the small piazzas where the market stalls set up during the day. She could still smell the sweet aroma of fruit and behind it the sharp salt smack of fresh fish. Rounding the blocky hulking shape of the church of San Giacomo she stopped and stood in front of its low, simple loggia, trying to get her bearings, which was never easy at the best of times, even during the day.

Ahead of her, across a patterned pavement of cobblestones with a low fountain in the centre, was a half-lit open space surrounded on three sides by arcades. To her left ran a line of low kiosks still lit by a handful of open tourist stands. On her right the taller buildings were occupied by what appeared to be a few restaurants.

She was in the right place but could see very little indeed except a moving procession of dark shapes, most of them in costume, criss-crossing the area beneath the shelter of the arcades.

The snow was starting to get heavier. From beyond an archway in the far corner of the piazza she could just make out flashing strobes, like multi-coloured lightning. She heard the low rumbling thud of dance music and remembered something from her teenage days: a disco in San Giovanni in Rome, Sofia leading her into this forbidden place, buying her a drink, trying to teach her to dance, not that this was ever going to be possible.

The music became louder. She closed her eyes and could see her aunt in this place, wandering it easily, comfortably, attracted by the promise of anonymous pleasure.

A group of young men and women, masked and in the costume of palace courtiers, walked by, one accidentally brushing her shoulder and apologizing immediately in French. She felt like a stranger in a different country. Rome had its darker corners. But none quite like this. The cold was biting. Swirling loose clouds of snow were starting to dash in and out of the ancient stone and brick colonnades. In a city that often appeared to go to sleep well before nine of an evening, the night was just beginning for those hidden behind the disguise of the carnival, masks frozen in expressions that seemed cruel and inhuman, incapable of any emotion except disdain.

As she crossed the piazza she could see crowds of revellers gathered beneath the galleries and in the open space beyond the archway, huddled together, chatting, dancing, flirting, she guessed.

Sofia . . .

A tall figure stepped out of the gloom ahead and caught her attention. Alberto Tosi wore what looked like a thicker overcoat and one more old-fashioned gentleman's hat. She walked over to join him. In each of his gloved hands was a plastic glass of liquid with an olive on a long cocktail stick. She could just make out the colour in the light leaking from behind him: bright red.

'Spritz!' Tosi declared. 'Here.'

This was all so ridiculous. She wanted to laugh and so eventually she did, and took the glass, and a sip from it. The Venetian drink: Campari bitter, prosecco, soda water, olive and a chunk of lemon. The strangest combination, and one that never made any sense unless it was consumed here, in the sharp marine air of the city, the briny fragrance of the sea mingling with the mould and decay of buildings that teetered on a hidden forest of timber buried deep beneath their feet in the mud of the lagoon.

'The police—' she began.

'To hell with the police!' Tosi interrupted.

She smiled at him and wondered whether this was his first spritz of the evening.

'I spoke with the *commissario*,' he went on. 'I'm sorry. They won't spend much time on Sofia's case at the moment. Not with that dreadful incident in the piazza to clear up. And all these people in the city. Venice is full. The pickpockets and the criminals have come from all over, from beyond Italy even, for such rich pickings. Until they go home a missing person . . . even the aunt of a famous Roman pathologist . . . I'm sorry.'

'No need, Alberto.'

'But there is a need! Your aunt is more impor-tant than all this . . .' His long arms waved around him, pointing, eventually, at the mingling crowd in the adjoining piazza. Some women in thick winter parkas were beginning to dance to the music. It was an incongruous, scarcely believ-able scene. 'All this nonsense. We never used to have it, you know. Carnival was a local affair, for the Venetians. Then the city saw the glint of money . . .' He rubbed the fingers of his black leather gloves in a familiar gesture. 'And look at it now. People dancing in the street. In February. I ask you.'

'That's probably what it was like,' she suggested. 'In the old days.'

'In the old days we used to string people up on those columns by the Doge's Palace and leave them there to rot. People forget that. Your Gobbo fellow knows. Why not ask him?'

She took another drink, sighed and waited.

Tosi moved to one side and she realized he was leaning against a set of iron railings that guarded a low statue of a crouching man, hewn out of what looked like grimy marble, head bowed, muscles straining as if in pain, bearing on his back and neck a heavy flat platform engraved with an obscure inscription in Latin.

'In the old days,' Tosi went on, 'a pompous city official used to climb up there and read out the odd death sentence from time to time. Or some poor soul was forced to strip naked in the Piazza San Marco and run the gauntlet of the crowds all the way here, until he managed to touch this chap.'

The bent back, the pained, contorted posture, face unseen, pointed to the ground.

'Gobbo,' she said.

'*Il* Gobbo,' Tosi emphasized. 'One must never miss grammatical detail. The definitive article is what gives it away, I think. Why use it if this was someone's last name? And if it were some kind of sobriquet . . .' He scowled. 'No one would call another human being something so cruel. Not in this day and age. I should have seen the connection straight away.'

He reached over the railings and patted the hard surface of the platform above the pained figure of the naked man.

'He's a local celebrity. The trouble is there's so much history in Venice one scarcely thinks about it for a while. I mentioned our problem to my granddaughter and she told me immediately. It's what the young say to one another when they're coming here. Meet you at Il Gobbo. Shorthand I imagine for a night out in the cold having what passes for fun these days.'

Teresa looked at the crippled statue, a stark, contorted monochrome figure in the tenebrous piazza, thought about the faceless people around them. The certainty that had been growing inside her since the moment she stepped into this part of the city, an underworld she never knew existed, finally fell into place.

This was where, before her disappearance, Sofia came for the evening.

To do what?

The same thing she did wherever she was, probably, the routine lonely people like her always fell into. To wander, to drink and mingle, looking for company among strangers, not caring that most were half her age.

'You're quite the detective,' Teresa Lupo said, with no small degree of genuine admiration.

'Time on my hands.' He tapped his head. 'And not enough work for this atrophied organ.'

'Sofia came here night after night,' she said. 'She would have talked to people. She always did.'

He chinked his glass against hers. The plastic made no sound.

'Then so should we,' Tosi said.

There was a sudden, deafening burst of music from the sound system round the corner.

'If anyone,' the old man added, 'can possibly hear.'

They started at the nearest bar, little more than a small compartment built into the arcade. Tosi bought another round of unwanted drinks – it seemed the best way of getting the busy woman behind the counter to give them a little of her attention. Then Teresa showed her the old photo and asked a few questions.

She was from Croatia, like Camilla. Venice appeared more an international city than an Italian one, hereabouts anyway. A couple of local men came over and stared at the photograph. They seemed interested.

'Sofia,' Teresa said. 'Her name's Sofia.'

The woman's eyes lit up. The men nodded.

'She comes from Rome?' one of them asked.

'Originally.'

'She was here.' He looked at his friends. They agreed. 'Nice woman. We talked to her.'

'About what?'

He shrugged.

'Whatever. Music. Food. Jobs.'

The woman behind the counter cut in, 'She was looking for work. A little . . .' She frowned, and looked a touch guilty. 'A little old for round here to be honest with you. Not that it bothered her. Where is she? I haven't seen her for . . . I dunno.'

The men looked at each other. They didn't seem to have a clue either.

'Who was she with?' Teresa asked. 'Friends?'

'On her own,' the woman insisted. 'Always, I think.'

The talkative man thought about this and said, 'I don't remember her with anyone. She just came for the company.' He looked at his companions and laughed. 'Must have been desperate.'

'And then?'

He grimaced, glancing round the corner, in the direction of the piazza with the music and the flashing lights.

'Then she went to the next place,' he said. 'Like we all do.'

He reached up and patted the Croatian woman on the arm.

'Unfaithful. That's how it goes.'

Wandering from one little bar to the next. Talking to lonely people like herself. The idea this kind of behaviour might be dangerous would never have occurred to her.

'This is important,' Teresa said. 'She's my aunt. She's missing. When did you last see her? Please. Try and remember.'

She waited, watching their faces, knowing this was pointless. In these cold, bleak arcades in the midst of the Rialto markets time no longer mattered. One night was much the same as any other.

'A week,' the Croatian woman said.

'Ten days,' the man added.

'Thanks.'

She must have sounded despondent. He looked sorry that he couldn't help more. As they were leaving he stopped her and said, 'Try the place round the corner. The one next to the Casa del Parmigiano. That's nice. It's a bit smarter than this. I saw her there sometimes.'

He thought for a moment.

'She talked to lots of people. A nice lady. You go find her.'

They went there straight away. The young Italian man behind the counter was doling out spritz and cocktails to a steady stream of people who came to stand outside. Tosi bought two more drinks they didn't touch. It wasn't easy to hear. The disco, with its flashing lights and deafening music, was just across the square, surrounded by costumed figures in masks, swaying and jogging, drinking, pulling on cigarettes. There was the strong, insistent smell of dope from a couple dancing uncertainly close by.

Sofia smoked, tobacco only as far as Teresa knew. She'd hated the fact she couldn't light up inside a café or bar or restaurant in Italy any more. This place would have appealed to her.

'What?' the barman asked over the noise.

She showed him the photo.

'Sofia,' he said before she'd even mentioned the name. 'Sure, I know her.'

Same question. Same vague answer. It was a week or more since she'd been seen here.

'Did she come with anyone?' she asked.

He thought for a moment and said, 'Oh yeah. The last couple of nights she was here. I remember now.'

'Who?'

Alberto Tosi crowded in close to hear the man's answer.

'Him,' the barman said, pointing at the crowd.

Desperate, excited, a little scared, Teresa turned and scanned the dark figures in the centre of the piazza.

'And him,' the barman added. 'And him. Oh . . . and him.'

Funny man, she thought. Tosi's gazed ranged across the people in the piazza. Then he worked it out and threw some abuse at the barman.

'This woman is missing,' the old pathologist barked at him. 'Don't play games with us.'

'It's not a joke,' the barman retorted. 'You asked. I told you. I didn't get it either. I mean, you see

132

people wearing masks here all year round. Not just carnival. Tourists mainly though. Not locals and I guess she was local, wasn't she?'

'The man,' Teresa persisted.

'Some guy in a cloak and a mask. Always that one. Sometimes she'd have a mask too. No costume. Just a mask. Not easy . . .'

He made the motion of removing the face mask and taking a drink.

'Not if you want to get a few down. And they did. Trust me.'

'What did he look like when he took off his mask?' she asked.

'Nothing special. Just some guy.'

'Italian? Foreign? Young? Old?'

'Old. Never heard him talk much. Kept his mask on mostly. Are you police?'

'If only . . .' Teresa murmured. 'Does the name Jerome Aitchison ring a bell?'

He shook his head. Then he thought for a second and added, 'I remember one thing though. Last time she was asking where they could get a gondola.' He laughed. 'A gondola? Jesus. At two in the morning.'

'And you've never seen him before or since? You've no idea who he is?' Teresa demanded.

'I told you.'

He pointed again. There were five of them now in the crowd nearby, probably plenty more if she wanted to look.

'They call him the Plague Doctor.'

Il Medico della Peste. The same deathly archetypal figure who had greeted Teresa and her mother at the Zattere vaporetto stop the day before, helping them onto the icy jetty. Which had to be coincidence. There were so many people dressed like that in the city during carnival. The same costume Aitchison wore when he shot at Luisa Cammarota then killed himself. That was no accident.

She took Tosi by the arm and led him away from the noise. Then she asked, 'Where would you get a gondola around here?'

'At this time of night? I've no idea. Perhaps . . .' He glanced back at the bodies moving to the music in the piazza. 'There could be a gondolier here. In this sort of place if you ask for something and you have the money . . .'

'But why, Alberto? Why would Sofia do such a thing? With a stranger here, in the dead of night?'

'If he was a stranger. They'd been here more than once. How do you know?'

I don't, she thought. I haven't a clue.

'I'll tell you one thing, though,' Tosi added. 'This man she went off with. He surely wasn't a Venetian. Not unless he had an ulterior motive. The gondola is a device for extracting money from visitors. No local would pay to go in one. Except for love, for a wedding perhaps, not that anyone gets married at two in the morning. Not even in the Rialto.'

'Where . . . ?' she began.

He took her by the arm and led her away from the piazza. Very soon the music had diminished. They were standing by the Grand Canal looking up at the Rialto Bridge from the deserted pavement of the markets next to a small private jetty. A set of upright poles stood like tree trunks set in the water, waving gently with its eddying flow. Between the timbers stood several black gondolas, shiny beneath the moonlight, their seats covered tightly in blue fabric to protect against the vile weather. A light dusting of snow had built up already. More, she felt, was on the way.

There wasn't a soul in sight. Then a voice came out from behind the arcades, a lilting tone to it, almost singing the words one heard everywhere in Venice that tourists and water were to be found.

'Gondola, gondola, gondola . . .'

A tall man in a thick hooped sweater and straw hat with a ribbon round it wandered out from the shadows.

He stumbled up to them and smiled. A burst of spritz filled the air from his breath. He must have been freezing, she thought.

'Fifteen minutes, a hundred euros,' he said, slurring the words a little. 'There's nothing like the Grand Canal at this time of night. No boats, no people, no noise. Just you and the water and the gentle sound of my *remo* in the *forcola*.' He made a suggestive turning, thrusting gesture, that of an oar in the rowlock, and something more physical, more human too. 'What you get up to in the back . . .' He sniggered and looked them up and down. 'That's up to you.'

Tosi let fly with a loud and unmistakably vicious burst of abuse, in Veneto she guessed since she could barely understand a single word.

The gondolier stood there and finally shivered a little, downcast, perhaps even ashamed.

'The photo,' Tosi ordered.

She got it out. There was another rapid exchange between the two Venetians. Then the gondolier nodded and said, 'Seen her.'

'When?' Tosi demanded.

'Week ago maybe. You think I keep a diary?'

'Where?' Teresa asked.

'Here.'

'I meant where to?'

He laughed.

'How far do you think I can go like this?' He nodded at the black, shimmering surface of the canal and the landing by the bridge on the other side. 'Just from here to there. Slowly, how they wanted. Then they were gone. Don't ask me where.'

'You must know . . .' Teresa began.

'Don't . . . ask . . . me . . . where.'

He stood there, sighed, wrinkled his nose.

'Didn't even charge them,' he said. 'How often do I get to say that?'

They waited.

'She was beautiful,' the man said. 'She looked so happy. The man in the mask too, I guess, not that I saw him or heard him say much.' He scratched his straw boater. 'Anything really.'

The gondolier leaned forward and his breath reeked of alcohol.

'Love,' he said, tapping the side of his nose. 'A man like me gets to recognize it. That was a woman in love. They didn't have a penny between them. A gift from a gondolier. She looked broke and scared and . . . kind of happy too. Like they'd made a decision about something. Who knows? I felt sorry for her. I envied that *Medico della Peste*. What else was I supposed to do?'

She left Tosi to catch the night vaporetto to his home on Sant'Elena, the quiet faraway island at the very tip of Venice beyond the Giardini. Then she set off walking back to Zattere on a long, circuitous route following the signs for the Accademia before diverting across the large open square of Campo Santa Margherita near the university. Even at this hour some of the bars were open, with crowds of young people huddled on the street, laughing and joking, some in costume, others, students, with laurel wreaths around their necks, signs of the same kind of success that she had once enjoyed herself.

When Teresa Lupo was getting mildly drunk in Rome with a circlet of green leaves on her shoulders Sofia was here in Venice, troubled, perhaps recovering from a suicide attempt if her mother was to be believed. Teresa still wished she'd known, even if the consequences could have been far-reaching. A sudden and overwhelming flood of sadness fell upon her as she crossed the broad expanse of Santa Margherita. She fell onto one of the benches there and found herself watching the gatherings of the young around her, all so carefree, oblivious to the future, with its challenges and uncertainties, already beginning to gather round them.

She was not, by nature, an introspective person, preferring action, logic and insight to rumination, doubt and indecision. But perhaps that facet of her character was simply an unconscious effort at self-deceit, a trick by which she allowed herself to survive each day unscathed by the insistent uncertainties that dogged everyone, whether they knew it or not. Sofia was a more sensitive soul than she. This, Teresa had come to realize, was one reason she envied her glamorous, free-spirited aunt. Yet with that gentler intuition came vulnerabilities too, ones that the deep affection Teresa felt towards her had kindly obscured over the years.

Love was the balm that tried to cure everything, the shutters in front of one's eyes, keeping out the harsh cruel face of the world.

Teresa took out her phone and, even though she knew from the screen there was no message there, went and looked for one anyway, wondering what Peroni was doing in Sicily at that moment. How safe he was. What concerns troubled him, for he was a man who was always devoted to the safety and well-being of others. That was as much a part of his nature as his rough and kindly features.

She thought about texting him again. Then she put the phone away. Rules were rules. She should never have sent that first message about the flowers. The fact he didn't reply said everything. Besides, their closeness was unspoken, accepted, like the seasons, like sun and rain. To mention it, to draw attention to the bond that had crept upon the two of them unbidden, would be to alarm him, perhaps at a time when his hands were full already. He would not come to Venice to help her find Sofia. Nor would Nic Costa or Falcone. This was not their responsibility. It was hers.

A group of young men and women wandered past, most in ordinary winter clothes, two in carnival costumes: a pretty girl in a voluminous silver ball gown and high white wig with an ornate gold mask dangling round her neck on silver string, and a man in the *Medico della Peste* outfit with its long probing nose, striding by her side, arm round her waist. It wasn't sinister really. Simply someone in disguise, one that during carnival seemed commonplace.

Teresa stared at the long white curving shape that bent down towards the ground, as if sniffing for something. Once, when Italy was riddled with plague for real, doctors did wear such things, with bunches of herbs placed beneath the ivory shell, as if a few fragrant plants could ward off evil. Like most cities, Venice had come to rely on superstition and magic to defeat the deadly sickness. No one at the time had the wit to realize the cause was not airborne but came from the bites of tiny fleas that merchants and soldiers, many of them Venetian, had brought back from Asia and foreign wars, an invisible, catastrophic cargo. In the absence of fact, of certainty and science, men and women always clutched at straws, at superstition, credulous ideas of faith. Or else they gave up and wandered into the dark in places like the shadowy corners of the Rialto seeking comfort in the company of strangers.

Facts, she thought.

There were some now, and none had come from the police. Shortly before she disappeared Sofia had spent her evenings carousing with the young around the outdoor bars of the Rialto. She had met someone there, a man who didn't like to show his face, preferring to hide his features behind the mask of the Plague Doctor. Some kind of relationship had been struck, one that pleased her.

The last time she was seen was when a drunken gondolier ferried the two of them across the black, deserted waters of the Grand Canal in the early hours of the morning a week before. She had then disappeared into the spider's web of alleys stretching into the sprawling *sestieri* of San Marco, Cannaregio and Castello. The opposite direction from her home in Dorsoduro, though it would have been easy for her – for them – to double back over the Rialto bridge if they wanted.

The story the night before said Jerome Aitchison stayed in Castello. Paola Boscolo, the pleasant if unhelpful police officer, had confirmed this when Teresa asked her during the intermittent interviews in the Questura. It was possible that Sofia was headed towards Aitchison's hostel. If so, she didn't get there. The woman who ran the place had gone on holiday a few days before but Boscolo had tracked her down. Aitchison had never received visitors, and he'd vanished too around the same time as Sofia.

One week later the Englishman tried, half-heartedly it seemed, to murder a TV starlet during the Flight of the Angel, killing himself in the most dreadful and spectacular of fashions on the hard patterned pavement of the Piazza San Marco when he failed.

Teresa Lupo could not countenance the idea that she would never know what had happened to Sofia. Or what that doubt might do to her mother, who was already crippled by guilt over her younger sister's disappearance. There was another possibility to be faced too, one that carried with it both hope and terror.

What if Sofia had not been harmed but simply imprisoned by Aitchison? That she was now trapped somewhere in the city, alone, unable to escape or make her presence known?

That idea almost seemed worse than the obvious, bleaker alternative.

Teresa shook herself out of this sudden, unwanted depression and began to think about how the following day might begin. Once that was clear in her head she walked down to the Zattere promenade and crossed the bridges towards the apartment. The snow was returning, the pavement was treacherous. Across the Giudecca canal the basilica of Redentore, the Redeemer, stood like a solemn grey ghost in the moonlight.

The small, crooked palazzo seemed uninhabited as she opened the green iron gates by the waterfront and walked down the narrow icy path to the front door. No lights, not a sound.

She thought of the mess in the living room, the jumble of papers and fabric, the tarot cards and crystal ball, the paintings scattered beneath the dead glass eyes of the stuffed pheasant. Sofia was still here in a way.

Then she stepped carefully over the slippery front steps and let herself in.

Her eyes went immediately to the letter box for some reason.

There was a manila envelope poking out of the slot. It was a little thinner than the one that Camilla brought the previous evening and there was no stamp. The postman didn't deliver on Sundays. This, somehow, had come by hand.

Her name was on the front, in the same plain font from a computer printer.

Teresa went upstairs and turned on all the lights. She opened the envelope as carefully as she could, with hands protected by a tissue. There was no plastic lining this time and the text appeared to be on ordinary white paper, not the thick mustard stock of the previous night.

Nevertheless the first thing she did was to go through every sheet and take a picture of it with the camera on her phone. This story was not going to disappear as easily as its predecessor.

After that she took the pages to bed.

THE ISLAND OF THE DEAD

On a balmy airless evening in May the small tourist launch *Tintoretto* cut a lazy path across the lagoon, meandering from the busy water-front of San Marco towards the distant slender strips of land that separate Venice from the Adriatic. The vessel's destination was a tiny island off Malamocco known as Poveglia, its cargo a gathering of forensic scientists assembled for the First International Symposium on the Genetic Analysis of the Skeletal Remains Attributed to St Mark.

The group comprised experts from Italy, Spain, France and Great Britain gathered for three days of intense debate and deliberation in the Faculty of Mathematical, Physical and Natural sciences at the city university, Ca' Foscari. The sole woman among them was Dr Teresa Lupo who had casually glanced at the scrap of paper thrown to the wind by Jerome Aitchison some five months before. By profession the senior pathologist for the state police in the *centro storico* Questura of Rome, she was unused to being so outnumbered. But the symposium was almost over and would, the following morning, vote upon its conclusions. It was time, in the natural order of these events, for delegates to 'wind down' in the accustomed fashion for those who followed the profession of forensic science: with a little food, a surfeit of drink for some, much professional banter and the odd arcane and mildly risque joke concerning cadavers.

Standing at the back of the boat, listening to the wily retired Venetian pathologist Alberto Tosi probing subtly yet insistently in order to elicit her opinions, Dr Lupo pondered the wisdom of accepting such an invitation. It had happened by chance the previous February when she was primarily engaged on business which had caused some sleepless nights. This visit to the city was more enjoyable. She had spent her time in the company of scientists who were likeable, professional, for the most part terrifyingly knowledgeable and, like Tosi, deeply religious. As an overworked atheist running a forensic department dealing with crimes that tended to the mundane, she felt little in common with any of them. Nor had it occurred to her until that afternoon that she might have been invited into this erudite company with a purpose, an ulterior motive which offended her sense of professional impartiality.

Three years before, a group of scientists had exhumed the remains of the poet Petrarch from his tomb in Arquà Petrarca, the little town one hour east of Venice which had taken the famous

145

writer's name after he died there in 1374. Using the very latest techniques – principally mito-chondrial DNA extracted from a rib and a single tooth – the study confirmed the long-held rumours that Petrarch's much-venerated remains were not what they appeared. The skull was male and the single rib tested undeniably female. Local archives revealed that in 1630 a drunken priest had been tried and exiled for attempting to rob the grave of its precious bones and sell them to passing visitors as valuable relics, hoping to replace the originals with objects of a more lowly origin. Thanks to twenty-first century science it was now beyond doubt that the intruder had been more successful than anyone had previously appreciated.

As a result the idea of mtDNA verification as a historical tool had caught the imagination of both scientific researchers and the Church. Venice possessed its own set of bones, ones allegedly much more holy in origin. They had arrived through another feat of grave-robbing though in this instance it had been applauded, and perhaps even planned, by those in authority. St Mark had long been associated with the Veneto region. An early legend held that, on a journey from Aquileia to Rome, his ship had put in at what was then the island of Rialto. There, close to the site of what is now the church of San Giacomo di Rialto, the apostle encountered an angel who blessed him with the message, *Pax tibi, Marce, evangelista meus.*

146

Hic requiescet corpus tuum – Peace to you, Mark, my evangelist. Here your body shall lie.

This seemed, to an atheist and affirmed sceptic like Teresa Lupo, decidedly convenient in the light of what was to follow.

Though north African by birth, Mark was reputed to have written his eponymous gospel while in Rome, later returning to Alexandria to found a church and suffer a suitably nasty public martyrdom in AD 68. A group of Venetian merchants stole what were believed to be his remains from a much venerated tomb there in 828, possibly under secret orders from the then Doge, Giustiniano Participazio, who wished to use the presence of an apostolic corpse to turn the city into the second most holy in Europe after Rome. Mark's emblem, the lion, became that of the Venetian republic. A great basilica was created around his coffin and later destroyed to make way for the even more splendid Byzantine structure of today, the very emblem of the power of La Serenissima and now the focal point for countless millions of burger-munching tourists. All this essential Veneto history was based, said the whispering atheistic gossips throughout Italy, on a common act of body-snatching, one that, had the boot been on the other foot – the Saracens stealing the remains of St Peter from Rome, say – would have ended in a mighty and holy crusade.

The situation was further complicated by the intervention of the Copts, Egyptian Christians who felt they had been cruelly robbed of the body in the first place. They continued to claim that they retained possession of the evangelist's head. On the thirtieth day of Paopi, the second month of the Coptic calendar, they venerated the object in their modern cathedral in Alexandria, built on the very site from which the Venetians purloined the skeleton that was shipped furtively across the Mediterranean and the Adriatic, wrapped in pork skin so that no curious Muslim would dare disturb it along the way.

Did they have a point? Were the bones in the basilica in San Marco real or fake? Or perhaps, like those in the tomb of Petrarch, fragments of more than one human being, assembled by charlatans who could never guess that one day science would unravel their dishonesty? Was it even possible, as a British author had lately claimed, that the body those ninth-century bandits stole from a grand tomb in Egypt belonged to someone else entirely, namely Alexander the Great himself?

These were the questions which this learned symposium sought to answer, after a brief exhumation and the release of a few fragments of the contents to be tested. Extensive and detailed scientific results had been assembled by a disparate team of experts in Barcelona, Cambridge, Rome, Parma and Mantua. For Teresa Lupo the difficulty was plain. Her fellow scientists, all, it now transpired, carefully selected for their connections with the Church, had clearly reached their conclusion, a very opportune one that, in some ways, was entirely merited. A single obstacle stood in the way of a unanimous verdict and that, they all knew, was a sceptical female police pathologist who possessed something they appeared to lack entirely: doubt.

Alberto Tosi, a charming, suave man of whom she had grown rather fond, had subtly started to apply a little pressure the moment they embarked from the jetty of Zattere, plying her with spritz and *baccalà cicchetti* as the *Tintoretto* steered a gentle path out to the distant bare reaches of the southern lagoon.

She listened to his polite, discreet comments, smiled and said, 'I know why you invited me, you know.'

'For your reputation, Doctor!' he responded briskly, stopping a passing waiter in order to grab a couple of anchovies spiked on caramelized onions then offering her one with a genteel, courtly charm. He was tall, well past seventy, still upright and stiff-backed, very proper in manner and word. 'What else?'

'You want an atheist's name on your document, alongside your army of Catholics. A police pathologist's too. I'll lend credence to your findings, won't I?'

'Of course you will,' he insisted. 'For your reputation and your extraordinary talents. Nothing else. I assure you.'

'Alberto—'

He put a firm hand on her arm.

'We live in irreligious times, Teresa,' Tosi interrupted. 'People need a little certainty in their lives. Don't deny them that without good reason.'

'The facts . . .'

'The facts are plain, aren't they?'

In a way, they were. That still left open the matter of interpretation.

'You've put me in an uncomfortable position, you know,' she told him.

He looked hurt. Almost sincerely so.

'I'm deeply sorry if that's the case. I never intended such a thing. I should have remembered you were a true Roman. That mutinous streak is always there, isn't it?'

'Mutinous? *Mutinous*? This is to do with the evaluation of scientific data. Not personalities.'

Tosi looked decidedly puzzled.

'Now you've lost me. Do the two never cross paths? The latter must interpret the former, surely. Even science is rarely black and white. Never mind. No need for an answer. I understand your position. It will not, I imagine, waver?'

'I doubt it.'

He raised his glass and chinked it against hers.

'So be it. See. We arrive!'

The *Tintoretto* was berthing at a ramshackle jetty on a very small island that seemed to lie about a kilometre or less from the flat, shallow line of land that ran, for the most part, the length of this stretch of lagoon, from the Lido to Chioggia. There was what looked like an old public building, a hospital or a monastery perhaps, lines of uniform rooms with windows two and three storeys high, covered in rampant ivy, surrounded by grounds that were overrun with weeds and unkempt in the extreme. The place was clearly abandoned, ruined. Behind it stood a modest campanile, much in the style of the church towers seen throughout Venice, slender, with a rose-coloured tiled steeple, rounded for once, with all the windows bricked in and a ragged black crucifix on the summit.

'We're here for a party?' she asked, astonished.

'A brief one, and we won't be disturbed,' he answered, happy again. 'This is a gathering of pathologists, isn't it? Where else would we go but Poveglia, the Island of the Dead?'

The guests, most of them in smart evening dress, unlike her, disembarked, glasses in hand, onto the modest patch of land by the jetty. The gathering was then treated to a brief lecture by a pale and elegant young woman in a long black gown who spoke in the monotone high-pitched drone of a TV presenter of late-night horror movies.

'My,' Teresa Lupo murmured as she listened to the tale of Poveglia, the most haunted place in the Venetian lagoon. 'I do feel terrified.'

She stood, automatically, a little way from the rest of them, finding herself next to a slightly built man in an old-fashioned though smart blue suit, white shirt and subtle dark tie. He had a kindly, handsome face that defied age, being anything

151

from pushing forty to mid-fifties. In spite of the heat he wore a crisp cream fedora which he lifted by way of greeting. His hair was very black though not, she guessed, artificially so, and his features spoke of Spain or the far south of Italy, a region where the dark features of the African dalliance in Europe, a thousand years before, still left their stamp. Some of the paintings of Mark had made him look a little like this. Nothing contemporary, of course, or even mildly authentic, if such a word could be used of images so antique. Like the legends surrounding the saint, they were simply one more diversion based on fantasy. While the apostle certainly came from north Africa, all the evidence was that he belonged to the Greek community, not the native one.

'One should not expect pathologists to quake and quiver in the presence of death,' the man said. 'I am the Count of Saint-Germain. You are Dr Lupo. It is an honour. Call me Arnaud.'

'Teresa. You're a count and a scientist? From France?'

'From many places over the years.'

'I don't recall seeing you earlier. At the symposium.'

His face wrinkled in the hunt for an answer. On reflection she put his age at the higher end of the scale, fifty perhaps, though he looked very well maintained.

'I'm a jackdaw, though less visible,' he answered. 'I toy with many things. Music was my first love, writing the second. But I'm easily bored. Time hangs heavy for a man like me, and I sleep little. Rarely, to be honest. It's only natural that an inquisitive mind should seek other subjects, science among them. You're the same. I can tell.'

The actress hired to send shivers down their spine – she could be nothing else, the pathologist surmised – continued with her horror story. Of how the island was used to isolate plague victims in Roman times and then became the burial pit for the dead when *La Peste* devastated Venice in 1630, introduced, on this occasion, by German and French soldiers engaged in the Thirty Years' War. That outbreak cost more than forty thousand lives, a third of the city's population. Many of its victims' bones now lay beneath a shallow covering of earth around the abandoned hospital and church of Poveglia, in this distant and, to most outsiders, forbidden corner of the lagoon. Nor did the tragedy end there. In the early part of the twentieth century the city opened a psychiatric hospital on the island, in spite of warnings from locals that the place was cursed by its black past. Inmates complained of tormenting ghosts and strange spirits. The doctor in charge experimented with cruel, crude practices, lobotomies and other unproven medical trials. When he began to see demons too he leapt from the church tower only to survive and be torn apart by his own patients. Deserted for eighty years, Poveglia was now nothing more than a curiosity for prurient searchers of occult thrills and a place where a few nonchalant locals raised vines on the massed corpses of those buried below.

At this point the actress reached down, scratched at the earth, saw something, and raised it in her right hand, feigning shock like a player from a B-movie *giallo*. From a distance it looked like a human femur. Some of the guests began grubbing at the ground around them with the toes of their shoes, digging for bones too, and a few even picked up what they found, displaying it, Teresa Lupo was glad to see, with something approaching shame on some of their faces.

'It's downright disrespectful,' she complained bitterly. 'They wouldn't dream of doing this somewhere that had a crucifix over the gate. In San Michele.'

'There is a crucifix,' the man said, in excellent Italian tinged by another accent she couldn't place. 'On the church tower. This entire island is a graveyard. Shattered corpse upon shattered corpse. One cannot expect order. Only the living may impose that upon the dead, and no one is fool enough to stay here long enough to countenance such a task.'

'They still deserve dignity, don't you think? All the more so if they have no grave, no place to leave flowers.'

He was looking at her, a curious expression in his face, one she couldn't quite read.

'And they wonder why people come to Venice

to contemplate mortality,' the Count of Saint-Germain mused. 'Is there a better place on earth?'

She studied this odd man, of an uncertain nationality. He wasn't like the others. Perhaps in one important way . . .

'Probably not, but it's a good place to study life too.'

'Precisely the same discipline,' he observed. 'Though most people miss that point. Shall we walk a little? I find amateur theatricals tedious.'

The pathologist readily agreed and so they slunk away from the body of the group by the launch *Tintoretto*, where a fresh round of drinks and food was being served amidst, no doubt, much chatter about bones and departmental budgets and the pleasantly Malthusian implications of plague.

Beyond the crumbling buildings of the hospital the island was delightful, a tiny oasis of well-tended green vines that were carefully manicured in dead straight rows and set on a single expansive field on the city side of the island. The sweep of lush grapes looked like the garden of a long-deserted country mansion, still fertile and mysteriously cared for after humanity had fled elsewhere.

The Count of Saint-Germain walked with a black lacquered cane topped with a silver handle though he seemed very fit and agile, stepping ahead of her, kicking stones out of the way, pointing out potholes in the overgrown path ahead, and, close to a wild and untidy apple tree, removing, with his fingers, a large black scorpion in their way. He deposited the creature carefully on an adjoining dry-stone wall with an admonition – to the arthropod, not her – to be more careful in the future.

They found a thicket of dense grass at the water's edge and sat there, admiring the view back to the city which appeared on the horizon like some petrified stone forest of campaniles, churches and palazzi, fed by a constant traffic of boats crawling across the still and mirrored surface of the lagoon.

'How do you intend to vote tomorrow?' she asked after a suitable interval, aware there was a note of pleading to her voice.

'Vote?' he asked, as if this were news to him. 'There's a vote?'

'The resolution's been written already. Alberto Tosi is to propose it. Some pompous prig from Barcelona will second.'

Arnaud, the Count of Saint-Germain, nodded and didn't speak.

'It says,' she went on, 'that, after suitable scientific analysis, there's an overwhelming probability the remains in the sarcophagus are indeed those of St Mark.'

'Probability,' he repeated. 'What a weasel word that's become. Did you know they now teach in universities that the origins of probability theory may be found in the correspondence in 1654 between Pascal and Fermat?' He tut-tutted. 'Have the idiots who feed this pap to the young ever read those letters? Shocking.'

'I'm sorry. Mathematics . . . It was a long time ago.'

'Pascal seemed a pleasant enough chap until he became ill. Pierre de Fermat was an honourable and knowledgeable gentleman, though I feel we could have done without his blasted last theorem, published posthumously by the way. He didn't dare deliver that devious little prank to the world while he was alive.'

She was unable to comprehend fully what seemed to lie behind his words.

'Arnaud. You speak of them as if . . .'

'Yes, yes,' he interrupted. 'The point is that never once in this correspondence does either man use the word *probabilité*. Only, and I find this instructive, the more alluring and everyday term *hasard*. Chance, luck. As in, to quote Pierre, "*la somme des hasards* . . ."You see the point? Using the word probable attaches, quite deliberately, some quasi-scientific rectitude to the notion. The idea of luck, of randomness is replaced by a relentless march towards certainty, a Darwinian destruction of the glorious wonder of doubt, a despicable act which is both immoral and, I would argue, entirely unscientific. I don't believe Pascal or Fermat felt party to such a conspiracy for one moment. They were explorers in an unknown land, grateful for what little knowledge they were able to extract. Religious fellows too, and they never saw any conflict in that either.'

Teresa Lupo watched two large car ferries manoeuvre past each other on the lagoon like elephantine ballet dancers performing a *pas de deux*.

'The vote, Arnaud?'

He looked at her and, for a moment, she felt something akin to a chill. There seemed to be an ocean of accumulated wisdom and self-knowledge in his deep, dark eyes.

'What about you?'

The question was welcome. This was the first time in three days anyone had asked for her opinion.

'It's very clear from the carbon-dating results that the bones come from around the first century AD. Simple forensic science proves they represent the remains of a single corpse. That head the Copts worship in Alexandria is nothing to do with the remains here. We can also rule out any possibility whatsoever that they might belong to Alexander the Great, not that I had much time for that nonsense in the first place.'

'Good for you,' he said, and tipped his hat.

'The mitochondrial DNA is remarkably similar to that of some modern samples from the remaining Hellenic community in Alexandria, which is a second reason for abandoning all thoughts of our Macedonian hero, since his would have been entirely different. This is a tentative link. Two thousand years ago there were a hundred and fifty thousand Greeks in the city. Today, fewer than a thousand. Nevertheless the probability . . .'

He coughed into his fist and stared at her.

'. . . the possibility,' she corrected herself, 'is that the remains in the basilica are those of a man of Greek origin, born in north Africa, around the time of Christ.'

'If you're lucky,' he added. 'Remember my friends Pascal and Fermat.'

'I will not put my name to a piece of religious chicanery,' she insisted. 'We know it's one body. We have a rough idea of its origin and age. To deduce a direct identification with Mark simply from the literature surrounding a body-snatching incident in Alexandria twelve hundred years ago is unscientific and irrational.'

He frowned then said, 'Yet Tosi and his friends may be right.'

'Which is not the same as saying they are. Besides . . .' Something larger, and more ill-defined, grated about this entire episode. Her obvious discomfort appeared to interest him. 'It's wrong. I don't understand why they're so desperate to achieve this result.'

'I believe they justify it on the grounds that the Church needs all the help it can get.'

'That's nothing to do with me. Or you, I imagine.'

The light was starting to fade. From somewhere near the campanile came the long, slow hoot of a waking owl.

'Strange, isn't it?' he mused. 'Here we are on an island built upon the skeletons of forty thousand lost souls. Just a few steps away is a learned conclave of self-appointed experts debating the identity of a few grey, fragile bones that have sat in a basilica, first in Alexandria, latterly here, for almost two thousand years, worshipped, adored on a daily basis.' He picked at the earth with his shoe. Those sharp eyes were on her again. 'No one asks their names, do they?'

'Too late now, isn't it?'

'I imagine so. Doesn't it worry you? Being here with a stranger? On a tiny island that's the resting place for so many who suffered an agonizing death not so long ago?'

She could only laugh.

'You should see what I do on a daily basis. The dead don't scare me, not half as much as the living.' She shrugged her shoulders. Teresa Lupo was a muscular, well-built woman, fit and active. Nothing, she felt, frightened her easily. 'They're not so bad either, so long as you speak your mind and tell them the truth. Four hundred years is a very long time ago, by the way.'

'Not for everyone,' he murmured ruefully, unable to look her in the eye at that moment.

This strange man toyed again with the pebbles at their feet. Another black scorpion, or perhaps the same one as before, dodged the movement of his shiny shoes and scurried off into the grass.

'How old are you, Arnaud?' she asked, willing to play this game for a little while anyway.

'That's a very personal question! What would you think of me if I asked the same of you?'

'I'm thirty-six. Anyone can ask my age. I don't mind.'

'Well I do.' He looked miserable, mournful. 'I have my reasons.'

'You mean Pascal? Fermat . . . ?'

His face turned grim and sad, and the words just poured out.

'For starters. I also mean Louis XV, Madame Pompadour, Voltaire, Frederick the Great, Casanova – who at one point had the nerve to impersonate me. A creature of the most enduring charm but an utter prune as a man – Beethoven, Cagliostro, Pushkin, Chopin, Marx, Abraham Lincoln, Bismarck, Theodore Roosevelt, T. E. Lawrence, that interesting American Ambrose Bierce, Thomas Edison, Robert Oppenheimer.' He brightened briefly. 'Oh, and those charming young men at Google. They're alive, for now anyway. Acquaintances all. Not friends. The longer you live, the fewer you have. I don't expect you to understand.'

He took something out of the pocket of his jacket. It was a small book, backed in black pock-marked leather and very old.

'I am the Count of Saint-Germain. I've written operas and concerti, swindled royal families of their riches, though only when they deserved it. Made love to a select number of beautiful women along the way then disappeared discreetly before the inevitable, usually anyway. I've dabbled in science and alchemy and commerce and politics.' He stared at the lagoon. 'And here I am, back in Venice, on Poveglia, the Island of the Dead, still breathing, still thinking, still . . . sleepless after all these long years.' He glanced at her. 'I could tell you more if you were interested.'

There was the sound of a ship's horn. It sounded like that of the *Tintoretto*.

'On the way back, I think.'

'You didn't laugh.'

'You didn't seem funny.'

His mouth screwed up in a wry smile, very like that of a child.

'I can be. Sometimes. But not now.' He looked around him. 'Not here.' He shook his aristocratic head. 'When that woman held up the bone of one of those poor creatures as if it were a trophy I saw the expression on your face. You were hurt. It caused you pain.'

'I'm a pathologist. I never forget that what passes through my hands was once a human being. The beloved child of doting parents, if he or she was lucky. Someone's wife or husband. What we are today, just as they are what we shall be tomorrow.'

This last sentence seemed to affect him. There was a second hoot of the boat's horn. Then he uttered a very mild and ancient swear word, an epithet Teresa Lupo had once heard from her maternal grandmother in a moment of rare heat.

'I don't believe it. They're leaving without you,' he declared, standing up.

The launch hove into view rounding the green promontory of the Poveglia vineyard, heading back towards Venice. It was already a good way out into the lagoon. She could see the crowd on the deck. They stood together with their backs to the island, still and silent, a little ashamed perhaps.

'They know the way you're going to vote,' Saint-Germain shouted. 'This is their way of stopping you. Hey! Hey!'

The *Tintoretto* carried on regardless, picking up speed.

'Us, Arnaud!' she insisted as she made her way along the narrow overgrown path to the jetty, blind to all potholes and scorpions. 'They're stopping us.'

He didn't seem to hear.

There was a hamper of food on the rickety wooden landing stage, a bottle of prosecco in an ice bucket, a selection of bedding, a sleeping bag, a roll of toilet paper, an electric lantern and a handwritten note signed by Alberto Tosi. It read, 'Dear Doctor. We looked for you, without success. So we assume you wish to be alone on this curious little island, for professional reasons which are only understand-able. This is not a problem. The place is safe. We leave food and drink and will send a launch back for you tomorrow around midday.'

'Midday,' she spluttered. 'By which time their

163

names will be on Tosi's resolution, making the declaration unanimous.'

She took her phone out of her bag. Her stubby fingers stabbed at the buttons. There was no signal.

Saint-Germain reached the landing stage a few moments later, a little out of breath. He retrieved a very modern BlackBerry from his jacket pocket, looked at the screen and shook his head.

'Nothing,' he said, panting. 'We're a long way from civilization.'

'And don't they know it! Damn Venice. There's trouble every time I come to this place.'

'Don't talk to me about trouble here.' He shook his head. 'That bastard Casanova . . .'

'Please, Arnaud. Not now.' It puzzled her that they'd left just a single sleeping bag, and not much food for two people either. 'I have to ask. You weren't a party to this, were you?'

He stiffened as if she'd uttered the most offensive of insults.

'I'm sorry,' she said immediately.

The long strip of Malamocco, dividing the lagoon from the Adriatic, lay less than a kilometre away. There were lights in the houses but they were so distant no one there would easily see anything on Poveglia, even if she possessed something more substantial than the small lantern Tosi had left.

'We're stuck here until they come back, aren't we?'

'A boat might pass,' he suggested.

She murmured a more modern epithet than the one he'd used earlier. Then Teresa Lupo uncorked the prosecco, poured him some in the one plastic cup they'd left and retrieved a spent one from the party for herself.

'And the probability of that, Arnaud?'

He raised his cup in a toast.

'With luck, who knows?'

Saint-Germain took the smallest of sips. He was still clutching his little black book in front of him.

She nodded at the battered leather cover, looked at him and said, with some resignation, 'Well I suppose you have my full attention now. Best tell your tale.'

To her surprise he hesitated, looking a little guilty.

'I'd rather you told me yours.'

Teresa Lupo sighed.

'What tale's that? I don't have one.'

Saint-Germain shrugged.

'Not true. I must confess. This meeting is not entirely *par hasard*,' he said. 'Not simply to do with the bones of the Evangelist or my own history. You do have a story. It's essential you remember it.'

She sat down on the single wooden bench by the narrow jetty and patted the space next to her.

'What tale?' Teresa Lupo asked.

'An important one,' he said, joining her. 'About the man you encountered here in February, during carnival. The Plague Doctor. The most important tale there is at the moment. Surely you know that?'

She felt a sudden chill on the warm summer air.

'Important? I don't even know a story about the Plague Doctor.'

'But you do,' he insisted. 'If you can only remember.'

'Remember what?' She was alarmed by the volume and intensity of her voice.

'This is going to be more difficult than I thought,' Saint-Germain declared.

'If I knew what you were talking about . . .'

'Then we'd have no business here at all. Very well. My story . . .'

He patted his jacket and the book underneath.

'You shall have it in due course. But in order to understand that you must first hear another . . .'

A RENDEZVOUS IN THE DARK

First thing the next morning she took a close look at the pages. The text was unchanged, readable though as baffling and impenetrable as the night before. She had no doubt what this meant: there was nothing in the documents that could possibly be of use to the police. This cryptic, unfinished piece of fiction was for her benefit alone, one piece in a puzzle yet to be revealed.

There was no answer from Camilla's door. Strozzi was playing the piano with such intensity and beauty that she felt unable to disturb him for the moment. Teresa let herself out of the block and walked down to the waterfront, heading for the vaporetto. Ahead, crossing the first bridge, she saw the young Croatian woman. So she ran and caught up with her, and the two stepped briefly round the corner for a coffee and *frittelle* – it seemed ridiculous to eat anything else for breakfast during carnival.

Teresa told her about the Rialto and Il Gobbo, nothing more. This latest story would remain private from everyone until she knew what to make of it.

Camilla nodded and stared at her cappuccino.

'Did you know that's where she went?' Teresa asked.

The young woman smiled and looked out of the window of the tiny *pasticceria*. There was a matronly middle-aged figure in a pink nylon jacket behind the counter, laughing and joking with the locals. Behind her stood a tall, serious young man in a baker's uniform covered with flour, as if he'd come straight from the ovens. Teresa couldn't help noticing he kept stealing glances at Camilla and that, when he answered the woman at the counter, he spoke cracked Italian in an accent that sounded English. His interest was returned once with a wry grin, nothing more. Camilla simply smiled and held on more tightly to her bags full of masks for the small shop that Strozzi rented near the Guggenheim.

'I think Sofia liked to go out,' Camilla said carefully, toying with her coffee. 'I thought I told you that.'

'Late at night? Drinking?'

'Not so much, I feel. Not often anyway. There were never any problems. Once she lost her keys. That was all. I had to help her in.' Camilla would not look at her. 'She wasn't in a bad way. Sofia was very happy. No money. No idea, I think, where she was going. But she wasn't miserable. Not just before she disappeared. I thought . . . I wondered . . .'

'She had someone?'

'Maybe. She never mentioned it. I didn't want

to pry. That would have been rude. There was something private about Sofia. Something she didn't want the rest of us to see.' She took another bite of her *frittella*. 'I don't want to be party to someone else's secrets. I don't pry into matters that are none of my business. I would hate it if someone did that to me.'

Peroni always said you had to listen to the words people didn't say just as much as the ones they did.

'She wasn't always so happy then?'

Camilla sighed and said, 'Not always. Not until lately.'

Teresa Lupo looked at the young woman's hands. They were fine, artistic, slender, covered in paint and what looked like white dust. Everything about her seemed so pale, almost bloodless. She'd been up early making masks that morning. Carnival came once a year. The opportunity could not be missed.

'If there's something you know and you're not telling me, something that may seem insignificant . . .'

The young woman's eyes turned again to the window and the bright day outside. She stayed silent.

'Camilla. I'm worried. I think Sofia met this man, Jerome Aitchison. The one who died yesterday after he tried to kill that actress in the piazza. No one's seen Sofia for a week. No one's heard from her.'

'No,' she said. 'It's not possible she went off with such a horrible person.'

'How can you be so sure?'

'Because she was happy! Smiling. So content. I can't believe she was involved with someone bad. Not for one moment. She was no fool.'

'Sofia wasn't always what she seemed. I've known her all my life and I'm starting to realize that. There was something else going on.' She picked a mask out of one of Camilla's bags, a woman's in gold and ivory, beautifully painted. 'She could be like this, I think. Beautiful, fetching, adorable. But deceptive.'

'No. That's not true.'

This conversation seemed to depress Camilla Dushku for some reason. She traced the face of the mask with her fingers then placed it back in the bag.

'Filippo says I'm better at making these stupid things than he is now,' she said. 'What an idiotic way to earn a living. This place, this city. It's unreal. And yet I don't know how to leave. If I did I'd only come back. It gets to you. Like a disease. Like a virus.'

She finished her coffee and pushed the cup to one side then added, 'Like it got to Sofia. So she came back too.'

Teresa waited in silence until finally Camilla asked a little nervously, 'What?'

'Yesterday, when I told you Sofia lived here once before you said you didn't know. Today . . .'

This felt strange. Like an interrogation, and it wasn't meant to be that way. She liked Camilla Dushku. All she wanted was the truth.

The young woman sighed, pushed back her long hair with one hand and then said, 'Yesterday I lied.'

'Why?'

There was pain on her pretty face, not for herself either.

'Because she made me promise. I was never supposed to know. It was an accident. Something she blurted out. Like me just now. Damn!'

'When she was drunk?'

'Just that one night! She locked herself out. Around Christmas. She was miserable. And lonely. I'd never seen her like that before. Filippo had a spare key. Signor Ruskin gave him a set for the block because he was never there. So I got it from Filippo and I helped her in. I stayed with her because I was worried.'

'About what?'

'About her state of mind. She seemed so desperate. Miserable about something I guess. Nothing was working out. It was Christmas. She had no one.'

She had us, Teresa thought, if only she could have picked up the phone. If only we'd made her believe that was easy, and right.

'Filippo and I took care of her the next few days. It was just one bad night and too much to drink.'

'And she told you she once lived here. What else?'

'I promised!'

She was close to tears. This had to be made as easy as possible.

'Sixteen years ago,' Teresa said, 'Sofia had some kind of breakdown. I was never told at the time. It was kept from me. My mother came here and looked after her in hospital. She says she never really understood what happened either. She thought . . . she thinks Sofia tried to kill herself.'

'No . . .' Camilla said, shaking her head.

Teresa gripped her slim, talented fingers.

'I was kept in the dark then,' she said. 'It's not going to happen now. Not with what's at stake. Camilla . . .'

'Sofia lost her baby!' she said so loudly that the tiny café became quiet and still as every face turned to stare at them. The cheery woman behind the counter looked shocked and suddenly serious. So did the tall young man next to her. The genteel calm of this charming middle-class haven in Dorsoduro had been briefly punctured by the world beyond.

'A baby?' Teresa whispered, scarcely able to believe what she'd just heard.

Camilla took a deep breath, removed her hands from the table and leaned a little closer.

'That's all I know. Sofia was pregnant. She lost the baby for some reason. It still got to her. At least it did at Christmas. She said that was the worst time. She saw all the families. Thought about them.'

Teresa tried to remember the last time Sofia had been in Rome for the holiday. She couldn't.

'What else did she tell you?' she asked.

'Nothing. She was very upset. I didn't ask questions. How could you? The following morning she was so embarrassed. She swore me to secrecy. I never told anyone, never would.'

'Did she mention the father?'

Camilla shook her head vigorously.

'No! It was as if there wasn't one. As if she was on her own back then as well. As if that's how she spent all her life. Until lately. When she was happy. And then.' A click of her fingers. 'She's gone.'

That was Sofia in a nutshell. Alone. In Italy or elsewhere, wandering, searching, hanging round anyone who'd talk, looking for something she couldn't begin to name. This, Teresa felt sure, was what caused her mother so much pain. She had seen the desolation in her younger sister decades before, recognized the gaping emptiness in someone she loved and found it impossible to fill.

Then here in Venice, in the middle of a bitter winter, someone, Jerome Aitchison perhaps, came along and met that need. Shortly after, Sofia disappears.

A child.

It was hard to think of more questions. Motherhood was something Teresa hadn't associated with her aunt and, when she thought about it, that in itself seemed shocking. She'd never thought of motherhood herself. There were medical reasons. But even without those, children didn't seem to fit in with her career, any more than it suited Sofia's peripatetic meanderings throughout Europe and beyond.

There was also the question of identification. She had told herself, 'Because I'm like Sofia, she's also like me.'

Neither assumption made the slightest sense in the way she'd originally intended, as a compliment to both.

'That's all she said,' Camilla added. 'She was so upset I never mentioned it again. I put her to bed and sat with her. We talked for a while, about other things. About Venice. When I was sure she was asleep I cleared some junk off that sofa of hers and slept there. The next couple of days we never let her out of our sight. It didn't take long before she was happy again. She wanted to be happy. She wasn't . . . suicidal or anything. It was just a black mood, a bad memory. Then . . .'

'Then she found Il Gobbo and a man who wore the costume of the Plague Doctor. And off they went across the Grand Canal on a gondola. And no one's seen her since.'

'The Plague Doctor?'

'The last time anyone saw her she was with a man dressed like that. Does it mean anything to you?'

'Not to me.'

'She must have brought people back from time to time,' Teresa said.

'No. I don't remember that at all. I thought it was odd. She could have done, you know. There's no reason why not. Especially lately. That last week. I wondered if she had a boyfriend. I asked her.'

'What did she say?'

'She went all bashful. Shy. I almost thought . . . scared. It was as if she wanted to keep something secret. Maybe . . .'

Camilla looked into her coffee cup.

'Maybe what?'

'Maybe he was married or something,' she said and sighed. 'Who knows? Sofia was happy. You could see it in the way she looked, the way she bounced out of the place. You don't know who this man was?'

Jerome Aitchison. Or so it appeared.

'I'm not sure,' Teresa said. 'One week ago Sofia left the bars in the Rialto with him. It was two in the morning. They took a gondola across the canal and no one's seen her since.'

Camilla sat there open-mouthed, plainly astonished.

'Two in the morning? You have to talk to the police,' she said finally.

'I have talked to them. They're too busy to care. Besides, what do I have to show them? Some stray coincidences. Nothing that adds up. And a missing person. The world's full of those.'

'Sofia's disappeared before, hasn't she?'

Teresa watched her very closely and asked, 'Why do you say that?'

'You get to know them after a while. Venice is full of people drifting through, not sure where they're going.' A pause and then she added, 'Like me, I guess.'

'I never knew,' Teresa murmured. 'That was kept from me too.'

Worse, she thought, I never noticed.

The young woman leaned forward and said, 'Tell me what I can do.'

You could speak the truth straight out, Teresa thought. But she didn't say that or much else. No admonition was necessary.

She got up and went to the counter to pay for the coffees and *frittelle*. The large Venetian woman there smiled at her, clearly concerned. Then the young man in the white uniform came forward and said, in half-decent Italian, 'We couldn't help overhearing. Sofia came in here too. Everyone loved her. If there's—'

'Do you know something?' Teresa cut in, a little sharply. 'I'm grateful, honestly. But if I'm going to find her I need some . . . facts. Some certainty.'

'A beautiful, kind human being,' the woman behind the counter insisted. 'We know no more than that, signora. But if we can help . . .'

They gazed at her, she in an antiquated garish pink nylon uniform, he in the white short-sleeved gown of a baker. The doctor in Teresa Lupo couldn't help noticing the sticking plaster and cotton pad in the crook of his arm.

'You give blood,' she said, nodding at the small wound. 'That's a good thing to do. I wish more Italians did it so readily.'

'I'm English, love, not Italian,' he said with a chuckle. 'Can't you tell?'

The Venetian woman grinned and pinched his cheeks, the way a mother might a child.

'He is my saviour. My St George slaying the dragon that is the city council with their taxes and their thieving. Never such a baker and pastry chef have you met. Did you taste those *frittelle*? And he's *English*. He speaks so *funny*! Say something for the lady, Jason. Speak like a proper man from Yorkshire.'

A sly, shy expression crossed the young man's long pale face then he snuggled up to the woman behind the counter, put an arm round her shiny, old-fashioned jacket and cooed, in a very strong English accent, 'Ooh . . . you do look lovely, Mrs Rizzolo.'

She wriggled out of his grip, giggling, then paused for a moment and said, very seriously, 'Miracles do happen, signora. But mostly to those who believe in them.'

Teresa took her change, nodded and didn't say a word.

On the way out she asked Camilla about the envelope the previous night. Someone had put it in her mailbox.

'It was me,' she said straight away. 'I found it on the mat when I came back in the afternoon. Pushed through the door, I suppose. Very strange. The post doesn't come on Sundays. Who was it from?'

'I'm not sure. Maybe someone called Arnaud. The Count of Saint-Germain. Know him?'

Camilla burst out laughing, and Teresa was pleased to see her cheerful again. She had warmed to this young woman and knew she ought to feel a little guilty – though didn't – for extracting from her a secret Camilla felt duty bound to keep hidden.

'Do I look like the sort of person who knows a Count?' The girl thought for a moment then added, 'Though I met plenty of people who looked like one last night. Russian mainly. Not French. Not aristocrats either. Real ones anyway.'

'Carnival,' Teresa said.

'*Si*. Carnival!'

Camilla picked up her bags.

'I have to restock the shop now. We'll be open at ten. A long day ahead. Another party to wait on this evening. You have my number. Call me. About anything.'

I will, Teresa thought, and walked back to the vaporetto stop. The sign said she had to wait ten minutes for a boat. So she phoned Alberto Tosi and arranged to meet him at eleven o'clock outside the Scuola di San Giorgio degli Schiavoni, not far from the Castello Questura where she had spent so many fruitless hours the afternoon before.

In a little while she would see the Carpaccio painting that had so distressed the fictional Jerome Aitchison. It was time to attempt to divide fiction from fact.

★   ★   ★

178

This was her third day without email or the Internet and the absence of both was starting to hurt. When she got off the fast boat across the Basin she went into the commercial back streets near the Mondadori bookstore, found a phone shop and handed over her credit card for a cheap netbook computer with mobile broadband. Then she walked beneath the arches of the Museo Correr into the Piazza San Marco.

Carnival was still in full flow. A procession of brightly coloured and skimpily dressed drag queens was parading around the piazza where the day before Jerome Aitchison, in the black costume and white mask of the Plague Doctor, had plummeted to his death. There was nothing to indicate where the Englishman had met his end. The police and forensic scientists had done their job and the cleaners had followed with their mops and bleach. Teresa wondered whether she would have allowed the public to walk over those patterned stones so quickly had such a terrible event happened in Rome. If it was in the heart of a tourist area she guessed she'd have had little choice. The city authorities would be screaming for a return to what passed as normality. In Venice the pressure would be even greater. As Filippo Strozzi had pointed out, there was only one industry here now. Anything that got between visitors and their cash had to be removed, scrubbed away like the Englishman's blood-stains on the pavement of the piazza just a few short steps away from where she now stood. In truth if Aitchison's death was as simple as it seemed there was probably no good reason to preserve them. People were always uncomfortable around death, even though it walked the same streets as they, an invisible companion night and day.

She bought a couple of newspapers, took a deep breath and went into Florian, paying a price for a *caffè* that almost made her eyes water. But the place was elegant and largely deserted, she was able to spread out the papers and her netbook across an entire table in its mirrored interior and for that kind of money she would stay as long as she liked.

The violent incident during the Flight of the Angel was, unsurprisingly, the lead story everywhere. The papers were so certain of their facts – all of them identical – that Teresa felt like calling the Venice Questura's public relations office and congratulating them on doing such a great job.

In every edition the story had a depressing similarity. Aitchison was a sad Englishman, sacked from his job over an unproven accusation of sexual misconduct. He had come to Venice on a whim, spent much of his time drunk and, it would seem, becoming obsessed with the young TV starlet Luisa Cammarota, whose face and, more importantly, body had been all over the magazines thanks to her varied and highly public love life. The young woman had enjoyed 'flings' with rich businessmen, politicians, actors, footballers and, most recently, a young and talkative car mechanic from Naples who had a talent for photography. So notorious had she become that it was, the media seemed to argue, scarcely unexpected that some foreign lunatic should fix upon her as the object of his unobtainable desires.

Teresa read the stories, cursing every word. There was nothing tangible to link Aitchison to the young woman. No letters, no messages of any kind. The man had left his lodgings in Castello one week before when the owner went on holiday to Kenya. Since she was still there no one knew where he had been living in the meantime. The assumption was out on the street. How did a homeless man acquire an authentic and presumably expensive costume for the Plague Doctor? And a gun? No one seemed to know, or demonstrate much interest in finding an answer. The strange, murderous and incompetent Englishman was dead. Why waste time on the corpse of a fool?

All that was certain was that this curious bachelor had somehow secreted himself inside the campanile early the previous morning, waited for the event to start, then walked out onto the ledge beneath the open arches and half-heartedly tried to kill Luisa Cammarota before stepping out into thin air a hundred metres above ground.

The one loose thread that seemed to concern the papers was Aitchison's body. So solitary was the man that he had no relative or friends who wished to come to Venice to claim his remains. Nor did the British Consulate intend to pay to repatriate his corpse for a pointless funeral in England. Cue outrage on the part of the local media that the man who so shockingly disrupted the opening ceremony of the Carnival might end up being cremated locally at a cost to the taxpayers of Venice.

There were so many open questions here Teresa scarcely knew where to begin. The most important of all being, simply, why? Aitchison was a university lecturer in the obscure field of actuarial science at a famous Cambridge college until his fall from favour. What would make such an intellectual man develop a murderous obsession with a young Italian TV starlet? The woman was, according to the papers, unknown in England. Could such a deadly fixation really have occurred over the last few weeks? And where did this leave his relations with Sofia, a woman more than twenty years her senior, yet someone, it appeared, with whom he had an affair, one her aunt found close and satisfying?

The pages of the previous night's story were in her bag. She took them out and spread them across the antique glass table in Florian's, ignoring the surprised look of the waiter, who clearly did not associate the place with business. Some answers had to lie in this odd narrative and what details she recalled of its predecessor, now disappeared, presumably for good.

Teresa plugged her new computer into the wall and went online. She was grateful to be back in contact with the outside world. Already Venice was starting to feel as if it were detached somehow from the rest of Italy, even from reality itself.

The next twenty minutes confirmed several points that were raised by both stories. She established that there was such a thing as disappearing printer ink for sensitive commercial and government use, and that the paper stock for the commonest brand was, indeed, mustard yellow and simply required a special cartridge for an ordinary printer.

Then she typed in the name of the apparently fictional Arnaud, the Count of Saint-Germain.

A distinct and unwelcome chill came upon her as she watched the search page fill up with endless references, some literary, some historical, a few in the wilder reaches of the human imagination. She had assumed this character was, like much else she'd read, pure fiction. Perhaps he was. Perhaps not. According to the more reliable sites there was a man called Arnaud Saint-Germain active in European society in the eighteenth century, a musician and a philosopher to some, both wizard and con artist to others. Contemporary diaries cited him in Rome, London, Paris, Vienna, Madrid and Naples. He was also mentioned by Casanova in his Venetian memoirs.

Several literary references said that he claimed to possess the secret of the mythical Philosopher's Stone that could turn lead into gold, and relieved rich fools of their fortunes by promising to pass it on . . . and then disappearing. A similar number also recorded that he claimed to have found an elixir which gave him eternal life.

Much of this Teresa could take as fact. What followed veered into pure fantasy. A man claiming to be him appeared in Russia in the 1830s. In New York in 1876 the Theosophist Madame Blavatsky reported a meeting with a 'nobleman named Saint-Germain' who advised on some philosophical principles in her book *Isis Unveiled*. Twenty years later the name appears in records of spiritualist and bohemian circles in *fin-de-siècle* London, the same individual supposedly making the acquaintance, among others, of Arthur Conan Doyle, George Bernard Shaw and the artist Aubrey Beardsley. Twenty-five years after that a controversial Hopi mystic from Arizona 'revealed' himself to be Saint-Germain before disappearing when the police came to call, asking about money.

This was, Teresa surmised, a neat trick. The name was one that con men had used over the centuries in order to baffle and fool the gullible. A point Peroni had once made came to mind. There is no better way to make a lie more convincing than to clothe it in truth. Another memory returned too, of a line from that amusing English comic opera *The Mikado*. This kind of trick was 'merely corroborative detail, intended to give artistic verisimilitude to an otherwise bald and unconvincing narrative'.

There was cunning behind these stories.

She checked her watch. It would soon be time to meet Tosi. This prompted another search, one for 'the First International Symposium on the Genetic Analysis of the Skeletal Remains Attributed to St Mark'.

The results of that proved no surprise either.

Walking across the piazza, admiring the delicately ornate front of the basilica which glistened in the bright winter sun like the skin of an exotic tattooed jungle native, she steeled herself for the conversation ahead, then called Frascati.

Her father answered and, when he heard the tone of her voice, very rapidly passed the call over. There was a brief exchange of semipleasantries, then Teresa asked, 'Why didn't you tell me about the baby?'

The line went silent for so long she thought her mother had put down the phone. Then a tired old voice on the other end said, 'My, we are the detective, aren't we?'

'No. I'm not at all. I'm struggling here. I can't get the police interested. I can't make head nor tail of what's going on. I haven't the faintest clue what's happened to Sofia. Which makes me all the more worried. You *do* want to know, don't you?'

She hated the anger and outrage in her own voice.

'Perhaps I've a better idea than you,' Chiara said miserably.

'Stop this now, Mother!'

'You think you know her.'

And you do? The question remained unsaid. It seemed kindest.

'Why didn't you tell me she'd lost a baby?' Teresa asked instead. 'How can I hope to make some progress if you hold things back?'

'She didn't *lose* the baby,' her mother said in a resigned, quiet, patient voice. 'She got rid of it. As if it was something unimportant. Then the guilt almost destroyed her.'

The basilisk faces of the saints and nobles on the façade of the basilica stared down at her, their stern frowns passing judgement. *Abortion*. Her mother was a good and faithful Catholic. Sofia, like her niece, never gave a second thought to what they both regarded as some archaic form of super-stition.

A sudden, sharp thought occurred to her. Was that something she'd picked up from Sofia too? Her atheism? Her dismissal of anything that couldn't be counted as part of the here and now? Possibly. One more reason for her mother to feel aggrieved by the easy, natural closeness they had for one another as Teresa was growing up.

'Sofia wouldn't take a decision like that easily,' Teresa said.

'What right do you have to say that? None of us understands her reasons. She never explained them to me. If it wasn't for the doctors I might not have known. She just lay there in that hospital bed, silent, tears in her eyes, staring at the ceiling.

Apparently she went to some private doctor across the water in Mestre. There were problems but she left the clinic before they could be remedied. Then she took some pills and walked into the hospital like a lost beggar, almost at death's door. She could never have children afterwards. There were complications.'

So many unknown facts. So much about Sofia that Teresa had never understood. The tears were starting at the back of her eyes and she had no idea whether they stemmed from anger or grief or both.

'Anything else to tell me?' Teresa Lupo asked her mother.

'No.'

'The father?'

'Never mentioned one. She was on her own in Venice as far as I knew. Perhaps she didn't even have a name for him. The life she led was shameful . . .'

'Do *not* talk about her like that.'

'Like what?' Chiara cried. 'Like one who knew her for what she was? Not worshipped her as some distant heroine? I looked after Sofia as if she were my own child. One day she leaves me. Goes out into the world thinking she's grown up, ready, able to look after herself. Not so. She was as much a baby as that poor infant she killed . . .'

Teresa took the phone away from her ear. Religion, decency, the mores of the twenty-first century . . . these were all subjects on which she and her mother had agreed to differ in silence for years. It was the only way there could be peace between them.

'I want you to hear some names,' she said, fighting to keep calm. 'Please think about them. Tell me if they mean anything.'

She listed all she could think of. Jerome Aitchison. Alberto Tosi. Filippo Strozzi. Arnaud Saint-Germain. And finally, out of nothing more than desperation, Camilla Dushku.

In a way she felt guilty bringing them all into the equation. But they were the only names she had. And Venice was an island, a city divided from the world by that shifting slab of silver sea. It made sense to start with what was here.

Her mother paused for a moment and said, 'I do read the newspapers. That Englishman who killed himself yesterday was called Aitchison. What's he got to do with this?'

'Probably nothing,' Teresa lied. 'Do any of these names sound familiar?'

She knew what the answer would be so it came as no surprise. There was a note of resignation, of mourning even in her mother's voice. Chiara was preparing herself for the worst of news because, in her heart, she felt that was what any rational person ought to expect. Sofia had struggled to survive on her own, embroidering the sadness of her lonely life with lies and self-deception. Sixteen years before, that fantasy had briefly fallen apart. She had almost slipped beneath the surface. Chiara had somehow dragged her back only to let go again, inevitably, as Sofia appeared to find herself once more.

There were deep scars here, ones that still itched and ached.

'How did you find out? About the baby?' Chiara asked with some trepidation for once in her voice.

'She told someone. In the apartment block. At Christmas. When she was down one night. And after that she got better. She was happy. Very happy, I think. Which makes it all the more odd. Mother . . .'

'I don't want to argue with you. Please . . .'

'No. This isn't an argument. I need you to know. Sofia wasn't miserable before she disappeared. She was bright and cheerful. She had a man, I think.'

'The men were always the problem.'

The two of them were just a single step, a few short words, from another explosion. Teresa was determined to avoid this.

'Are you sure there's nothing else I ought to know?'

'That was my only secret. You think it's a small one?'

'You should have told me. It might have saved some time. And yes. I think it's not such a big secret that you should keep it to yourself. In the circumstances.'

'That's why we're so different.' A brittle judgemental tone had entered Chiara's voice again. 'Don't raise your hopes too highly. Sofia never

189

meant anyone any harm. That doesn't mean she wasn't capable of inflicting it. She was my sister. I loved her. I still do. But she was always careless, with herself, with the emotions of others. She never once noticed the damage she did.' Her mother took a deep breath, audible on the line, then said, 'Don't let that part of her touch you. The scars don't heal easily. I know.'

After the call she walked to the waterfront and stared at the lagoon and the stately shape of San Giorgio Maggiore across the water. People seemed so small next to the grandeur of this city. It was as if Venice had created itself somehow, or been built by a lost race of giants. It was hard to imagine how any modern man or woman could possess such wild and seemingly impossible dreams of a magnificent world built on nothing but mud and water. Sofia would feel at home in this oddly unique place. That was one good reason for her to return, and not a morbid one.

The phone rang again.

'Mother . . .'

'It's not your mother,' said a voice down the line.

'Silvio . . .'

Her deputy sounded both cross and a little scared, which lifted her spirits somewhat. He immediately launched into a rant about reports and meetings and how very, very furious the malevolent grey-suited, bean-counting bastards

190

upstairs were getting about her lengthening absence from the Questura.

'Tell them to go screw themselves,' Teresa said. 'It's just been a couple of days. People have gone sick for longer.'

'You didn't go sick and you didn't say you'd be away this long,' he pointed out.

'I didn't know! Tell them it's something personal. God knows I'm owed the time.'

Silvio Di Capua muttered a barely audible curse.

'You really don't get it, do you? If you'd handled this properly from the beginning no one could possibly object. But you didn't. You just walked. Handed that bastard Orsini the opportunity to screw you. On a plate. And . . . he . . . will.'

This was tiresome.

'Oh for pity's sake, Silvio. No one hired me for my communication skills. Go sort it out.'

'This is not a joke,' he cried. 'They've cancelled the quarterly budget review meeting because you can't be there and you haven't even started the departmental report.'

'Oh my. Don't let the criminals find out. They'll run wild.'

'That's not funny.'

'Listen,' she went on. 'Scribble some numbers on a piece of paper. Go along in my place. Nod and smile. That always works. I'll deal with it when I get back.'

'Which will be when?'

'When I'm finished here.'

'Teresa!' She didn't ever remember Silvio Di Capua yelling at her like this before. 'Are you listening to me? You've walked out on us without asking anyone's permission. This is serious. Job-threatening serious. They want you back. Today. Catch a plane. Now. Tomorrow at the latest . . .'

'Not going to happen.'

'In that case prepare to get suspended.'

He rang off after that. She couldn't help but laugh.

Suspended? For bunking off for a few days on personal business?

Impossible. She'd done them so many favours in the past. She was good at her job. Couldn't remember the last time she'd gone off sick.

True, she could be a little . . . unpredictable at times. Unruly.

There was the occasion she punched some mouthy *commissario* on a nasty murder case in Testaccio. Repercussions followed. But he'd deserved it.

These were needless distractions. Reminding herself of this fact, then dismissing Di Capua's concerns from her head completely, she strode east towards Arsenale, took out her map, found the right canal and cut in towards the narrow street that ought to lead to the Scuola di San Giorgio degli Schiavoni.

It was as she imagined from the lost story: a small white classical building next to a fetching low brown brick bridge.

Alberto Tosi was outside, a tall, reserved figure in an black ankle-length coat and a hat of a similar colour which he raised like a gentleman as she arrived.

'Have you news?' he asked before they went in.

'Not really.'

Teresa looked at him and decided to get this out of the way first. She didn't feel confident enough to talk about the stories in any great detail. Not until she understood them more. That didn't mean she couldn't try to use what information they contained. And perhaps that was one of their purposes.

'When we first spoke, you said you had something in mind for me, Alberto. That was why you rang—'

'It's not important now,' he broke in.

'Was it to do with the remains of St Mark by any chance?'

His long face was broken by a ready grin.

'You're so quick! I should have known you'd have realized. It's been in the papers, of course. We're still finalizing the team. I haven't released any names but they'll be prestigious. You'll be in good company.' He rubbed his gloved hands. 'And there'll be expenses too. The Vatican has deep pockets.'

She smiled at him.

'I'm afraid I'm not a believer. You really shouldn't invite an atheist into your midst. Not if you want me to rubber-stamp some saintly death certificate on behalf of the Pope.'

She could tell from Tosi's face that he was offended and she regretted that.

'Nothing could be further from my mind,' he assured her. 'For what it's worth I'm a Catholic so lapsed I doubt I'd get out of Purgatory in a thousand years. They only asked me because I'm local and know everyone. This is about science. About truth. I wouldn't have undertaken it otherwise. Let alone have had the temerity to ask for help from one of the most admired forensic scientists in Italy.'

'I'm just a pen-pusher in the Rome Questura,' she told him.

'Nonsense. I've watched you work. Many of us are good scientists. That's our job. But you . . .' He took her arms and she felt doubly embarrassed. 'You sometimes have this faculty to combine your intellect with some sense of the imagination that goes beyond anything the rest of us can hope for. We are all rational. But you . . .'

'I'm irrational?' she asked.

'No. You're *super*-rational. That's the word.'

'A new one on me. And I don't think it's true.'

'A good one,' he said, and looked proud of himself. 'And yes, it is true, even if you don't realize it yourself.'

She felt a brief moment of discovery. The story from the night before was, in respect of Alberto Tosi's character, largely inaccurate. As if it had simply been copied from a newspaper, without the slightest personal knowledge.

'You said the Vatican was paying?'

'And we all know why,' Tosi replied. 'That doesn't mean we have to deliver what they want, does it? Facts are facts and I would be honoured if you saw fit to help us find them. I won't be party to some piece of chicanery just to keep the crowds coming to the Basilica San Marco. As if they need our help.'

'Quite.'

'Besides.' He patted her arm. Any offence, such as it was, appeared swiftly forgotten. 'This is a small matter next to that of your aunt. Let's concentrate on her, shall we? So why are we here?'

She told him as much as she felt able, leaving out the missing story about the dog, replacing it with a vague intuition that Sofia had visited this place and possibly met the dead Englishman Jerome Aitchison.

Tosi listened attentively and asked a few questions. Then they went in.

There was a brisk, efficient-looking middle-aged man seated behind a small table at the door. He looked up as they entered then glanced at a donation box. Tosi quickly put in some coins and got two very old-fashioned tickets by way of thanks. The warden wore a pinstriped grey suit and the thick horn-rimmed spectacles of a minor civil servant. From what she recalled of the lost story this could be the very man it described.

There was, however, no opportunity to talk at that moment. The hall was very like a small chapel but with the main three walls covered in paintings. It was occupied by a party, all teenage girls, with the insignia of a Catholic school from London on their uniform. A guide or teacher was talking them through the art around them in the entertaining and slightly condescending way that adults sometimes adopted when addressing the young.

He was a tall man in an unseasonal pale summer suit, much crumpled as if it had just come out of a suitcase. A costume perhaps to keep their attention through some theatrical posturing as he inserted a little factual academic and religious knowledge into his lecture. So he pointed out the strange beasts in the various Carpaccio canvases – dragons, monsters and the lion which St Jerome adopted, a charming animal that could be seen howling with grief in the painting of the saint's death. Alongside the amusement he talked a little about Catholic theology, the role of St George, England's patron saint but that of many other nations too, and Jerome's work on the first Latin Bible, the Vulgate.

Teresa sat next to Tosi on a hard bench, listening to the teacher's florid language, some of it a little beyond her own usually good grasp of English. She found herself entranced by the man's charming theatrical manner and musical voice. He was fair-haired, perhaps older than the forty years he first appeared and possessed a fund of information and spurious, engaging facts designed to ensnare the casual listener into paying attention.

Till that moment she'd never heard of *The Golden Legend* of Jacobus de Voragine, a medieval bestseller composed of mythical lives of the saints, source of many of the fanciful tales about George and the Dragon which had inspired not just the Carpaccio paintings on the walls of the Scuola di San Giorgio degli Schiavoni but the entire canon of literature about the saint and his monster-slaying habits. All from the mind of an ancient monk who had fabricated the stories out of nothing more than pure imagination.

The speaker's frankness was praiseworthy. Perhaps some of the Catholic scientists roped in for Tosi's commission would be equally assiduous about the truth. Legend and myth sprang from fiction and fancy, the man insisted, so much that at times the imagination only served to hide or disguise genuine facts that lay hidden like precious gems lost in a forest of fabulous whimsy.

From these same two competing sources came beauty too. The paintings around them, while bizarre in the extreme at times, were extraordinarily compelling. Fantastic mythical landscapes in which heroic figures conspired to challenge dreadful monsters alongside more subtle and real terrors, war, age and death. Mostly the players were portrayed with fetching features, real human beings, not religious icons but inward saints. Teresa could imagine why Sofia would be drawn to such an intimate, emotional and intellectually fertile place as this, could believe implicitly that part of the lost story on those mustard pages was indeed true.

The guide wrapped up his presentation with a talk about the painting that interested her most of all: the one she knew already, St Augustine in his gorgeous academic study, working at a desk surrounded by the detritus of an intellectual life, staring out of the window beyond the books and instruments, hearing something that clearly both puzzled and intrigued him.

Close by his feet, unnoticed, eager and alert, was a small white dog, a breed unknown to her.

Volpino. Little fox.

That was what she'd read.

The teacher spoke about the painting for a good five minutes though, in truth, he had very little to disclose by way of hard fact. Its meaning was obscure. Even the identification with St Augustine was questioned by some art experts. And the cartellino . . .

She shivered, though it was not cold in the hall of the *scuola* at all.

'As you'll know – I hope from your Latin lessons – the tense of the verb is strange. Quite wrong. Nowhere else does Carpaccio use the imperfect in such a way. Why should he? The painting's complete. Finished. What is he trying to say?'

Teresa found herself putting up her hand like a school pupil.

The Englishman laughed and said, in a sound Italian accent, 'Signora?'

'If Augustine is hearing about the death of Jerome, through some mystical intervention, perhaps Carpaccio is reminding us, through the saint, that life goes on,' Teresa said, half-wondering where this idea came from. 'The dog's doing that too. It's looking at him as if it wants to go out and play. Not watch its master sit at a desk writing all day.'

'Or painting!' Tosi chipped in. 'Perhaps Carpaccio was saying enough of this work. It's time to knock off for some supper and a glass of wine. A man, a saint even, can read and write and think all day long. But life's to be lived. And isn't it an affront to God not to enjoy it?'

The Englishman took it well, laughed and said, 'Nice try but it's not an idea that would have appealed to Jerome, I suspect. He loathed jollity in all its forms.' He bowed. 'But thanks anyway. Class? Do you have questions?'

There were three. Two about the lion. One about the dog.

Then the talk was over and, very quickly, without another word, the schoolgirls followed their guide out of the building.

Tosi leaned over and whispered in her ear, 'That was very good. I didn't know you understood art. And religion.'

'I haven't the foggiest about either,' Teresa said, still amazed by her own intervention.

The lost story must have been nagging at her unconsciously ever since she read it. The odd suggestion was quite out of character.

'Good explanation though,' the old man added. 'I must admit these are lovely paintings but they've always baffled me. And they seemed a little . . .' He shuddered. 'Spooky to be honest.'

'You're a pathologist, Alberto,' she scolded him. 'How can anything be spooky after a career like that?'

He stared at the floor and she wondered if she'd gone too far for some reason.

'You'd be surprised,' he said in a soft, low voice.

She got up and walked over to the man on the door, taking out the old photo of her aunt.

'I'm trying to find someone,' Teresa said. 'Her name's—'

'Signora Bianchi,' the warden interrupted. 'Sofia. That's a very out-dated picture. Do you really have nothing more recent?'

'No,' she said.

'It must have been taken before.'

'Before what?'

'Before she came back.'

She pulled up a spare chair and sat down next to him. Then she explained how Sofia had gone missing and that there was concern for her whereabouts. The man had a very immobile face, officious, a little dour even. He listened patiently, unmoved, betraying little interest.

'You knew my aunt when she was here the first time?'

'No,' he said immediately. 'She told me herself

she lived here before. She's a very talkative and charming woman.'

'Did Sofia say why she came back?'

He closed the donations box, as if expecting no more customers.

'I think she said something about having no choice. It was in her blood. Outsiders have strange ideas about this city sometimes.'

Tosi had come over to stand by them. He cast the man a sour glance, unhappy with the curt answer.

'You want the truth, don't you?' the warden responded. 'She seemed proud that she'd come back for some reason.' He took off his glasses and polished them with his tie. The man looked older and, with his bulbous eyes, rather owl-like without them. 'As if it was some kind of victory. Over what?' He scowled. 'I don't understand. Is it such a penance to live in Venice? I was born here. I like it.'

'I think she liked it too,' Teresa said. 'Didn't she?'

The warden thought about this. He was not a man to make swift or rash statements.

'Lately yes. To begin with . . . I'm not so sure. She seemed lost. She would come here looking for tourists to talk to, asking if they needed a guide. I had occasion to speak with her about this. It was not something I relished. She looked very sad and miserable back then.' He sighed. 'And poor to be honest. I didn't like asking her not to approach people, and she didn't stop, not entirely. But . . .'

'But what?' Tosi asked. 'Come on, man. The poor lady's missing. This is her niece. At least try and help.'

The sound of a gruff Venetian voice seemed to have some effect. These people never liked talking to foreigners, Teresa thought, and being a Roman that was precisely what she represented.

'Sofia – she insisted I call her that – was a very captivating woman,' the warden told them. 'Pleasant to talk to. Intelligent. Very well informed. One of the best tour guides for this place. She knew everything about Carpaccio. Not just his paintings here. Elsewhere. In the Accademia too. I recommended her to many people. None ever complained. She wasn't like that . . .'

A sour expression wrinkled his grizzled features.

'That English popinjay you just saw. All wind and piss, if you'll excuse my language. *The Golden Legend*. Fanciful rubbish. That man annoys the life out of me. These are paintings about real people, real life. Not stupid fairy stories for teenagers.'

'My aunt . . .' Teresa prompted him.

'We reached an accommodation,' he said. 'Sofia was always welcome here, and would often arrive with her customers already on the hook, as it were. But if not, she was to approach them slyly. In casual conversation. Nothing that disturbed the atmosphere.'

Which was, Teresa thought, that of a crypt.

'When did you last see her?' she asked.

He opened a drawer in the table, removed a diary, flicked through the pages and said, 'Eleven days ago precisely. In the morning.'

This was not what she expected.

'You're sure of that? Not more like a week?'

He showed her the page.

'I'm sure of it. I'm the principal guardian and I keep a record of our commercial visitors. They're expected to make their donations too.' He opened the donation box and pushed it forward. 'As is anyone who receives special service.'

Teresa pulled out a twenty-euro note and popped it in with the coins. For some reason she recalled the café, the cheery Venetian woman behind the counter, and the young foreigner in the baker's uniform, covered in flour, a sticking plaster on his arm. St George come to slay the dragon.

'There was another Englishman here,' she said.

'There are many English visitors to the *scuola*.'

'A particular one. His name was Jerome Aitchison. He died yesterday, in the Piazza San Marco. Dressed as the Plague Doctor. He tried to kill that young woman who was the angel.'

He frowned, shook his head and pulled a copy of *Il Gazzettino* out of the drawer. Aitchison's passport photo was blown up to fill a large part of the front page.

'So many people,' the man muttered. 'Am I supposed to remember every one?'

'This one spoke to Sofia, I think,' she said, probing, hoping, wondering if that disappeared piece of fiction could really, in any sense, be 'true'. 'They talked about the painting of St Augustine. What the cartellino meant. And the dog.'

'Ah!' He thought for a moment, looked at the picture again. Then his face fell and he shook his head and said, 'No.'

'The dog,' she persisted.

'The dog is a volpino. A very rare breed.' He shrugged. 'Some people think it is a little special, I believe. Local people. Superstitious people.'

He looked at Tosi and said, 'You're a Venetian. Help me out.'

'I've never heard such nonsense in my life,' Tosi declared. 'A dog's a dog. What on earth are you talking about?'

The warden wriggled on his seat.

'If one met a volpino . . .' Teresa asked.

'Then one would treat it with kindness and respect, I trust,' he responded. 'As with any dog.'

She was unable to speak for a moment. The words were so similar to those she remembered from the story. Were they his in the lost piece of fiction? Or Sofia's? She couldn't recall. But they were aimed at Jerome Aitchison, with no small degree of concern on the part of the person who uttered them.

'Lunchtime,' the man declared, getting up off his seat. 'If there are no more questions . . .'

Teresa scribbled out her mobile number and gave it to him.

'If you think of anything. If you see my aunt . . .'

'Then I shall call,' he said, shooing them to the door.

In an instant they were gone, pushed abruptly into the harsh midday February sun.

Inside the Scuola di San Giorgio degli Schiavoni the man turned off the lights one by one. Then he went to the picture of Augustine at his desk and found his attention drifting, as always, to the small, off-white shape of the little animal, taut and alert on the floor, staring up at its master with a bright and quizzical expression.

He hadn't been entirely truthful on that particular point. There was a dog much like this in the neighbourhood. He'd seen it from time to time and for some reason felt minded to give it a wide berth.

With a shrug he returned to the door, looked at the phone number the woman had given him, thought for a moment, then screwed the scrap of paper into a ball and tossed it in the bin.

Tosi took her to a tiny local bar down a back alley near the *scuola*. She stood outside for a moment and stared at the sign over the door: the Cason dei Sette Morti.

'Morbid name,' the old pathologist said. 'It comes from some old lagoon tale.'

'About what?'

He huffed and puffed awkwardly then said, 'Ghosts and spectres and dead men walking and talking as if nothing untoward had happened.'

Teresa went in and immediately interrogated the pleasant old bartender behind the counter about an odd Englishman named Jerome Aitchison who might have been here recently. Her questions drew a blank, genuinely she believed. The story on the yellow pages was mostly untrue. Yet Jerome Aitchison did exist and had tried to murder the young actress Luisa Cammarota the day before. Whoever wrote those words knew about him, knew this place and the nearby *scuola* and Sofia's connections with it.

Tosi announced that he remembered from her previous visit how much she liked salt cod.

'The *baccalá* here . . .'

The bartender beamed as Tosi lavished fulsome praise on the small puddles of white, puréed fish being set in front of them.

They sat down and she realized how right he was. The taste, so delicate, so redolent of the sea somehow, took her back many years.

The place looked more like a junk shop than a bar. It was full of bits and pieces accumulated over time. Old amusement machines, clearly out of order, shelves of books, fishing nets, agricultural implements, scores of sepia and black-and-white photographs of long-dead Venetians staring at the camera as if it had intruded upon some private ceremony. Three grandfather clocks, none apparently working, stood in shady corners. An obscure fortune-telling device was attached to the wall next to the toilet, a sign declaring 'broken' taped over the coin slot.

'The owner likes to collect things,' Tosi said by way of explanation.

Reluctantly she told him about the fiction that had disappeared from the mustard-coloured pages sent to her the previous Saturday night. Told him everything she remembered. Then she explained how she knew about the First International Symposium on the Genetic Analysis of the Skeletal Remains Attributed to St Mark. He sipped his *ombra* of weak white wine, eyes glassy with shock and bafflement.

'What can it possibly mean?' he asked when she'd finished.

'I can't imagine.'

'To think I'd treat a lady in such a way. That any of us would. Abandoning someone to a place like that.'

'You know Poveglia?'

He shuddered again and said, 'I know *of* it. The Island of the Dead. As you said. Well that's one thing I can guarantee about our symposium, should you turn up. There'll be no boat trips.'

She finished her *cicchetti* and bought him another *ombra*. The wine was prosecco spento, so weak it scarcely counted. He seemed terribly upset, by Sofia's absence and the idea that he had somehow been introduced into the mystery almost as a villain in the piece.

'Let's go and see the police again,' Tosi suggested. 'My name still carries a little weight here, I think.'

But it didn't and they both soon knew it.

They walked round to the Castello Questura and, after waiting for thirty minutes, found themselves sitting side by side in an interview room, Tosi getting somewhat red in the face as Paola

207

Boscolo explained what was being done about the case of the missing Sofia Bianchi.

Everything and nothing was the answer. The beaming *sovrintendente* explained how she had followed the procedures in the book, alerting neighbouring police forces and the national missing persons register. She had personally called every hospital and homeless hostel in the region without success, leaving her own mobile number and emailing them the last photo they had of Sofia.

None had any record of a woman answering her description.

Then she listened carefully, sympathetically, as Teresa told her about the baby Sofia had lost here sixteen years before.

'I'm sorry to hear that,' she said. 'I don't understand why a Catholic nation allows abortion.'

'Because we're not a Catholic nation,' Teresa responded through gritted teeth. 'I'm not here for a conversation about the morality of terminations. There must have been a father. It's possible Sofia came back to see him . . .'

'I thought you said she had something to do with this Englishman? Aitchison? The one who died in the Piazza San Marco?'

'I . . . I . . .'

She struggled for the words, for some kind of logic. Both were absent.

'Teresa,' the policewoman continued, with that same infuriating familiarity. 'If your aunt had an abortion here all those years ago it was a private matter, nothing illegal. The police would never have been involved. There would be no need of any official record. No requirement to register the father's identity. As I said before, if you wish to pursue these matters you may find it easier to do so through your family, through Sofia's friends—'

'I'm trying!'

Tosi intervened and told Boscolo about their conversations in the Rialto the previous night.

'Here are hard facts,' he insisted. 'Sofia went to these places regularly. She was seen leaving in the early hours of the morning, with a man dressed as the Plague Doctor. They took a gondola.'

The police officer opened her hands, smiled and said nothing.

'You could ask,' Tosi went on. 'Make inquiries.'

Boscolo was staring at Teresa, knowingly.

'Ask what?' she said. 'Did someone see a woman in the night? Teresa understands we have nothing to work with here. No evidence of a crime or of wrongdoing. A woman in a delicate mental state goes missing—'

'With a man!' Tosi said rather too loudly.

'With a man,' the policewoman agreed. 'Listen to me. Venice is a small and crowded place. On the rare occasions we have crimes of violence we know about it. In Rome, in Naples, in Milan, a woman might scream and no one cares to notice. In this city everyone hears everything. Had Sofia come to some harm a week, ten days ago, we would have found something by now. I understand that this uncertainty is disconcerting but believe me. Sometimes no news is good news, as they say. Now . . .'

She shuffled the documents on her desk.

'Carnival continues. There is paperwork to be concluded with regard to the dead Englishman. I have much to do. We will continue to look for your aunt. Be assured of that.'

It was starting to get dark by the time they left. Tosi stayed with Teresa as they walked back to the waterfront.

By the lagoon Teresa kissed his cold, whiskery cheek, held him for a moment and said, 'Thanks. I don't know what I'd do without you.'

'Cope,' he said forcefully. 'You're a champion at coping. I knew it the first time we ever met. In circumstances like these coping is a powerful antidote to doubt and misery and despair. Perhaps the best there is.'

She laughed.

'It's nice that I don't have to cope alone.'

He shuffled on his stiff legs.

'That policeman of yours . . . Peroni. He's a very lucky man. I hope he realizes it.'

'We're both very lucky, Alberto. And yes, we know.'

He took her arms and gazed into her face with a stern, determined expression.

'I will make inquiries, my dear. Be assured of that.'

She walked to the vaporetto stop and took the

fast boat back to Zattere, her heart a little lighter. Alberto Tosi was a charming, intelligent, fiercely dedicated old man. He desperately wanted to help. They all did.

But what could any of them do without the next envelope? The next marker along the trail?

As the fast sleek boat pulled into Zattere she ached to see it, to know what happened next.

There was nothing in the downstairs mailbox. Teresa walked up and checked the stone steps in front of the green door of Sofia's apartment. Nothing there either.

She stood on the cold winding staircase for a moment, unable to believe this. The tale of the Count of Saint-Germain and her visit with him to the Island of the Dead was not simply unresolved, like that of *Carpaccio's Dog*. It was blatantly unfinished, left hanging in the air, demanding answers. Where else could they possibly be found?

Laughter rose from two floors below. She walked down and entered through the half-open door. Camilla was there by the side of Strozzi who was now away from the piano, a hunched, bulky figure in his wheelchair. The two of them were fighting frantically with paper and paste and paint.

'Busy times,' he said, nodding at Teresa as she came in. 'So many people. So many orders. So much . . .' He breathed a deep sigh, as if of relief. '. . . money. Any news?'

'No,' she said simply.

Every wall of the room was occupied by masks, all of them white and ghostly, some waiting for paint to give them a little life, a good half, she saw, Plague Doctors like elongated crows' skulls mounted as trophies on display.

'The postman . . .' Teresa began.

'Has been,' Camilla said. 'Bills, bills, bills.' She stopped what she was doing, which appeared to be applying paste onto some kind of a template, and asked, 'No news at all?'

'None that means anything,' Teresa muttered.

The two of them stared at her, clearly concerned.

'Camilla told me about the Rialto,' Strozzi said. 'And this man in the costume of the Plague Doctor. They went off together? In a gondola?'

'Just across the canal,' she confirmed. 'After that . . .'

'Inexplicable,' he said. 'A gondola? What could she have been thinking?'

'I think she was in love,' Teresa said, though she wasn't quite sure why. 'Infatuated, I guess. Acting on a whim.'

'Lots of people are like that,' Strozzi replied with a shrug. 'Look at us.'

He gestured at the paper and the masks.

'I was supposed to be a concert pianist. And Camilla?'

They both looked at her.

'Still thinking about that,' the young woman said, and splashed some more paste onto the mask in her hands.

'Did Camilla tell you about the baby?' Teresa asked him.

His face was stony, blank.

'No,' the young woman said quietly, a little offended. 'I do not tell tales.'

'That's a good thing,' Teresa observed. 'But sometimes tales are necessary.'

She explained what had happened during Sofia's previous time in the city. About the baby. About the abortion. And the overdose. Strozzi listened attentively, shaking his head sadly. Then, when she'd ended, he asked, 'Do you know who the father was?'

'No. I thought perhaps . . . you might.'

'Why me? I'm just the man downstairs. I liked Sofia. I wanted to help. We both tried to cheer her when she was down. But that's as far as it went. I was not party to her secrets.'

'If it wasn't for the drink,' Camilla added, 'I don't think I would have been either. There was something very private about her. I respected that. So did Filippo. How else should we behave?'

Now she seemed to have offended both of them, and for no good reason.

He took Camilla's arm and said, 'This work . . .' He put aside the small, feminine mask in his hands. 'It's nothing next to finding Sofia. But help us help *you*. Otherwise we're lost.'

I can't, Teresa thought. Not without some insight. Or the next instalment of the story.

'I'm sorry,' she said. 'It's been a long day. I'm tired. I apologize if I appeared rude.'

'Ah!'

Filippo Strozzi raised his hand.

'No need for apologies. I remember! One thing I have to tell you. It may be nothing at all and it's too late to do anything about it now, I'm afraid. But that costume you found in Sofia's apartment. The one you believed was for the carnival?'

'What about it?'

He scratched his beard.

'I could be wrong but I think I know where it comes from. Or at least the original. There's something round the corner in the Accademia.'

'A painting?' she murmured.

'*Si*. By an artist called Carpaccio. A very beautiful, very disturbing series of paintings in some ways.'

Teresa Lupo closed her eyes. The thought of staring at another of Carpaccio's finely detailed dead Venetians sent a shiver through her. There was something in the work she'd seen in the Scuola di San Giorgio degli Schiavoni she found deeply unsettling. The saint gazing through the window, hearing the news of his friend's death as if by some mystical medium. The panoply of books and scientific instruments around, all the trappings of the academic, the man of the world, the scientist just like her. And the dog on the floor, staring up at him, asking a simple, unanswerable question that still eluded her.

'Tomorrow at nine thirty,' Strozzi's voice boomed, bringing her back to her senses. 'If you

have the time. We should go and look. As I said . . .
I may be wrong.'

'I doubt that somehow,' Teresa told him.

She went back upstairs. There were only two
emails waiting. The first was from Silvio Di Capua
and ranged from threats to pleading, all with one
aim, to bring her back to Rome immediately.

'Poor Silvio,' she said to the glass-eyed pheasant
in its case. 'Always living in fear.'

She saw the name on the second and went into
the kitchen to make herself one of Sofia's curious
mugs of tea. She'd still not found the time to stock
the apartment with food. Now it was too late
again. She would have to go out and a part of her
knew already where she was headed.

Beyond the kitchen window a liner glided along
the canal, its vast dark hulk ribboned with cabin
lights, its might sending a tremor through the
building. She didn't mind this now. It was a
reminder that there was a world outside, one that
could reach into the interior enclosed community
that was Venice and touch it, if only for a little
while.

She called Di Capua. From the noises behind
him she guessed he was in that bar he loved so
much near the Piazza Navona. She'd left Rome
only two days before. It seemed like weeks.

'You're coming back?' he said straight away.

'No. I'm not.'

'Teresa! I'm telling you! This is serious. Career-
threatening serious. No one's sacrosanct. Not the

way things are today. You've been here so long you earn twice as much as the rest of us. And I mean that word. Earn. I know how much we need you. That doesn't mean those penny-pinching bureaucrats upstairs do.'

'You know, you're the smartest minion I've ever had,' she said, and meant it. 'I taught you well.'

'Don't talk like this. Get on a train first thing in the morning. Walk in and say you're sorry. It's just a few days. If you come back now the worst that can happen is a suspension or something.'

'Silvio . . .'

She heard him move somewhere. Outside perhaps, for a little privacy. She could imagine the street of Governo Vecchio in her head, see him standing on the cobblestones in the cold winter night.

'I shouldn't be telling you this,' he continued. 'They'd kill me if they knew. Peroni and company are coming back. Probably by the weekend. They could help . . .'

'Peroni's a cop in Rome. I'm in Venice.'

And besides, she thought, there was something here he couldn't understand, any more than she at that moment.

'You can handle things,' she said. 'And you will. I've got to go now. Goodnight.'

She ended the call and felt a little guilty.

The second message was from Orsini, the senior civil servant responsible for the administration of the department. The man who hired and fired. A decent enough individual. An obedient and thoroughly unimaginative servant of the state. One who resented her occasional recalcitrant moment and disregard for the rulebook. That was his problem, not hers.

They couldn't dismiss her, not on the basis of a few days' unauthorized absence and the occasional past misdemeanour. Suspension. Demotion. Maybe even some formal hauling over the coals. There wasn't a lot else they could do.

The decision was hers, had to be. She thought of Augustine at his desk then leaned over her new computer and typed out a reply. It was formal and polite. Her absence was due to pressing personal reasons. She apologized for not explaining these earlier. They were family matters, of no concern to the Questura. If he looked at the duty rosters he would, she suggested, see that she was owed at least a week of extra time, as well as due holiday. While it was unconventional to take this without warning it wasn't unknown.

Orsini had made it plain in his email that he wanted a date for her return. As politely as she could, she told him this was impossible. When her business here was done, she would be back. In the meantime he had Silvio to rely upon, a skilled and intelligent officer who possessed all of her finer points and none of the weaker ones.

When she was done she pushed back the computer and read the message again, carefully, word by word. Her emails were, on occasion, notorious for their intemperate language and judgements. This would not be one of those.

Her finger hovered over the send button for a moment. Then she hit it.

She was aware of an unexpected sense of freedom, of having turned a previously unseen corner. Until Sofia was found she would remain in Venice, whatever the consequences.

Teresa wandered into the bedroom, lay down and fell asleep almost immediately. The shivering passing of another cruise liner woke her around eight o'clock.

She climbed into the cracked enamel bath and stood under the dribbling, lukewarm shower for a while. Then she found her best clothes, investigated Sofia's compendious make-up drawer, did her best with what little she understood, including some lipstick. It was clumsy she guessed, though not as much as a mask. But who'd really notice in the dark?

Just after nine she set off into the night, much as her aunt must have done, walking through the intermittent snow to the Salute stop where she caught the number one vaporetto to the Rialto, the one that stopped everywhere along the way.

It was busier than before. A crowd of people in costumes and masks obscured the statue of Il Gobbo, almost filling the square opposite the church of San Giacomo. From the adjoining *campiello* came the deafening blare and hypnotic strobe lights of the outdoor disco. She had to remind herself again: this was the Rialto, the place where the tourists came and gazed at stalls of exotic gleaming fish and colourful vegetables.

The vaporetto had pulled in at every last *fermata* on the Grand Canal. It was now almost ten and she'd not eaten a thing since the *baccalà* at lunchtime with Tosi, in the little bar that looked like a junk shop. Teresa bought herself a couple of small panini and, without thinking, a spritz, served in a plastic cup. Then she stood on her own in the square next to the hunchback's statue, trying to stifle the nagging thought that this was pointless. She didn't know what to do any more, what to ask, who to talk to.

She was, it seemed to her, very like Sofia must have been when she found herself back in Venice after a gap of sixteen years. Friendless? That was how it appeared. But clearly it couldn't be so.

Teresa quickly devoured the two panini and bought herself another drink. Out in the dark and the cold, jostled from time to time by anonymous, disguised strangers, it was easier to think somehow. Easier than it had been with Tosi and Strozzi and Camilla all asking the same question: how can we help?

'I've no idea,' she said to herself.

She thought of what Tosi had said about Peroni, somewhere in Sicily, and the odd single life she'd led before she met him. Men came and went, mostly the latter if she were honest, and she didn't mind because attachment carried with it such difficult and demanding conditions. Until Peroni turned up, with his gruff voice, quick smile and a sense of humour that never failed to lift her spirits, she'd never really understood what it meant to be swept off one's feet. But he'd managed it somehow, and never once made her feel less than free, independent, her own woman.

There was no sense to the relationship whatsoever. That's what love's like, she thought. A condition that couldn't be explained, measured, or defined. It was a word the two of them rarely, if ever, exchanged because it was so unnecessary. A platitude, a truism. Like pointing out the presence of the sun during the day and the moon at night.

'Where's the logic there?' she muttered.

'Logic? You want logic?'

A man was next to her. She recognized him from the night before. Heavily built, with a beard that was a little too tidy to be anything but arrogant. He'd stood close to the helpful one at the bar, not saying a word then, just listening. And watching.

'Talking to myself,' she said. 'A bad habit.'

'Dead right. Talk to me. Much more interesting.'

He was wearing the costume of what she took to be some kind of medieval count. A heavy cloak, fancy trousers with stockings and buckled shoes. A broad-brimmed velvet hat. But no mask.

'I'm looking for someone,' she said, and immediately realized the words had come out badly.

'Aren't we all?' he grinned.

'No. You were here last night. With your helpful

friend.' She pointed to the bar in the hole in the wall. 'Over there. I explained to him . . . My aunt . . .'

'Ah. Want a drink?'

She smiled briefly, said nothing and walked off into the next piazza, the one with the disco and the lights, where the barman had recognized Sofia immediately. He wasn't there this time, just a woman in a ridiculous flimsy cartoon-character costume and mask, holding out plastic glasses of spritz at people the moment they came near. Teresa bought one and tried to talk to her. The noise was too loud now. It was late. People were getting a little drunk. This was all a waste of time.

She shuffled over and stood outside the fancy cheese shop, staring through the glass at the lumps of parmesan and provolone that lay beneath the dim interior lights like cuts of meat.

Sofia came here and did much the same thing. Why?

Because she was lonely. Because this was what she did everywhere she lived. Hung around with a fast-changing bohemian crowd, never putting down roots, never once forging a stable relationship. And then moving on.

Except here, before, something had gone wrong. The mask of the solitary, footloose wanderer had slipped. She'd become pregnant. She'd terminated the child for some reason. Then, briefly, her world collapsed until, nursed by Teresa's own mother, she recovered enough to return to her old way of life elsewhere.

More than a decade and a half later she'd returned, in spite of the memories. They were still bad, still real. The drunken conversation she'd had with Camilla at Christmas – one that still stung, for Teresa – proved that.

A man in a straw hat and a familiar hooped shirt walked past. The gondolier. She followed him, caught his arm, stopped him.

'Last night . . .' she began.

He was staring at her, puzzled, maybe interested too.

'What about it?'

It wasn't the same man. Or maybe it was. She couldn't be sure.

'I talked to you about my aunt. You said you took her somewhere.'

'Didn't take her anywhere.' He winked. 'What are you really looking for?'

'I don't know,' she said and walked off into the darkness, starting to like the way it folded round her like a vast, enveloping cloak.

There was another bar on the far side of the square, the biggest she'd seen so far. She bought a drink from the stand outside, stood in the midst of the crowd, letting her head spin a little as she tried to think. The music was so loud here it was impossible for anyone to speak. All around her people, some young, some much older, danced to the rhythm and the lights, bodies moving, in costume, in heavy winter coats, laughing, locked in the stupidity of a strange masquerade in which they could lose their identities completely.

Was that what Sofia sought too? Anonymity? Some mundane comfort, the warmth of another? Anything to blank out her own lost personality and all those restless years travelling the world, looking to escape something, never quite accepting it might be herself?

The longer Teresa stayed in Venice, walking in Sofia's footsteps, the more she felt at one with her, able to see this place through the eyes of the woman she'd come to regard as a sister, someone to be admired, emulated even. In the black night of the Rialto, behind masks, engrossed with strangers in the shadows, there was no guilt, no sense of failure, no elder sister or mother to look down on you from on high and pass a cruel and exacting judgement.

Time slipped by unnoticed, in a semi-drunken haze. Just as it was doing now.

'It's me again,' said someone by her elbow.

The badly dressed count with the too-tidy beard nudged her shoulder, looking cocky and expectant.

'If you and I were the last two human beings on the planet,' she said very slowly, very carefully, 'I'd be happy to leave the place to the ants.'

Feeling a touch cheerier she walked off, depositing the remains of her drink in the nearest bin.

Sofia's secret lay here, hidden in the shadows of

these bleak, chill *campielli* and arcades. But at that moment Teresa lacked the wit to find it, or to locate in her own underused imagination some clue to where it might lie. Even if her head was clear, not muddied by the three or four strong glasses of drink she'd found herself downing as she wandered among these faceless, pointless crowds.

For some reason the next episode in the story, the essential, cryptic clue, had failed to materialize and she didn't want to wonder why.

The stories could come from only one of three sources. Someone who held Sofia and was, for whatever reason, determined to taunt Teresa to find her. Some ally, a friend who understood her plight and was powerless to unravel its origins themselves. Or Sofia herself, trapped, scared, intent on communicating through cryptic riddles, piece by piece, for reasons Teresa couldn't begin to guess.

An old, welcome sound rang out over the racket from the disco. Church bells from somewhere, San Giacomo perhaps, or one of the many other towers close by. She counted the tolls, realizing she had no idea of the time. Everything became lost and malleable in these dim alleys and corners and archways. A part of her, the same facet she shared with Sofia if she were honest, half-enjoyed that.

Midnight. Two hours had slipped by since she stepped off the vaporetto on the far side of the canal. Now the boats would be on the night service again, and she wasn't willing to wait for that.

The bearded count had followed her. Ignoring his continuing half-hearted attentions she set off eastwards, back towards Dorsoduro, down the long winding alleys that led to the Campo Santa Margherita and then Zattere, a route that was now sufficiently familiar for her to walk it without thinking.

Twenty minutes later she crossed the broad empty space of the Campo Santa Margherita. There was no one around this late, not even a few drunk students or carnival revellers. Her sharp, quick footsteps made a rhythmic loud tapping sound, like the ticking of a metronome, as she crossed the wide paving stones. From behind came something similar.

An echo. Had to be.

All the same she didn't turn, telling herself it was the cruel chill breeze blowing from the direction of the Rialto that she didn't want to face. Instead she quickened her pace down the narrow street towards the Ponte dei Pugni, the Bridge of Fists, a low, curved crossing over a narrow *rio*.

In the darkness she could just make out the boats that, during the day, sold fruit and vegetables, shiny peppers, bright green chicory and zucchini, on the far side of the water. Now they were covered in tarpaulins, slumbering, like the city itself. The only light came from the sky: a hazy moon dimmed by high cloud. What little moisture that remained on the cobblestones had turned to glittering ice. The freezing night air left her face and fingers numb.

She'd had too much to drink, talked to people who didn't care about her questions, discovered nothing from any of them, only a mounting sense of ignorance and frustration in herself. The harder she tried to understand, the less she saw.

This investigation needed to be personal, not forensic. The kind of intimate, prying peek behind the scenes of individual lives that real cops like Peroni, Costa and Falcone pursued. Not the logical, dogged deduction that was second nature to her as a scientist, trying to force the truth out of a smear of blood, a knife wound, a trace of humanity on a wall or a footprint in the mud.

As she strode across the bridge she was met by the first living thing she had seen in minutes. It was a dog, small and white, trotting purposefully across the stones from the other side.

The little animal stopped in front of her and lifted its pert, curious head. She was aware of being judged by two black and beady eyes.

A familiar dog. It sat down on the hard cold stone, staring at her, as if determined to make this point.

Except it couldn't be. These things were impossible. Just as the fictional – or half-real – Jerome Aitchison had said in the story she had lost.

The dog was quite motionless, waiting. Teresa

had never been much of a one for pets, but she remembered something Peroni, who loved all animals, had taught her. Remembered what the warden of the Scuola di San Giorgio degli Schiavoni had said too, twice over, once in the story, the second time only earlier that day.

Treat it with kindness and respect.

This was ridiculous. Irrational. Or as Tosi had put it, *super*-rational.

The fictional Jerome Aitchison had mistreated this animal – no, she thought quickly. An animal *like* this. She would never dream of doing something similar. Yet the warden in the *scuola* seemed to indicate that more was required. Not simply inaction but a positive act of gentleness and courtesy. Doing nothing was insufficient, just as it was with Sofia in the lost, hazy years before she vanished.

Teresa Lupo looked at the dog and said, with only the slightest of slurs, 'You will never know how happy I am that not another living soul will see this.'

Slowly, in an open and friendly fashion, she removed her right glove, bent down and offered the animal the back of her hand, stopping just short of its black shiny nose. Exactly as Peroni had taught her.

The dog blinked, moved its head forward, sniffed and then – this could not be real – appeared to nod. She raised her hand and, just once, stroked its head gently, slowly with her fingers.

The fur felt hard and stiff as if very old. The animal waited a second or two then got up off its haunches and trotted off into the darkness, back towards the Rialto.

Alone, on the Bridge of Fists, she felt a strange sense of freedom. As if she'd rejected a familiar part of herself, an important aspect of her own character but one that had overwhelmed some other subterranean side.

Her breath remained short and it was not from the night or the rapid route march home any more. Another corner had been turned, some rusty mental lock freed.

She looked at the bridge and the canal beneath it and a memory returned, of visiting Venice as a tourist, on her own, when she was young. Wandering around, head alternately deep in a guide book or staring about her, amazed by the city's distinctive beauty.

There was a story about this very area. Of Katharine Hepburn here, making some long-forgotten movie in the 1950s, falling into the San Barnaba canal during a scene, swallowing the grey, foul water of the lagoon. And getting sick, ill with some strange, persistent malady that followed her for years. An infection no doctor could quite diagnose. An unwanted memory of Venice, circulating in the blood, unwilling to leave.

Something similar had brought Sofia back. A recurrent, obsessive need to return.

Another thought occurred to her. Whatever that

curious, illogical virus was she felt at one with its persistent nature. Sofia's failings – her inner sense of loneliness and impatience, the endless, pointless curiosity that had taken her around the world – were traits that Teresa knew she shared, tendencies she'd managed to stifle over the years. Only just. Had she known about Sofia's agonies here sixteen years before she could easily have become as lost in these dark, narrow lanes as her much-loved aunt, the sister she'd never had.

Perhaps now she was. And that was the point, of Sofia's mysterious disappearance, of the cryptic, unresolved pointers to its unravelling. Of the dog.

The masks of the carnival served several purposes. To disguise the identity of the wearers from those around them. But there were other masks too, more subtle and disquieting ones. Masks that fooled the wearer, provided a veneer a man or woman might use in order to hide their own identity from themselves.

Was that what stood between her and Sofia's mystery? Some lack of self-knowledge, or personal insight?

Sometimes a mask is there to fool others. Sometimes to fool oneself.

'This is too damned hard,' she muttered, wishing for the umpteenth time that day she had Peroni and Costa and Falcone to help her, knowing the assignment in Sicily made that impossible. She felt out of her depth here, in a city where the rules of everyday life seemed not to matter.

Teresa looked down and another recollection came back. Centuries before, close to where she stood, two marble footprints had been carved into the paving stones of this bridge. They marked the point where Venetians of old gathered to fight. These were vicious pitched battles, to the death sometimes, between the Castellani of the east, workers for the most part in the Arsenale boatyards, and the Nicolotti of the west, tough, unforgiving fishermen.

These marks were the starting point of their war for mastery of this small piece of masonry over an insignificant stretch of water.

Men fought for the most trifling, fleeting of prizes. Yet it was part of human nature to labour, to struggle, to contest for whatever others coveted. Wasn't that what she was doing now? So badly? With an excess of zeal and energy and precious little insight?

So many arguments, with the police, with fleeting figures in the night in the Rialto, almost with Tosi and Camilla too, people who were on her side and wanted to help. There was something here she failed to understand. No, more than that. Failed even to see.

And she'd patted the head of a small dog, one that, logically, could not in any sense be 'real'.

A sound caught her attention, a noise from behind. Footsteps. She hadn't moved.

Teresa Lupo turned, the anger rising within her again, ready to confront the buffoon with the beard, to use her fists if necessary, as surely and as viciously as any Venetian fisherman or boatyard worker would have done in this very place a few centuries before.

'Don't even think . . .' she began in a loud, firm voice.

Words left her.

It wasn't the ugly man in the costume of a medical count. This figure stood at the foot of the steps and the very sight of him made her feel cold and dead inside.

He was tall and broad and imposing, a big man, though the full black cloak was so flowing and capacious it was difficult to decide how much of this was bulk, how much muscle or fabric. Standing at the foot of the steps of the Ponte dei Pugni he looked up at her with his white, ghostly face, tilting the long shiny nose to one side like a quizzical bird waiting for a question.

She knew the Plague Doctor so well by now. His broadbrimmed hat with the buckle, the ebony ruff at his neck. The ivory beak the colour of the moon and above it the crystal eyes, impenetrable, inhuman.

A fit and active man, she guessed. There was no point in trying to run, even if that was in her head.

He didn't speak. Simply stood there, head cocked to the left like a deathly dark cockatoo.

'Who are you?' she asked.

The head turned from one side to the other, as if thinking. The creature in black said nothing, simply held out his gloved hands and made a gesture of incomprehension or despair, turning them inwards then out.

'Where's Sofia?' she yelled.

Teresa took two swift steps down the bridge and snatched at the long white bill in front of her, determined to remove it. The man retreated backwards, then, so quickly she lost sight of him for a moment, fell into a dark *sotoportego* beneath the building behind.

She followed, walking quickly, chasing the flowing black cloak that whirled ahead of her. Almost immediately she found herself in a small, grimy courtyard strewn with litter, the walls covered in graffiti. There was a pale white wellhead, ornately carved, at the centre.

The Plague Doctor stood next to it, a black glove on the metal lid, leaning on the thing casually, relaxed. The little white dog sat next to him, a tiny triangle of pale fur, erect, alert, just like the animal in the Carpaccio painting.

There were no windows on any of the buildings that faced onto this grim little place, none that were illuminated anyway. Only a single iron street lamp, the bulb flickering uncertainly. For the first time since she came to Venice Teresa was aware of the smell of drains: a rank, fetid odour of decay and age.

She walked up to the man and asked the question about Sofia again. The beak didn't turn away this time. The black eyes simply stared at her. She wondered whether the cloak exaggerated his bulk. It was hard to tell.

'For God's sake,' she said. 'Talk to me.'

He took his hand off the metal cover of the well-head and reached inside his cloak. Then the Plague Doctor withdrew a large manila envelope of the kind she knew already, too well.

She didn't want to get angry. It was important to think clearly, to talk to this man. To understand.

He held out the envelope more forcefully. She thrust the thing aside with a wave of her hand.

There was an unfamiliar stinging in her eyes. She felt desperate and lost and not in the least afraid.

'For God's sake . . .' she begged him.

The black figure stepped forward, thrust the thing at her and ordered, in a voice that was muffled by the large, heavy mask, 'Take it!'

'Why?' she demanded. 'What kind of charade is this? Masks and mysteries and stupid, stupid games. *Where's Sofia?*'

It seemed impossible but, as she spoke those words, the man appeared to shrink a little in front of her, bowed by doubt or guilt or shame.

The dog got off its little hind legs, stared at her, as if outraged by the tone and volume of her voice. Then the animal trotted off into the darkness at the corner of the *campiello*, out through another *sotoportego* just visible as a dim and dingy arch in the shadows.

'In the end it's the mystery that lasts,' the Plague

Doctor said in the same muffled, fuzzy voice she'd heard before. 'Not the explanation.'

'Enough damned riddles I . . .'

His black-gloved hand went to the mask's thin, inhuman lips, right finger upright, a gesture for silence.

She had no idea why she obeyed.

He placed the envelope on the dull metal cover of the well and then said simply, 'I'm grateful you were kind to my dog.'

After that he walked off into the pool of darkness that had swallowed up the little animal a few moments before.

She wanted to follow but she couldn't. Something about his manner told her he was strong and fast. And that if she did manage to tear off that eerie white mask whatever lay beneath would offer no answers whatsoever.

'He doesn't know where she is either,' she murmured in the noxious, grubby courtyard, her words falling on walls tattooed with inane graffiti and spray-painted murals.

He's giving me these things so that I find out. Because, for some strange reason, he's powerless himself.

Teresa Lupo picked up the envelope, thrust it beneath her jacket, then walked back to the Bridge of Fists and on to home.

The sense of helpless bewilderment followed her up the winding stone staircase of the crooked little palazzo close to the Ponte agli Incurabili, past the closed doors of Filippo Strozzi and Camilla Dushku, both apartments in darkness and silence. It was almost one o'clock. Physically she felt tired but her mind was alert, almost elated somehow. She had seen, touched, something that was real, not myth or fantasy on a sheet of paper, not cryptic paint on a five-hundred-year-old canvas.

There was someone in this city who needed to prise open the secret of Sofia's fate too. For some reason he was unwilling to reveal himself, and chose instead to wear the garb of the Plague Doctor. Just like Jerome Aitchison high on the San Marco campanile.

This man possessed, or was perhaps merely accompanied by, the dog that seemed to run through this affair like a meandering Delphic thread.

She was now inclined to the view that this was the person who greeted them that first day on the vaporetto stop at Zattere. It was also feasible – she had to face this – that more than one interested party had assumed this disguise. It was common. Aitchison had adopted it for his performance on the campanile. The purpose of masks and cloaks was to deliver anonymity, to fox the unwary. To lull the innocent into seeing safety where there was danger, fact where there was nothing but lies and fiction.

One man was dead, a young woman had been lucky to escape a terrible yet amateurish attack. Danger lurked here, and perhaps it did not come from the direction she'd expected, the figure of the Plague Doctor, at least the one she'd just met. She'd heard his muffled voice in the darkness of the cramped *campiello* near the Bridge of Fists and there was something unmistakable inside it.

Trepidation and a sad, almost resigned anxiety.

He thinks I'm not up to this, she thought, staring at the envelope, half-reluctant to open it. And maybe he's right.

A light was flashing on the netbook, indicating a message.

Teresa pulled the machine over, ran her finger across the keys to bring it back to life, sighing as she saw the name on the single email waiting there.

It was unknown for Orsini to work at night. He was a bureaucrat, an admin drone from upstairs. A grey man in a grey suit who approved budgets and hirings and firings. Someone who handed over clocks at retirement parties, signed off purchase orders and internal reports, never once coming close to the base material of the Questura's work, humanity *in extremis*, ordinary people in extraordinary circumstances.

Yet there he was, writing only two hours earlier, just after eleven at night. Perhaps, she thought, reading it, Orsini had been drinking too. The tone was different, unexpected. Intemperate, aggressive, finger-pointing in the way it raised old grievances, some she'd forgotten, a few she'd never realized were much of an issue in the first place. A button had been pressed and it unleashed such venom in her direction that she would have been offended if his petty complaints weren't so pathetically amusing.

She pushed back the computer and gazed out of the window. There were few lights out on the water at this time of night, just a handful of distant vessels moving on the Giudecca canal, and some illumination from the houses and the streets of the island opposite. Sofia had been missing for more than a week. If she wasn't found soon she probably never would be. Not alive anyway.

Some crucial part of this task was hers alone. A man in a black cloak and ivory mask had made that perfectly clear. There was no time for distractions. When she reached down to stroke that strange little dog Teresa Lupo was aware that she had invited something into her life. She'd once have damned it as superstition. Now she felt another word was necessary. Faith? Or plain, simple doubt? An acceptance that the world was, perhaps, more complex and more unpredictable than she had hitherto accepted?

The drink was making her head hurt. A decision was needed.

Teresa Lupo copied Orsini's email to several key people: the *commissario* in charge of the Questura, Silvio, several other administrative officials who worked alongside the man. Above it she typed out a simple note of resignation, stating plainly that she was unable return to the Questura to reassume her old position under any circumstances.

With immediate effect she was quitting her post as the chief forensic officer of the Rome Questura and would not seek anything in the way of compensation or paid notice.

She looked at the words. A career of thirteen years, built with care and sweat and dedication, stood in the balance in front of her.

Without a moment's hesitation, she hit the send key then took the envelope and whatever it contained to bed.

EVERY LAST DROP

Jason Cunningham never had a dog at home. Too much trouble, Auntie Flo said. Messy. Bothersome. A pest.

This one didn't look messy. It was small and white and perky. Friendly little thing with a pointy nose and gleaming black eyes. Unlike him the dog didn't look lost, stranded in some back alley in Venice, wondering where to go.

He bent down, made tutting noises and patted its little head.

'You're a nice chap,' Jason said, though he knew it wouldn't understand a word of English.

He'd idly followed as the dog trotted into a constricted dead-end lane, a tunnel of black brick and mould that ended in a sullen line of canal. The water there was a blue-green colour swilling around idly as if wondering where to go, a faint medical odour rising from the surface. There wasn't a sign, let alone a fence to keep people from falling in. If it was dark or someone was blind or sick or drunk they'd step off the slimy paving stones and tumble straight into the viscous depths of the lagoon. This shocked him. Must happen all the time, the young Englishman muttered to himself and then heard a little voice inside his head add: maybe on purpose once in a while too.

Someone at work had killed himself a year or two back. Young man. About Jason Cunningham's age. Hanged himself in the woods. No one really knew why.

Jason was abroad, alone, for the first time in his life. *Abroad*. He remembered the way some folk used that word back home in Yorkshire. It carried the same kind of chill scariness Uncle Arthur and Auntie Flo used when talking about vampires and black people and the Conservative Party.

He thrust his hands deep into his pockets and felt the coins there. There was no need to count them. He'd done that three or four times already. Money didn't grow on trees, his auntie said, repeatedly. It was seven euros an hour ago and would still be seven euros now. Enough for a sandwich and a bottle of water. It was winter in Venice. Bitterly cold. Yorkshire cold. Dry and bright but chilly enough to leave patches of ice on the worn cobblestones. Not the weather he'd expected at all though he felt he'd managed all right at first. And then . . .

The thieves who'd snatched his wallet at the station had ripped from his waist the little pouch he'd bought down Wakefield market. He still had his clothes in his rucksack: all neatly folded and as clean as he could keep them. And his passport too. Some elusive memory told him he could find the British consul, whoever he was, and throw himself on the man's mercy. He had an idea of what a consul would look like: some southerner in a suit, with a posh accent and a snooty expression. If Jason was lucky maybe he could get repatriated. Sent back home like a beggar. The whole process sounded humiliating. Finding himself dumped back in Britain with no job, no money, nowhere to go, and a big label round his neck that read, 'Failure'.

'Sod that,' he muttered, staring at the canal with its funny colour and faint aroma of disinfectant, wondering whether the water was as cold and nasty as it looked.

He turned round, still puzzled how any sane person could know which way was up or down or in or out in this place. He'd been in the condition his late father would have called discombobulated ever since he arrived the night before. The free map he'd picked up at the airport was useless. It tried to describe a real city, one with turnings and landmarks and some logic to it, not the maze of nameless alleys that had swallowed him up the moment he stepped off the Alilaguna ferry at a long-lost place called Fondamenta Nove.

He was by the side of a broad stretch of water that looked very like the sea. Ahead was a white island surrounded by an ornate wall with a church somewhere to the left. Beyond it was a larger shape he'd seen from the boat stop. They'd been calling the name for the place when he arrived. He remembered because it sounded nice: Murano. To his right was what looked like a castle wall, in bright, handsome yellow-brown brick rising out of the water, with stone pikes on the top. He was at a dead end, the corner where one smaller canal met the larger stretch of lagoon ahead, with no bridge across to the forbidding-looking castle place to one side, and nowhere else to go except back into the alleys behind or left, past a succession of largely derelict warehouses.

Ahead of him, at the end of a narrow and rickety bridge over the lagoon, was a strange little house set all on its own, standing above the water on a low platform stained with algae and seaweed. Two storeys tall, its white marble walls were streaked with dark stains like the running mascara on some teary-eyed tart. The place looked as if it had been some kind of miniature church once upon a time, one that had decided to shrug off its spire and crosses for some reason and start a new life beyond the influence of God.

As Jason watched, the little white dog got up off its haunches and trotted across the bridge to the front step, moving with a happy, rolling gait.

There was no sign saying 'keep out' or anything that looked like it in Italian. So out of curiosity he followed the animal. A notice had been posted in a holder next to the polished wooden door. He walked up for a closer look. In English it read, 'Blood donors needed. Generous rates for suitable applicants. With perks.'

Perks.

The word reminded him of Uncle Arthur. He was always asking, 'But where are the bloody perks?' The week before, as part of what the money men down in London called the 'credit crunch', the bank had closed the bakery where the two of them worked. They'd found out what a perk really added up to then: eight weeks' wages and a place in the dole queue, alongside half the men in Yorkshire it seemed.

He'd lived with Arthur and his wife Flo since his dad, a good baker, a dedicated one who got him the job in the first place, died of emphysema two years before. One room in a tiny terrace in Garibaldi Street. It cost him most of his pay packet though if he whispered the slightest murmur of complaint Arthur and Flo quickly gathered together, elbow to elbow, and catalogued with pointing fingers the breadth and depth of his ingratitude. There was washing and food included, they told him. The grub was good. He had a home.

It still seemed a lot of cash.

Then along came the men from London with their layoff envelopes, smiling grimly as they slipped them into the hands of the silent bakery workers.

'Bastards,' Arthur had said, grasping for his.

Straight away Arthur had gone down the pub with some of the other men, got steaming drunk and wound up with a kicking from some blokes he'd turned mouthy with.

It was the most money Jason Cunningham had ever seen. That was a perk all right and it had got him out of Garibaldi Street and Wakefield. Out of the clutches of his Uncle Arthur and Auntie Flo. He was nineteen. Lost and now, since he'd got robbed at the station, skint.

He stepped up to the door and pulled the rusty iron stay of what he took to be a very old-fashioned bell. It was a while before someone answered.

Jason Cunningham stood there, shuffling awkwardly on his big feet, blowing on his hands to keep them warm. The dog had trotted back across the bridge and disappeared.

When the door opened Jason said, 'I've come about the blood.'

The man who took him into the house was a middle-aged Italian with a kindly smile. He wore a white nylon collarless jacket, like a dentist. They went into what appeared to be a doctor's room with a large mahogany desk, lots of books, a computer and a variety of medical instruments. The strange house, a little palace, was surrounded by water on all four sides which made every sound, the man's soft and amiable voice, the whirring of the computer on the desk, the squawk of seagulls and the steady rhythm of the waves, seem to hover in the air.

'We require one specific blood type only,' he announced. 'What is yours?'

'Don't rightly know.'

'Shall we find out?'

The man reached into the drawer of a metal cabinet and retrieved a plastic envelope with a sheet of paper and a little plastic gadget which he opened to reveal a short, sharp spike.

'Needles,' Jason murmured, shivering. 'Is this a hospital or something?'

'It's a private clinic. I'm the doctor. My name is Marco. We pay one hundred euros per donation.'

'And the perks?'

'Vouchers for four nights' accommodation in a very nice hostel close to the station. I can also offer a free ticket which will get you into some of the historic sites. If that is your . . . thing.'

'Seems very generous.'

The doctor spoke good English and smiled pleasantly. A nice chap, Jason thought.

'Only if your blood is the right type, I'm afraid. If not I give you twenty euros for your trouble . . .'

It didn't hurt really. Just a little prick on the finger then Marco smeared the blood in several places on a sheet of card and waited a minute or two, watching the stain on the paper for some kind of sign.

'Bravo!' he declared finally. He seemed genuinely delighted. Perhaps even a touch relieved. 'For future reference you are blood type AB positive. It's worth remembering. Only three per cent of the English belong to this group. Congratulations.'

He asked for Jason's passport and wrote down some details.

'You mean I'm special?'

'We're all special, Jason.'

'But I'm special enough to flog you some of my blood?'

Marco's head went to one side. He had bushy grey hair, a long, beak-like nose and keen icy blue eyes. Something about him reminded Jason of a bird. Like the kestrel a young lad kept as a pet in an old film that was set in Yorkshire, one his dad had taken him to as a treat years ago.

'Flog? I mean you no harm. Why would you wish to flog me?'

'Flog. *Flog!* It's Yorkshire. Means sell. For money, like.'

'Ah. Strictly speaking we will take some plasma. It comes from your blood. The red cells . . . you get them back. You'll see. And after . . . I give you the money. And a cappuccino and some *biscotti* if you wish.'

'I'd prefer a cup of tea and a sandwich if you don't mind.'

'Tea with milk the English way, and a panino, then.'

'Ta.'

He frowned again then led Jason through to a large whitepainted room with some old religious

246

prints on the wall. The heavy blinds at the windows were drawn so that the dazzling winter sun from the open lagoon was completely excluded. But the space was bright with artificial light and it had the smell of a hospital: soap, fresh sheets, chemicals and antiseptic. A complicated machine sat on a trolley beneath the window. It looked a little like a fancy food mixer, but with knobs and wires and tubing.

There were two beds, both broader than normal single ones, as if someone couldn't quite make up their mind whether to have a double or not. On the left lay a girl around his own age, eyes closed, fast asleep on the sheets. She wore jeans and a white tee-shirt bearing a picture of a grinning gondolier holding up his thumb. Her left arm was extended onto the bedclothes. On the inside, near the elbow, was a small sticking plaster enclosing a piece of cotton wool. There was a faint stain of blood on the fluffy material.

'Not the only customer then,' Jason said, realizing the idea cheered him. 'You're a busy chap.'

Marco didn't answer. He was doing something with the machine.

Jason took the opportunity to look at the sleeping girl, more closely, more bravely than he would usually have dared.

She had long dark hair that fell back onto the pillow in tresses as if it had been arranged, though that was obviously impossible. Her face was incredibly pale, almost pure white, and quite the most beautiful he'd ever seen. Like an angel or one of those impossible women in paintings, unblemished, unreal, without any of the flaws and visual imperfections that marked most of the girls back home. A few of the bakery tarts – their words, not his – were pretty. He'd watched a couple slyly in the early hours of the morning, noting the way they gossiped and cackled about boys and what had happened at the weekend. He used to think: I know that type. Coarse.

Then he checked himself. This was a Cunningham family habit: judging people instantly, on their looks, a single word they said, anything really. It was wrong. He was glad his Auntie Flo wasn't there at that moment. She'd have stared miserably at the young woman asleep on the bed next to him, tut-tutted at the sight of that full tee-shirt and let loose with all her foul-mouthed venom, at him, for his shyness, at the slumbering girl for her perfect beauty.

Busty. That was one of her favourite words of condemnation. The girl on the bed was slim, tall, about his own height. But she wasn't skinny, not all over anyway.

'I prefer to think of it as full-figured,' he said out loud. 'Shapely.'

'Excuse me?'

The doctor had a needle in his hand. It was long and attached to the machine by a snaking transparent tube.

'S-sorry,' Jason stuttered. 'Me and my gob.'

Marco appeared puzzled.

'Camilla's sleeping. Let's not wake her, shall we?'

'Camilla. Righteo, Captain,' Jason said, making a little salute with his hand before he climbed onto the bed.

It didn't take long. It didn't even hurt much. The mattress was so soft and the pillow so inviting. The funny machine whirred happily as something passed from him to it, got swirled around then sent back down the tube, the precious part removed he supposed, some of it anyway. Not that he looked when the blood started to flow. Marco advised that was for the best.

Jason closed his eyes once and found himself drifting off into a pale white paradise, one that included the girl from the bed next to him. Camilla. No one ever got called that in Wakefield. She was smiling and talking to him and he didn't feel any of that heat, the muckiness that came up out of nowhere back home with the bakery tarts and their dirty talk.

He opened his eyes and checked his cheap LED watch, bought a couple of weeks before, two quid in the market. Six o'clock. He must have slept for three hours or more, which was odd because in the delightful dream nothing happened. Nothing at all.

The needle was gone. He turned his head and saw there was a cup of milky tea on the table next to him along with a ham and cheese sandwich in that funny Venetian bread he'd come to recognize.

The drink was still hot. Someone, Marco he imagined, must have woken him.

Starving, he took a big bite and then a swig from the cup before realizing the young woman was awake too, propped up in bed against the pillow, staring at him.

'Got to finish this,' he said, pointing at the sandwich. 'Could eat a horse.'

She smiled and he saw she had the most perfect teeth he'd ever encountered, every one white and uniform like teeth were supposed to be and rarely were.

'Oh my. So you're English? I'm guessing.'

Camilla had a soft, musical voice, with a touch of foreign in it that made the sound all the more engaging.

'Yeah. Sorry. Jason Cunningham.'

He held out his hand then stopped. She was still attached to the machine. The girl glanced at the tube joining her to it and shrugged.

'Camilla Dushku.' She nodded at the window, glancing at the closed blinds. 'I come from across the sea.'

Jason thought for a moment and asked, 'Germany?'

She laughed.

'No. Dubrovnik. Croatia.'

'Sounds nice. Why are you in Venice then?'

She thought for a moment and said, 'Why not? It's beautiful.'

'I got the sack, me. Took redundo and bought

a ticket on the first plane going anywhere. I were a baker. You believe that? A baker. What kind of a world don't want someone who can bake bread?'

'Are you a good baker, Jason?'

'That I am.' He held his hands out in front of him and felt a slight twinge in the left where the needle had been. 'My old dad reckoned there were magic in these fingers. He said he'd never seen anyone work a batch of loaves like what I can. It is magic too. You got flour. You got water. You got yeast. Don't mean nothing on their own. Not till the right person puts them together and treats 'em proper. I can do that.'

She was gazing at him. Her eyes were dark and kindly, amused, but not in the sarky way the girls had back home.

'Then what happens?'

'Then you mix them together, just right, and you put them somewhere warm, somewhere they're happy, and they can talk to one another, yeast to flour and water and the like. And you watch, if you can, and they rise. Like Jesus did. They rise and they're all warm and soft to touch, like, like . . .' A thought came to him and he wondered if he dared utter it. 'Like your mum must feel when you're a baby. And you're hungry. These fingers . . .'

Jason Cunningham looked at his hands. They were fine and strong, not that anyone ever noticed.

'There's life in them, my old dad said.'

'There's life in you then.'

'S'pose so!' He took a swig of the tea and swung his legs off the bed. He felt wonderful after the sleep. 'You want to come out and have a cake or something? Don't know where. Don't know Venice at all.'

'I haven't finished yet,' she said, glancing at the tube again. 'Sorry.'

'Seems a long time . . .'

The girl smiled and said nothing.

Marco returned, brisk and businesslike. He had an envelope with money in it, a voucher for a hostel, some museum tickets, and a very good map, marked with lines and arrows to make sure Jason found his way to places.

'Thank you,' Jason said. 'I wish doctors back home were this helpful.'

'No. Thank you. If you wish to come back in three or four days for more . . .'

The offer surprised him.

'Can you do that? Take blood from people like it's . . . milk or something?'

Marco's bushy eyebrows rose.

'I told you, Jason. I gave you your blood back. It was just the plasma I removed. Three or four days will cause you no problems at all.'

'I'll think about that, Doc,' he said, taking the money.

It was bitterly cold outside but there was no wind. From the moment he stepped onto the narrow little bridge that led to the promenade he could see the sky was full of bright, twinkling stars.

He felt happy, settled, for the first time in ages. Jason looked at the map and realized it would be easy to find his way to the hostel. Venice didn't seem so difficult once it had lines and arrows attached.

Then he thought about the girl, Camilla. He could have asked how to get in touch with her. Tried to get her phone number, not that he had a phone. An address then. Shown some interest anyway, since she seemed, unless he were dreaming, to show some interest in him.

If she were at a loose end maybe they could do something. If only . . .

'Sod it,' he muttered to himself, and set off for the hostel, walking towards the shape of a lustrous full moon shimmering in its own reflection on the flat black surface of the lagoon.

The next few days disappeared in a blur of sights and sounds and experiences. With Marco's money and free tickets in his pocket Jason Cunningham visited places that seemed to come from a mad, wild dream. Great cavernous churches with dark dusty paintings that were unlike anything he'd seen in England: bold and violent and, on occasion, full of naked flesh and all manner of suggestive notions. Astonishing palaces so grand and majestic it was impossible to believe any ordinary human being could really have lived in them. And the markets. There was one near the funny bridge called the Rialto that had so much stuff he'd had to buy a postcard, a picture of all these strange fish and vegetables, in colours that would never have been deemed edible in Yorkshire. He sent it home to Wakefield with a message for the miserable old couple in Garibaldi Street: *Am all right here don't worry.*

Like they would.

Everywhere he went he kept his eyes peeled for Camilla. But he never saw her. There were lots of people in Venice. Locals crammed into the little alleys, heads down, never looking you in the eye. Tourists wandering around aimlessly, lost like him a lot of the time, getting in everyone's way. Nowhere among them was the lovely slim pale-faced figure he'd hoped to see. Not that this surprised him. Jason Cunningham never thought of himself as lucky or special, except when he was in the bakery, casting a spell over the loaves-to-be.

He travelled on the busy little boats that wove their way down the Grand Canal. Then he discovered those that sailed even further, out onto the open miniature sea that ran like a silvery hem around the crumbling, ancient skirt of the city. After a little while he didn't even ask where they were going. He didn't understand the answer anyway, and his ticket meant he could catch any he liked. This was, he came to understand, not a real place at all. More like a little universe of its own, without cars or motorbikes or most of the trappings of the modern world, its boundaries marked out by nothing more than the chill, lazy waters of the lagoon.

The hostel was all right too. And the food after a while. He even found something called *sarde en saor* which turned out to be just like the soused herrings his dad used to make: cold pickled fish in vinegar and spices, dead delicious.

He took to buying them from a little shop near the Zattere waterfront, getting a bit of bread from the cheery woman in the bakery next door who spoke a little English and took a bit of a shine to him when he told her he was a baker too. Then he'd sit hunched up in the cold on a bench by the Giudecca canal, watching the boats and ferries go to and fro, eating with gloved hands. The bread was good. They knew their stuff in Venice.

Yorkshire wouldn't leave him entirely though. And the memory of that last row, after they cashed their cheques and came home from the bank flush with money.

'What you going to do with that little lot then?' Arthur asked eagerly, unable to take his eyes off the envelope in Jason's hand.

'Still thinking.'

Auntie Flo came out from the kitchen with three cups of tea, took a big gulp and announced, 'Ooh . . . I'm spitting feathers.'

She wagged a long finger at him.

'No point in leaving it with men in suits, Jason. Is there? Not when they might go belly-up any moment. I don't know. If you can't even trust the Yorkshire Penny Bank . . .'

'I never trusted them,' Arthur declared.

She made a rasping noise, as she usually did when she heard something she thought ridiculous, which was often.

'Pah! You never trusted no one.'

'Not except family,' Arthur replied. He glanced in Jason's direction. 'That's what it's all about in the end, int'it? Family. Who else has your interests at heart?' His foxy eyes narrowed. 'All that dosh is burning a hole in your pocket, eh?'

'No. I thought mebbe next week I'd go see the bank and ask 'em if I could get a loan to start me own bakers.'

They laughed. And then they laughed some more, holding each other, slapping their fat sides, wiping imaginary tears from their eyes.

'You're a one, I'll give you that,' his uncle said when he got his breath back. 'You? Start a business? *You*? On two months' redundo?'

'I said I'd get a loan.'

'Our Jason knows his baking,' Flo declared, in a way that told him there was a sizeable 'but' coming. 'His dad always said that. Best bread man in the family. Shame no one's interested in that kind of thing any more. Not when you can get it sliced and wrapped down Tesco for half the price.'

'That muck's not bread.'

Arthur pulled his sourest of faces.

'Tell that to the punters. You think them shit-fer-brains know the difference?'

'Language, Arthur,' Flo scolded him.

'Well he'd make a parson swear, he would. Look at him. Nineteen years old. Got some brass in his pocket at last. And what's he want to do? Turn the clock back. A . . . bakers.'

'It were good enough for me dad.'

'Yer dad's dead!' Arthur shouted. The room went quiet beneath his sudden outburst. 'I'm yer dad now and I'm telling yer some home truths. It's the twenty-first century, Jason. This country is about selling stuff, not making it. Not any more. Consumer electronics. That's the thing.'

'I don't know nothing about electronics.'

'You don't need to. Them Koreans do all that. You just have to sell it. Now . . .' He went over to the sideboard and took out something that looked like a shiny metallic matchbox. 'I've been meaning to bring this to your attention. Can I interest you in the latest personal entertainment centre direct from the manufacturer? This little beauty does MP3 and video and you can watch telly on it too.'

Arthur thrust the thing under his nephew's nose. Jason refused to touch it.

'Telly? I hate telly.'

'I can get these from some bloke in Leeds for thirty quid a pop. They go for a hundred and fifty in the shops. We flog 'em to suckers on eBay for a hundred and we're rolling in it. There's lots more crap like this besides. All you need do is move four or five a day and you're making more than you ever did in that bakers. Don't need to get up at two in the bloody morning either.'

'I like making things. Giving 'em life.' Jason stared at the stupid little gadget. 'Where's the joy in that?'

Auntie Flo sat down in the big armchair by the fire and placed her tea cup on the small nest table next to it. This was always a sign events had taken a serious turn.

'Jason,' she said with a very grave face. 'Listen to your uncle for once. These are hard times. Families need to stick together. Blood's thicker than water, y'know. We need to back each other up 'cos no one else will.'

'I don't know what you mean.'

Arthur took over.

'Businesses need capital, lad. I can't get me margin on these things without paying for them upfront. I need you in with me. As a partner. Fifty fifty. We'll clean up, no problem. Provided I've got the dosh to get us going in the first place. Which on me own I haven't. So . . .' He held out his hands and made a grasping, familiar gesture with his fingers, one he used every month when it was time for Jason to pay for his board and lodging. 'Make with the readies, eh?'

Arthur was a big man. He often got into fights down the pub. A couple of barneys had got him in court.

'This is my money, Uncle Arthur. Not yours.'

'*Our* money. And lots more of it to come.'

'No,' Jason said simply, then thrust the brown envelope into his trouser pocket and folded his arms across his chest.

Flo and Arthur exchanged baleful glances.

'We've talked about this,' his aunt said.

'Not with me you haven't.'

'We've talked about this,' she continued, as if he'd never said a word, 'and we've come to an agreement. We've looked after you like we was your own loving parents since your dad died . . .'

'I paid you.'

'And frankly,' Flo went on, 'it's been a thankless task. You're an odd little sod. Should have known something was up when Kathleen died having you. Like she knew what were coming and didn't want nothing to do with it.'

The red heat of embarrassment rose in Jason's head. They threw this at him from time to time.

'Wasn't my fault.'

'She'd still be here if it wasn't for you, wouldn't she? Like I said . . . you're an odd little sod, and it's not been easy looking after you since Ron left us. We're both agreed, Arthur and me. If you won't support your own family now, after all we've done, you can sling yer hook. We don't need an extra mouth to feed especially if it's one that don't know how to say thanks.'

Arthur was holding out his hand and making the grasping gesture.

'So make with the readies,' he said again. 'Where else are you going to go, eh? Got no one in the world except us two, have you? Not a living soul.'

Jason thought about it for the best part of a second then went upstairs and got out the rucksack he'd bought for the brief holiday he'd taken the previous year, camping on his own in Keswick. He packed the money and found his passport. It had been used just once, when they made him come along on a package deal to Fuengirola, which he'd hated, and not just because it seemed to cost an awful lot of his money. He picked out his favourite clothes and folded them neatly into the rucksack with his passport. The cash went into a nylon belt with a big pocket that he'd bought for Spain.

When he came back down they were seated in front of the unlit fire, already pretending he didn't exist. Flo was sobbing into a tissue.

'The sheer ingratitude of it,' she sniffled as he walked past. 'Our Jason. Our flesh and blood.'

Arthur looked up and couldn't stop himself. He was on his feet, roaring, his rough and ugly face turning puce with rage.

'Don't ever darken our door again, boy,' he screamed, waving his big, clumsy fist. 'Don't ever . . .'

'I won't,' Jason said quietly and walked outside, wondering how much a taxi to the airport cost. He was determined to take the first flight out, wherever it went. Anywhere had to be better than this.

It amazed him he could remember every word, every gesture, every angry moment of this encounter almost a week later, seated on the Zattere waterfront watching the exotic vessels go by, ferries with cars, little boats carrying household goods, detergent and toilet paper and furniture, burly serious men at the tiller looking back at him as he sat there eating a sandwich – panini, they called them – with his gloved hands.

His dad, dying in hospital, had said something about pain. It stuck to you like flour. You thought you could wash it all away, out of your clothes, out of your hair. But some stray grain always persisted, slyly avoiding your well-meant attentions and the drugs the doctors had. Life was like that. The only thing to do, he said, was your best. Be a good man. There wasn't anything else.

Jason felt down remembering this. Then he thought about the funny white house on the water that looked as if it used to be a church. Flo was right about one thing. Blood was thicker than water. Helping out like that was a decent thing to do. He could use the money again too.

The lines and arrows on Marco's map meant it was easy to find the place once he walked down a few narrow, winding alleys through the area known as Castello, heading in the direction of Murano. Half an hour after he set off Jason strode across the little bridge over the lagoon feeling no concern whatsoever about meeting the needle again.

The sign was gone. There was nothing there at all except the ancient bell pull. His heart fell. He experienced a mild panic about cash and wondered where, in this foreign country, he could possibly find work. Then the door opened and Marco was there, smiling.

'Jason! How pleasant to see you again. Is this a social call? Or do you have a . . . gift?'

'You don't have your sign up.'

'I said you could come back any time, didn't I?'

'Yeah, but . . .'

There must have been a video surveillance camera somewhere. Posh houses had them, not that he could see a lens on the wall.

'You do want to give blood, don't you?'

He stayed on the doorstep. Something seemed funny about this place. Perhaps he should have noticed before, except the first time he was confused and a little desperate.

'I thought you said it wasn't blood.'

'It is when you donate it. I was not being literal when I used the word "gift". There will still be a hundred euros and the voucher for the hostel. As to the museums . . . I imagine you have seen most of them by now. Would some free meals in a few restaurants I can recommend be of any interest? I know a place that does fried fish. Similar to your own fish and chips only better. If you want . . .'

Jason licked his lips. He was starting to like the food here. A lot.

'You bet,' he said and marched in.

The blinds were still closed, blocking out entirely the persistent sharp afternoon sunlight. The fluorescent tubes seemed even brighter. Beneath the window the machine sat silent, waiting. Jason was both pleased and alarmed to see that Camilla was in the same bed as before, asleep with a fresh plaster on her left arm. She seemed dreadfully pale.

'Do not disturb her, please,' Marco whispered. 'The poor girl is very tired and needs the rest. The young. The lives they lead . . .'

The way he said that last part made it sound as if Camilla had been out at a disco or something, which didn't seem right at all.

'Are we the only two who give you . . . ?'

'Quickly now,' Marco insisted, getting the equipment ready and almost pushing him onto the bed. 'Even doctors go home sometimes, you know.'

It all seemed to happen much more rapidly this time. He watched too as his blood trickled into the machine, got whirled around inside a glass jar then returned to his arm.

Camilla didn't stir at all. She looked sick, he thought.

Marco went outside. Jason coughed loudly. The girl began to wake, rubbing her eyes with the back of her hands, the way a toddler did. She was wearing a different tee-shirt, one that was a little tight over her ample chest. The emblem of the winged Venetian lion was on it this time. He was aware that his heart was fluttering at her presence, that he'd been waiting for this meeting to happen for days and hiding the desire by burying himself in the city.

'Jason?' she asked blearily. 'Is that really you? You came back?'

'Yeah.' Her lovely skin seemed so translucent he could imagine it tearing at the slightest touch. 'Not the only one who comes here, am I? Are you all right, Camilla? No offence but you look terrible.'

'This is English flattery, I think,' she said with a weak laugh.

'No. I mean it. I know . . .' He glanced at the door, wondering if Marco was listening, and then realized he didn't care. 'I know he says we can keep on doing this time after time. But looking at you I'm not so sure.'

She yawned, stretched her arms and got herself more upright. His breathing stopped for a few seconds as he watched.

'Marco is a good and kind doctor,' she told him. 'What he does is called apheresis. This machine here separates the blood, and takes out the part he needs. The rest goes back . . .'

'So he said. If you could see yourself in a mirror . . .'

She laughed again and he could not take his eyes off her.

'I don't want to see myself in a mirror.'

'Why not? You're beautiful. But very, very pale if you ask me.'

'Don't worry,' Camilla said. Then she leaned back on the pillow and placed her hands behind her head, staring at the ceiling. He had to fight hard not to stare. 'Tell me about these cakes you bake.'

That's what women do, he thought. Change the subject.

'Well, I do bake them. Eccles cakes. Bakewell tarts. Bread-and-butter pudding. Curd tarts. Custard tarts. But they're pastries really and I'm not a pastry chef. I'm a baker.'

She turned and looked at him. Her eyes didn't seem as young as the rest of her.

'The difference being . . . ?'

'You don't need yeast for cakes, not usually. Bread's different. Water and flour and yeast.'

He stole a glance at her.

'Milk loaf's my favourite. Not everyone can make that. You have to treat the milk first or the crumb's all wrong. If you don't get the temperature right it can turn out as flat as a pancake.'

'You make this bread come alive?'

'It's a gift.'

The young girl on the bed placed a thin white finger to her cheek and said, 'A power, surely?'

'A power. I suppose. Want a cup of tea and a sandwich after? I'd quite like to get out of this place. Gives me the creeps a bit, to be honest.'

She shook her head and said, 'No. Sorry. I need to talk to Marco.'

'Don't you let him take any more from you.'

'More what?' the doctor asked. He was almost by the bed already, and began unhooking the needle from Jason's arm. In his jacket pocket was a wad of cash and some vouchers. He'd got there without making the slightest noise.

'Scared the life out of me, you did,' Jason complained as the spike came out of his flesh.

He got up and rubbed his arm. He felt a little woozy which was odd, as if this time round was more of a strain.

'I apologize. What is it I shouldn't do?'

'Take too much blood from her. That's what.'

Marco's gaze grew stony.

'I had no idea you possessed medical knowledge.'

'I've got a pair of eyes, haven't I?'

'Jason.'

He felt something touch his arm. It was Camilla, standing next to him, peering into his face, concerned. She seemed a little unsteady on her feet and he felt sure she was holding onto him for support. Her face was that of an adult, wise, kind, yet sad somehow. It made her even more beautiful. He wished he were better with words, with emotions, because the sight of her did something to his heart which was new to him, something he couldn't quite control or comprehend.

'Please . . .' she murmured. 'I appreciate your concern but it's not necessary.'

'I would like to have a cup of tea some time though,' he pleaded.

'Of course. Soon. But not now . . .' She glanced at Marco. 'I can't talk.'

The doctor led him to the front door by the wonky little bridge then said, rather frostily, '*Ciao*.'

'I'm sorry, Marco,' Jason said, stopping as he stepped outside. 'I didn't mean anything. She looked so poorly. I made a fool of myself.'

'These things happen.' The Italian shrugged. 'If it helps I believe she's staying at a little *pensione* in Cannaregio. Near Misericordia. Perhaps if you are around there tomorrow in the afternoon . . . Camilla rises late.' He winked. 'Who knows?'

'Good man!' Jason said cheerily, and nudged him with an elbow. 'Tell her I'll be looking out for her, will you?'

'I promise. Good evening,' he said, and closed the door.

Fondamenta della Misericordia was a long straight street by a canal, not far from a place called the ghetto. A few Jewish people wandered round there in dark clothes, some with skullcaps and what Jason thought had to be dreadlocks of some kind. By the time he got that far he noticed the street had changed its name to something entirely different, and did so again not much further on. Venice tried to get you lost even when everything looked dead simple. So he retraced his tracks and worked out where Misericordia ended, realizing the place wasn't quite as extensive as he first believed.

There were three or four cafés, some restaurants and a few bars. He had his first cappuccino around two – he didn't really know what Marco meant when he said Camilla got up 'late'. Four hours and three coffees passed and the area was still pretty much empty. He talked to one of the waiters who spoke good English and asked, exactly, what counted as afternoon in Venice. The answer didn't make much sense, something about how *'buon giorno'*, good day, could turn into *'buona sera'*, good evening, any time around three o'clock, or even earlier, without any intervening period for afternoon at all. Jason felt even more lost after that and decided upon a practical plan, one he wished he'd thought of earlier.

Marco said that Camilla was staying in a *pensione* in Misericordia. All he had to do was find it.

He walked up and down then checked to make sure there really was no other street with the same name. He couldn't find a *pensione*. No hotel. Anywhere to stay. When he went back to the café the friendly waiter confirmed this.

Jason stood outside by the canal, thinking. Three jazz musicians in heavy winter coats were starting to play on a little boat moored on the water: bass, electric piano and sax, fast and noisy. This wasn't the sort of area someone like Camilla would live in at all. It was too noisy, too public somehow.

She liked quiet places. And for some reason he felt she didn't like to be seen.

Marco had lied.

He didn't like being angry but sometimes it was impossible to avoid.

'. . . make a parson bloody swear,' he muttered as he marched across the rickety little bridge, so forcefully the structure seemed to shake beneath his feet.

The stars and the moon were out again, bright and distant. He yanked on the bell then, for good luck, started pounding on the door with his fists.

It was all lies. About Camilla being in a *pensione* in Misericordia. About Marco having to go home at night. Jason had watched the way he walked round this big old house, set on its own over the water, a place apart. Somewhere you could get away with anything. Marco was familiar with it, every last step, every turn, every floorboard. He lived here. It was his home. His clinic. His . . .

Jason didn't want to think too much about anything else. The familiar, birdlike face opened the door, smiling, looking a little puzzled.

Jason pushed his way in.

'I know she's here,' he said without fear. 'I know what your game is. I may be English but I'm not stupid.'

Marco was making soft noises of protest but did nothing to stop him as he stormed into the room with the machine and the needles and the two broad beds.

The blinds were closed as ever. No wonder, Jason thought. Camilla lay on the bed on the left, the usual one. This time she wore some kind of nightdress, the sleeve rolled up to her pale, thin shoulder. A pipe red with blood ran into the faint blue line of a vein at her elbow.

'You take that thing out of her now,' Jason roared, and felt he heard the angry voice of his Uncle Arthur egging him on from somewhere. 'I want to see that needle gone. I want you nowhere near the lass. After that I'm calling the police. After that . . .'

He could feel his face going red. He wasn't scared. Not one bit of it.

Camilla stirred with all the noise, woke up, her big, dark eyes rolling around, looking at the room, at him, at Marco, trying to make sense of what she saw.

Jason dragged up a seat, sat by her and took her free hand. Her skin felt clammy the way his father's had.

'Don't you worry.' He tried to look into her eyes, but she seemed more interested in Marco at that moment, perhaps out of fear. 'He's not taking any more blood out of you. I'm getting you out of here.' He turned and stared at the doctor. 'I said I wanted that thing out of her.'

The Italian didn't seem angry or threatening or anything but sad, in a way that made Jason feel decidedly uncomfortable.

'Marco, I said . . .' he repeated.

Camilla's cold hand closed on his, clutching at Jason's fingers tenderly, squeezing, with the same delicate weakness he'd felt in his father's grasp towards the end.

'He can't take it out,' she whispered.

The doctor pulled up a chair and shrugged.

'If I remove the line she will die,' Marco said in the same resigned, matter-of-fact manner Jason recalled the hospital people using back in Wakefield. 'Don't you understand? Camilla isn't the donor here, Jason. That was you.'

'You mean . . . ?'

He wondered why he was so thick sometimes. Why he couldn't have worked this out for himself.

'Camilla is the patient,' Marco went on. 'My only one. I thought I'd lost her. Then you came along and . . .' Another shrug. He looked baffled too. 'I don't know. I thought we had some hope finally. Not that I understand how.'

Jason felt her shuffle along the bed, squeeze his hand once more, then, very carefully, kiss him once on the cheek, the way foreign people did.

'Thank you,' she whispered.

Marco stood up.

'Shall I make some tea?' he asked.

'That would be nice,' Jason said automatically.

'What kind of illness?' Jason asked, sipping at what he now knew, from his earlier visits, to be Earl

271

Grey, something that had never found its way to Garibaldi Street. 'Is it catching?'

Camilla and the doctor exchanged worried glances.

'Not infectious in a normal way,' Marco said finally.

She placed her hand on Jason's arm and looked into his eyes.

'I wouldn't harm anyone intentionally,' Camilla told him. 'Ever. I couldn't. I inherited this disease. It's not my choice. But I can keep myself like this, in quarantine. With Marco trying to find a cure.'

Her concern for others explained why she was here, Marco said, repeating a point he'd made earlier. Why she'd come for help in the first place. There were what he called 'potential side effects' to her illness. But with the treatment these could be kept in check. Stabilized.

Jason felt bold enough to take her hand, to hold her pale, slender fingers in his.

'You look as weak as a kitten. As weak as . . .' My dad, the night he died, Jason almost said. 'I want to know what's going on here. I'm not a kid.'

She turned to Marco and said, 'Please tell him.'

The doctor issued a long, agonized sigh.

'Camilla's not getting better, I'm afraid. With the technique I came up with – the transfusions of AB-positive plasma – I've managed to keep her alive. But I feel I've been fighting a losing battle. Something in this . . . condition defies me. I've

272

consulted all the experts I dare confide in. We're all baffled.'

'You should never give up,' Jason insisted. 'Never.'

The doctor's eyes met Jason's. They were thoughtful and reticent too, as if there was something Marco wished to say.

'And then you come along,' the doctor said, scratching his chin.

'I've got the right blood,' Jason told him. 'You can have as much as you want. I can stay here forever. Move in if you like. Just take it. I want to help.'

Camilla's fingers moved inside his.

'It's not just the right blood,' she said, and placed another soft, warm kiss on his cheek. 'It's . . .'

She fell silent.

Marco filled in.

'It's special somehow,' the doctor said. 'Don't ask me to explain. I can't see any difference between your AB-positive blood and any we've used before. But something's not the same.' His face became more fixed, almost fierce with indignation. 'Had you not stepped through these doors I believe Camilla would have died this week. Nothing I could do seemed to arrest the illness. Then . . .' The faintest of embarrassed smiles crossed his face. 'You arrive and . . . I don't know.'

'There's a little bit of magic in me,' Jason said eagerly, smiling, waving his fingers in the air. 'My dad always reckoned that. You said it yourself, Camilla. There's life.'

'There is,' she agreed.

'Then have it!' He took her hand away and unrolled his sleeve. 'Take as much as you want!'

'You're a kind and generous man,' Marco told him.

Jason Cunningham wondered whether anyone had ever called him a man in Yorkshire. He couldn't remember.

'I have something else to ask,' Marco went on. 'All I've done is slow Camilla's decline. With your . . . special blood perhaps I could do more. Though it's not without risk. To Camilla. To you. It's important you both understand.'

Jason listened out of politeness. This was one of those doctor's conversations they had to have so that they kept themselves covered. The sort where they offered to cure you but reminded you it might get sticky along the way. It took a good ten minutes and Jason couldn't wait for it to be over. The details, the get-outs, the possible side effects . . . they seemed interminable and completely beyond his compre-hension. Besides, he'd made up his mind before Marco ever started down this path. If there was a chance he could save Camilla, for good, not just for one night, he'd take it, whatever the risk.

When the doctor finally finished he looked at her and said, 'I'm game if you are.'

She kissed him again. There were tears in her beautiful eyes.

'But I want that tea and cake when we're done. Maybe a fish supper too. Somewhere that's not here.'

'Anywhere,' Camilla murmured, then lay back on the bed, smiling, ready.

For some reason he passed out halfway through the transfusion. Maybe it was watching the blood too closely. Or the amount Marco was taking.

When he came to the room seemed completely dark except for the whirring illumination of the machine beneath the window. Jason wasn't sure whether he was awake or dreaming.

He was beneath the clean ironed sheets with no clothes on. Camilla was with him, naked too, straddling his chest.

'Excuse me,' Jason murmured in a voice that sounded slurred and sleepy.

She placed a finger against his lips then reached down, took his hand, clutched it to her.

His head didn't feel right. He couldn't think straight. Camilla was touching him in places where no one else's fingers had ever been before and it felt good, felt wonderful, sent delicious images and thoughts racing through his head. He was exhausted, he knew. Drained. But her presence revived him, and the movement of her warm skin, the loose soft fall of her breasts grazing against his chest as she angled carefully over him, made him feel more alive than he'd ever known.

'I ought to tell you . . .' he whispered.

'Hush,' she said, and put her index finger to his lips then slipped the soft warm tip into his mouth, moving it to and fro on his tongue.

Her long black hair fell softly on his shoulders. Her lips came down close to his ear. Hot, damp breath filled his head.

'Jason, Jason . . . kind, kind Jason,' she murmured.

He sucked on her finger, not knowing why. Then she withdrew it and slowly, inch by inch, worked her way down his chest, nails scratching gently, playing with his navel, sliding a little further, hesitating, as if uncertain or shy.

'I haven't never . . .'

It wasn't happening right. He was nervous, afraid.

'I know,' she said, and leaned forward until one of her breasts, he wasn't sure which, fell to his mouth.

The nipple was hard, as if it had a life, an identity of its own. He thought of Wakefield and the mother he'd only ever seen in a faded photograph. Then his lips closed on the full white shape hovering over him in the darkness of the clinic room, like the moon fallen to earth.

He wasn't quite sure what happened after that. Liquid entered his mouth, warm and salty, not like milk, not human milk. More like . . .

Before his conflicting thoughts could coalesce they departed his head altogether. As his teeth closed more firmly around Camilla's breast, and the warmth of her entered him, she found the place, the position, the perfect union between them, and with that the omission which had troubled him disappeared.

I want to remember this forever, Jason thought,

276

as she rocked above him, crying, calling, beckoning, murmuring sighs of passion in a language he couldn't begin to understand.

He threw his head back on the pillow. The warm stream of fluid from her breasts spattered his face and chest.

Something precious and important began to pass between them, him to her, her to him.

Camilla's teeth clenched, her voice, guttural and hoarse, cried out, almost snarled, 'Every last drop, Jason. Every last drop.'

'Oh my goodness,' he gasped. 'Oh . . .'

When he woke up he was in the bed on the left, the one he thought of as Camilla's. His nose was pressed into the pillow. He was wearing a pair of soft cotton pyjamas that he'd never seen before. The smell of her was everywhere, a soft perfume like flowers and rose water. And soap too, hospital soap. Jason sniffed his wrist and realized it was him. He'd been cleaned up, the way nurses did.

It took all his strength to turn over. Then he tried to get up and found it was impossible. He didn't have the energy.

Marco came in, put a thermometer in his mouth and felt his pulse. The Italian looked concerned, not that he said a word.

Jason remembered the funny dream, and recalling it felt at odds with himself, pleased and frightened, ecstatic and a little ashamed.

'Where's Camilla?' he asked, and realized he sounded a little croaky.

'Gone,' Marco said. 'Bounded out of here this morning with a spring in her step.'

'Lucky her. I feel terrible.'

He looked at the other bed, the one he'd been in. They'd been in.

'It wasn't a dream, was it?'

'What, exactly?'

'Last night. Me and Camilla.' He wondered if he was blushing. His cheeks felt as if they ought to be going red but somehow he doubted he had the means to achieve this. 'Something happened.'

'Something happened,' Marco agreed. 'What exactly?'

'I don't like to say.'

The Italian sat on the bed and looked worried.

'I think it's important you do, Jason. For your sake. For mine. Perhaps for Camilla's too. Please . . .'

He seemed very earnest and he was a doctor. So Jason told him, as simply as he could. Even the part about the milk, if that was what it was. Marco listened carefully. He looked both fascinated and appalled.

'I thought I was dreaming!' Jason protested. 'You know. One of *them* dreams . . .'

'I can imagine.' Marco went to the window and raised the blind. It was the first time Jason had seen real daylight enter this particular room. When it fell on him he felt a sudden pain on his face, the kind you got when you put vinegar on a cut.

'Ow!' he exclaimed. 'Ow!'

The hurt was getting worse, becoming unbearable.

'It's only daylight,' Marco said.

'Stop it! Stop it now!'

'Of course.'

The doctor closed the blinds then came back and sat on the end of the bed.

'What's wrong with me?' Jason asked.

'I don't know. I never really knew precisely what was wrong with Camilla. I had . . . ideas. Sometimes they seemed ridiculous.'

Jason asked the question, though in his heart he didn't want to hear the answer.

'What do you think it's called? The thing she had?'

Marco shook his grey head.

'I told you before. There are no names. No medical ones. Only common, pejorative terms which I will never utter in your presence.'

'Pejora . . . ?'

'Bad. Nasty. Horrible. Names you could never have applied to Camilla.'

Jason swallowed. It was hard. His throat was dry. His skin still felt itchy from the sunlight.

'Have I got what she had?'

'I think so. The light. Your pallor. You seem to have the same symptoms.'

'Does she still have it?'

'No. I think I can say that with certainty. She couldn't have walked out of here if that were the case.'

'Camilla didn't know this would happen,' Jason cut in, desperate to defend her. 'It wasn't deliberate. Besides . . .'

He remembered her beauty, and what he understood of her courage, her decision to be in this white, clinical prison.

'I'd still have done it anyway.'

Marco nodded.

'I believe you would. You've cured her. For now anyway.' He scratched his grey head. 'With your blood. Your presence. Your bravery. Your love, and the fact it was quite, quite selfless. I don't know. I'm a doctor. I can only speak of things that can be measured, observed, analysed. With this . . . ?'

'Well that's something, int'it?' Jason felt proud. 'I mean. I wanted to help.'

'You did. It was very valiant, very generous of you. How do you feel? Physically, I mean.'

'Bloody awful.' Jason thought for a moment. When he closed his eyes he could see himself drinking from the warm, soft generosity of her breast. 'Spitting feathers too.'

'Pardon?'

'Spitting feathers. It's Yorkshire. Thirsty. Dead thirsty. Can I have something please? Right now?'

'Coffee? Tea?'

At first Jason didn't say what came straight into his head. It seemed a stupid idea. Marco would think him bonkers. Or down-right odd.

Then he thought, in for a penny . . .

'A tomato juice would be nice if you had it.'

'Tomato juice . . .'

Marco folded his arms for a moment then reached beneath the bed and pulled out the cardboard sign Jason first saw by the front door, the one asking for blood, at a price. With perks.

'I'll find you a tomato juice. I'll put this outside too.'

Jason didn't want to think about outside. Not at all. Not in the sun.

'Will I be here long?'

'Possibly.'

'As long as Camilla was?'

The Italian thought for a moment and said, 'I don't know how long Camilla was here exactly. I inherited her. From the doctor before me . . . I didn't want to ask.'

'Oh.'

Marco waved the sign.

'I'll find you someone, Jason. I promise. In the meantime I will fetch books. I will teach you Italian. You can teach me . . . Yorkshire. Whatever you wish. You can have fried fish. I'll bring it. Whatever you want. There'll be time. Plenty of it. Perhaps . . .' There was that shrug Jason had come to recognize. 'There will be someone else to teach you after a while. As there was for Camilla. With me.'

Then he left.

Jason Cunningham thought of Wakefield. He knew he'd never return to grey, bleak Garibaldi

Street, not in a million years. He looked at the freshly made-up sheets on the bed beside him and wondered where Camilla was now, where she'd end up, and with whom. She was beautiful. He wasn't. Not on the outside anyway. He'd had something, though. Something that set her free. And put him in her place.

He closed his eyes and slept immediately. There was a dream, or perhaps a dream of a dream. Camilla was back in his bed once more, her taut, naked form moving rhythmically in the space above, low, short words he couldn't understand tumbling from her mouth as she made love to him with a steady, determined passion.

Fighting, wrestling to become one, a single conjoined beast, they were consumed by a milk-white dust storm of flour and yeast gathering round them like a grainy fog that wanted to cling to their sweating bodies, take nourishment from it, become something else, something alive.

The sudden, agonizing moment of sharp liquid heat happened again, together, and this time he screamed, as did she.

Afterwards, clinging to one another in the whiteness, her hot mouth found his ear and she whispered, 'One day I will come for you, Jason.'

'That would be nice,' he murmured, only to realize that he was alone and awake beneath the fluorescent lights of the room with the shuttered blinds. There was a line in his arm. It was hooked up to the whirring machine on the wall.

He went back to sleep and when he finally woke Jason Cunningham felt as if he'd been out of it for days. Weeks even.

A plump and rosy-cheeked girl with a long, horsy face and a bob of blonde hair was putting her rucksack on the floor as she sat down on the adjoining bed. He watched as she rolled up her sleeve. Her arm was as well-padded as the rest of her, with a prominent blue vein running from elbow to wrist as if it had been drawn there with a child's crayon.

'Ooh . . . you do look lovely,' he said.

CARPACCIO'S SAINT

Teresa left her phone turned off overnight. The next morning – which was grey and filled with swirling clouds of light snow above the canal – there were three messages waiting for her, two from Silvio Di Capua, one from Orsini.

Ignoring them, she walked downstairs to Strozzi's apartment.

The two of them were working away at the masks again. Camilla had her sleeves rolled up. Teresa walked over and gently took hold of her left arm. The young woman seemed too surprised to object. There was a plaster there and, around it, several marks of earlier transfusions.

'What's wrong with you?' Teresa asked.

'I'm sorry!' Camilla stuttered, flushing with anger and embarrassment. 'What is this? What business of yours . . . ?'

'I don't know the answer to that,' Teresa admitted. 'Yet. But it's some business. It has to be.'

She'd brought the previous night's story with her. This was on ordinary paper again. Whoever was writing them no longer felt the need to hide

284

the words. Only the first – which would surely have interested the police, since it mentioned both Aitchison and Sofia directly – required that.

'Please,' Teresa said, showing the pages to Camilla. 'Read this. I think you should call Jason and ask him to come round.'

The girl's bright, darting eyes opened in amazement.

'Jason? What's this got to do with him?'

'Read it,' Teresa ordered. 'Then tell me.'

Strozzi watched them both in silence, taking in every word. Camilla put aside the delicate female mask she was working on and began to turn over the pages, blushing so lightly it was barely noticeable. From time to time she would exclaim, mostly in Croatian, a language Teresa could not begin to comprehend. The young woman dashed through the first few sheets at a steady pace, swearing and crying out in outrage from time to time.

After a few minutes she thrust them to one side. She stared at Teresa and demanded, 'That's enough. Who wrote it?'

'The same person who wrote all the others,' Teresa said with a sigh. 'The Plague Doctor. Or one of them. I simply don't know. But that's not the most important question, is it?'

They both stared at her.

'Why?'

Strozzi, who didn't seem much minded to move, said, 'Unless this is too personal, may I?'

He nodded at the pages.

'We'll finish them together,' Camilla said, looking at Teresa. 'Give us time.'

She left them alone for a while, dodging more phone calls, but sending a short and, she hoped, sensible email to Silvio Di Capua to say that if he had any questions about taking over the department he should pose them, and she'd answer freely, happily.

After half an hour she went back downstairs. Camilla and Strozzi sat at the table in silence. The pages were there, face down.

'I'm sorry if this seems offensive,' Teresa said. 'I felt you ought to see them.'

Camilla checked her watch then said, 'Jason will have finished his morning shift by now. I need some fresh air.'

'And coffee! And *frittelle*,' Strozzi announced, trying to brighten the mood.

Two minutes later they were out of the door, heading across the Ponte agli Incurabili, the musician taking the wooden gangplank in his humming electric wheelchair, a black beret on his head, a scarlet scarf tied over the top, then round his ears and beneath his chin.

Teresa followed Camilla in silence as she stomped across the steps head down, upset, dabbing at her eyes with a tissue. It was bitterly cold but that was not the reason for her tears.

Signora Rizzolo, who ran the *pasticceria*, took one look at them then directed all three to a back room. It was a bare place that probably hadn't been decorated since the 1950s. The single oven was still cooling down in the tiny adjoining kitchen, which made the place uncomfortably hot. Jason Cunningham, a tall, pleasant young man, Teresa thought, kept slapping his hands to get rid of the flour as he listened to what they had to say.

'Read it for yourself,' Camilla ordered as they sat down at a bare, bleached wooden table, Strozzi manoeuvring his electric wheelchair alongside the rest of them with ease then untying the scarf from his head and placing his beret in his lap.

'I don't think I want to from what you've told me,' Jason said. 'Where's this rubbish come from?'

'From someone who's trying to guide me towards Sofia,' Teresa told him. She thought of the figure in the dark, the long white mask, and decided to keep the meeting with him the previous night to herself. 'The Plague Doctor, whoever he is.'

'How would something like this help?' he asked, wide-eyed.

'I don't know,' she said. 'But I think you should look at it.'

'All right,' Jason replied then sat down and skimmed quickly through the papers, Camilla nudging him with details at times.

They devoured *frittelle* and sipped coffee in silence. When he was finished he was blushing too, and scratching at his fair hair with a floury hand.

'Bloody 'ell,' he said in English. Then, in good Italian, added, 'Someone's got quite an imagination, haven't they? They should be doing this for a living, not giving it away without . . .' He turned over the title page. Jason, in real life, was a lot smarter than his ingénue namesake in the tale. 'Without even putting their name to it.'

Teresa waited. Eventually it was Strozzi who leaned over, stroked his beard nervously, as if by way of apology, and said, 'But some of this is true, Jason. Some . . .'

'Some!' he burst out. 'But not that about me and . . .' His eyes found Camilla's for a moment. 'Not about us two like that. We're just friends. Nothing more. Good friends. It's disgusting to think someone could even imagine a thing like that. Whatever it's meant to be . . .'

Strozzi glanced at Teresa and she knew immediately what this older, wiser man was trying to say: that there was more than affection here, even if it was on one side alone.

'Making fun of Camilla's sickness like that,' Jason went on. 'What sort of person thinks it's a laugh being ill?'

'Whoever it is seemed . . . I don't think they found it funny,' Camilla said. 'It was a sad story. With a little hope in it. And love and sacrifice and goodness, I think. They were trying to make a point.'

She gazed at Teresa and asked, 'But what?'

'I imagine that's for me to work out. This story has a conclusion, but it's part of something longer that isn't finished. Something to do with this man Arnaud, the Count of Saint-Germain.'

All three of them looked clueless, as did Signora Rizzolo, the proprietress, who stood blatantly listening from the door. Strozzi stared at her until the woman coughed, muttered something about customers, then went back into the café.

'I don't wish to pry,' Teresa said carefully. 'But it would be useful to know how much exactly is true, or close to it.'

Some details she'd guessed already. The medical details, before ranging into fantasy, matched the treatment for a range of blood diseases. Camilla quickly confirmed, in a very matter-of-fact fashion, that she was suffering from a rare form of leukaemia. The treatment included transfusions of blood stem cells from someone with a matching tissue type. In Croatia the only amenable donor she could find had vanished. Desperate for help, Camilla had used a friend in Venice to gain treatment within the Italian state medical system, which had better and newer techniques. By accident she'd met Jason in this same café the year before. Keen to help he'd offered to be tested for compatibility. The doctors said they were a perfect match. Now, his blood kept the illness at bay during more longterm treatment for the condition.

'It doesn't harm me,' the young Englishman said. 'What that story was making out . . . that Camilla gave me some kind of sickness in return . . . that's a load of tripe.'

'Of course it is,' Teresa told him. 'I'm a doctor.

I know. Medically the whole thing is . . . a load of tripe. The idea . . .'

Mystery not explanation. The words she'd heard in the dark before the Plague Doctor and his dog fled back towards the Rialto returned to her.

'It's not to be taken literally.'

'The treatment's working too,' Jason added, and took Camilla's hand. 'She's a lot better than she was last year.'

'I am,' she agreed, and slowly, with affection, unwound her fingers from his.

Teresa's heart went out to them both. The truth was there in their faces, and in Strozzi's sad, downcast eyes. Jason loved this beautiful young woman. She, in return, was grateful and fond of him. Nothing more.

I love you. You love me. How can this possibly change?

It won't, Teresa thought. It can't. The heart's a wilful, selfish instrument, deaf to reason, intent on following its own desires, nothing else. Was this a lesson she was supposed to learn too? A harsh truth that was part of the solution she was seeking?

'Does this man . . . whoever wrote this know you, Jason?' she asked.

'Not very well,' he insisted. He told how he arrived in Venice. The facts were similar to those outlined in the story, though he had been in the city for nearly a year and found the job with Signora Rizzolo almost immediately, simply by knocking on her door and offering, at the outset, to work for free. There were, however, significant differences. He'd never been close to destitute, and his father was still alive and – Jason added proudly – a small businessman who had once been the deputy mayor of Wakefield.

'Your mother?' Teresa asked. This aspect of the story seemed important.

'Mum's a member of the Townswomen's Guild,' Jason said straight away. 'Don't have an uncle or aunt at all. Wicked or otherwise. My folk are lovely. Mum and Dad came to visit here only last October. That stuff's all . . .'

'Tripe,' she said quickly. Teresa looked at Camilla. 'And your doctor?'

'A consultant at the hospital,' she said at once. 'The big one near Zanipolo. Not called Marco either.'

As for some strange miniature palace stranded on the water . . . Camilla was lost for any clue to its identity. She knew of no such place, she insisted. Nor did Strozzi or Jason.

'Yet whoever wrote this,' Teresa pointed out, 'must have met you both. Or talked to someone who has. Someone who's aware of your medical condition. Of Jason and where he came from.'

The Englishman cast a quick look at the door.

'Doesn't really narrow it down,' he said. 'Bella – Signora Rizzolo – is a lovely old girl but she's a one-woman loudspeaker system for the whole of Dorsoduro. Plenty of customers know I give blood for Camilla, Sofia for one and, without telling tales, she isn't exactly discreet either.'

Tenses, Teresa thought, watching, listening intently.

Jason paused then added, 'And this bloke of yours is called the Plague Doctor. Maybe that's a clue too. Maybe that's what he really is. A doctor. Have you thought of that?'

No, she hadn't, and his words made her all the more convinced the story had underestimated Jason Cunningham greatly. He was, it seemed to her, very quick off the mark indeed.

Filippo Strozzi cleared his throat and said, 'Unless I'm mistaken, the author of these stories – I am assuming there is just the one, by the way – knows much more than this. He – or she – was aware that you would come to look for Sofia, for one thing, and was able to deliver an envelope to the house, with your name on it, before you turned up.' His arm swept the room. 'How could some customer here know that?'

'Whoever it was knew that Sofia went to the Scuola di San Giorgio degli Schiavoni,' Teresa pointed out. 'And something about the Englishman, Jerome Aitchison . . .'

'You mean that nutter who took a pot shot at the lady in the piazza?' Jason Cunningham asked. 'He's involved in this?'

'He was,' Teresa said. 'Or at least so the story claimed.'

'Police,' he said emphatically. 'This is a job for them.'

'The police aren't interested,' Camilla told him. 'The Englishman's dead. Sofia's vanished.'

Strozzi nodded, thought for a moment, then said, 'If those stories were coming to me I would feel the possibilities are very limited. The person who's writing these things must surely be someone who knows Sofia very well. Or, more likely I think, she is writing them. To help you find her.'

'Why doesn't she just call me?' Teresa asked. 'Why is this all so hard?'

Strozzi leaned back in his wheelchair and sighed. Then something, some spark of recognition, struck him.

'Carpaccio,' he said. 'You reminded me. The dress. The gown in Sofia's room. The one you found on the tailor's dummy.'

Camilla's eyes lit up at that moment.

'Of course! I was thinking carnival all the time. What a fool. It's her, isn't it?'

'Who?' Teresa asked.

'Ursula. The beautiful saint. Who else? She's just round the corner. You must see!'

'And you must work,' Strozzi said. 'Masks, Camilla. Masks. I'm playing later. Jazz for a boat party. I will take Teresa to the Accademia. Jason? Would you care to join us?'

'Paintings?' the young Englishman asked, screwing up his nose. 'Not my thing, thank you. I've got loaves to bake.'

The electric motor of the wheelchair whirred. Filippo Strozzi, an active man in spite of his disability, was the first out of the door, strapping on both scarlet scarf and black beret as he went.

The great gallery by the Grand Canal was wrapped in sheets and vast, ugly posters for a new movie. Refurbishment. She tried to remember what it looked like underneath its present shroud. One more Venetian church or *scuola* converted to another purpose. Now it stood like some hastily covered stone corpse abandoned next to the hand-some low curve of the wooden bridge sweeping across the Grand Canal. A scattering of tourists shivered outside in the light snow as they queued for tickets at a temporary booth.

Strozzi was having none of this. He buzzed up and down the front of the gallery as if trying to remember something. Then Teresa saw the sign for the disabled entrance, pointed it out and they went up a low metal ramp by the side and dealt with a polite woman in an office there.

'So many things change,' Strozzi complained as she stared at his resident's card. 'One minute you come in one way, the next somewhere else.'

'Works,' the woman said grumpily, then, when he seemed completely lost for directions, pointed them to a small lift with a cracked and peeling disabled sign stuck to the door.

It was still a little chilly inside the Accademia. Strozzi merely removed the scarf but left the beret in place, whirring around the corridors, muttering to himself. In the end they had to ask an attendant, and found themselves guided to Room XX half-hidden down a narrow corridor.

Teresa walked in and found herself for a moment quite lost for breath. The chamber was filled with large, spectacular canvases, all clearly the creation of the same artist she'd seen working on a much smaller scale in the little *scuola* in Castello. Here the artist's imagination ran riot and the result was so panoramic, so vivid and full of narrative power, it was like encountering a three-dimensional movie that had leapt, brimming with life and colour and violence, straight out of the final few years of the fifteenth century.

'Here's the one,' Strozzi said, heading straight for what had to be the last canvas of several, on the right.

'No. This is a story,' she said, picking up the card that described the collection. 'Bear with me. I want to start at the beginning.'

Stories are important, she thought. More than she had once appreciated.

There were nine canvases in all, telling a fable that came, like St George, from *The Golden Legend*. In this case it was the tragedy of a mythical princess, Ursula, the daughter of a king of Brittany, who was betrothed to a pagan prince in return for his conversion to Christianity. The works – bold, sweeping images of a medieval Europe that seemed so real one might step up from the gallery floor and enter them – filled the walls with ships and castles, noblemen and soldiers. They ran in sequence beginning with the ambassadors organizing the political arrangements for the wedding in cities much like parts of Venice still.

There was a brief, polite and formal meeting between Ursula and the prince, taking place on a stretch of water that might have been a reimagined Grand Canal. Then came a strange and disturbing image. Ursula asleep in bed, alone, stiff, almost corpse-like, with an angel standing by the door delivering a message that could be just one thing: a warning of her forthcoming martyrdom.

Teresa Lupo stood in front of this painting feeling cold and a little distanced from reality, unable to force from her head a picture of Sofia in the same situation, beneath the crumpled sheets in the tumbledown apartment a few hundred metres away, a solitary figure, unaware of what lay ahead.

In the next canvas Ursula and the prince were meeting the Pope in Rome, outside the recognizable barrel-like shape of the Castel Sant' Angelo.

And then to the final vast panorama, divided into two sections like a modern split-screen piece of cinema.

On the left the pilgrims were in the midst of a battle outside Cologne, attacked on all sides by fierce and gaudily armoured Huns. There was bloodshed everywhere. Men and women lay on the ground, in agony, hacked by swords, pierced by knives, shot with arrows. The Pope from the previous frame was pinioned to a tree by a soldier's dagger, stabbed through the neck, in the throes of an agonizing death. It was a dreadful, despairing scene.

Yet in the foreground, kneeling on the earth, praying calmly, awaiting her fate, was the figure of Ursula. The similarity to the figure on the tailor's dummy in Sofia's apartment was so close it sent a sudden shiver through Teresa Lupo. The mythical saint cut a humble yet courageous figure as she waited on the ground, her long blonde hair falling down her back onto the crimson cloak that covered the skyblue dress with a gold braid collar and shawl. In front of her an extraordinary archer, face hidden, tumbling curls of yellow hair falling past his shoulders, drew back a bow, aiming the arrow directly at her heart.

His pose – tense, determined, muscular – seemed the epitome of male power and cruelty. On his head stood a circular red feathered hat, almost a carnival prop in its own right. Strapped to his right leg was an ornate quiver decorated with strange pagan emblems. The arrow was in place, the string fully stretched. His entire posture, from the sinewy legs to the athletic arch of his shoulders, mimicked the strains and pressures of the bow itself, as if he were as much a deadly weapon as it. Around this faceless yet beautiful man other soldiers gathered to watch, waiting for the heartless slaughter of the young woman praying on the ground, hands tight together, eyes fearlessly set on her executioner. Death was a moment away yet she could not have been more serene, more composed.

The dress, the collar, the shawl, the crown . . . all the things that had fallen to the floor when Teresa had forced open the door were here. Sofia's apartment possessed an exact copy for some reason and Teresa could not imagine for one moment what that might be. The only possibilities seemed trivial, mundane. Some historical pageant perhaps, associated with the carnival but not trapped in its rigid, formal adherence to tradition? A theatrical event?

These, she knew, were not the answer. Nor could she remember much of Sofia's embroidery skills. Could she really have made such a detailed and beautiful copy?

'I've only seen the photo on my camera,' Strozzi said. 'But . . .'

'It's the same,' Teresa told him.

She walked back round the room, examining each canvas again very carefully. The wheelchair whirred behind her.

'What are you looking for?' Strozzi asked after a while.

'This,' she said, pointing to the small notice painted at the foot of the nearest canvas.

'What is it?'

'It's called a cartellino. The painter used it to show it was his work. A signature, if you like, but one that becomes a part of the canvas itself.'

Strozzi, who seemed to know only a little of painting, asked, 'Is that significant?'

'Every picture here has the simplest, most obvious of cartellini. Carpaccio's name, suitably disguised in Latin. And the date of the painting.'

He waited.

'There's another canvas in this story. In a *scuola* in Castello. It seems to be important somehow. The cartellino is very different. It uses an unexpected verb tense. That one says, "Carpaccio *was* painting me."'

'Was painting me when what?' Strozzi asked straight away.

'Precisely.'

Teresa turned three hundred and sixty degrees, taking in each panel, following the movement of the story and the same characters towards their dreadful end. The right-hand half of the last canvas, divided from Ursula's death by a column, depicted the slow, formal ceremony of her interment. There was a complete narrative of an adult, Christian life here, one recreated with the utmost care and dedication. Teresa felt she could sit in this room for hours, knowing that if she waited long enough the faces on the walls would find their voices and begin to speak.

'I haven't helped at all, have I?' Strozzi said miserably, playing with the controls on his wheelchair, flicking a lever from side to side like a fidgety child.

'Of course you have,' Teresa told him.

'You're very generous.'

'No, Filippo. I'm not. Not at all.' Answers came from synthesizing fact and fiction, ignorance and knowledge. Guesswork, in other words. 'Usually I'm the most logical and prosaic and . . .'

What was the phrase Arnaud, the Count of Saint-Germain, had used about the kind of scientist he detested?

That they were embarked upon a relentless march towards certainty, a Darwinian destruction of the glorious wonder of doubt.

'Inflexible of people,' she concluded.

Ursula's beautiful face, composed and ready for sacrifice, would stay with her for a long time, she thought.

There was something here she was supposed to notice too. She thought back to that lost, first story, the tale of *Carpaccio's Dog*, that had first set her on this path.

This lovely invented saint from a mythical Brittany was not the first Ursula she'd encountered in Venice.

Her phone rang the moment Teresa Lupo got back to the apartment.

'You said you'd call,' her mother complained immediately.

'If I had anything to tell you. I'm sorry. I haven't.'

'That's something, isn't it?'

Teresa sighed. Her mother was right.

She sat down at the table, talking as she navigated the computer.

'Yes it is. I've been distracted.'

Quickly, in a matter-of-fact fashion, she recited again the routine actions the police were taking. The missing person register. Photos and briefings for hospitals and other government agencies. She left out any mention of the Plague Doctor or a gondola at two in the morning. There seemed no point. It would only kick off an old and now well-exercised argument.

'I know that!' Chiara complained when her daughter had finished. 'Are we just supposed to wait until they find something?'

'That's certainly their idea.'

'Perhaps they know best. Aren't you coming back to Rome? Your office won't be happy. That idiot deputy of yours called here last night, babbling like a child. I didn't understand a word he was saying. Why would he want to talk to me?'

Silvio, she thought. He wouldn't give up.

'I don't know,' Teresa told her. 'I'll make sure it doesn't happen again.'

Damned sure she thought, and started to type the beginning of an email to his personal address as she spoke.

'Come home,' Chiara urged her. 'What more can you do?'

'Something,' she murmured.

There had to be more that her mother knew. A question she hadn't covered already.

In desperation she asked, 'Where did Sofia live? When she was here before?'

'I don't have an address,' Chiara replied. 'Why would I keep something so long?'

'Didn't you go there? When you came over to see her in hospital? Surely you had to pick up some things. When she moved to Rome. Her belongings.'

There was a pause on the line, then Chiara said, 'No. I never saw where she lived. Sofia said she never wanted to go back to the place. Ever. Too many bad memories. Whatever things she had there she left behind. Didn't want them.'

'You never found out?'

'She was adamant. Why would I argue? There was never any point in that. I know you only ever saw a lovely aunt bearing gifts. Sofia could be as stubborn as a mule too.'

'I think I did see that actually,' Teresa said, half-remembering a few incidents from the past. A pleasant firmness rather than tantrums. Sofia had a mind of her own. That rebelliousness in her was attractive to any teenager.

The call ended with a touch more warmth than most of late. Teresa dashed off a warning message to Silvio asking him to keep his long nose out of things unless she asked for his help.

She needed to talk to Tosi. Filippo Strozzi, Camilla and the charming young Englishman had little if anything to offer her. Little that she could discern at the moment anyway. The old pathologist, with his connections and boundless knowledge of the city, could surely prove more useful.

There was a knock on the door. It was Camilla. She looked exhausted. There was an envelope in her hands.

'This was pushed under the door when I came back just now,' she said. 'I thought you'd want it straight away.'

Teresa's name was on the front, printed the usual way. She looked at it and felt the need to apologize for the very awkward and embarrassing scene in the *pasticceria* that morning.

'No matter,' Camilla said. 'It's funny really. Who on earth could dream up something like that?'

There was a knowing look in her eyes.

'Sofia wanted to be a writer,' the young Croatian woman added.

'She used to tell me that too. But she never finished anything. Not that I know of anyway. Your illness. I'm sorry. I shouldn't have pried like that.'

'It's no great secret. Not among my friends anyway. And you're one of them now, aren't you?'

'I'd like to think so.'

Teresa took the envelope.

'He's never sent anything in the middle of the day,' Camilla asked, 'has he?'

'I don't think so.'

Camilla kept looking at the envelope.

'Then I suppose it must be important,' she added.

THE COUNT OF SAINT-GERMAIN

'Y ou managed the accents very well,' Teresa Lupo said after Saint-Germain had finished telling his story, entirely from memory it seemed.

'Not really. That voice was north Yorkshire, not west. I stayed with the Sitwells at Wood End in Scarborough for a while after the Great War. Sacheverell was working on a small book about baroque art in Italy and Spain and required a mentor. A decent man, much mocked as if he were some upper-class prune, which was unfair and untrue.'

'I have to say, Arnaud, that your facility for name-dropping would be rather more impressive if they were ones I'd actually heard of.'

His right hand went to his mouth and a laugh, a little like a hiccup, emerged from behind it.

'I do apologize. The Sitwells were an interesting English family. Once famous. Largely forgotten now, I imagine.'

Arnaud seemed content with his story. She was not. Teresa Lupo sat next to him on the bank, watching the sun die over the ragged low horizon of the thin line of littoral land that separated the lagoon from the Adriatic. It struck her once more that she felt trapped inside a swirling, formless painting by the English artist Turner, a canvas of undefined horizons framing an indeterminate world that challenged the viewer to fill in the gaps.

'The point of this story being what exactly?' she asked.

'That one never knows what lies inside the blood. Nothing special, mostly. But on occasion . . .'

He smiled then frowned then shrugged, a jumble of gestures that seemed to mix the French with the English and the Italian. The universal man.

'Blood is blood,' she pointed out.

'That's a very simplistic view. Sacheverell's sister, the more famous Edith, suffered all her life from Marfan syndrome. It made her extraordinarily tall and gaunt, much mocked like her brother. A freak of nature or so her vile peers believed. It was only two decades ago, thirty years after Edith died, that someone established for certain that Marfan is a genetic condition which may be inherited. Paganini had it, I suspect, which probably explains a little about him, though not everything. Blood is the gift our parents hand down to us, not knowing for one second what lies hidden inside. The colour of hair, one's chances of being fat or skinny, teeth, eyes . . . If a father or mother can pass on a predisposition to cancer or short-sightedness who's to say that something else might not slip from generation to generation? The entire population of the earth consisted of fewer than eight hundred million human beings when I was a child. By the middle of this strange century I expect to witness it surpass ten billion, even with the current penchant for sophisticated mass destruction. Think like the scientist you are. And then – this is important – think a little more. On a simple statistical basis alone can you possibly hope to predict what random chromosomal mutations such impossible numbers might bring? Leaving aside the invisible demons that lurk inside those genes. Depression, depravity, criminal wicked-ness . . .'

'Criminal wickedness!' she cried. 'Don't try and tell me that's passed on from generation to gener-ation too.'

'If you'd known as many villains as I . . .'

'I've known my share! They're the product of circumstance. A want of love. Cruelty on the part of others. Poverty. Misery . . .'

He nodded and said, 'Those things too.'

'Those things only! If you're trying to say a man or a woman is condemned at birth to being a thief or a murderer by nothing more than their blood then . . . what's the point? We're nothing more than robots walking to a predestined fate. It would be so unfair . . .'

'It's unfair to have cancer in your genes,' he pointed out. 'Or Marfan.'

'You've no choice about that!'

'Could Hitler have elected to be someone else?' he asked. 'A mere house painter?'

'Of course!'

Arnaud shook his head and stared sadly at the ground.

'Not so. I spent some time in Berlin in the Twenties, until a few bullet-headed idiots thought I had a touch of the Jew about me. Let me tell you. Wickedness was in that man all along, waiting for the spur which history so readily supplied. Had the Great War not humiliated Germany and given him both motive and platform from which to spout his hate-filled lunacies perhaps he would have been one more half-crazed nonentity with grandiose dreams. Nevertheless the material for what he became was there from the beginning. Do not misunderstand me. I don't believe one's fate is inevitable. That dark seed requires watering, germination. A catalyst. Like any other disease.'

She wanted to argue. Yet he seemed so certain, so convinced.

'Something brought your Plague Doctor to life,' he said. 'What was it?'

'I don't know!' she replied immediately.

'Try guessing,' he suggested. 'It's a useful trick. I recommend it highly. Particularly to those of a fixed disposition.'

'True love,' she said.

It was the first thing that came into her mind. Yet it felt apposite.

A sudden sour scowl crossed his face.

'You made that up!' Saint-Germain said in a sharp, accusing tone.

'You told me to guess. Don't you like the idea?'

'Nothing but good comes of true love. Even an old fool like me knows that. So I can only assume you mean one of the masks that wickedness wears, like some carnival character chasing around in the dark, hoping to hide his true identity. Like your *Medico della Peste* himself. Beneath the disguise, what? Lust. Envy. Covetousness. Hatred.'

'Not necessarily,' she murmured. 'It's possible I mean true love. Gone wrong, of course. No less true for that. And I don't mean him. I'm not . . .' She tried to reach for the words. 'I'm not at all sure about *him*.' She gazed at the man next to her and asked, 'Are you Marco? The doctor in this story? Someone struggling between science and sense and . . . whatever else there is?'

'Possibly,' Saint-Germain replied straight away. 'I'm many things. This is about you. Not me. Don't you see that?'

He harrumphed and grumped for a while, watching her with his keen, bright eyes, wanting to hear something, she thought, not that she had any idea what it was.

'Perhaps,' he continued, 'this capacity for evil is in all of us then and it's largely down to fortune whether we encounter the circumstance that breathes life into it or not. Just as it's luck that deter- mines when or if that faulty gene breaks and gives you cancer or Marfan or the physique of an Olympian.'

'Free will . . .'

'. . . is the label we attach to actions we want to do, choose to do, consciously in any case, whatever the circumstances. Perhaps ten per cent of our daily behaviour, no more. Everything else . . .'

He winked at her, broke into the slightest of grins, leaned forward and said, 'I have to say it's odd hearing an atheist argue the case for redemption.'

His fine black eyebrows rose.

'The point of your story . . .' she continued.

'. . . is that we carry within us invisible burdens, surprises, perhaps good, perhaps bad, all slumbering, dreaming. Waiting for the circumstance, the catalyst, the trigger that will rouse them from their sleep. That happened to me and now I must bear the consequences. The cost is curious but given the sheer weight of humanity it would be arrogant indeed if you were to assume I must be alone. And arrogance, before you ask, is a wasteful, petty thing. A product of the vestigial cerebral appendage known as the ego. I removed that unsightly little birthmark somewhere around the turn of the nineteenth century and frankly I feel well shot of it.'

There was a noble sadness to this man that seemed almost physical, like a crippled limb, real enough to touch.

'This Camilla had the same affliction as you?' she asked.

'You think this Camilla exists?'

'I don't know.'

'If she did, or does,' he replied, shaking his head, not meeting her eyes, 'then it was something entirely different. Something older, perhaps. Something rather more vile in that it pursued and damaged the innocent, those who never sought or deserved its attention.'

'Are you really asking me to accept she was a vamp—?'

'Please don't use that word. It's inaccurate and judgemental. My inkling is that, if the unfortunate child does exist, she suffers from some unknown variant of porphyria. An obscure disease of the blood.'

'What kind?'

He sighed.

'I really don't know. You must understand the position of those of us who are, for want of a better word, freaks. Physical or psychological or both – the two do tend to go hand in hand in my experience. There's an army of people out there only too keen to hand us over to some university, some laboratory. To be turned into an object of curiosity, a specimen. Quite unacceptable. It will never happen to me, I promise. I'm much too clever to be caught by their traps. In return it means I avoid acting and interacting in their world too directly. It would be dangerous. And wrong, for them and for me. Also . . .'

He looked a little shame-faced.

'I know my limitations. Lord knows I ought to. I've lived with them long enough. I'm not blessed with an inquisitive, deductive nature. I'm an artist, not a scientist. The dread tedium of rationality, of work, has been beyond me for centuries. I need practical people like you for that. As badly, as urgently, as Camilla needed whatever it was that brave young man gave her.'

The melancholy seemed to envelop him like an invisible cloud.

'"In the end it is the mystery that lasts and not the explanation."'

'Who said that?' she asked.

'My late friend Sacheverell Sitwell in one of his books. Easy for him. He could see both. I see one only, as, I'm afraid, do you.'

Teresa thought of the bones in the coffin in the Basilica San Marco. They were human. Blood once coursed over them, flesh clothed the limbs they formed.

'You don't have a vote, do you?' she asked. 'In the symposium?'

He looked a little guilty and asked meekly, 'What do you think?'

'If you did,' Teresa went on, 'which way would you go?'

'The third way,' he said immediately.

She laughed in spite of herself.

'What third way? He's either St Mark or he's not! Please . . .'

He smiled at her and said nothing. She felt like

a schoolchild foxed by a question that was beyond her.

'Who are you?' she asked.

'I am Arnaud, the Count of Saint-Germain. Allow me to elaborate.'

'Let me start a little way in, with Pushkin,' Saint-Germain began, licking his fingers then turning the pages of his book. She could see the contents were handwritten with a quill or fountain pen, in a very old-fashioned script that leaned vertiginously to the left. 'This is from Aleksandr's short story *The Queen of Spades* which he wrote in 1834. Three years later the idiot was dead in a duel with his brother-in-law, that vicious French prune d'Anthès. St Petersburg was a rum old place in those days, I can tell you.'

He cleared his throat and began to read.

'"You have heard of Count Saint-Germain, about whom so many marvellous stories are told. You know that he represented himself as the discoverer of the elixir of life, of the Philosopher's Stone, and so forth. Some laughed at him as a charlatan; but Casanova, in his memoirs, says that he was a spy. Be that as it may, Saint-Germain, in spite of the mystery surrounding him, was a very fascinating person, and was much sought after in the best circles of society. Even to this day my grandmother retains an affectionate recollection of him, and becomes quite angry if anyone speaks disrespectfully of him."'

Saint-Germain frowned.

'It's true I appear in Casanova's memoirs, dressed up in the most ridiculous garb. An Armenian cloak and sporting an ivory wand, for God's sake. That was as much a work of fiction as *The Queen of Spades*. I have never claimed knowledge of such nonsense as the Philosopher's Stone, nor would I have offered up card tricks for money, as Aleksandr suggests in the story. Happily Tchaikovsky left me out of the opera he wrote from this little tale. Although to be honest I couldn't have sued, could I? By then I was supposedly fifty years in the grave – I first faked my death in February 1784, rather poorly if I'm honest. It takes a few goes to get the hang of that particular trick.'

'Impressive,' she observed.

'Thank you. Now here's something about my musical abilities. Jemima, Marchioness Grey, was a charming hostess when I lived in London in the 1740s. A great supporter of the songs I contributed to *L'Incostanza Delusa,* a little pastiche of an opera we put on at the Haymarket Theatre for a few months in 1745. Largely, it has to be said, to annoy Handel, who was desperate to drag people into his oratorios at the King's up the road. Infantile, I know, but I was younger then. Jemima writes of an evening recital I gave at a house in Upper Brook Street . . . "His Play indeed is delightful! The violin in his hands has all the softness and sweetness of a flute, and yet all the strength of the loudest strings. His execution is not of that rapid prodigious kind such as that of Veracini and Geminiani; but his style is more easy and harmonious and his excellence is softness. He piques himself you know upon the expression of the passions in his music, especially the tender ones, and both his composition and his manner are almost all *affettuoso*, for his music is entirely fitted to his own way of performing and would be nothing I am convinced from anybody else."'

Teresa Lupo raised her plastic cup and said, 'Praise indeed.'

'Bloody times though. This was the middle of the Jacobite rebellion. When Bonnie Prince Charlie's men got as far as Derbyshire the English did what comes naturally to them in a crisis: arrest the foreigners. Here's that sad old stick Horace Walpole writing to a friend in Florence on 9 December 1745 . . . "We begin to take up people . . . the other day they seized an odd man who goes by the name of Count Saint-Germain. He has been here these two years, and will not tell who he is, or whence, but professes that he does not go by his right name. He sings, plays on the violin wonderfully, composes, is mad, and not very sensible. He is called an Italian, a Spaniard, a Pole; a somebody that married a great fortune in Mexico, and ran away with her jewels to Constantinople; a priest, a fiddler, a vast nobleman. The Prince of Wales has had unsatiated curiosity about him, but in vain. However, nothing has been made out against him; he is released, and, what convinces me he is not a gentleman, stays here, and talks of his being taken up for a spy.”'

Saint-Germain shook his head and took a bite on a ham sandwich left by the crew of the departed *Tintoretto*.

'Was this true?' Teresa asked.

He looked exasperated.

'If you believe in fashionable theories about infinite universes I suppose Walpole's tendentious drivel is bound to be true in one of them, isn't it? But not any I know. When people arrest someone like me as a spy it's decidedly difficult trying to explain things, particularly to the numskulls in the police and security services. So I may have manufactured a few stories, as did they. I have never stolen from commoners, not in the conventional sense of the word. A life like mine makes it easy enough to build a fortune without resorting to larceny. I have always invested sensibly, from the beginning of the railways, to oil, banking, commodities, futures, technology, alternative power. Also I didn't go to Mexico until the liberal constitution of 1812, have never pretended to be Polish – the language is too difficult for a simple soul like me – or a priest for that matter. Saint-Germain is not my real name . . .'

'What is?' she asked.

'I never did know,' he replied, looking at her with eyes clouded by some distant memory. 'It was not what one might term a conventional upbringing. I had a brother. I know that. The family tree ends there. Children were never easy to father. I think that's part of the condition. But enough self-pity. Are these quotations true? Of course. You can buy the books and read them for yourself, along with plenty of others. You might want to track down an obscure work from 1905 by a Scot, Andrew Lang. Published in London by George Smith, a man you may also know as the publisher of the *Pall Mall Gazette*, the favourite newspaper of Sherlock Holmes, and, in real life, as you would think of it, the first employer of the most ill-tempered vegetarian I ever met, George Bernard Shaw. These things are mostly in the public domain now, which is one of the benefits of age.'

The BlackBerry appeared in his hand, and a business card.

'I have scans. I can send you PDFs if you like. Once we're close enough to civilization to get a signal.'

'Email from a three-hundred-year-old man,' Teresa Lupo said, taking the card and handing over hers in return. 'Now there's a thought. What I meant was . . . how *can* this be true?'

He frowned, seemingly puzzled himself, and when he did so Saint-Germain's appealing features seemed clown-like in their obvious frustration.

'I can understand why you'd think I ought to be able to answer that but in all honesty I can't.

Not fully. It's not magic, if that's what you mean. Prick me and I bleed. Shoot me and I die. I've been very careful over the centuries to avoid physical harm. It wasn't always easy.'

'How?' she insisted.

'I was born this way. Do you ask a man with red hair where he got it? My first memory is of the monastic orphanage in Beaumont-de-Lomagne in southern France where we were brought up. Pierre de Fermat came from the same town, which is how I know so much about him. My first language was Occitan, the second French. The monks taught me to follow a very specific regime. No alcohol except wine, red preferably and that in moderation. Only hard cheese, never soft. Water from a known source. Regular exercise, never too violent. I am, I should say, a very fine swimmer, strong and with great resilience.'

He reached into his jacket and pulled out a small antique glass medicine vial with a silver stopper.

'Oh, and this. The monks made it for sale to the locals. They disappeared in one of Napoleon's purges, and their note of the formula with it. My copy is the only one that remains, though a competent chemist could surely reverse-engineer the ingredients from a sample. This is the elixir to which Pushkin and so many others refer, not that I ever flaunted it in their faces. In fact I only ever offered it once to another human being, and that was a beautiful lady called Maria Cerny in Vienna in 1793.' His expression became bleak. 'Not that it made a blind bit of difference.'

'I'm sorry. What is it?'

He shrugged and said, 'Herbs mainly. It tastes rather like a Calabrian bitter, Vecchio Amaro del Capo, but with a different kind of kick. Very similar ingredients too. Hyssop. Ginger. Cascarilla. Quinine. Cochineal, the real thing, from Lanzarote beetles, not a test tube.'

'Calabrian bitter has kept you alive for three centuries?'

'Of course not!' he said quite crossly, only to apologize immediately for his ill temper. 'I'm sorry. I haven't spoken of this with anyone much. Ever, really. Least of all a knowledgeable scientist. Perhaps these things help, but on their own . . . ? I don't know and I've never sought an answer. I take them. I stay alive. Would you stop just to see what happens?'

'I imagine not.'

'The truth is . . .' He wiped his forehead with a hand. There was a bright, strong moon in the night sky now. Whoever this strange man was he looked remarkably handsome under its silver light. 'I didn't understand what was happening until I was in my sixties and people started to notice. Then . . .' His hands opened wide in despair. 'Those same people were no longer there. Until that point, until I saw death begin to cross Maria Cerny's lovely face, I regarded myself as an artist. A composer. A violinist. I painted. I wrote, discourse and poetry and fiction. When I was unable to save Maria, and felt and looked not a day older myself, something changed. Since that day I haven't touched an instrument, written a note, or a word without good reason.'

He shook the little black book at her.

'I read you a few of the interesting parts. There's much more. I was there in Bologna when Galvani thought he might reanimate a frog with static electricity. Go and read Darwin's diaries from the *Beagle* and look for mention of a Frenchman with unusual opinions on what you would now call genetics. In Strasbourg with Pasteur. With Pierre and Marie Curie in *fin-de-siècle* Paris. Watching Fleming work on staphylococci at St Mary's in London.'

'Arnaud . . .'

'You think I'm mad?'

'I think this is . . . improbable.'

He gazed at her for a long time, silent underneath the watchful silver moon. Then he said, 'Doubt and faith are bedfellows, inseparable if only they knew it. I was in those places, Teresa, never under my own name, naturally. I could no longer use it in official circles any more, and I possessed enough money to own a multitude of identities. But I was there. Read their notes. If you can't spot me I'll be very surprised.'

'And then . . . ?'

Nothing that he came to encounter, he said, in universities, laboratories and private institutions spanning the globe, provided a single clue to the strange condition that kept Arnaud, the Count of Saint-Germain, alive.

'After the Second World War, which I spent in Paraguay by the way, ever more desperate for answers, I returned to England again. Cambridge. A beautiful city, my favourite in that cold, nervous country. One day in 1953 I was sitting in the saloon bar of the Eagle pub, with a half-pint of warm bitter and a cheese and pickle sandwich. Francis Crick ran in from the Cavendish Laboratory, looking like a lunatic and bellowing to all and sundry that he and his colleague James Watson had, in his words, "discovered the secret of life'."

Saint-Germain tapped the side of his nose.

'Cambridge is a wonderful city, full of answers for those with the sense to ask the right questions. Whatever birth gave me it includes, as you may now appreciate, a fortuitous sense of timing. You know as well as I what Crick and Watson achieved that morning. They had unlocked the structure of the DNA molecule, the double helix. Our hereditary gene map. The secret code behind every creature, great and small. Where else in the world was I supposed to be at a moment like this?'

'I can't imagine.'

'Not,' Saint-Germain continued, 'that things happened quickly thereafter. So much of the science I needed had yet to be invented. Researchers required money. Biotech companies had first to be invented and then plied with resources. Half of my time was spent seeking answers, the other half applying my several fortunes placing bets on where some new breakthrough might lie. How else do you think I got to know those nice Google lads? Stanford is a wonderful place, full of the brightest and the best. All the same it was forty years before I was able to view my own DNA sample in a way anyone might begin to analyse. And then . . .'

He sighed and poured her a little more prosecco.

'It's different?' she guessed.

'Very. Strictly speaking, I wonder if I'm human at all. Not that the casual bystander, or even pathologist, would notice. It's very subtle indeed. You have to look very hard.'

'I wouldn't worry too much about pathologists, Arnaud.'

'Perhaps not,' he conceded. 'Nevertheless, as I have already said, like the beautiful Camilla Dushku, if she exists, I am a freak. In ways that, try as I might, I cannot begin to comprehend.' He watched her intently. 'This is all beyond me. I was born to be a violinist and a poet. When the true nature of my affliction became apparent I turned to studying mathematics, physics, computational science, medicine, anything that might help me understand what makes me this way. I'm aware that some freak of nature inside my genetic code means that I simply do not age beyond what . . . fifty or sixty? There's nothing sinister or supernatural in this. I am what I am, a genetic oddity, perhaps the result of some recessive disorder, like an albino.' He pointed a slender, tanned finger at her. 'If you accept this, as I've said, you must also realize I cannot be alone. That's impossible. The others . . .' His face grew sombre. 'I thought I met a woman by accident once. There was something in the way she spoke. The way we . . . were. She committed suicide. One understands the temptation after a while.' He shook his head. 'The lack of sleep. Time dragging. Dead lovers . . .'

There was a long, awkward moment of silence, then he resumed.

'My funding of certain biotech companies in the DNA field allowed me to examine my own without bringing it to the notice of others. As to how this sport in the blood works or what triggered the change . . . I'm at a loss. This is hardly surprising. You – and by that I mean the scientific community at large – still disagree about why human beings age in the first place. There are so many competing theories . . . telomere, somatic mutation, free radicals, mitohormesis, entropy . . . where does one ignorant and very old man begin testing what little he knows against any of them?'

'You need a team, Arnaud.'

'I need a team,' he agreed then added hopefully, 'So you do believe me?'

'I don't disbelieve you,' Teresa Lupo said carefully after a long moment of thought. She glanced at the jetty where the *Tintoretto* had docked a few hours before. 'That team was meant to be us?'

'Meant to be. Where else was I likely to find so many distinguished scientists with knowledge of DNA and medicine and basic physiology? More fool me. I didn't see the religious connection, any more than you. I thought if I lurked on the side-lines, met the right people. I'm desperate. I can't . . .' His eyes grew glassy. 'My head won't hold any more. It's fit to burst already. Every answer begets a million new questions. It's impossible.' He stared at his feet, miserable again. 'So I bribed my way into Ca' Foscari to take a look at these men, my saviours, and my heart fell. If only I'd understood how dreadfully mundane they'd be. Such closed minds. Such a lack of basic curiosity. They'd probably want to dissect me and put the cadaver in a glass jar for an exhibition somewhere.'

'That's a little harsh,' she suggested.

'Is it?'

He took out the silver-topped flask. Then he removed a packet of tissues from his jacket, spat into one, and placed it inside the plastic cup. Saint-Germain's dark, unfathomable eyes gazed at her as he held out both the elixir and the evidence of his DNA.

'You were the exception,' he said. 'I've only ever offered this potion to one other human being. She was a woman I loved. It was a freezing January night in Vienna and what I gave her was as worthless as the talcum-powder remedies those plague-doctor quacks sold to the poor souls who lie beneath our feet.' He shook the paper cup. 'Not now. Not with this. It may take years to see the difference between your DNA and mine. You need to start work. Find the right people. They exist. Here . . .'

Dr Teresa Lupo didn't move.

'Imagine . . .' He looked around them. 'No more death, except by accident or design. No growing old, growing feeble, in the body, in the head too.'

She was silent. He placed the cup and the flask beside her on the grass of Poveglia and grasped her hands in his.

'A life that lasts forever,' he added.

He had long, strong fingers, without the hard pads they would once have possessed thanks to the unforgiving strings of a violin.

'Would that still count as a life?' she asked.

'Of course . . .'

He struggled for something else to say. She hesitated, surprised by her own reluctance, yet, with only a moment's thought, certain of its source.

His mouth hung a little open. She could see perfect white teeth, all real, she felt sure. There seemed nothing flawed about him whatsoever.

She felt trapped by the sharp sparkle in his eyes, and wondered whether he might reach forward at that moment and kiss her, and what she would do if that occurred.

'Are you saying your answer's no?' he asked, bewildered.

'I'm not quite sure, Arnaud . . . I thought I had

unfinished business myself. Perhaps more pressing.'

'*Victor Carpathius Fingebat*,' he said.

She felt cold, frightened after a fashion. It was that old sensation, the one her mother always said was someone treading on your grave.

'I beg your pardon.'

'The imperfect, the incomplete tense,' he said. 'The state we all live in, without knowing. Die in too.'

'I've heard that somewhere before, I'm sure.'

'You'll hear it again if we're to get anywhere with this. It seems to me . . .'

Saint-Germain stopped. Something had crossed his face. A sharp stab of physical pain.

'Had a twinge,' the count confessed. 'I'd quite forgotten what one of those felt like.' He breathed deeply, rhythmically, for a few seconds then smiled the way some men did when wishing to hide a sudden discomfort. 'It's interesting in a way. I'm sorry. I've been dreadfully rude. This entire spectacle on Poveglia . . .' He stood up, rather shakily. 'Engineered by Alberto Tosi. I seem to have taken advantage of his outrageous deceit. This is just as bad, if not worse, though I wouldn't have wished it otherwise.'

He closed his eyes and she thought he winced.

'You must excuse me. I've been thinking of this moment for a very long time. It didn't quite turn out as planned. I need a minute or two on my own.'

Saint-Germain retrieved his hat from the ground, placed it on his head, then turned to her and said, 'I forget sometimes. Time for me is never in short supply. For you on the other hand . . .'

Teresa waited, unsure whether he lacked the words or the breath to utter them.

'I fear the opposite may be the case.'

'Why?' she asked.

'Because we're both searching for the opposite sides of the same coin. And you are looking for mine, while I see nothing but yours.'

'You're too cryptic, Arnaud. Are you all right?'

He sat down again and he seemed pale.

'Yes. Listen to me, Teresa, please. If I'm cryptic it's because I have my reasons. Whatever you feel, I'm no nearer the source of the mystery than you. Why else do I send you these stories? To make you do what I cannot: think and then act. What we seek here is the trigger, the catalyst. If we're to find that I require from you the specific, the balanced and sane. What you need of me is the general, the irrational, impossible, the foolish even, or at least foolish in your eyes. Do I make myself even a little bit clear?

She could think of nothing to say.

'No,' Saint-Germain murmured. 'I'm sorry.'

He got up again, took off his hat, scratched his head for a moment, then said, 'Here's an idea. What if the trigger is something particular? An event, say. What if, as an infant, I was left out in the sun when there was an astronomical occurrence, the falling to earth of a meteorite, one of those alignments of the stars and planets they call a syzygy?'

'Unprovable, surely? Unless you know the date of your birth.'

He broke into a brief and wan smile then said, 'There goes the scientist in you again. Though I should point out you sound more like a fortune-teller. They need those dates, don't they? In order to know your star. As to the scientist, you need to gag that child and leave her in the corner for a while. Sometimes she talks out of turn. Oh . . .'

He flapped his arms about himself in exasperation.

'Why am I wasting your time like this? I need a lie-down.'

The idea of losing him alarmed her.

'Don't go, Arnaud!' Teresa cried. 'Please.'

'What use am I? Really . . .'

Some, surely. There was a picture in her head, an image, invented or perhaps a memory. Of sitting in front of a computer in a dilapidated apartment on the Zattere waterfront, feeling the building rumble as a cruise ship edged along the canal outside, searching desperately for answers to questions she had yet to formulate with any great conviction.

'That bird in its glass case, looking down at you, has as much of a grasp of the matter as either of us at this moment,' Saint-Germain said somewhat severely.

'So you can read minds now?' she shot back at him. 'Then what am I thinking?'

He hesitated for a while, leaning on his stick, looked down at the ground and said, 'You're wondering why this should happen now, of all times. The other you, I mean. Not the one here, in this form of the present.'

'I . . .'

'Silence, please. You're asking yourself whether the trigger might not lie in something so obvious, so large, so visible, so close that it has quite passed you by because you are looking in all the wrong places. As a scientist you're accustomed to hunting for answers where you most expect to find them. Among microscopic detail. In the detritus, the debris that remains once your neat and tidy experiments are done.'

'That's just common sense,' she complained. 'Where else would I look?'

'Then what you require is uncommon sense,' he said. 'What if the trigger were something so simple and everyday it seemed invisible? A habit? A ritual? A recurring date in the calendar?'

'Like Christmas?' she suggested.

He stared at her.

'Like carnival,' Teresa said.

'Possibly. Or a place perhaps. The city itself. The stones of Venice are remarkable. Never forget those. They're your world now. They enclose everything that matters. Including your answers.'

'Such stones,' she murmured.

'Meaning what?'

'Meaning every time I walk somewhere in this

328

city I find myself lost! Every promising *calle* leads to a dead end and black water.'

'In that case it's not a *calle*,' he pointed out. 'Now is it?'

'Pedantry . . .'

'Not at all. Words have specific meanings. We should take heed of them. The Venetians inhabit an odd world, I'll admit. But it's there for the learning. If a child can navigate these stones then so can a foreigner. I learned, though I'll admit it took a while.'

Arnaud, the Count of Saint-Germain, nodded, as if agreeing with himself, then shambled off along the path to the vineyard without another word.

THE HOUSE OF SPIRITS

There was an invitation there, one that could not be refused. Teresa began searching for some of the more obvious references from the manuscript. Pushkin's tale. The opera *L'Incostanza Delusa*. The quotation from the memoirs of the English politician Horace Walpole. The reference to a history, readily available on the web, by an obscure Scottish journalist called Andrew Lang.

In a very short space of time she was able to ascertain that every last mention of the Count of Saint-Germain cited in the text was true. Or, more correctly, accurate, in the sense that each existed and could be used by anyone pretending to be the mythical figure.

There was more. Recent books and articles that talked of Saint-Germain appearing throughout the twentieth century. Even a strange memoir from a member of the Theosophists that referred to him as 'one of the hidden immortals who manipulate history'.

'Tripe,' Teresa muttered, and was briefly amused by how the peculiar vocabulary of Jason Cunningham had affected her.

The stories she was being sent were obscure and cryptic. They had a specific purpose nevertheless and, it was becoming clear, an arcane kind of meaning. They now told her that whoever wrote them knew not just Sofia and her close circle of neighbours and their friends in Venice, but the very apartment where Teresa now sat. That the author appeared to be aware of her progress, or lack of it, in finding her aunt. The latest instalment also seemed to hint that she ought to feel some kind of urgency in her quest.

And there was even, surely, a direct nugget of hard information. A hint to an answer in the riddle. A *clue*.

She reread the pages quickly and found the section she wanted, repeating the words, 'Cambridge is a wonderful city, full of answers for those with the sense to ask the right questions.'

Jerome Aitchison came from Cambridge though his speciality, unlike that of the famous Crick and Watson, lay in unravelling the secrets of death, not life.

She retrieved the police ID badge from her bag to remind herself of the number in case it were needed. There were rules about impersonating officers, though she was unclear whether that applied to her. She'd resigned her post the night before. The wheels within the administration moved painfully slowly. It would take days at least before she was formally removed from her position.

Teresa Lupo experienced a brief moment of self-realization. This was the old her, trying to rationalize everything, to find a reason to act, to believe, to feel. Arnaud – she had begun to think of him this way – had firm views on that.

'You're gone,' she murmured, reaching for her Questura card.

She retrieved the number for the police in Cambridge from the web and, using her Rome police ID, finally got through the switch-board to a duty detective inspector, a gruff though not unfriendly man called Postlethwaite.

'How's your weather?' the English officer asked.

'Cold. Freezing cold.' Why did the English always want to talk about the weather? 'I'm calling about Jerome Aitchison. The lecturer who died here in Venice at the weekend.'

'Cold here too. I thought you said you were from Rome?'

'On attachment.'

'Dreadful story,' the man said. 'Glad he's your customer, not ours.'

'Thank you. The student who complained that Aitchison had assaulted her. She was called . . . Ursula something.'

'You speak very good English,' Postlethwaite complimented her. 'That's a funny name. Ursula something. Why do you want to know?'

'There are loose ends, Inspector.'

'Usually are, don't you think? What's it matter? Poor bloke's dead.'

Teresa took a deep breath and thought: they're the same everywhere.

'This poor bloke tried to shoot dead a young woman here. In front of several thousand people. I would like to know why.'

'Does it matter? Honestly and truthfully?'

'Honestly and truthfully, yes. There may be other issues.'

'I find that hard to believe,' he said.

'Why? The student, Ursula . . .'

She could hear the clack of keys on a computer.

'That wasn't her name,' the man said. 'She was called Imogen Hardwick. I spoke to her myself and if that idiot Aitchison hadn't shot off to Venice like a scalded cat none of this would have gone anywhere. I didn't like that young woman one little bit. Jumped up little madam with a very high opinion of herself. Seemed to me she was angling for something from the college. Happens from time to time.'

Teresa tried to understand what he was saying. This was yet another inaccuracy in the stories she'd been receiving from the man pretending to be the Count of Saint-Germain. Was it possible they were all simple mistakes? Or was there something deliberate here? A thread for her to untangle, unwind, then follow to its conclusion?

'Aitchison did assault this girl, didn't he?' she asked.

'Her word against his. It was a very minor offence if anything. I mean, would some Italian get arrested for patting a lady's bottom in Rome?'

'If I saw it the ignorant bastard would be in a

cell in five seconds flat. Do you know Italy, Inspector? Has anyone updated your national stereotypes of late?'

'I'm sure someone at headquarters is putting together just such a course as we speak. To be frank this whole business was so flimsy I wasn't even sure it was worth sending a file to the prosecutors and letting them decide whether to take him to court. I put the fear of God up Aitchison a bit, I suppose. Not that much. He was an odd sort. Miserable. Confused. Not a ladies' man at all, though that can work both ways, of course. As far as I can work out he was a little smitten by this Hardwick girl and just got spooked by what she was putting around. So he upped and legged it without a word to a soul. Ridiculous really. No one at the college, on the staff that is, believed her. Next thing he's in Venice wearing some bloody stupid costume and shooting at a starlet no one's ever heard of. Then topping himself. So perhaps Imogen Hardwick was right, and it was me who got taken in all along.'

There was a pause.

'What other crimes?' he asked.

'I didn't say there were other crimes. Other issues. It may be nothing.'

'Well, my impression was that Jerome Aitchison was the sort of pain in the arse who'd find a five-pence coin in the street and take it round the police station and hand it in as lost property. As honest as they come.'

'You're sure he wasn't a ladies' man?'

'As sure as I can be. Not a confirmed bachelor, if you get my drift.'

'My English fails at a certain level of subtlety, I'm afraid.'

'Gay. He wasn't gay. Or so people said. Just very awkward and shy around women. Never had a girlfriend. Or many friends at all.'

She thought of the starlet Luisa Cammarota floating over the piazza in her snow-white angel's gown, and the blood on her feathers.

'Not a fan of celebrities?' Teresa asked. 'This girl he shot. She was a TV star, an actress. There could have been a secret obsession with women he saw in the papers.'

She could hear the English police officer sigh down the line.

'Jerome Aitchison was a meek little Cambridge lecturer who lived in a tiny college room full of obscure books so boring any sane human being would want to fall asleep the moment you set eyes on them. His idea of light reading was the *Financial Times* and I don't think you find many starlets in there. Wouldn't say boo to a goose. Probably wound up blushing if a woman so much as asked him the time. At least that's what I was told. Fits with how the man looked to me.'

She blinked and said, 'You're sure?'

'As sure I can be. Listen. This is a university town. You get to know these college bachelors after a while. They live in college rooms. Rarely have any friends outside. They're a type. We never have any trouble from them. More the other way round. People making trouble for *them*. Like that Hardwick girl.'

'You must have a photograph of him,' Teresa said.

'Why must I? He wasn't even charged.'

'The college . . .'

'Ask them. Not me. Good luck. He's an unperson now. They went cold on the poor bastard the moment that girl started making her accusations. After what happened at the weekend he's gone for good. I checked their website on Monday out of interest. These academics . . . they don't hang around. It's all about reputation and ego, isn't it?'

'What do you mean?'

He laughed, as if he couldn't quite believe what he was about to say.

'Come Monday morning Jerome Aitchison had completely disappeared from that college even though he'd spent most of his adult life, student and lecturer, there. His name was gone, his entry in the department, his photograph . . . everything.'

'There must be a picture somewhere,' she pointed out.

'I imagine there must. If you come up to Cambridge I'd be happy to point you in the direction of some people who might have one. But right now I'm really rather busy, and this case is so very closed for us. Honestly, I don't wish to be rude . . .'

Nor was he, she thought as the policeman in Cambridge said goodbye. And perhaps Detective Inspector Postlethwaite had proved rather more helpful than he realized.

It was Silvio Di Capua who first taught her how to recover information that had supposedly been removed from the web. There were so many ways if you knew them . . . search-engine caches being among the most popular. She'd tried that with Jerome Aitchison already and got nothing more than the same brief dreary mentions she'd found in a normal inquiry: references to academic documents and some lectures the man had given at a few specialist actuarial conferences around the world. Not a photo anywhere.

There was one more place to look though: the Wayback Machine. According to Silvio some non-profit organization in the US had taken to archiving the web, sometimes in a fairly haphazard fashion, site by site, year by year.

She found the archive, typed in the college address, and got a list of the most recent versions of the website. Slowly, patiently, she worked her way through the different iterations until she found the faculty page.

Aitchison's name was there. The photo was missing. She wanted to scream. The archive did this sometimes. Text was deemed more worthy of storage than a simple mug shot.

The next hour she spent wading through every

version of the college site right back to the very first, which was launched in 1994. Each one listed Aitchison on the faculty. In every case the photo was nothing more than a blank box with the missing graphic symbol.

'Damn,' she yelled, and banged the table.

If only the words hadn't disappeared from the mustard-yellow paper. If only she remembered more.

The building trembled. One more liner meandered past the window, distant figures staring out from the porthole windows on the side. Another reminder of a physical world beyond this strange, dilapidated room, Sofia's last home before she vanished into the black Venetian night.

In *Carpaccio's Dog* Aitchison had mentioned another painting, one that was surely from real life, just as much as the canvas of St Augustine. The depiction of a politician, a pioneer of the science of actuary, who had been slaughtered in a random act of rebellious violence.

Early in that very first lost story Aitchison had remembered walking into another gallery and being shocked by this canvas, perhaps as a portent of something terrible to come later, in Venice.

It happened at a convention. She typed Aitchison's name and a few keywords into the archived websites.

Amsterdam.

He'd been there as part of an academic conference two years before. She remembered that part of the story quite clearly now.

Teresa Lupo's stubby, anxious fingers sped across the keys of her cheap little computer, searching, trying combinations of words and places and names.

It took another twenty minutes. Then she found it. A photo of the guests at a dinner in the Mövenpick Hotel, not far from Centraal Station, part of a report of an actuarial conference in an industry newsletter. It was the kind of formal academic event she had to attend herself from time to time, one that gave her the shivers. Dinner jackets and evening dresses. Floral arrangements and presentations.

The caption beneath was part of the photograph, an image, not text. This was why the search engines had missed Aitchison's name even though it was spelled out clearly among the others, all, the story said, leading experts on actuarial study from around the world. The Englishman was third from the left, a round-faced stocky individual smiling in a childlike, embarrassed fashion, sand-wiched between two rather elegant women in cocktail dresses.

He looks happy enough, she thought, if a little uncomfortable in female company, the way some academic bachelors are. Just as the English police inspector had said.

Teresa walked across the room and got the copy of *Il Gazzettino* she'd kept from Monday. She checked the picture of the passport photo she'd found on the corpse on the pavement close to

339

Florian. Then she looked at Jerome Aitchison, smiling for the camera in Amsterdam just two years before.

The man in the paper seemed a good deal younger, with a narrower face, more hair, different, hooded eyes. The owner of the lodgings where Aitchison had stayed had closed the place and left for Kenya on holiday around the time he'd disappeared. It was entirely possible that no one in Venice had identified the body of this solitary and mysterious man. Nor, according to the paper, had any relative from England. Perhaps all they were relying upon was the passport found beneath his cloak.

Paola Boscolo had an email address on her business card. Teresa sent her the document from the web and, from the newspaper website, a copy of the passport photo.

Alongside them she wrote a short message.

Dear Paola,
This is the real Jerome Aitchison, taken under the circumstances explained in the article. If you place this picture next to the passport photograph you have from Sunday you will, I think, come to the clear conclusion that the man who fell to his death in the Piazza San Marco is someone else entirely. The real Aitchison is, I believe, alive and probably in Venice still. I am now, more than ever, convinced that he is holding my aunt Sofia here against her will.

I have a suggestion regarding the individual you thought was Aitchison. It's been apparent to me since I saw him on the campanile that, while he may have felt he was supposed to harm Miss Cammarota in the first instance, he was unable to do so with any great conviction when push came to shove, as it were.

My hunch is that he was under some kind of pressure to put on this sinister performance and, perhaps out of fear or a simple sense of decency, buckled in regard to the young woman's death at the last moment. Whatever this pressure was, it resulted in his suicide, as we all saw.

If you check, your Questura lawyer will confirm that this makes the party responsible for any such pressure guilty of manslaughter at the very least and just possibly, depending on the circumstances, simple old-fashioned murder.

I leave this information in your hands since doubtless it will take the Questura a day or two to digest it in these oh-so-busy times. When I have more news I shall, my own pressure of work permitting, pass it on to you.

Oh, and on a purely practical matter I feel I should point out that manslaughter and murder do, in all parts of Italy under the jurisdiction of the Polizia di Stato, Venice included, count as more serious crimes than pickpocketing, fleecing tourists and being drunk in charge of a stupid mask.

I trust this helps.
Teresa Lupo.

She read the message again before she sent it, trying to remember if she had ever in her life used the word 'hunch' in any context whatsoever. As a formal police document it was a fraud. She had no reason to believe Aitchison was holding Sofia. The ideas about the motive of the man who fell to his death dressed as the Plague Doctor were imaginative in the extreme.

All this was deeply out of character, she thought, hitting the send key, hoping that Arnaud, the Count of Saint-Germain, if he existed, would approve.

She estimated that the young policewoman would read it immediately, take a deep breath, curse her impudence, file the message for later consideration, and, just possibly, make some brief inquiries of her own before knocking off for the day. The two pictures were dissimilar. But passport photos could be old and unrepresentative. It was obvious to Teresa that these were not of the same man, and a fairly rapid forensic examination could establish this beyond doubt. But an overworked police officer tended to see what he or she hoped for, and was never in a rush to involve another department.

Falcone would grasp a curious anomaly like this in a shot. She wondered what he and Peroni and Nic were up to in Sicily. Whether their trip had proved successful. How soon she'd see them – something that she would look forward to with the greatest pleasure once the present task was out of the way.

There was another line to follow, one that had occurred to her hours before, when she spoke to her mother. She called Alberto Tosi and politely listened to his fulsome greeting and incessant apologies.

'Any news?' he asked finally.

'A little,' she said. 'But not for the phone.'

'Coffee then?' Tosi asked, full of excitement. 'Or dinner. It will take your mind off things.'

'That's very kind, but not tonight,' she said straight out. 'I have two favours to ask.'

'The first?'

'I want you to get me into that big hospital near Zanipolo. The one where Sofia was treated sixteen years ago. I need to talk to an administrator—'

'They won't show you her medical records,' he said quickly. 'Not even with me there. Privacy. Privilege. You know the score.'

'I don't need her medical records. Bear with me.'

'I will *always* bear with my dearest Roman friend and colleague!'

His constant politeness and enthusiasm were so old-fashioned, and called up the very picture of him, erect and alert in a smart, ancient suit. She had, she realized, become exceptionally fond of Alberto Tosi over the last few days.

'You're so kind,' she told him.

343

'Nonsense. You're a visitor and my guest in Venice, in a way. And the second?'

She hesitated.

'The second, I forget,' she said.

'That's not like you.'

'No. Perhaps not. Will you call me back? We could go to the hospital this afternoon if you like.'

'Let me see what I can do,' he promised, and rang off.

Teresa Lupo still couldn't quite believe the request she had so nearly put to this decent, honourable, law-abiding old man, though she understood only too well what had prompted the thought. It was the recurrent image of the archer in that last canvas in the Ursula cycle, face turned away from the viewer, body taut and stretched, ready for the kill.

There was danger here somewhere. What she had so very nearly said to Alberto Tosi was that it might be better for everyone concerned if, from now on, she carried a gun.

'I must be going mad,' she murmured.

As Sofia did. Sixteen years ago. And perhaps more recently.

Half an hour later Tosi called back, full of good cheer and enthusiasm. They had an interview at four thirty.

She knew this place from the assignment a few years before when Leo Falcone was shot and badly wounded in Murano. The main Venice hospital was, like so much else in the city, unique, a compromise between ancient and modern, the practical and the spiritual. On the waterfront side, facing – unfortunately, it always seemed to her – the graveyard island of San Michele, it was a sprawling line of buildings, some recent, some centuries old, a ragtag collection of linked wards, clinics and theatres so labyrinthine a newcomer would require a map to navigate them. Ambulance boats came and went from an emergency stop on the canal next to the main building. The sick and the recovering who could transport themselves emerged from doors near the Ospedale vaporetto stop and were taken, some hobbling on crutches or hunched in wheelchairs, to the boats that ran round the island.

The canal was the way she always came. Tosi knew another, guiding her from the San Zaccaria vaporetto stop near San Marco through the dark, winding lanes and alleys of Castello, so purposefully and with such a knowledge of every turn and diversion that she was soon hopelessly lost, and clueless about the direction in which they were headed.

Then they passed one more fashionable shop of carnival costumes and masks and emerged into the light again in a broad open space she recognized. They were next to the old-fashioned *pasticceria* of Rosa Salva, opposite the great church of Giovanni e Paolo, Zanipolo to the locals, with its vast, cold interior full of dead doges and sundry nobles.

Adjoining the imposing basilica was another smaller façade, a contrast to the classical brick of Zanipolo since it was of white marble as ornate and Byzantine in appearance as the front of the supposed resting place of St Mark himself. A sign by the door revealed it to be the Scuola Grande di San Marco, a larger, more affluent version of the same kind of charitable fellowship that was the abode of Carpaccio's dog.

Tosi walked briskly through the front door. Teresa followed and found herself surrounded by the sounds and smells of a modern hospital, soap and disinfectant, low, querulous voices, the ringing of telephones.

'I taught here for years,' Tosi declared. 'The police may have short memories but the medical profession . . .'

In the space of fifteen minutes they found themselves in the office of a friendly female administrator who kissed Tosi on both cheeks and listened carefully and with great patience to his fulsome introduction of 'the famed professor from Rome' before he handed over to Teresa to outline her problem.

The woman let her finish then sighed and said, 'As a doctor you must appreciate the issue of confidentiality. That and the fact we are talking about records from a long time ago. An attempted suicide, a termination elsewhere, a patient who left the city shortly after and was never treated again . . . Would you keep such records in Rome?'

'Probably not,' Teresa admitted. 'I'm not asking for anything other than practical information. An address. Any details of friends or relatives that may have been left as contacts.'

'She was your aunt. Did you not have an address yourself?'

Teresa took a deep breath and said, 'I didn't know any of this was happening. My mother had lost touch with Sofia when she came here. The first she heard was when she was called to the hospital.'

Tosi seemed puzzled.

'Sofia must have had an address in the city, surely. Your mother would have fetched clothes for her. Dealt with the mail.'

'No,' Teresa insisted. 'She said that Sofia was in such a state she wouldn't talk about what had happened in Venice. When she was well enough she came back to Rome. After that, when she was better, she went her own way.'

The administrator shook her head and said, 'This is very strange.'

'I couldn't agree more.' Teresa heard the desperation in her own voice when she added, 'Can you help me?'

'I'll ask for some coffee and see what records we have,' the woman said.

They waited for the best part of an hour, staring out of the window at the vaporetti, the ambulance launches and the white, still outline of San Michele and its hidden cemetery across the narrow stretch of water. The afternoon turned to a beautiful, soft, pale dusk. Then a gentle darkness seemed to fall from the sky and night swiftly descended on the lagoon.

To pass the time Teresa asked Tosi to tell her more about the First International Symposium on the Genetic Analysis of the Skeletal Remains Attributed to St Mark. She had to admit it sounded an interesting prospect, an adventure almost, one that attempted to unravel the truth of a mystery that went back two millennia.

'Which way do you think you'll vote?' she asked, recalling the fictional conversation with Arnaud in the story that had appeared earlier that day.

'Whichever way the evidence suggests,' he answered immediately.

'For or against?'

'One of the two,' he answered, a little puzzled.

'Unless there's a third possibility.'

Alberto Tosi stared at her. He looked baffled.

'What third possibility? Either it's Mark himself. The apostle. Cousin of Barnabas, if I recall correctly. Didn't he bring a jug of water to the Last Supper?'

She laughed.

'Why ask me, Alberto?'

'Because you posed a very odd question. It's Mark, or at the very least the body of a man of Mark's origins, antiquity, race perhaps. Or it's someone else. A stranger. Some skeletal cuckoo in the nest, an impostor revealed through his DNA.'

He stared at her and added, 'Unless you have another suggestion?'

'No,' she answered, though she felt she was supposed to know one.

When the woman finally returned she had a blue folder containing a single sheet of paper.

'We do still have some records,' she announced. 'I can't show you them. As I've already said that would be improper, though I can tell you they reveal nothing you don't know already. Miss Bianchi suffered complications after a termination. She'd also taken an overdose of barbiturates and was very distressed on both counts. She was here for a week, no more. Then we discharged her into the care of her sister. These are the only address and contact details we hold.'

She passed across the single sheet. It contained the family's old address in Rome, before the move to Frascati, and the number there. Next to it was an address in Venice, marked as Sofia's home. Like so many Venetian house names it was simply a *sestiere*, Castello, and a number.

'What's wrong with street names?' Teresa asked, once again in despair at the opaque way Venetians wrote their addresses.

Tosi peered over her shoulder, glanced at the woman and said, 'Celestia, surely?'

She nodded, played with the computer in front of her. It came up with a map and a circle over a single building, seemingly set on its own by the waterfront close to the Arsenale, jutting out into the lagoon.

Alberto Tosi was staring at the screen, his kindly face frozen in a stern expression, one of disgust, of fear even.

'Are you absolutely sure?' he asked.

'That's the address we have. One stop away,' the administrator said. 'I hope that's—'

'Thank you,' Teresa said, and nearly dragged Tosi out of the building, down to the vaporetto.

It was a short ride on one of the faster small boats. Tosi sat in the front, uncharacteristically silent, staring at the floor. Opposite them five cheery workmen played cards across the seats in the bows, laughing and telling jokes. A cloud of beer fumes hung around them.

'What's wrong?' Teresa asked.

'Nothing,' he said. 'Nothing.'

'Alberto. I think we know each other well enough now. Please. Tell me.'

He took off his hat and placed it on his lap then shook his grey head.

'Sofia can't have given them this address,' Tosi said. 'No one lives there. No one would dare.'

'You know it?'

He peered at her. There was, when she was this close to him, a terrible sense of resignation, of sadness, in the man, she thought. He'd expected to be the Venice pathologist till he died. The modern world had ejected him from that post: one, she felt sure, he was quite capable of performing. He was a widower, lonely, lost, in need of something to fill the day. She had provided that, and been grateful for his assistance in return.

But now, in the bows of the little vaporetto as it rode the choppy lagoon swell, she saw another side to him: the man who emerged when the day was empty, and there was no one to help or amuse, no academic institution to entertain, no quest, no sense of adventure.

He was a child at heart, she realized, and like a child both easily bored and, perhaps, frightened too.

The boat was coming to dock at a tiny jetty marked Celestia. No one else got up to leave. No one stood on the gangplank waiting to board. This was a stop in the middle of nowhere, some back alley on the ragged, half-derelict north-eastern strip of Venice that attracted no tourists, and not many locals either.

'I was a Castello brat,' the old man said eventually. 'We had a house off the Via Garibaldi where the Arsenale workers used to live once upon a time. Those years after the war when I was a child . . . they were a magical time for me. We used to roam among the ruins, day and night, scavenging for wild chicory, fishing in the canals. Everyone was starving for a while. There wasn't anywhere you wouldn't look, not if it meant you could bring home something to eat.'

The boat banged hard against the jetty, jolting them as they climbed to their feet. He took her arm and said, 'Come. Let me show you something.'

* * *

This was the first night she'd noticed much in the way of cloud. A dull grey circle above them marked the presence of the moon but did little to illuminate this lonely backwater. Beyond the light of the jetty Castello looked pitch black. Most of the waterfront buildings hereabouts seemed to consist of deserted, abandoned warehouses and industrial units. One solitary figure got up as they left, as if remembering something, joining them when they disembarked, scuttering off down an alley towards what looked like a residential street with a few shops a couple of hundred metres away at its foot. Something ran close to the disappearing stranger's legs. A dog, surely.

Tosi turned left into the pool of darkness along the waterfront and casually pulled a torch out of one of the deep pockets of his winter coat, flicking it on as they walked.

'No one lives here,' he said.

'Sixteen years ago . . .'

'No one lived here then.'

They walked for a few minutes without seeing another soul. Then he stopped by the side of what looked like a small abandoned mansion, once grand with Palladian columns at the front, now crumbling and stitched together with scaffolding and timber. Tosi was running the beam of the torch up and down a patch of the front wall as if searching for something.

'I used to come here fishing. Just little ones mainly, lots of bones, hardly any flesh. Nothing tasted too good. The lagoon was dirtier then. But we were hungry. Even the city pathologist – did I mention my father held this position before me? – didn't find it easy to put food on the table after the war.'

Teresa stood next to him watching the flickering, moving torch beam.

'I can imagine,' she said.

'No you can't.'

He stopped and looked at her.

'This city is full of strange stories. You think you know that, but you don't. Some of them are so strange we're reluctant to share them with foreigners.'

She felt like laughing, but refrained. This mood of his was new to her, and she understood he would be offended.

'Alberto,' Teresa said lightly. 'Once we've found Sofia – and we will – you want me to help verify the bones of an apostle who's supposed to be lying in a crypt not far from here. A man from north Africa, a friend of Jesus. Here in some cold tomb in Venice. I'm not unused to your peculiarities, honestly.'

He looked briefly amused.

'I wasn't talking for one moment about *him*. No, the real oddities are much smaller. Much more personal. Like this one . . .'

The torch moved to a part of the wall next to a lined column by the door. She looked and saw what appeared to be a figure scratched there in the white Istrian stone. A childlike scrawl, etched deep into the marble, stained with soot and dirt. It appeared to portray the upper torso of a man wearing a large and tall turban. In his right hand he held what looked like . . .

She leaned in closer to look and felt a sudden start as the scrawl became clearer.

It was a heart, visibly spouting blood, small fountains of it, as if freshly released.

'I remember the day I heard this story,' Tosi announced. 'I can't have been more than ten years old. One of the older boys, a little tyke with bony fists and a vivid imagination, took great delight in telling me. A long time ago there was a man who lived nearby, half-Venetian, half-Turk. A madman. Violent and insane. His mother cared for him, kept him out of trouble as much as she could. Then one day, for no good reason but rage, he murdered her. *Butchered* her. Ran along the waterfront here afterwards, screaming, crying, holding the heart he'd just ripped from her body.'

Teresa examined the wall more closely. The scratched figure there must have been centuries old.

'When he got here, in front of what was then a local *scuola*, he stumbled. Or God tripped him. You choose.' Tosi took a deep breath and she could hear his old lungs wheezing. 'The heart fell out of his hand, rolled along the ground and then . . .' He paused for a moment. 'Then it spoke. In his mother's voice. The heart said, "Poor son! Poor boy! Have you hurt yourself? Have you scraped your knee again? Come here. Mamma will make it better. Come to me. Come to me, son . . .'"

Tosi took a few steps to the edge of the pavement by the dark churning waters of the lagoon.

'He threw himself in, clutching the heart, and drowned immediately. All of this was witnessed by a mason who'd been working here. Immediately after he scratched this image in the wall to record what had occurred. This was the early eighteenth century, I believe. The young man wore a turban because of his Turkish lineage. A terrible story.'

'Terrible,' Teresa agreed. 'We've lots of ghost stories like it in Rome. The Italians are a superstitious bunch.'

'I'm Venetian, not Italian. We all believed this place was haunted. Being children, that meant we'd come here, of course. We'd walk up to the house over the water where they'd lived – it was abandoned, had been for years – and try to peek through the windows, rattle the door.'

He flicked the torch further along the *calle* then out over the lagoon. She saw something emerge out of the darkness. It was a low, narrow ramshackle bridge. As the beam moved further she began to make out the shape of a building in darkness at the end. It looked like a small palazzo or an abandoned chapel, set on a platform above the water, a solitary place. Beyond, across a narrow *rio*, stood the castellated exterior wall of the deserted Arsenale dockyards.

'That was the house,' Tosi told her.

'I need to see,' Teresa said. 'Sofia lived here.'

'No!' Tosi said, almost shouted. 'She didn't! That's not possible.'

'How can you be so sure?'

'They call it the Casino degli Spiriti.'

'I don't believe in spirits. And even if I did, I doubt they'd need a house. What happened here . . . the mad Turk, the mother . . . even if it was true, as you said yourself, it was ages ago.'

'You didn't let me finish my story,' he said, staring balefully at her.

She folded her arms and waited, watching her breath turn to mist in the bitter air.

From somewhere over the lagoon a solitary gull began to caw into the night. It made a lonely, desolate noise.

'We would come here as children. The fishing was always good for some reason. No adults bothered us. The locals . . . this part of Castello. They're all superstitious. They said they heard voices from that place. Saw ghosts, the mother walking along, holding her own heart, crying for her son.'

'But they didn't,' she told him. 'Did they?'

Tosi looked cross for a moment.

'Do you never have doubts?' he asked. 'Does the fact our profession shows us the very stuff of which men and women are made . . . does that blind us to the obvious sometimes? To things that others can see?'

'No,' she said immediately. Then thought for a moment, and added, 'Or rather I mean . . . I don't think so.'

He smiled and said, 'The answer you're looking for, then, is yes. You do.'

'You have me there,' she admitted.

'When I was eleven years old,' Tosi continued, 'I came here alone and began to fish just there.' He pointed to the dilapidated narrow bridge. 'It was always the best place for some reason. The fish seemed to like it and they were always . . .' He took a pained breath. '*Fat* fish. That day I caught a squid, the biggest I'd ever taken. The sight of it . . .'

He stopped.

'What?' she asked.

'It had the eyes of a woman. Not a squid at all. I was young. I didn't understand. I thought I'd made some extraordinary discovery. So I ran all the way to the fish stall in the Via Garibaldi, to show it to the man there. He was a good fellow. He loved us little rascals. He didn't even look at what I gave him, just took it. I'll never forget the expression on his face when he saw what it was. He screamed and crossed himself and threw the thing on the ground, cursing me as a fool, yelling at me.'

'Some genetic mutation . . .' she suggested.

'That's what we'd say today,' he agreed. 'The fishermen didn't think so. They said that whenever a woman had been murdered and dumped in the lagoon they'd catch squid like that. With the eyes of a human being, not the little black ones of a fish.'

She waited. There was more.

'But I was eleven years old,' he went on. 'A brat who wasn't scared of anything. Who didn't believe in ghosts or fairy stories.'

'So you came back?'

He pointed at the low dark shape of the building ahead and the bridge over the water.

'The very next day I walked here with my little rod and tackle and bait. And I fished in the very same place. The next thing I caught was the body of a woman with no eyes and no heart.'

She couldn't look at his face at that moment.

'After that,' he said, 'I knew I'd become a patholo-gist too, like my father, like his father before him, even though I'd always wanted to be an airline pilot or a soldier. Something different. When I looked at that sad, torn body in the water I finally understood. Death asks such difficult questions of us on occasion that it's only right someone takes on the job of trying to answer them.'

Tosi hugged himself in his thick winter coat. He looked a little relieved to have told this story.

'Not that I or anyone else had any answers about that poor woman. No one wanted to talk about her. I was only eleven, remember. Some things are never said in front of children. But when I turned twenty-five, after I qualified as a doctor in Bologna then returned here as an apprentice pathologist, I finally found the means to read the files on her from the Questura.'

She watched him as he hesitated.

'The woman was a prostitute working in the docks. Murdered by an unhappy client, the police assumed. Not that they ever found the culprit. She was half-Turkish, strangely enough. The eyes were the result of fish feeding – there was other damage too. Her heart had been removed by whoever killed her, of course.'

'I'm sorry I dragged you all this way,' Teresa told him.

'No. The hospital gave you the address. It was important you should come and see for yourself. No one has lived in that place in my lifetime. No local would dare.'

'Sofia gave the hospital that address.'

'A mistake. What else could it be?'

'Someone must own it, Alberto.'

'I checked that too. It's one more piece of unwanted property belonging to the Church. As if they don't have enough spare ruins on their hands already.'

'May I look?' she asked, offering to take the torch. 'Just from the outside? I don't mind if you stay here.'

'I will *not* stay here,' he said and led the way.

It was very much as she pictured it from the story about Camilla and Jason Cunningham that she'd read the night before. White walls streaked with dirt that looked like smeared mascara. A solitary exposed position where the constant lazy lapping of the lagoon must have entered through every window, day and night.

But this was not the house of Marco, the mysterious doctor and his patient, a fictional version of the real Camilla Dushku. The narrow bridge, metal on rusting posts stuck into the lagoon at crazy angles, shook so wildly as they crossed it she wondered whether the thing was safe at all. The door had a padlock and chain over it. There were iron railings covering the nearest windows. The shutters behind were boarded up and covered in peeling paint.

'No one's been here for years,' Tosi said. 'There was talk of the Church selling the place to some gullible foreigner at one point. The locals said no. Their opinion of the Casino degli Spiriti is very well known. They made it clear any potential owner would understand it too. This is not the Grand Canal where there's always some hotheaded halfwit ready to buy that cursed place, Ca' Dario. Not even the boldest of strangers would take on a hovel like this out of pure bravado.'

She stepped forward and took a professional look at the area near the door, the state of the step, the chain and the padlock. Teresa Lupo had worked with Leo Falcone and his crew for a long time. They were good teachers.

'You're right,' she said. 'It's impossible Sofia could have lived here.'

'The hospital must have got the address wrong,' he said eagerly. 'These things happen. It was a long time ago. One number could put her several streets from this place. I did tell you.'

'And I should have listened to you in the first place.'

Tosi shook his head and said, 'No. That would have disappointed me greatly. Because it would have meant I didn't know you at all.' He leaned forward and patted her shoulder. 'You're a very persistent young woman, you know. I only wished we'd worked together on more than just a single case.'

'We're working together now,' she told him. 'Very well, I think.'

He laughed a little at that. They went back across the flimsy bridge. When they were on the pavement she linked her arm through Tosi's and they wandered towards the vaporetto stop.

'I'll walk home from here,' he said. 'Through all those back streets I used to play in as a child. It seems like only yesterday, you know. Where do the years go? What do we do with them?'

'We help people, Alberto. You haven't retired from that.'

They stopped by the narrow alley that led down to the houses and shops she'd seen earlier.

'I'll walk too,' she said. 'I can find the Arsenale from here.'

'You're sure? You're in the labyrinth now.'

'I'm good at labyrinths. Or at least, I'm getting better at them.'

The street, when they reached it, was busy and lively and quite unlike any near Dorsoduro or San Marco, broad enough to be a *rio terà* or a *piscina* perhaps. The shops, which were just beginning to close, seemed local. The cafés were full of cheery, red-faced men drinking wine and spritz. There were busy lines in the bakery, the butcher, the green-grocer's store. It could have been Rome, Testaccio maybe.

Except . . . meandering slowly up the wide *calle* was a carnival band, making a joyously dreadful noise with their drums and ragged collection of instruments. They were dressed like medieval characters: jesters and knights and soldiers. The solitary woman wore the long velvet gown of a princess and a headband of cheap pearls. She tapped away at a xylophone in what seemed a random fashion. A happy middle-aged drunk followed them, dancing and clapping to the music, shouting for the locals to come out and see.

Icy sleet was starting to fall. No one seemed to mind.

'I can find my own way,' she said and kissed Tosi's cold rough cheek.

Teresa Lupo watched him walk back towards Giardini and the bridge to Sant'Elena. Tosi had a very upright, certain gait. Good for his age, she thought. No, wonderful.

When he was out of sight she retraced her steps to the general store she'd seen earlier. The place was starting to close. She walked in briskly, determined she would not be thrown out till she'd found what she wanted. The place seemed to sell everything. One wall was given over to artists' materials, canvases, brushes, and paint mixes with extraordinary labels: 'Tintoretto's Scarlet', 'Caravaggio's Black', 'Raphael's Sky Blue'. The display next to it was full of detergent and rat traps. The shelves below contained dusty plastic children's toys for the beach.

'We sell everything,' the man behind the counter said.

'So I can see. I'd like a crowbar, a hammer, a screwdriver and a torch,' Teresa said, thrusting a fifty-euro note at him.

That was enough money to keep him open an extra five minutes. She was out of there in three, with all the items safely stowed in a plastic bag in case she accidentally bumped into Tosi again.

There was no one between her and the Celestia vaporetto stop. Not a soul on the waterfront as she walked back to the abandoned building sitting on its perch above the lagoon next to the wall of the Arsenale.

The torch was more powerful than Tosi's. She flicked it along the rattling iron bridge as she walked across. The state of repair was shocking. Even sixteen years before it must have been too bad for regular use. Tosi was right. Sofia didn't live here. But someone had used the place. Someone had put the very same building in the story about Camilla and Jason and their need for one another.

Teresa got to the door and shone her torch on the padlock and chain. Under Tosi's weak light the evidence had been barely visible. But now she could see clearly and there was no mistaking the signs. Scratch marks, fresh on the metal around the lock. They were shiny and recent.

The sort of thing Falcone wouldn't miss in a million years.

'Thank you for that, Leo,' she murmured.

Then she turned and looked back at the city to make sure no one was watching. It was a ridiculous precaution. From this distant promontory in the back streets of Castello, Venice appeared dark and dead to the world.

Teresa Lupo put the torch on the stone steps, took the crowbar out of the bag, placed the head in the first loop of chain next to the padlock, twisted it into place, then heaved with all her might on the lever she'd made. It took two turns to break the thing. After that she inserted the corner of the bar in the narrow crack in the door frame and began to work at it, slowly, patiently.

In a few minutes she had enough space to force the thicker end through, then to lean back and place her weight against the iron bar, levering it against the door.

There was a loud crack, not unlike the sound of the shot that had rung across the Piazza San Marco just two days before. The door sprang open with a sudden, violent lurch. Beyond it she could see nothing. The interior ahead was so black, so

364

lacking in shape and form, it might have been the place where the physical world came to an end.

She reached for the torch. As she was doing so something came to her, both familiar and terrible, triggering so many memories. Of work, of Rome. Of events like this when she was never alone but surrounded by police officers and her own forensic staff.

It was the rank, cloying smell of decay, of physical corruption, one a police pathologist came to know well over the years.

She picked up the tools in the carrier bag, then the torch with her free hand, and walked ahead into the stinking dark.

A narrow, empty interior hall ran the width of the building parallel to the waterfront. Flashing around the beam of the torch she saw scrawls on the walls, graffiti in curled, painted lettering that looked as if it might have been hundreds of years old. The floorboards were cracked and, in places, shattered altogether so that brittle, rotten shards of wood projected upwards, ready to trip or spear the unwary.

There was nothing here except a ludicrous, battered hat stand leaning drunkenly next to the interior door ahead. She walked forward and shone the torch at it. A single piece of fancy headgear was perched on the top. It rang a bell she couldn't place at that moment. Circular, theatrical, with a long feather peeking out of the back. The colour, as she got the torch closer, was a rich shade of scarlet, the material velvet.

It looked old-fashioned. But not old.

The door was ajar already. She pushed it fully open and turned the beam on the floor ahead, checking it was secure.

The room seemed in a better state of repair. The smell was becoming stronger. She flashed the light around the walls. This might once have been some kind of private home but now it seemed more like a derelict chapel. Vast canvases hung from every inch of spare space, old Biblical scenes, mostly violent: crucifixions, martyrdoms, the flayings and whippings and beheadings she'd seen enough of in Rome.

She walked on slowly, carefully, watching the floor. There was no furniture that she could see. Just the paintings and, as she got to the centre of the room, what looked like a vast Murano chandelier, dangling uncertainly above her.

It seemed incongruous somehow, all the more so when she saw that it was festooned with electric light bulbs, some of which seemed quite recent.

The place had power. It was probably hot-wired into some conduit from the promenade. Wouldn't be hard.

She thought about looking for a light switch. But that would only draw attention.

Not yet.

Edging sideways, forgetful for a moment, she

bumped into something solid and the physical shock made her shriek briefly. Her high, pained cry echoed off the damp walls and the closed wooden shutters that covered what must have been high, long windows giving out onto the lagoon.

She flashed the torch at the object. It was an old dining chair, high and formal, the fabric seat and backing torn to shreds. A small dark shape squeaked and ran away from the light.

Mice. Rats.

There was another sound and it came from above. Light and scratchy. More vermin. Or birds. Pigeons. Gulls. Fighting their way through what had to be a wrecked tiled roof, taking shelter from the bitter night where they could.

Teresa turned back towards the wall facing the door and flicked the beam over the area furthest from the point where she'd come in.

A shape was visible on the ground, dimly human. Kneeling in front of some kind of makeshift altar with what looked like a small gilt cross and above it a painting of the crucifixion.

Please God, she thought. Not Sofia.

She stepped forward and the smell became so strong she started to breathe in short, rapid gasps. The beam flickered towards what lay there and she reminded herself of all the corpses, all the violence she'd witnessed over the years.

Never like this. With such a possible connection.

It was a woman and she was tied to a low pole

set in a wooden base. Under the bright light of the torch Teresa could see that she wore precisely the same kind of dress Filippo Strozzi had shown her that morning in the painting in the Accademia. Sky-blue, with a scarlet cape, shining ribbons, golden hair and a crown decorated with pearls. The jewellery was cheap and theatrical. A plain female mask, bright white, the area beneath the mouth stained with dried blood, covered her face. The elastic band holding it was still visible around the back of the long, flowing hair of a cheap wig. Her hands were in front in the gesture of prayer, kept there by several loops of dark hessian rope.

The shaft of an arrow, its feathers shiny and black, stood out of her breast at a sharp angle. The point, Teresa guessed, had gone directly into her heart. The shot must have come from close up: a man standing above her, aiming down, just as in the Carpaccio canvas.

She shook her head. Why was she thinking like this? She wasn't here as a police pathologist. She didn't even fit that description any more.

All the same it was impossible not to see this from a professional point of view. The man had taken this woman, tied her to the low post, some ship apparatus perhaps, and forced her to kneel, binding her hands, placing the mask over her face.

'Bastard,' Teresa muttered.

She could see now that the rope was drawn viciously, cutting deeply into the skin. Her nails were ragged and broken and there was still black caked material beneath some of them.

Good for you, Teresa whispered. You fought.

A wooden church lectern rose behind the body, with an empty shelf for the Bible and the rearing, bold body of an eagle, wings outstretched, at the top. She put a hand on it to steady herself. For the first time since she'd been a rookie pathologist the acrid fresh tang of recent blood made her feel faint.

Teresa bent down and faced the mask, desperate to remove it though her personal instincts clashed with the professional, the strict rule of the criminal investigator whose first commandment was, always: Do not touch.

Struggling with this internal dilemma, she looked at the wound in the woman's chest. The blood had congealed in a black sticky mess around the entry point of the arrow. Ragged flesh was just visible near the rough-edged tear where the shaft pierced the fabric of the gown. She could picture the coming procedure in the morgue. The naked body on the shining silver table. The necessary incisions, the injuries a pathologist would inflict in the search for fact, plain and obvious or hidden inside veins and wounds and bloody tissue.

She placed the bag with the tools on the dry wooden floor, the torch by its side.

The mask had to go, however much her counterpart in Venice would shriek. But first she took the dead fingers in front of her. They were still a little mobile and it wasn't difficult to imagine how, just a few short days before, they must have moved with life and warmth and, in this tiny room, during those last moments, the most awful sense of terror.

'I'm so sorry,' she said, hearing her own voice echo in this small, dank, reeking room. 'If I could have been here . . .'

There was a noise from behind. An animal, perhaps. A large one. So distinct was the sound it stopped her dead at that moment, made her mind go blank, fighting for rationality, for some response or explanation.

Teresa crouched there, turning towards the source, flicking the torch in that direction too. The beam was broad and, in the space of a few steps, tall enough almost to reach the ceiling.

A man stood there. He wore the uniform of a medieval soldier, one she recognized. One she now realized she probably saw close to the little carnival band in the street beyond the waterfront, following in the wake of the woman with the xylophone and the costume of a princess. Except for the hat with the feather she'd seen outside by the door.

The bow in his hands was fully drawn, the arrow tight to his cheek. A golden wig of flowing curls fell around his shoulders yet the curve of his body, as taut and as powerful as the straining bend of the bow, meant that his face remained out of sight, just as it had in that final painting in Room XX at the moment the mythical Ursula was meant to die, on her knees, praying.

'Who are you?' she asked simply.

'Who do you want me to be?'

There was no reply to that. None she could imagine.

'Kneel,' the archer ordered.

Teresa didn't obey, just stayed as she was, crouching.

Her right arm was wrapped round the base of the wooden lectern. Her left was close to the bag with the tools in it. She could just touch the torch on the floor with her foot if she wanted.

Both doors were open behind the erect, tense figure of the archer. She could see nothing there but she could feel the icy breeze working its way into the building like an inquisitive thief allowed entrance to a place that had kept its secrets for years.

The wind brought with it the smells of the lagoon. Salt water and the faint stink of diesel. They mingled with the aromas of death and damp and decay, making her head swim a little, blurring the figure in front of her in the yellow light of the torch.

She could just make out a single gleaming eye behind the golden wig. It was focused on her entirely, alert, sombre and quite devoid of any emotion.

'Kneel,' he said again, and stretched the bow to its fullest extent.

By his side, she now saw, there was a sword, bright and gleaming, tucked beneath the belt. One arrow wasn't much of a weapon in a fight with a woman. He needed something else.

She listened to the sound of the wood arching, the string straining, and said, 'Do I have to pray too? If I don't, does that break the spell? The magic?'

He didn't utter a word. She wanted to launch herself at him. Tear the beast to pieces.

Instead she asked, 'Or do you just require belief on your own part? Say something. I'm interested.'

'I told you what I want. Now do it.'

His accent was unidentifiable. Not northern. Not southern. Simply flat. He might even be a foreigner who spoke Italian well.

In the darkness her fingers clutched the lectern more firmly.

'I don't kneel for a man who kills a defenceless woman,' Teresa Lupo said, shaking her head, watching the angle of his arms, the power there. 'I don't pray for some cowardly animal who takes pleasure in the pain and terror of others.'

She gripped the wooden support of the lectern in her fingers. Its fierce beaked head was silhouetted against the corona the torch made as the beam flooded the room.

'I don't . . .'

Afterwards she'd no idea whether it was luck or reaction. Whether she heard or felt or saw something on his part or simply guessed the moment, dragging down the lectern in front of her, screaming, screeching, not words, just sound.

Fury and fierce emotion released like a fire from within.

There was a frantic, violent rushing commotion through the air, like the swooping of an enormous invisible bird of prey. As she dragged the heavy wooden structure forward, finally feeling it begin to tip beneath its own weight and momentum, she turned herself, falling to one side, scrabbling for the bag of tools, the hammer, the crowbar, fingers clawing, hunting for bare, hard metal.

The arrow struck and its power was so great that she screamed in pain at the impact, wondering where the thing had hit her, what it had done.

Then the noise. Almost musical, a thrumming, vibrating sound like the song of a gigantic vocal insect.

It had hit the lectern as she'd planned, was rattling under its own momentum as it bit somewhere into the wooden structure she'd pulled down around her as a shield. The eagle stared her in the face. The arrow, with its flight of black feathers, was buried deep in its dead eye.

Now, she thought, aware of movement ahead. She arched her arm back and launched the hammer from the floor, rolling sideways, clutching the crowbar to her chest, fighting to get upright on the splintered, fragile boards.

He screamed. She liked the sound of his pain. When she found her feet he was half in the torchlight, half out of it, waving the sword around wildly, yelling obscenities, Italian, English, some language she didn't know.

She retreated further into the darkness beyond the beam of the torch, trying to make herself invisible, fighting for reason, trying not to breathe or move, aware any sign of life might betray her.

Then there was another light. It was narrow, like a long yellow pencil, focused, hunting. As her eyes adjusted to its anxious searching finger of brightness she understood. On his forehead, beneath the golden wig, he had one of those torches that walkers and mountaineers used, strapped to a headband so that it went whichever way he turned, leaving his hands free for other work. On his forehead, close to the source of the beam, she could just make out something dark and liquid. Blood. The hammer had hit him, a glancing blow perhaps, but it was something. He was *hurt*.

The archer took one step forward, bellowing threats and curses. The little beam of his head torch flickered from side to side, never quite reaching far enough. He raised the sword in both hands and slashed away at emptiness.

Angry people lose perspective. Angry people make mistakes. She knew this instinctively. She was one of them.

Very carefully, with the gentlest, slightest of movements, Teresa reached into her jacket pocket with her free left hand and drew out a few small coins. His narrow beam was on the still corpse tethered to its stake now. She still couldn't make out his face. The wig was too long, too full for that. But from the way he stared down at the dead

374

woman there, nodding, she guessed he was proud of his handiwork.

Anger, she thought, stemming the emotion.

She threw the coins across the room, away from him, into the furthest distant corner. Then she watched as he turned to follow them, aiming the narrow torch beam into dust and cobwebs and what looked like some once-grand fireplace surmounted by an ancestral shield rotting into nothing but mouldy plaster.

Thirty-six years old. Average height. Average weight. Average looks on a good day. She didn't have any illusions. But she was stuck in this place with a man who'd slaughtered someone. Sofia, perhaps.

She had a crowbar too.

Teresa Lupo tiptoed up behind him, holding her breath, getting ready to swing the heavy lump of iron gripped tight in both her hands. He didn't hear too well, perhaps. You get that with wigs.

She stole in close, raised the crowbar, moving it behind her head to get some swing, started to bring the weapon down with all the force, every muscle, she could bring to bear.

It crashed into something on the way towards him. The blow was blocked. She heard the sound of glass tinkling, shattering, felt a light, hard rain on her face.

The chandelier.

The archer was reeling round as she recovered. She got in an uncertain half-blow that couldn't have hurt much, then another. By that stage he

375

was screaming too and it wasn't anger this time. It was pain. There was a spatter of blood on the wig and the flash of skin she saw on his temple showed she'd hurt him more than she thought.

The crowbar swung easily through the air, low and certain. It caught his hands. The sword cart-wheeled out of them as the black iron fetched against the hilt.

No weapon.

She moved closer, arcing the bar in front of her, flailing the thing crazily, spitting meaningless words at the figure retreating into the darkness that had, just a few moments before, hidden her.

'Bastard!' she shrieked, and more, so many words, so many curses they streamed out of her without a second thought.

The pencil beam disappeared, turned off. She was out of the pool of the torch she'd set by the dead woman in front of the makeshift altar. Scared suddenly, trembling, aware of the aftershock of that sudden rush of adrenaline and emotion.

Teresa edged back towards the centre of the room, clutching the crowbar to her chest, sweating, panting, waiting for the attack. When she got there she swept her feet across the floor until she found the torch, grabbed it, skimmed the beam across the space ahead of her anxiously, screeching at him still.

She wasn't ready any more. The fight was gone. All the anger and pain and strength. There was just fear left at that moment.

The torch swept the room, right to left and back again. She was alone with the tortured corpse tied to the stake. Still holding onto the crowbar she walked forward to the door, checked there, checked the narrow hall running the length of the front. The hat stand was tipped over. The feathered cap was gone. The front door was open. Sleety rain was issuing in from the black night along with the salt smell of the sea.

She flicked the torch towards the rickety bridge and the waterfront. No one.

'Bastard!' she shrieked again, this time out into the endless empty night.

Exhausted, unable to think straight, she leaned back against the wall and knew that, at that moment, she'd have given anything for a cigarette, though one hadn't touched her lips in more than a year, not since she'd come to that deal with Peroni: I'll look after myself a little, if you'll just do the same.

'God, I wish you were here,' she murmured.

It took her a couple of minutes to find enough composure to make the call. Then she phoned Paola Boscolo, expecting that she'd have to make a fulsome apology for interrupting whatever cosy dinner the young Venetian woman would be enjoying with her family.

Instead she heard the busy buzz of an active police room behind the officer's anxious voice.

'Why do you not answer your phone?' Boscolo demanded immediately. 'How am I supposed to help if you're impossible to reach?'

'I needed a little privacy,' Teresa replied. 'I didn't think you'd be so interested . . .'

'What? *What*? Do you think we're fools? Much has been happening. It's important we speak. When can you come into the Questura?'

'I think you'd rather pay me a visit,' Teresa said.

It took a little while to describe what she'd found, what had happened, as succinctly as she could.

'You could have been killed,' the policewoman spat at her.

'So it appears. Are you coming?'

Ten minutes, Boscolo said. That was all it would take for them to get there, by launch and on foot.

It was enough.

Teresa went back into the derelict palace, back to the dread room with the smell and the dead woman in her ornate, archaic dress. Returned to what she was about to do before a man dressed as a medieval archer tried to shoot an arrow through her chest.

Like the figure in the Carpaccio painting in the Accademia.

Something jarred. That was wrong. In the painting the archer was about to fire the arrow. He was in the process of murder, not the act.

Tenses mattered. She just didn't quite comprehend how.

With the utmost care, in the light of the torch, she bent down over the corpse there, removed the mask and looked at the face beneath.

Then she sat down on the hard cold floor, amidst the sharp wood splinters and the fragments of broken glass, and began to weep.

By ten in the evening the deserted building Alberto Tosi knew as the Casino degli Spiriti, the House of the Spirits, was bathed in floodlights inside and out, surrounded by police launches, crowded with officers and forensic staff walking around quietly in white bunny suits.

Teresa sat on the old chair she'd found in the main room, not far from the body. She watched, envious of their detachment, wishing that she might have access to the secrets that surely lay in this cold, deserted place set above the shifting waters of the lagoon.

The lights made it a little warmer. That only served to make the smell worse.

She'd insisted on being interviewed there. It was important to get the sequence of events straight in her head, and that could only happen in the light, in the place where everything had occurred.

'You're lucky to be alive,' Paola Boscolo said when she, and a duty inspector, had listened to Teresa's story.

'I imagine so,' Teresa replied.

Beneath the police floods she could see more clearly the lectern with the arrow in the eagle's eye. It was close to the edge of the bird's body. The wood there was so thin the point had burst through to the back of the head. Another few centimetres to one side and it would have hit her with a penetrating, deadly force.

'Why did you come here?' asked the inspector.

'As I told you . . .'

She'd mentioned the address she'd found for Sofia when she first lived in the city, though she hadn't revealed where it came from. The resemblance of the building to the palace in the story was something she didn't care to talk about. It seemed pointless. Even if they believed her they wouldn't understand, any more than she did.

'I don't believe Sofia actually lived here,' she added.

'The building is owned by the Church,' Paola Boscolo told her. 'It's supposed to be closed to the public.'

'They obviously don't check too often, do they?' An idea struck her. 'If I can help with the forensic investigation—' she began.

'No,' the inspector cut in. 'That would be inappropriate.'

'Inappropriate,' she echoed.

Teresa Lupo despised that word, and the way it was used as some kind of talisman against original thought.

'I'm sorry about Sofia,' the policewoman said. 'Let me organize a launch to take you home. We should talk in the morning.'

'About what?'

'About anything else you remember.'

Teresa Lupo stood up and looked her in the eye.

'Paola,' she said. 'I've been trying to tell you there was something strange about my aunt's disappearance for days now. It takes this . . .' Her hand swept the room. '. . . for you to treat it seriously. And now you expect me to turn up at the Questura for an appointment. At your convenience . . .'

'I know this is a stressful time . . .'

'It's not Sofia!'

Teresa's voice was a little shrill. She regretted that. Even more when she realized that Paola Boscolo was not in the least surprised by what she'd just said.

'You knew already?' Teresa asked, trying to fight back the anger.

'I meant I was sorry we haven't found Sofia. I knew this wasn't her the moment I looked at the woman. I told you on the phone. We were trying to get hold of you. When you sent me that passport photo. And the picture of the Englishman . . .'

Teresa had expected that Boscolo would put it to one side for another day. She was wrong. The young policewoman explained succinctly what had happened next. The Questura had checked its file of missing males, and the photo log there. Very soon they came up with the name of Massimo Gabrielli, a truck driver from Bologna who'd failed to turn up for work the previous Friday. Gabrielli's picture matched. The Bologna police had checked his apartment and discovered his wife, Fiorella, was also missing. Talking to neighbours they'd come to the conclusion that Gabrielli had a side-line pimping his wife using sex lines and small ads in newspapers across northern Italy. The two hadn't been seen since the previous Wednesday. Their computer showed a booking for train tickets to Venice and an exchange with a potential client on an adult website.

Teresa glanced at the body, which was still kneeling on the floor.

'Fiorella Gabrielli?' she asked.

'Without a doubt,' the inspector said. 'Massimo was an opportunistic little man. His neighbours said they'd never seen him so happy. Fiorella was no innocent. She had convictions for soliciting. From what they told the neighbours the two of them thought they'd struck it rich. Some wealthy foreigner here for the carnival wanted company.'

Teresa recalled the figure on the ledge of the campanile in the Piazza San Marco. His reluctance when it came to firing at the disappearing figure of the starlet.

'What kind of couple were they?'

'The loving kind,' Boscolo said with a shrug. 'In spite of everything. You mentioned the idea of pressure . . .'

What could make a man try to murder, then kill himself when he fails?

It was against Teresa's principles to guess, but the answer seemed so obvious.

'He told Gabrielli that if he shot the girl his wife would be safe,' she said. 'Gabrielli couldn't do it.

It's a long way from a pimp to a murderer. He couldn't have escaped anyway. Besides . . .' She thought of what she had seen. 'The woman was dead already. He probably knew that.'

'All this is conjecture,' the inspector responded. 'We can't work with—'

'Hunches?' Teresa suggested.

'Precisely.'

'What do you have?'

'Signora,' the man said grumpily. 'That's our business.'

'The purpose of what happened in the piazza,' she went on, 'was to convince you Jerome Aitchison was dead. So that you'd stop looking.'

He edged a little closer. 'Well, we're looking now. We have your photograph of him. We'll talk to the English police and get more. This is a priority.'

'At last,' she said, and looked him in the eye.

She thought of the conversation she'd had with the officer in Cambridge, Detective Inspector Postlethwaite.

'There's a problem there, you understand,' she added. 'Whoever this man is, he is familiar with the city. He's been coming here for a long time. At least sixteen years if he knew Sofia here. If he was the father of her child.'

The inspector actually laughed at that.

'These are such suppositions! How can one possibly know such things?'

'I don't. Aitchison was a stranger to the city . . .'

'According to your story?' Paola Boscolo interrupted. 'The one that disappeared?'

The one that disappeared. Quite. Teresa didn't intend to labour that point.

'Forget the story,' she said quickly. 'The clothes this woman was wearing. Sofia had something like them in her apartment. They're from a painting in the Accademia. A Carpaccio. The Ursula cycle.'

Paola Boscolo was scribbling all this anxiously in her notebook and Teresa wanted to scream at her. To shout, 'This is more than peripheral detail. More than a line on someone's pad. This is the heart of the mystery. Somehow. In ways I can't even begin to guess.'

Then she realized from the expression on the young policewoman's face that Paola Boscolo actually thought this might be evidence against Sofia. Not just Aitchison.

'I don't believe this,' Teresa exclaimed. 'Can't you see? Someone, Aitchison if you wish, is obsessed with Carpaccio. Obsessed with the Ursula painting in particular. For whatever reason he sees women as victims, as objects, to be used then cast aside. Murdered, if it pleases him. Sofia was on his list.'

And I'd be dead too, she told herself, if I hadn't fought back. This was not what he expected of a woman. He wanted beauty, subservience, an innocence he could ruin.

'Just like the English,' the inspector observed.

'What? You think that kind of obsessive behaviour is restricted to the English? Don't you ever read the papers? Or is Venice a world apart?'

He glared at her.

'It is a world apart, signora, and for that we're grateful. What I meant was it's the lot of the English to come here and be obsessed. To see us as some kind of architectural freak show, not a place where real men and women and their families try to live in conditions that are sometimes difficult. Aitchison is not the first to suffer such an obsession. Nor will he be the last . . .'

Teresa threw her arms around herself, trying to stay warm. There was a murdered woman in this room, and all he could talk about was the eccentricity of foreigners.

One of the men in white bunny suits wandered over and said something about moving the body. She wanted to tell him to stop. To wait until daylight. Police floods didn't uncover everything. She would have wanted to see this place with the shuttered windows thrown open and the winter sun streaming through.

Instead she looked at Paola Boscolo and said, 'If there's nothing else, can I go now?'

It was almost one in the morning when the police launch moored at the private jetty by the Ponte agli Incurabili. The sleet had turned to steady snow. The uniformed police officers made a fuss of getting off the boat and helping her onto the slippery promenade. In the past few days she'd warmed to the Venetians. They could be stand-offish, brusque and occasionally obtuse. But they intended none of this and were sensitive and thoughtful when it mattered. More than anything, she felt, they were self-absorbed, not much interested in the world beyond their city. They possessed, too, mannerisms and customs that were starchy yet polite, almost gracious, in a very antiquated fashion. Alberto Tosi, with his energetic enthusiasm to help and his solitary inner sadness, typified them in many ways.

None of this had occurred to her before. She had only seen the place, she realized, not the people. Or, more truthfully, she had regarded them as adjuncts to the panoramic landscape before her, props on a gorgeous crumbling stage.

As the launch set off on the moonlit glittering canal, with one of the officers waving back to her from the stern, she marvelled again at the astonishing view that lay at Sofia's doorstep. There was nowhere in the world quite like this. It was, as she often thought, like something out of the imagination of the English painter, Turner. But Turner had never painted people much, not that she could recall. That was an omission.

Another recollection. Her fictional self, meeting Arnaud, the Count of Saint-Germain, was struck by the connection with Turner too. Whoever wrote those stories must have spoken to Sofia. Teresa had talked to her about Venice and painting, she felt sure. It would have been so like her aunt to have thrown into the conversation, 'And my clever niece, who finds killers for the Rome Questura, once noticed . . .'

The problem was that Sofia would say such a thing to anyone. A stranger on a vaporetto. Someone at the next table in Signora Rizzolo's lovely little café. Even a man in a mask.

Coming through the door into the cold stone hallway, every light out, she wondered whether there'd be anything in the post-box. Hoped not, if she were honest with herself. The rising tempo of the delivery of these fragments of the story had begun to concern her.

The envelope was there in the mailbox but it was so thin it seemed impossible that it could contain anything meaningful.

Teresa took it and trudged upstairs, turned on the light, felt moved for some reason to check every room in Sofia's decrepit apartment to make sure she was on her own.

Then – avoiding the document for the time being – she looked at the computer. One message from Silvio, the usual pleading. Nothing else.

Rome seemed a universe away.

She glanced at the tailor's dummy by the door. The gown there, sky-blue, the red cape, the gold brocade, the crown of pearls . . . these things sent such a shudder through her she had to walk across the room, take the grubby cover off the sofa and throw it over the still form of the torso for some peace of mind.

She found it impossible to stem the flood of thoughts, of possibilities, racing into her head. Ideas she would normally have dismissed as ridiculous speculation, entirely devoid of any basis in fact, as Paola Boscolo and the surly inspector had intimated the moment Teresa had first tried to imagine them out loud in the foul smelling room in the Casino degli Spiriti.

The first was this. The woman, Fiorella Gabrielli, had been summoned to Venice through her husband, a common if affectionate pimp, days after Sofia had gone missing. She'd been murdered in Sofia's place. Second best. A substitute. While her husband was despatched to the Piazza San Marco, told to shoot the young starlet and throw himself off the campanile. Luisa Cammarota was chosen at random, purely to make a show. There was no other link at all.

What kind of husband would agree to such an ultimatum?

A desperate one. A fool. Someone who loved his wife and hoped against hope to save her. Or perhaps the very opposite. Someone who understood the fate he'd brought her to and couldn't live with the knowledge.

What would be the purpose of such a subterfuge? To fool the authorities into thinking Jerome Aitchison was dead.

St Jerome, the cop from Cambridge had said. A novice in Venice, according to the story, captivated by Sofia in the little *scuola* by the bridge.

These two portraits of the man couldn't both be true. Was it possible Aitchison had been visiting Venice for years? That he was, in reality, the man Sofia met before? The one who made her pregnant then did something so terrible she aborted the child and tried to kill herself?

The picture she'd built up of the Englishman – from the stories and the conversation with the police inspector in Cambridge – had become so clear she'd started to believe it. To wonder whether *he* might be the one writing the stories. The Plague Doctor of the previous night. Arnaud, the Count of Saint-Germain. The worried, caring doctor Marco, baffled as he tried to treat the fictional Camilla. All desperate for answers, lost for a way forward.

Could a man like Aitchison write such good Italian? With such style? A lecturer in actuarial science? And why?

She looked at the computer and knew she was too tired to do anything useful with it. Then she remembered a single, inescapable fact, one that offered some comfort.

If the gown Sofia was supposed to wear was still here, and some-one else's body lay in that desolate mansion, her aunt, by rights, ought to be alive somewhere. In hiding. In fear. Waiting.

First things first.

She opened the envelope. This time there were just two pages inside. One way or another this narrative was coming to its conclusion.

ONE AMONG MANY

Teresa Lupo stayed by the jetty feeling a little light-headed, from the strangeness of the evening, not Tosi's prosecco. The resident owl hooted again and was joined by another nearby. A thin finger of cloud moved slowly across the moon, an indication of a coming change in the weather.

It was hot and stuffy on the lagoon. She much preferred Venice in the autumn or winter, and would return then, in October, November perhaps, to remind herself of this meeting and attempt to find some perspective on its significance.

In the distance, moving quickly, the lights of a low, swift vessel emerged from the night. She was on her feet in a flash, shouting, as loud as her lungs allowed. The boat disappeared in the direction of Chioggia as quickly as it came, not stopping for a moment, not hearing her over the sound of its whiny outboard motor.

Vaporetti and larger boats circled the distant outline of Venice constantly, as out of reach as spaceships coming in to land on a far-off planet.

391

She and Arnaud would be trapped here until Tosi's launch returned in the morning, perfectly timed so that she would miss the final meeting of the symposium, and the crucial vote. They had planned well.

There were only two possible decisions. She was still unable to imagine what her odd and amusing companion could possibly have meant when he spoke of a third.

She laid out the sleeping bag and by the side of it the sheets Tosi had left. Then she picked up the torch, not that it was truly necessary on a night like this, and wandered down the winding, stony, overgrown path Arnaud had taken, back to the vineyard, the only place it led.

He'd had enough time, she thought. They needed to talk again. Aspects of his story required clarification. Perhaps they might help her see more clearly the way forward through the fogbound mystery in which she found herself.

There was no one to be seen in the low patch of open ground where they had sat together earlier. Only the distant twinkling windows of the houses on Malamocco.

'Arnaud,' she called. 'Arnaud!'

A large bird rose up from the water margin, startling her. She flapped her hands, fearing it would fly into her face. Stumbling on the soft, soggy ground, her foot caught something and Teresa Lupo found herself thrown rudely to the earth.

The grass was soft and accommodating and gave no indication of the hard white layer of bone that must lie somewhere beneath. When she recovered her equilibrium she saw his face a short distance away on the ground, and the sight frightened her for the first time since she'd set foot on the Island of the Dead.

Arnaud, the Count of Saint-Germain, lay on his back on the thick vegetation, arms crossed over his chest, black lacquered cane in hand, face to the starry evening sky. He wore a half-smile and his eyes were wide open, unfocused, without the bright, sharp spark of life she'd seen there from the moment they first met. His mouth was a touch agape. She leaned forward, listening for breath. Then she picked up his left wrist, trying not to recoil from the coldness of the skin, and felt for a pulse.

There was nothing.

Over the years she'd seen so many corpses. She knew what death looked like, could sense its presence as if it were some everpresent actor waiting in the wings of the theatre that was life, ready to be called when his lines were due.

'Oh Arnaud,' Teresa Lupo whispered.

Wearily she went back to the jetty, picked up the things Tosi had left. When she returned she placed a cheap tartan blanket over his body and the sleeping bag next to him.

She found it impossible to cover his face, for a

little while anyway, until she realized there was no real alternative. There were bugs about, and proprieties to do with the end of a life, a remarkable one if he were to be believed.

It was a ridiculous story. She knew that. As ridiculous as the idea that an ancient skeleton in the Basilica San Marco might be the bones of a man who once served water to the – perhaps equally fictional – human being who called himself Jesus.

Yet Arnaud believed every word, as if he'd lived them. That mattered, surely. If enough people trusted, with all their hearts, in something that was no more – or less – than legend, did that fairy story cease, at some stage, to be fable and take on, instead, the mantle of truth?

Cautiously, with what the pathologist hoped amounted to a semblance of tenderness, she pulled the fabric over his handsome features then curled up inside the harsh, thin nylon bag beside him. One more corpse among many. A sea of ancient bones beneath him, anonymous, unmourned, for a hard, cold bed.

She was determined not to cry, and almost managed. But she was tired, bewildered, and, in spite of herself, a little scared.

THE ARCADES

He lay on the bed in the studio above the shop, watching the TV news. It was three thirty in the afternoon. Dusk was falling. Outside the long night would soon begin. Drunks in masks. Tourists wandering the alleys and dark porticos looking for something, some place, some person, they would never find.

Now was the between time. Only a few visitors meandering the freezing streets.

He'd barely slept. The image of the woman in the Casino degli Spiriti haunted him. Not the Roman. It was the dead figure on the floor, the whore from Bologna in the magical dress.

Ursula.

A saint waiting to be transformed. A virgin about to enter into the greatest secret of all.

It infuriated him he didn't dare return to the Accademia any more and sit, as he used to, staring at her face in each of the canvases, following her journey from innocence, through promise, into the shadows.

He was torn between two canvases most of all. The image of her asleep in bed, beautiful, waiting for the husband, the physical revelation that would never come. An angel at her feet, a creature of God delivering the portent of her death. A murderer with wings.

And the final painting. The kneeling saint, praying in that dress he'd recreated here, in the studio. The unsullied maiden, ready for sacrifice, for martyrdom above a life tainted by the pagan, the physical, the unclean.

Real women were different. He knew that. Had all along, if he were honest with himself.

He wouldn't set foot outside the door again until darkness was here entirely. The TV and the radio spoke of nothing but the murder in Castello. The event had, they said, cast a pall over the carnival itself. The very idea made him laugh. Men and women hiding their identity, seeking to pretend they were something else. What did they expect? A light interlude of pleasure, an absence of responsibility? And then normality resumed?

They were fools. The police too. What photographs they had of Jerome Aitchison were everywhere. The public was warned not to approach the man. They were also asked to look out for Sofia Bianchi, though the fat policewoman who spoke for them made it clear that she was not necessarily considered a suspect in the crime and was, perhaps, one more victim.

If only they knew.

He walked to the tiny bathroom, turned on the

single light and stared at himself in the mirror. The wound wasn't as bad as he'd first thought. A skin-coloured plaster now covered that part of his forehead. But his arm still ached from the effort of the previous night. His body wasn't what it used to be.

That fine wooden bow had cost him more than a thousand euros from a specialist manufacturer in Austria. It now lay in pieces scattered among a variety of public rubbish bins stretching from Zanipolo through the Fondamenta Nove to the Rialto. The shiny black-feathered arrows he'd smashed to pieces and placed in a restaurant's rubbish containers behind the tiny, too-perfect church of Santa Maria dei Miracoli. Long before that, in a back-street Castello *sotoportego* that stank of dogs and rotting refuse, he'd changed out of the archer's costume. It now lay at the bottom of the lagoon, stuffed inside two supermarket carriers which he'd weighed down with abandoned garbage and the sword. After that he walked the rest of the way in the simple, everyday clothes he wore beneath, shivering, teeth chattering, trying to think.

Scared.

No. Never that. Fear was a distant memory, not quite real.

He'd spent the last eighteen hours naked, flitting between sleep and consciousness, watching the TV, picking at food, drinking water from the tap. He liked being this way. Pale skin.

Bony bald head with not a single whisker of hair, a scalp so easily transformed by one of the many wigs he owned. It was an everyday, functional body, one he knew so well he didn't even think about it any more. Naked, he was one more mannequin waiting to be clothed. Waiting to be transformed, metamorphosed, into whatever he wanted. Over the years he'd learned to shrug identities off and on like the second skins they were. It was a useful talent.

The bathroom was on the first floor at the back, above the studio storage space. The floor was plain, cracked terracotta tiles, so cold at that moment his feet felt numb. The place was airless, rank with his sweat and odour. Not his favourite in the city. It was a prison, functional, nothing more.

Yet there was nowhere else that was safe. Sofia Bianchi had dictated that. Then along came another, a relative. And matters got worse.

When he thought about his present position the icy, bleak anger inside him rose and consumed his every thought. He hated this city. Had ever since the news, sixteen years before. The few brief, faceless weeks of carnival apart, winter was the worst. The pale, bleached landscapes. The people with their heads bowed against the wind and sleet and snow.

The festival here, like so much else, was tied to the pointless fairy stories of the Church, a brief moment of gaiety, of life, before the lean time of

Lent. As if a man needed to break from his true nature. As if there was, in truth, some aspect of him that rose beyond the everyday.

He went back into the bedroom and took out the small leather case he kept with him always, even when it had to be strapped to his chest beneath a medieval archer's tunic. There were five passports in it, all for different countries. Three open tickets provisionally booked for the same day out of Fiumicino the following week. First class, all under different names, changeable with a phone call. One to Rio de Janeiro. Another to Cape Town. A third to Melbourne. The southern hemisphere. Summer to Europe's winter. Warmth and promise.

The naked man leaned forward, stared at his pale, unremarkable face in the tall mirror on the wardrobe, bared his long white teeth, remembering. Then he snarled, 'That child was *mine*.'

Those four words were all he wanted to utter before finishing her. All he needed her to know.

The curtains were closed at every upstairs window. On the ground floor two sealed displays showed some mannequin stock. Behind them the solid metal security barriers were down. A notice on the front door said: 'Closed due to mourning'. It had been there a week. He'd used that trick before. The Venetians were a sanctimonious bunch.

Still naked, he walked down the narrow, steep staircase. The place below was both store area and workshop when he needed it, full of objects for sale and for his own use too. He had a drone to handle the public, seamstresses and pattern makers to deal with the costumes at whim. When the woman disappeared he'd sent them away with some money, told them to take some holiday. With carnival coming this looked a little odd, so he said he felt sick. Needed some privacy.

They knew not to argue.

He liked the place when it was empty. Behind the shuttered bay windows costumes stood on mannequins everywhere, men's in gold brocade and black velvet, women's in ornate white gowns, flowing, tight, sensual, cut in all the traditional styles. There was nothing fancy, nothing modern or jokey here. He hated that. The old ways were the only ways.

No sky-blue gown with a scarlet cape either. The last of those was gone. Needs must.

Naked, cold, the man padded barefoot around the room looking at the forest of still and silent dummies. He thought about the night ahead. Outside carnival was starting to return to life. He could hear the odd distant, drunken voice, the sound of the same stupid band he'd seen in Castello the evening before.

The outre was common at that moment. He went back upstairs and looked in the wardrobe in the studio. Sifting through the clothes – expensive suits and shirts from Savile Row in London, designer jackets and trousers from Milan – he chose a simple well-worn dark blue cotton workman's overall, a thick plaid shirt and heavy boots. Then he selected a chestnut wig, a full head of hair, badly made. So obvious it would generate smirks and behind-the-hand remarks. The fringe would tug down far enough to hide the plaster on the wound. No one would look twice at a face like this.

When he went back to the mirror he saw an anonymous labourer born to pull and shove and load, one of the strong-armed porters who ran the streets of Venice, dragging their wares around them on big-wheeled trolleys, bellowing for humanity to get out of their way.

No one ever took any notice of them. They were like canal rats, permanent fixtures, invisible. The disguise seemed perfect. Appropriate too.

Getting dressed he thought again about the woman from the building on Zattere.

Why had he tried to kill her?

Because she was an intruder. She had no place there.

What was she doing?

Defying him.

When he told her to kneel she just looked. Stared. Then fought back.

The woman was a kind of cop. A good one, Sofia said. The best in Rome. Not like the stupid Venetian kind. She was smart enough to find that place of his near the Arsenale. How? The hospital. Had to be. Sixteen years before when he went there trying to see Sofia they'd

401

pressed him at the desk. They'd no idea where she lived either. He had to tell them something, even if it was a lie. So, like an idiot, he gave them the first place that came to mind because the truth would have been much too close to home. And still it didn't work. Still she lay out of reach, refusing to see him, her fragile beauty beyond his touch.

He stopped as he dragged on the pair of heavy black boots.

Sometimes he was, he knew, slow-witted. Rigid in his ways. Blind to possibilities. Sitting there on the unmade bed, half-dressed, he wanted to punch his head with his fist, stamp some sense into it.

What did the bitch say to him?

Do I have to pray too? If I don't, does that break the spell? The magic?

What didn't she say?

Where is she? Where's Sofia Bianchi?

The niece was smart and relentless. Sofia couldn't stop telling him that all those years ago whenever her name came up. The Lupo woman wasn't looking for Sofia last night. She was searching for him. Determined to bring him in, a prize for the Romans, a slap in the face for the locals.

She wasn't looking for Sofia for one very good reason.

The bitch knew where she was already.

★   ★   ★

Think sideways.

Someone smarter than him had said that. One more tedious unwanted aphorism among so many. Though a few made sense.

His head felt clear for the first time in days. He now knew what to do.

He went downstairs, opened the front door and walked up the narrow dark alley out into the arcade along the approach to the bridge. There were only a few porters tugging at their trolleys, carrying vegetables and meat and fish, cartons of tourist tat, anything the dismal parasites of the streets desired. Just a handful of figures in costumes lurking in the shadows, waiting for the night to begin.

There were a couple at the little bar by Il Gobbo when he went there and ordered a cappuccino and a panino of prosciutto.

The piazza in front was being swept by the city cleaners, made ready for the coming wave of night-time revellers.

He went and stood by the statue, leaning on the black iron railings, then phoned the cripple, making out he was the proprietor of a costume shop on the other side of the bridge, in San Marco. He spoke like a local then, using the hard Venetian accent.

'You want what?' the cripple asked.

'You heard.'

He rattled off an order that was bound to make the man's ears prick up. Twenty masks in all. The most expensive.

'You got them?'

'Yes, yes . . .' Strozzi answered anxiously. 'Of course.'

He offered a ridiculous price. One the man would never refuse.

'And I want that girl to bring them. The pretty kid. The Croatian. I like her. What's her name?'

There was a long pause. Then the voice on the line asked, 'We've done business before?'

'Sure. I got a lot of shops. Here and there. Stalls too. I'll pay cash. Don't you worry. These masks are good? They're yours? Not some junk from Taiwan?'

'Of course they're ours.'

The cripple sounded offended by the question.

'I'm going for a coffee,' he said. 'Tell her to bring them to me. What's she called?'

'Camilla,' Strozzi said.

There was a place just round the corner. It was more secluded and closed for renovations. Not, he guessed, that she'd know. They were Dorsoduro people. No time, no money to explore much elsewhere.

He passed on the location and said, 'I'll meet her there at five thirty.'

'What name should I put on the bill?'

This was important. So much so he'd worked it out earlier, would have told the man anyway, even if he'd never asked. It was important to sow the seed, to throw the corn.

'Make it out to L'Arciere. That's the company. My name too. Cash, remember.'

He returned to the deserted shop, went upstairs, undressed and lay naked on the bed, thinking, imagining.

Forty minutes later, back in the blue workman's clothes, he went out again. At the end of the narrow dead-end alley that led from the shop back towards the bridge stood a small white dog. It sat on the paving stones beneath the arcade staring at him, blocking his way.

He hated dogs. Every last one of them. He would have fetched the thing a kick if there weren't a few people around. An act like that would draw attention. The Venetians adored these stinking little things.

Instead he simply walked up to the animal, bent down close to it, smiling, turning his head to one side.

Anyone who saw him would think this was an affectionate gesture.

The thing knew differently somehow. The dog sat there in a stiff little triangle, head erect, watching him with its gleaming black eyes. It was trembling as he got closer.

He reached forward for its neck. There was no collar. Just hard, white fur, a little matted and dry, as if the animal was very old.

He squeezed the skin beneath between his finger and thumb. The animal began to whimper and squeal in his grip.

'Be gone,' he said then let it loose, watching happily as it scampered, scared and anxious, across the patterned paving stones of the Rialto arcades, back into the darkness beyond the soot-stained statue of the pained and crouching man.

When Filippo Strozzi took the unexpected order that sent Camilla out into the foul afternoon, Teresa Lupo was still in the Questura, for no good reason she could see. Paola Boscolo had been true to her word. Too true. That morning, at seven thirty, Teresa was woken by the sound of the doorbell. Boscolo and three detectives were waiting outside to take her and all the material she had assembled about Sofia over to Castello.

She was allowed only a little time to wash and get herself ready. While she did that the cops poked and prodded around the apartment without asking. Teresa knew suspicion when she saw it. They were looking for evidence. Not just about Sofia's disappearance. But also her involvement with the man called Jerome Aitchison.

Teresa came out of the bathroom towelling her hair and said, 'If you told me what you were looking for perhaps I could help.'

'In this mess,' one of the men grumbled.

She didn't like the look of him. A little politeness would not have gone amiss.

'My aunt left in a hurry. She's never been the most tidy of people.'

406

'Did you find anything that suggested she knew this Englishman?' Paola Boscolo asked. 'Emails? Letters? Anything.'

Teresa smiled and said, 'I've already told you . . .'

The policewoman scowled.

'I meant something factual. Something I can touch.'

'As far as I can see Sofia didn't use email. She never did with me anyway. Just phone calls and texts.'

'Give me her number,' the policewoman ordered. 'I can talk to the phone company.'

Teresa waited for a moment then said, 'I gave you the number on Sunday. You mean you did nothing with it?'

Boscolo scowled at one of the men.

'I'll check,' he muttered and went to the window to make a call.

In the end there was nothing to take but the remaining stories and the blank sheets of mustard-yellow paper that once contained the first, presumably incriminating episode. The one that linked Sofia directly to Aitchison. Teresa pointed out that some simple forensic tests would show that the yellow paper had a particular purpose, even if the words once printed on it were now surely lost. The single sheet she'd sent Silvio would prove that once it was analysed, saving the Venetians time and money.

'We will look for ourselves,' Boscolo said, and then they went to the launch.

The rest of the day proved equally infuriating. Obstuse questions. Books of photographs. Long periods of inactivity spent on her own, sitting in a windowless room, listening to voices outside. She'd seen all this before, but from the other side. She knew what was going on. They were dancing in the dark.

Around three o'clock when Paola Boscolo came back with one more set of obscure questions Teresa asked, 'Am I a suspect here?'

The Venetian policewoman wriggled and muttered, 'Of course not.'

'So I can walk out right now?'

'If you like. We are discovering things. I was going to tell you.'

But only what you want, Teresa thought.

'Go ahead.'

The policewoman took a deep breath and said, 'First, let me be honest. See this from our point of view. This man Aitchison has murdered someone. Almost killed you too last night.'

'He was a man in a medieval costume,' Teresa told her. 'He didn't give a name.'

'Please. He made this arrangement with the Gabriellis. He organized a false passport with his own name and Gabrielli's photo. Gave him a gun. Told him to secrete himself in the campanile, shoot at the Cammarota girl then kill himself. Or his wife would die. The motive is obvious.'

'Tell me.'

408

Boscolo did not appreciate being dragged through this.

'He was aware that he was about to be exposed. By putting Gabrielli through this game Aitchison would lead us to believe that he was dead. We need look no further.'

'Sofia's still missing,' Teresa pointed out.

'At the time we had nothing to connect her with Aitchison except this vanished story of yours. Still we have nothing, frankly. The address of the place from last night connects Sofia to the crime.'

'That address was from sixteen years ago! And she never lived there at all.'

Paola shrugged.

'A link nevertheless. We have to consider that perhaps Sofia is a part of this man Aitchison's scheme. Unwilling possibly. Or not . . .'

Teresa Lupo sat there stony-faced and said, 'I know my aunt. You don't.'

'I rather had the impression you were beginning to doubt that yourself,' the policewoman said a little smugly. 'Besides. You've been in this situation. How often have you heard a relative say such a thing? They would *never* do this. How many times?'

'I'm telling you.'

'I know you're not a police officer any more . . .'

Teresa tried to stifle her disbelief then asked, 'You've talked to Rome?'

'Of course! How could we not?' Paola paused. 'They speak highly of you. For the most part.'

'I want to see what so-called evidence you've assembled.'

'You're a civilian. You know that cannot happen.'

'If it wasn't for me . . .'

Paola Boscolo nodded graciously.

'Thank you. I have no more questions. Do you?'

A million, Teresa thought. None of which wanted to appear at that moment.

'Sofia's phone. Have you tracked down the calls?'

The policewoman wondered whether to answer that. Then she said, 'The number you gave us has not been used for ten days. It's been switched off all that time. The last location the phone company had for it was in the Rialto.'

That could mean so many things.

'Of course she may have another phone,' Paola went on. 'She and Aitchison—'

'Sofia's terrible with anything technical,' Teresa broke in. 'Why do you think she didn't use email? She couldn't get the hang of it.'

'Possibly.'

'What about the police in Cambridge?'

'The man there told us you called pretending to be an officer,' Boscolo said. 'This is a criminal offence. For now I'm willing to overlook it. But no more such games, please. We will not brook any interference from a . . .'

She stopped.

'A what?'

'An outsider. A civilian witness. Someone close to a person of interest. Please . . .' She indicated the door. 'Feel free to go. If you wish to return to Rome . . .'

'Why would I do that?'

Boscolo seemed puzzled by the question.

'It's your home. This matter is in our hands now. We'll let you know if there's progress.'

The policewoman leaned forward to make her point.

'That would be for the best I think, Teresa. Interfering with a murder investigation is a serious matter. I have no wish to make a difficult situation worse for you. But if you leave me no choice . . .'

There was no friendly police launch this time. Teresa had to find her own way back from the Questura. The wind was getting up. Violent bursts of icy, squally rain were starting to chase across the water. The fast vaporetto across the basin lurched so much that a young American kid by the railings threw up into the seething waves.

Someone laughed.

Teresa called home and had a brief conversation with her mother. The murder was everywhere. Somehow Paola Boscolo had kept Teresa's name out of all the stories, nor did the papers link the death in Castello with a missing woman called Sofia Bianchi. Was this kindness on the

411

part of the policewoman? Or a simple precaution out of suspicion?

Probably the latter, she thought. They thought Teresa hadn't been entirely honest with them about Sofia. In a way, she guessed, they were right. She had two good reasons. They hadn't taken her seriously until she – not the police – found a young woman savagely slaughtered in a derelict place that had some hazy connection with Sofia in the past. And, more importantly, she wasn't yet sure what to make of events herself.

She felt grubby when she came through the door of the apartment. The Questura had done that, had placed some insidious uncertainties in her head. For the second time that day she climbed into the old bath and stood underneath the leaky, unreliable shower, listening to the gas boiler cough and wheeze.

Finally able to think for herself, away from prying cops, the previous night kept coming back, and with the memories came bafflement and a little fear.

The Count of Saint-Germain, the figure supposed to lead her in the search for Sofia, was dead. In the story anyway. What did that signify? That she was alone now. Some kind of climax was approaching, and it was one that no one else, it seemed, could tackle. Not that she felt capable of the task.

She went to the kitchen. One last exotic teabag remained. She boiled some water, made the final mug and sat at the computer. Messages from Rome. Yet one more plea from Silvio Di Capua asking her to get in touch. Not a word from Peroni. He would still be in Sicily with Falcone and Nic. Police work was never nine to five. Not their kind anyway.

Back to the search. Back to typing random keywords and hoping for the best. Beyond the grubby windows the weather was changing rapidly. The wind was howling outside. Rain, thick and greasy, was starting to lash down constantly from a rolling mass of angry, churning clouds. There were few craft in the channel separating her from the distant low shape of Redentore. Only one or two pedestrians fighting against the gale, struggling with umbrellas, staggering in the wind along the cobbled pavement that glistened under the street lights and the illumination from an unnaturally tall passing cruiser.

The building shook once more as it passed.

What was it Saint-Germain had said? She couldn't check the exact words any more. The Questura had taken them and in her astonishment she'd forgotten to ask for a copy for herself.

It was something about the stones of Venice.

'Never forget those,' she said out loud. 'They are your world now. They enclose everything that matters.'

She finished the tea, dimly remembering something. Then she went back to the computer. It took just a couple of minutes to track down, and when she did she wanted to scream.

The reason she missed the clue was that, unlike everything else Saint-Germain had told her, it was so very literal. The stones of Venice. Or, more accurately, *The Stones of Venice*. A book, by one of the most famous Englishmen ever to visit La Serenissima. His drawings, his words, his love for some aspects of the city and loathing for others, had electrified Victorian England and helped spread the fame of Venice to the world.

Teresa knew the name vaguely, and associated it with academic works about art and architecture. Not tragedy and madness, though when she looked more closely that was there too.

As she read about what had happened here a century and a half before she felt a grim sense of dread proximity to this strange and brilliant Englishman. Once he had lived no more than a few short steps beyond the Ponte agli Incurabili, in the Pensione Calcina, now a hotel to which, she'd promised herself earlier, she would return during the summer to take tea on the private wooden jetty over the lagoon, enjoying the view and, by then, the weather.

His books here were concerned with hard fact: the complex, shifting face of the city and how it might be interpreted. Behind this famous façade lay a tragedy so personal, so disturbing that its existence seemed to have been scrubbed from the public consciousness.

His name was John Ruskin and in 1858 he met a deeply religious Irish girl called Rose La Touche. A brilliant scholar and polymath, he was famed for his literary criticism, his commentaries on painting and architecture, and his precise and meticulous documentation, with his own highly detailed illustrations of the physical form of Venice. Every last portico, every quatrefoil, each window and stone and statue on the faces of the great buildings, from the Basilica San Marco to the distant reaches of the cathedral in Castello, had come to the punctilious attention of Ruskin's pens and pencils.

So taken was he with Rose La Touche that shortly after they met he declared his absolute, unshakeable love for her, a devotion that he regarded as sacred, as blessed by God, intended by the Almighty. No small promise to someone as religious as Rose.

She was eleven years old. He was forty-four.

When she turned seventeen Ruskin proposed and was turned down. A decade on she died, insane and hysterical. Mad with grief, Ruskin returned to the Adriatic to live in the Pensione Calcina, trying to find solace in the city where he won fame for the long and detailed illustrated chronicle that became *The Stones of Venice*.

There was none. At some point during his stay he visited the Accademia and walked into Room

XX, surrounding himself with the panoramic imagination of Carpaccio, transfixed by the stern faces, dead, but not entirely so as they stared down at him from the walls of the Ursula cycle.

No contemporary account existed of what happened that day. Ruskin never wrote about it, and scarcely spoke a comprehensible word on the subject during his madness or later. Before seeing the Carpaccio canvases he was one more miserable, broken individual, mourning the loss of a loved one who had rejected him. When he walked out he was a man deep in the tempest of insanity, racked by an obsessive belief, rooted in the portraits of Ursula, that would shatter his ability to write, to think, to deal with the world outside for years.

Teresa broke off at this point and tried to calm herself. These ghosts were so close they seemed to walk the same narrow alleys she'd followed herself in pursuit of Sofia. Just as obsessively as Ruskin had, and without much in the way of solid, well-founded reason.

The room closed in on her for a moment. All the details – the scattered collections of bills and books, of clothes and sewing material, the medieval gown by the door, still on its dummy, crown perched on the pale wooden head, hidden beneath the grubby cover of the sofa – spoke of chaos, the disorder of an irrational mind. That was why she had never looked too closely. It offended some inner judgemental, narrow-minded sense of propriety.

She thought of Saint-Germain and went back to the computer to read the rest.

After visiting the Accademia Ruskin became convinced that Rose La Touche was somehow a universal spirit, a creation of God existing outside the bounds of time. That she had lived in Venice centuries before, and it was *her* likeness that Carpaccio had captured from life in the face and figure of Ursula in the paintings on the wall of the Accademia. For several long months he'd laboured in Venice, crazed, delirious, captivated by the paintings, kept alive only by the loving support of friends. Then the first in a series of absolute breakdowns ensued and he was taken back to England by those same admirers, to begin a slow and uncertain recovery.

Away from Venice, from the calm, beautiful face of Carpaccio's Ursula, he began to improve.

Teresa called up some images of the paintings from the Accademia website. They did the original no justice. The detail was lacking, as was the tormenting intensity of the players in what was meant to be a sweeping universal drama.

Seen this way the differences between the Ursula cycle and the Carpaccio she'd first met, the canvas in the *scuola*, with St Augustine, the small dog and the strange cartellino, were even more marked. The Ursula paintings were vast and expansive. They sought to describe and contain an entire world, and a great tragedy within it. The painting of Augustine, which she much preferred, was about one man's doubt, his inability to interpret something just beyond reach. A single question left both unanswered and imperfectly, cryptically framed, perhaps by nothing more than a single small dog and some words on a painted note.

Thinking, imagining, alone in the front room of Sofia's ram-shackle flat, she felt, finally, that Saint-Germain's enigmatic tales were becoming a little clearer. The man she sought was a player in the greater story around them, an actor, the archer with his taut bow and arrow, moved and defined by events. Someone who appeared on the surface ordinary but contained within him an imperfection like Saint-Germain's own aberrant gene, a sport within the blood that required only the right catalyst, the correct trigger, to become active.

A mannequin clothed and made real by coincidence, by fate, by chance.

She was meant to play the role of Augustine. Solitary, bewildered, focused entirely on seeking enlightenment. Unable to reach a conclusion because, as the cartellino intimated, this strange, small personal odyssey was a work in progress, still in motion.

'*Victor Carpathius Fingebat*,' she murmured. A painter's enigmatic boast: *Vittore Carpaccio was creating this* . . . Teresa recalled the remnants of a line she felt Saint-Germain had spoken thereabouts in the story.

'Incomplete, unfinished. The state we all live in, without knowing it. Die in too.'

Dammit, Arnaud, she thought. If you are real and we ever meet I will give you such a tongue-lashing for these riddles.

She looked around and realized she'd spoken out loud. Talking to a ghost. Or not even that perhaps.

If Peroni or Falcone or Nic had been here they would have seen the point immediately. A wise man learns more from his mistakes than his successes. Revelation sometimes comes more from what's uncertain than from what is known.

She felt, once more, a fool. Why had her inquisitiveness never strayed into such a spec-ulative area before? Because, a lone voice answered, you are what you are. A scientist. Literal. Used to seeking answers only in the light. Afraid, in a way, of anything that can only be found in darkness.

'Enough,' she said, and got up for her coat, grab-bing her phone, reaching for Alberto Tosi's number which was now so used it sat on speed dial.

They could not possibly be relations. She'd established that already on the web. But the name on the bell for the empty apartment upstairs was that of Michael Ruskin. The owner of the block. Someone who rarely appeared and seemed almost unknown to Strozzi and Camilla. A rich man who travelled freely.

She did not believe in coincidences, any more than she believed in ghosts or God.

The weather was turning from squall to storm. Some streets were beginning to resemble *acqua alta,* when the lagoon rose so high that the city flooded in its lowest parts and wellington boots became everyday wear.

Camilla Dushku took the fast vaporetto to the Rialto carrying the precious masks in six bags, three on each arm. Struggling beneath a flimsy umbrella, she fought her way against the wind as she crossed the bridge then stumbled down into the arcades beyond.

The café she was looking for lay beyond the markets which were now deserted, with just a few bedraggled men and women soaking in their costumes and masks, hiding in the arcades, forlornly sipping at drinks. It took her a minute or two to locate but finally she found the narrow *salizada,* and then the *sotoportego* and the sign: *Do Spade.* Two swords.

It was closed. Another burst of freezing rain flew down from the sky, filling the dark arch where she stood. She put down the carriers for a moment, in the driest spot she could see, and started to take out her phone.

A man in blue overalls came out of the empty space by the corner. He smiled at her and nodded towards the bags.

'I won't pay if they're damaged,' he said in an odd and artificial accent.

'I'm sorry?'

'The masks? You're bringing them for me.'

She wasn't best pleased.

'The café. You said to meet you there. And it's—'

'Closed. Sorry. Venetians. What can you do? Listen. Let's dump these things off in the shop. Then I'll buy you a cappuccino and a *frittella*. You could use something warm inside you.'

Camilla Dushku did not like the look of this man. She had an idea she recognized him from somewhere, which was surely imposible.

'I'll just leave you with the masks,' she said and picked up the bags, offering them to him.

'Happy to carry,' he said with a smile. 'But the money's in the shop.' He leaned forward and looked at her. 'You're Croatian, aren't you? I can tell from the accent. Beautiful country. Shame it's so . . .'

He winced.

'You know. Screwed.'

She walked with him back to the arcade by the bridge. He kept close to her beneath the umbrella but he didn't carry the bags. On the eastern side, by some tourist stalls that were closing because of the gale, he guided her into the shadows with his arm.

'Filippo told me your shop was across the bridge in San Marco,' she said.

'Got lots of shops. Lots of money. Places all

around the world. But don't tell the tax people, huh? We all know what they want.' He nudged her arm. 'I don't need to tell *you* that, do I?'

After a minute or so they were in a deserted blind alley with a single store just visible, dimly lit at the end. It was off the main arcade. She didn't understand how anyone could run a business from a place like this. No one would find their way here accidentally. It was too dark, too hidden. The wind and rain were blowing damp newspapers and trash into the cul-de-sac. The gutters overran with black filthy water. There was that rarest thing in Venice, a real and noxious stench of bad drains.

The man kept walking and she felt she had to keep up. Finally he stopped outside the shop door and began fiddling with a set of keys. Quickly, anxiously, he pressed the button for the electric security shutter. As it rose it revealed a plate glass door. She looked through into the interior. The stock was limited from what she could see, but expensive, authentic. All the characters of the carnival, and the Commedia dell'Arte too. Harlequin and the female servant Colombina. The Captain and the pot-bellied villain Pulcinella.

And the Plague Doctor. Three of the last, though the costumes were all identical. The white mask with its beak, unadorned, the way purists liked. The dark gown, the broad, buckled hat. A ruffed collar, two black, one starched and white.

'Everybody likes him,' the man said, catching

the direction of her gaze. 'Don't they? Inquisitive little bastard if you ask me. Sticking that long nose where it's not wanted. Still, the drones enjoy a little . . .' He leaned close to her and she caught the smell of tobacco on his breath. '. . . .terror, eh?'

The costumes looked dusty and so did the faces of the mannequins wearing them.

She'd packed the masks herself. They were all female, small, easy to carry.

'If they're so popular why didn't you ask for the Plague Doctor?' she said, staring at the grubby glass and the faded and featureless plastic dummies behind.

He'd got the door open and was beckoning her inside. Camilla Dushku was frightened and she didn't know why.

'You ask a hell of a lot of questions,' the man in the blue overalls told her. 'Do you want the money or not?'

She dropped the bags on the damp ground, in the filth and the trash, and turned to run. But he was on her so quickly, and the place they were in was so remote, so hidden.

There was no chance to scream, no opportunity to fight. He'd dragged her inside the shop before she knew it. Then he struck her once in the face, knocking her to the hard, cold floor. While she floundered there he got a rag out of his pocket, tied it round her mouth, rolled her onto her front, legs kicking, arms flailing, and hit her a couple of times till she was still.

She was barely conscious. Just enough to see him go back to the door and close it, bringing down the shutters.

After that he set to work.

When Filippo Strozzi eventually answered the door he looked flustered.

'Something wrong?' Teresa asked.

'Not really. We had an order from someone.'

'That's good, isn't it?'

The big scruffy man in the wheelchair frowned. He wore a voluminous sweater, faded blue, threadbare, with holes at the elbows.

'I suppose. Camilla's gone to deliver it. The man who called . . .' He looked guilty. 'He said he was an old customer. I can't find any trace of a company called L'Arciere. I don't understand . . .'

She blinked, felt cold. He didn't know the details about what had happened the previous night. About the archer. Even that she'd been involved. The police hadn't released much more than the news of the murder to the media.

'Michael Ruskin,' she said.

'What?'

'He uses you as a kind of caretaker?'

Strozzi glanced at the wheelchair.

'What do you think?'

'You keep the keys, Filippo. Spares for whoever rents the apartments here?'

'True,' he agreed.

The phone was in his lap, as if he was expecting a call.

'Do you have them for his apartment too?'

His dark eyebrows rose.

'There's a window open or something up there,' she said quickly. 'If I can go in I can close it.'

'Has anyone ever told you you're a terrible liar?'

'Lots of people. It's important. For Sofia.'

He hesitated.

'Ruskin's not the kind of man who'd like people poking round,' Strozzi said.

She held out her hand.

'He's involved,' Teresa said. 'Don't ask me how exactly. But I know.'

Strozzi thought for a second then whirred over to a sideboard covered in half-finished masks. From the top drawer he took out a hefty key ring, handed it over, pointed out the right ones.

'When did you last see him?' Teresa asked.

'November. December. I can't remember.'

'And before that?'

'I don't know. He doesn't live here. Just uses it from time to time. There's a staircase at the back. It leads down to the little lane that goes round to Salute. He used to come in that way.'

'What's he like?'

Strozzi frowned.

'I don't really know. I've lived here ten years or so. Never see him much. He's got places in London. New York. Australia. All over, I think. I suspect this isn't the only house in Venice. We pay our rent. If there's something needs doing to the building I just take it out of the same bank account. It's easy. It works. He's the best landlord I've ever had. Ten years here. No trouble. No bother.'

I bet, she thought.

'I never really know when he's here or not,' Strozzi added. 'As I said. He can come and go through the back. Someone's been there lately. I pay the electricity bills. You can tell. Whether it's him or someone he's let in there . . .'

Strozzi stared at her and asked, 'You really think this is something to do with Michael Ruskin?'

She waved the keys.

'Later. I need to talk to you, Alberto and Camilla. Not in the café either. Let's meet here. Half an hour. Can you phone her?'

'Of course,' he said. 'Whether she'll back in time . . .'

She set off up the stone staircase, calling Tosi on the way. He was in San Marco already, with a friend, and could be there in minutes.

This was the first time she'd been to the top floor. The door was polished oak with a brass handle. Heavier, more expensive than the rest. There was a painting there of a centaur, half-man, half-horse, with something in his arms. A bow.

The picture jogged a series of unpleasant memories.

She returned to Sofia's apartment and picked out the sharpest knife she could find in the kitchen, a short and well-worn Sabatier. When she ran her finger across the edge it felt anxious to cut into her skin.

She put on her heavy jacket, stashed the knife in the right-hand pocket, and returned to Ruskin's floor.

The door had three locks, all of them heavy mortise mechanisms, fully turned. It took her five minutes to get them all open. The handle felt stiff, as if it was little used, but with some force she got it open.

Her right hand fell instinctively on the light switch, pressed it, then reached for the knife.

There was one vast room, the same shape as those on the floors below. But this one was tidier, with a single table, a sofa and flatscreen TV, and more modern windows giving out onto the lagoon.

Every apartment in this block was so different. Strozzi's with its grand piano and the careful arrangement of furniture to allow him to move around in the wheelchair. Camilla's, more a mask workshop than a home. Sofia's a confused mess of clothes and belongings, scattered everywhere as if she'd never found the time to call the place home.

And this. Michael Ruskin's apartment. Teresa walked into the extension. An extra bathroom, two bedrooms and a small office that led to the outside staircase. Like the main rooms in the older part they were totally without character. Tidy, with the minimum of modern furniture, a little dusty. No cleaner had been here lately, though the place had surely been occupied. Two of the bedrooms had clearly not been used for some time. The largest, at the back, away from the main building, had a double bed that looked as if it had been made that very day.

The position meant that no one below could hear. She realized now that he could have been here all along.

Something nagged her about the office. She went back and looked at the desk. There were two screens. One was for a computer. It was locked with a password. No time to waste there. The second was connected to what she now realized was a closed-circuit TV control board.

She looked at the labels on it. They listed every floor except the present one. She pressed the power button and the default view came up. It was Sofia's apartment, the messy living room. The bedroom. Teresa chose another view. Camilla's floor was in darkness. When she flicked the switch again she saw Filippo Strozzi seated at the grand piano. She hit the controls and zoomed in. He was making a phone call, listening, as if hearing his call ring out unanswered. He looked anxious.

A light appeared on the monitor. A bell sounded. She pressed another button and saw Alberto Tosi at the front door. He wore his usual old-fashioned hat which he took off to smooth his hair. Always the dapper gentleman.

She changed the camera, found the hall, watched

Strozzi let him in. The two shook hands and then went into the ground-floor flat.

'Wonderful,' she murmured. 'You saw everything.'

There was a volume control on the unit. She turned it up. Strozzi and Tosi were making puzzled small talk.

So he heard everything too.

A heavy cable ran from the back of the control desk to a web router by the PC. He had net access even if no one else in the building did. The entire surveillance system was hooked into a private connection. The man could spy on the people here from anywhere. He could be in Cambridge or Kathmandu but he still had the occupants of this crooked little palazzo in his sights.

She reached round the back of the router for the wire to remove it. She hated these things. There were too many already, legitimate ones, spying on ordinary people as they walked down the street. To her surprise the jack had been removed already. Any connection to the web was broken for some reason. She couldn't imagine why.

A tiny metal safe sat next to the desk, built into the wall. It had a conventional lock, not a combination. There was a small, short key on the ring Strozzi gave her that seemed out of place, too small to open any important door.

People who owned a string of properties around the world appalled her. How many places could a man or woman occupy at any one time? They never knew these so-called homes, not properly. They never looked after them well, made them personal, gave them character. And sometimes they became careless. They handed over the keys – all of them – to a trusted person nearby, asking them to become proxy owners, someone who could call the plumber when water started to run through the ceiling.

She tried the little key and it turned.

There were three envelopes inside the safe. She took out the first and knew from the feel what it was. Photographs. A tidy bundle of them, twenty or more.

Teresa went through them and felt her heart begin to ache. Every one was of a younger Sofia, a time when she was even more beautiful and a touch slimmer. Sofia by the lagoon, close to the Zattere vaporetto *fermata*. Out on the islands, by Torcelo, eating fish on the terrace at what looked like the Locanda Cipriani, staring into the camera lens, bright-eyed, mouth open, fork full of spaghetti. In San Marco. By the Rialto. Wearing a skimpy bikini on the private beach of the Hotel Des Bains on the Lido, fanning out a set of fortune-telling cards, not tarot this time, but old-fashioned ones covered with the signs of the zodiac, like the pictures she'd painted for the doors here. All part of the same nonsensical game she tried to play with Teresa when she was young until the child, for once, rebelled.

Then, a change. This was Venice still, a bench

seat on the Zattere promenade with Redentore across the canal in the background. Teresa could sense the shift in the seasons. The colours had leached from the bright, loud pigments of summer to the softer, washed-out shades of autumn.

Sofia was different too. Her face was more strained, her eyes had lost their vivacity. There were lines by her mouth. Her smile for the camera became ever more forced with each picture.

The last were around carnival. There were street lights and, in a shot by the Rialto, the same gigantic blue snowflakes that still ran down from the bridge into the arcades, towards the markets and Il Gobbo.

One photograph remained, beneath the shot she was staring at. She could guess it was bad somehow and she didn't want to see it.

Teresa blinked then forced herself, flicking away the penultimate picture.

The last was of Sofia inside the apartment where Teresa now sat. The main room, the one at the front. That was obvious from the windows and the view beyond them. She wasn't smiling. She was staring straight into the camera lens with a mixed expression, part fear, part resentment. And despair too. That was something Teresa had never seen in her.

This must have been days before she terminated the child. The last moment before her world fell apart, and that of the man behind the lens.

She flicked back through all the shots again. He wasn't in any of them. Just Sofia. An obsessive, intimate record of her journey from bright happiness, the kind that can only have stemmed from love, to some desperate form of misery.

The second envelope contained a bundle of passports from around the world: British, American, Canadian, Australian, French, German, Italian, Mexican. Different names. Michael Ruskin. Jonathan Archer. Miguel Manara. Hugo Massiter.

The identity pages were still loose. None contained a photograph. The seal was unfixed. A new image could be inserted as required. Forging passports was not easy. This was just the raw material. Each would be recreated at will, probably elsewhere using a specialist. A man with money could buy anything. A man with money needn't even exist, if that was what he wanted.

At the bottom was a loose passport photograph, old and used. She stared at it and recognized the face from the industry newsletter she'd found the day before. This, she felt sure, was a portrait of the real Jerome Aitchison, the man pictured when he appeared at the actuarial convention in Amsterdam. He seemed very unremarkable.

She picked up the envelope with the photos, made some notes then took out her phone and called her deputy, Silvio Di Capua, in Rome.

He listened to her greet him as if nothing had happened.

Then he said, 'Finally!'

'I've been busy, boy. Don't you start. I've got a job for you.'

'Busy? *Busy?* Firstly, I'm thirty years old. Not a boy. Also, you quit, didn't you? Secondly . . . I forget what the second part is. But given the first it doesn't really matter. You're history.'

He always made her laugh.

'Oh come on, Silvio. I resigned. That's not the same as quitting. Everyone knows that. Do you honestly think I can't deal with a bunch of penny-pinching bean counters in suits when I get back? I've handled worse than this. Good grief . . . I *am* handling worse than this now. Roll with it, kid. I'm nearly there. Once I'm in Rome I'll smile at a few people and handbag the rest. When did that not work?'

'You're delusional!' he yelled.

So would you be in my place, she thought. All she needed to do was find Sofia. Or Michael Ruskin. Or Jerome Aitchison. One of them was surely getting closer.

'Are you going to help me or not?' she asked.

'No.'

'Fine,' she barked. 'Ring off then.'

'You ring off!'

'Oh for God's sake. One small favour. That's all I ask. You read about that murder in Venice last night?'

'Yes,' he said more quietly. 'This has something to do with you?'

'Well, I found it. While our Venetian colleagues

433

were busy stuffing their faces with *frittelle*. So I imagine the answer is yes.'

He was silent for a long moment then he said, 'They never mentioned that in the newspapers.'

'They never want to hand anyone else the credit, do they? Trust me. That was *my* murder.'

'You're supposed to be there looking for an aunt who's gone bananas or something.'

'Don't tell me why I'm here. Even I don't know that any more. *I* found that murder. The bastard who committed it wanted that dead woman to be Sofia. She's escaped him somehow. So far. Until I find her – or him – I'm stuck here. This is my problem. Now are you going to help me with it or not?'

Silvio Di Capua ummed and aahed. Then finally, he said, 'We've a general call out on the network for information on this Englishman Aitchison. If you've a lead I can chase . . .'

She gave him the address of the crooked little palazzo and told him to look up the ownership details. The Questura had these online, ready for instant access. A few seconds later Di Capua came back and said, 'It's a company. Name of Schütze Enterprises. Registered in Monaco.'

'Schütze?'

'German, I guess. No way can I see anything in Monaco for a day or so. You know that.'

Wonderful, she thought.

'Anything else registered to the same company that you can see?'

The distant keyboard clacked.

'Someone's got money,' Di Capua said. 'Apartment in Florence. House in Orvieto. Place in Bologna . . .'

'Venice?'

'Nothing. Sorry. Wait. I'm trying Aitchison. That *is* why we're doing this, isn't it?'

Waste of time. As if that was a surprise.

'Keep looking,' she said. 'See if you can work out who's behind this Schütze company. Whoever owns this place has other property in Venice. Don't ask me what kind. Find it.'

Another pause.

'That's it?' he asked.

'If this was easy I'd be giving it to the locals, genius.'

'True. I'll call if I get something.'

She put away the phone and walked round the apartment again. Bare. Without any sense of identity, just like the man himself. A temporary home, nothing more. So why were the photos here, not somewhere else?

Because Sofia stayed here too, sixteen years ago. In the downstairs apartment possibly. To begin with anyway.

Another detail from the stories came back. When Saint-Germain asked her what the root of this was she'd said, 'True love.'

In a way, she guessed, the man who wrote those things had got that right. Not that she was any clearer how.

She returned to the hall and locked the door

435

behind her. It was time to talk to Tosi and Strozzi, and Camilla too if she was back.

The phone in her pocket rang as she walked down the stairs. She stopped on her own landing, grabbed at it anxiously, wondering about Paola Boscolo's reaction when she gave her this lead, and said, 'That was quick!'

'What was?' said a flat male voice she didn't recognize.

'Who is this?' she asked.

He laughed as if the question were stupid. Then he said, 'Who do you want me to be?'

'Look at the phone.'

Teresa stood on the cold stone landing and stared at the handset as he ordered. He wasn't there. Camilla was, in a white carnival dress, frills around her neck, a gag around her mouth, red lipstick smeared across her face, a cheap crown on her head. She gazed into the lens, wide-eyed with terror. A hand came and ripped the gag from her mouth. The picture was live. He wanted to prove that. So he shouted at her, slapped her, and held the phone closer as she cried.

'Stop it,' Teresa yelled and heard her voice echoing up and down the stairs.

The video disappeared before she could see his face.

'You're as smart as she said. Is it enough?'

'Probably not.'

'That's a shame. Bad for the Croatian kid. Bad for you. Bad for me too.'

'What am I supposed to say?'

'You really don't know?'

'No,' she told him.

'You're supposed to say, "Here she is. Here's Sofia. The cheating, lying, murdering bitch. Take her. She's yours."'

There was a sound and she felt sure he'd done something to Camilla.

'Don't hurt the girl,' she said. 'It's not her fault.'

'Whose is it?'

'No one's. Sometimes things just happen.'

'No they don't. People . . . do this.'

It was like talking to a child.

'People don't always mean things. They get confused. Events change them. They meet . . .' She tried so hard to remember the stories. 'Triggers.'

'Here's a trigger,' he said. 'Bang!'

His voice was so loud she had to take her ear from the phone.

'What do you want?' she asked.

'I told you. Sofia.'

'I don't know where she is.'

'Liar.'

Camilla shrieked again.

'I'm telling you the truth,' Teresa insisted.

He whooped down the line.

'Liar, *liar*! Lie to me again and she's dead right now.'

Teresa didn't know what to say. What might make a difference.

He went quiet as if he was listening to something. She heard it too. Bells. Not the kind of peal you got to mark the hour. A practice. He didn't say a word till they were over.

'You're her favourite little girl,' he said. 'The smart one. She told me. Couldn't stop. Night and day. The kid she envied. The strong one who made good. The oh-so-bright genius who always finds the answer.'

No, she thought. I envied her. Not the other way round.

'I'm not that bright.'

'You found that place last night, didn't you?' His voice sounded cold and dead. 'What you did was so . . . *unspeakable*. Sticking your sharp nose where it doesn't belong. Prying.'

I didn't put a camera in anyone's bedroom, she nearly said.

Instead she murmured, 'Sorry.'

'You should be.'

'Tell me what to do.'

He sighed, a long, jaded sound then ordered, 'Look at the phone.'

Camilla had a noose round her neck now and a folded piece of fabric over her eyes. The rope was taut as if held somewhere.

An arm came into the image from the left. Blue material, not carnival this time, not the colour of the Ursula figure in the Accademia either. Everyday. Industrial. Overalls maybe.

He shook the chair and Camilla screamed, desperate to stay upright.

Teresa watched, aghast, trying to think.

He stopped. Camilla stood there sobbing, head bowed.

'Tell me where she is,' he said.

'I can't.'

The picture wobbled. He was shaking the chair more violently. Camilla was shrieking with terror.

'I can't because I don't know!' Teresa yelled.

The dress was unusual. Archaic somehow. There were items around her. Mannequins possibly. Mirrors. The kind used in tailors' shops, only these seemed to have ornate ormolu frames.

The picture disappeared. She put the phone back to her ear.

Silence.

'If you don't know,' he said, 'I might as well deal with this pretty little thing right now. Don't you think?'

'I don't know because she keeps moving. It seemed safest. Give me time.'

It was so desperate, so invented. She wondered whether he'd believe her.

'Time doesn't work around here any more. You've got to do better than that.'

'I don't know. I can't reach her by phone. This evening . . .'

'Hear that?' he asked.

The church bells again. They were marking the hour. Tolling six o'clock.

'When I hear eight of those I will call you,' he said. 'If you've no news for me, nothing I can find and touch for myself, the girl is dead and I am gone for good. No prize to take home then. Just one more body.'

The last peal struck.

He laughed then added, 'If you want to know how to find me ask Sofia. Tell her to give you a sign.'

The line went dead.

She turned off the record button. It had been running almost since the moment he began speaking. Capturing everything, words and pictures.

Downstairs, at the table next to Filippo Strozzi's grand piano, the three of them watched and listened as Teresa replayed the conversation. When it was over the big bearded man in the wheelchair buried his head in his hands.

'We've got to call that young policewoman now,' Tosi insisted. 'After what happened last night . . .'

He'd already had his say about the Casino degli Spiriti, scolding her like a cross parent for going back there after he'd left.

He took out his very old mobile phone and asked, 'What better time than now?'

She waved it away.

'Alberto. You know as well as I what will happen. Paola Boscolo will tell her inspector. He will tell his superior. A meeting will be called, officers assigned, possibilities explored. They're already bewildered by what's happening. You said yourself. How often is Venice afflicted by murder? If we had something concrete to give them, an address, say, they'd be there in five minutes. But we don't and in the circumstances, without something more substantial, we'll only add to their confusion. You heard him. If he sees a uniform he'll kill her. Do you think for one moment that's an idle threat?'

'The police!' Tosi barked.

She stabbed her finger on the table.

'Not yet. Not now. He thinks I know where Sofia is. I can't disappoint him. Can I?'

The old man fell quiet. Filippo Strozzi muttered a few words of self-recrimination.

'How were you to know?' Tosi asked him.

'Of course I should have known,' Strozzi snapped. 'An order out of the blue? Some stranger asking to meet her in a café? This is no way to do business.'

He briefly closed his eyes.

'Tell me exactly what he said, Filippo,' Teresa demanded.

She listened carefully. Then she replayed the phone call again, pausing on the video though the sight of Camilla clearly caused Filippo Strozzi intense distress.

'Does the name Schütze mean anything to you?' she asked.

Strozzi nodded.

'It's on the bank account,' he said. 'For the property.'

'Why would a man ostensibly called Michael Ruskin give his property company a German name?' she wondered.

None of them could begin to guess.

'He does have a shop,' Tosi said, pointing at the phone. 'That's a real costume, surely.'

'A shop that's closed,' she added. 'In the middle of carnival.'

'It can't be anywhere central,' Strozzi said. 'Someone would notice. Venice is a small world. I know the competition. We talk to one another. It's not possible.'

'It's a shop!' Tosi insisted.

'I don't know . . .' Strozzi looked lost. 'A studio maybe? A place they make things?'

'And you've never done business with any company called L'Arciere?' Teresa asked.

Strozzi thought for a moment, shook his head, checked his address book anyway.

'Not that I know. Companies come and go. People stay the same. Maybe. Under a different name.' He looked desperate. 'You're telling me this is Michael Ruskin? The same man?'

His big, bear-like face contorted in bewilderment.

She threw the photos onto the table and told them where she'd found them.

'I think it's just one of the names he uses,' she said. 'He and Sofia were lovers here sixteen years

442

ago. She became pregnant. The relationship soured. She had an abortion. He took that very badly. This obsession with the painting in the Accademia. The name he came to use here . . .'

'Ruskin?' Tosi repeated. 'Like the Englishman?'

'Quite.'

Strozzi seemed genuinely taken aback.

'This seems impossible.'

'It's not. She came back for some reason. It wasn't coincidence. It wasn't a rental apartment she picked out of the paper. Did you know?'

'No!' His hefty arms flailed the air. 'None of this. Sofia never mentioned a thing.' He thought for a moment then said, 'I didn't see them together. Not once. Though . . .' Strozzi scowled. 'If he came in by the back way . . .'

She stood up and looked at the ceiling. There was a small chandelier there, dusty and cheap. She stood on the chair, reached into the uppermost circle of glass and pulled out a small, tube-like lens. Then she sat down, leaving the thing dangling over them.

Both men looked at her aghast as she told them what she'd found in the office upstairs.

'So we were some kind of zoo for him?' Strozzi asked. 'Circus animals he could spy on when he felt like it?'

'I suppose. Why's he so sure I know where Sofia is?' Teresa wondered.

'Because he's insane,' Strozzi said.

No. It was more than that.

'Sofia couldn't do all this on her own. Look, at the mess that's her apartment. Look at her life. She couldn't conceal herself in this city without help. And these stories . . .'

The stories said it all.

Teresa Lupo placed both her arms on the table and stared at them.

'Someone's hiding her. Someone who knows what's going on here is writing those things, trying to help me find her.'

'It could be him,' Strozzi objected, pointing at the dangling camera in the ceiling. 'Using you.'

'How would he know about Alberto?' she asked, nodding towards Tosi. 'About the investigation into the body of St Mark?'

Tosi frowned and said, 'I thought I told you. Anyone could read about that in the paper and put two and two together. You and I have been in the press in the past, remember. That case in Murano.'

'Then how did he find out Sofia had invited me here in the first place? That she frequented that *scuola* in Castello? About Camilla and that English boy, Jason? How? Even with those cameras . . .'

Strozzi shuffled in his wheelchair.

'He didn't remember Camilla's name,' he said. 'When he called me. I remember that. He had to ask. Twice, I think.'

'The man's a criminal,' Tosi cut in. 'He wants you to think this.'

'No.' Strozzi was adamant. 'I don't believe so. Why would he hide such a thing? If he didn't know that, how could he know she was sick? About Jason too?' He glanced at Teresa. 'Whoever wrote those things, it couldn't be him.'

'Well?' she said, waiting.

'You think it was me?' Strozzi asked, clearly amazed, pointing at his huge chest with a long, strong finger. 'A man who can't even stand on his own two feet? I'm flitting round Venice in the dark saving Sofia from the monster? I wish.' He slapped the arms of the wheelchair as if he hated the thing. 'Truly I wish. But it's not me. Nor do I write stories, of any kind.'

Silence. She watched Tosi. Finally he shook his head in amazement and said, 'If only . . .'

She glanced at her watch. Six thirty. In ninety minutes he'd call and demand some hard information he could check. A route to Sofia free of interference, of the police, of anything that might get in his way.

'Then who?' she demanded. '*Who?*'

Tosi put a finger to his cheek and said, 'We're wasting time. We need to call the Questura so they can start looking for this poor girl. You heard what he said.'

There was information in that phone call. She had to extract every minute piece of it.

The bells.

He was near the Rialto somewhere. They were the same peal she'd heard when she'd stood next to Il Gobbo in the freezing February night, sipping at a spritz, wondering how she could find Sofia.

Time doesn't work around here any more.

This was such a stretch, and so out of character, she could scarcely believe she was considering it. Some distant memory of a guide book told her the clock on the church of San Giacomo opposite was notorious for being the most unreliable in Venice. Time didn't work there, any more than it did for the Count of Saint-Germain.

She got up.

'Where are you going?' Tosi asked.

'Out. Here's my deputy's number in Rome.' She scribbled Silvio Di Capua's direct line and handed it to Tosi. 'Phone him first. Tell him all we know. Tell him to put it on his list. After that call Paola Boscolo. Tell her what you told him. If there's anything of use in the system, on the networks somewhere, Silvio will find it before anyone and get it to her. Make sure Paola Boscolo understands the threats. If they flood the city with uniforms he'll kill her anyway.'

'Teresa . . .' Tosi objected.

But she was out of the door, face down, trying to keep out the wind and the rain.

Signora Rizzolo's *pasticceria* would be closed.

There was only one person left who might be hiding Sofia from the vengeance of the man called Michael Ruskin.

Jason Cunningham lived above the little café, in a room Signora Rizzolo gave him as part of the job. She prayed he'd be there, had no idea what she'd do if he wasn't.

★   ★   ★

446

The rain was incessant. When she reached the café Teresa stood back in the narrow street, feet wet, shivering with cold, and looked at the upstairs windows. No lights. Curtains closed.

Then someone tapped hard on her shoulder and she almost jumped out of her skin. A large, round figure stood next to her, face in darkness, head completely covered by a clear plastic rain hood.

'We're closed, signora,' said a cheery Venetian voice. 'But if you want some bread, or *frittelle*, I can always let in a friend. Move into the doorway, please. I have no wish to drown in front of my own *pasticceria*.'

Teresa followed Bella Rizzolo into the shelter of the building. She was unlocking the door already.

'I was looking for Jason. I wanted to speak to him.'

'Too late,' the woman told her. 'Come in. I'll make you a hot chocolate. It's too dismal to be out there.'

'Jason . . .'

'Sofia's still missing, he tells me.'

She took off her hood and looked earnestly at Teresa.

'This is a mystery indeed. Such a lovely woman.'

'I really need to talk . . .'

Signora Rizzolo shook her head and the rain went everywhere.

'You just missed him. He goes out every night at this time.' She laughed. '*Every* night of late.

447

Choir practice, he says. The English. They have such a strange sense of humour.'

She winked.

'I think it's that pretty Croatian girl, you know. Camilla. Beautiful child. Jason's so shy. But I think they meet—'

'Camilla's been working these last few nights,' Teresa said immediately. 'Serving drinks at carnival parties.'

A puzzled look, then, 'Perhaps it is choir practice. Who knows?'

'You've no idea where he goes?'

Signora Rizzolo's finely sculpted eyebrows rose in surprise.

'Of course not!'

'I meant . . . none at all?'

She shook her strong shoulders, the way a bird ruffles its feathers, sending rain everywhere.

'The boy's a stranger here. It would be unkind to leave him entirely to his own devices. He catches the number two vaporetto. The fast one that goes to Rialto and the station and Piazzale Roma.' She shrugged. 'I've seen him once or twice when I'm out with Lancelotto.'

Teresa asked, 'Who's . . . ?'

Grinning like a schoolchild, the woman reached deep into her vast winter coat and retrieved the tiniest of chihuahuas. It wore a thick hooped jacket designed to look like a gondolier's sweater and a plastic hood fashioned after a straw boater. The tiny animal glared at her then let loose three falsetto barks.

'He has the heart of the lion. But I can't let the little dear walk in this weather. Not with such puddles.'

'Jason . . .'

'You can catch him if you hurry.' She pointed to the clock on the wall. 'The two minutes past seven. He catches it every night. The English. So *punctual*. It's always struck me that—'

'*Grazie*,' Teresa said, then patted Lancelotto so rapidly the little beast couldn't bite her, and was out of the door, marching towards the Accademia stop by the bridge.

The vaporetto was packed. She just managed to leap on board before it pulled out into the seething swell of the Grand Canal. The inside cabin was so full she was forced to stand in the open by the doors, staring through the misted windows at the people crammed together inside.

She could just make out Jason. He was giving up his seat for an elderly woman with a stick. Smiling as he did so. He had a large carrier bag in his right hand.

The boat skipped most of the stops on the canal, heading straight for the main destinations. They would be at the Rialto in minutes. Teresa called Tosi. He'd informed Paola Boscolo about the threat to Camilla. The police were incandescent that she had disappeared into the night without waiting for them.

'They want you to get in touch with them right now,' the old man insisted. 'That Boscolo woman was using language I would never expect of a lady.'

'Tell her I'll talk to her when I damned well feel like it,' she said. Then she thought a bit more and added, 'Correction. Say I'll call when I can.'

'Teresa!'

'You're breaking up,' she lied. 'Sorry . . .'

She had her hood around her head. Jason didn't even look her way. He seemed distracted. Not worried. Not conscious of the people around him, though many were in carnival garb: counts and princesses, a space monster and, at the back, she saw, two more figures in the black garb of the Plague Doctor.

Dogs, she thought.

Neither of the men was carrying one, but that didn't mean the little white animal wasn't hidden beneath one of those voluminous cloaks.

Plague used to roll around the city like the sirocco wind, an unwanted gift of the seasons, something that came and went. Redentore, the great church across the Giudecca canal, visible from the crooked block where Sofia and the man who called himself Michael Ruskin were once lovers, was built to give tribute to the end of the plague. Salute, its counterpart, behind Sofia's apartment close to the tip of Dorsoduro, was erected almost a century later to offer thanks for relief from a second epidemic – and prayers against a third. On the brisk, chill waters of the lagoon the fragility of life seemed too exposed at times, too naked, prompting the response – the richness of imagination, a luxury of buildings, of culture, of *life* – that made Venice what it was.

This city could swallow you whole. Entice you with its beauty. Ensnare you in its dark and winding alleys. Then, before you knew it, you were lost, like Sofia. Perhaps like Michael Ruskin too. Cut off from the rest of the world and its humdrum mundanity, just as this glittering dark chain of islands was detached from the mainland by a swirling strip of lagoon pierced by nothing more than the slender artifice of a bridge.

Cross that and for some all logic, common sense, any rational view of life disappeared. Sane people did not live on islands built on tree trunks hammered into banks of mud. Nor did they hide behind masks, slipping from one identity to another as easily as someone else might try on a different set of clothes.

Wasn't that what Saint-Germain was trying to tell her more than anything? That if she followed her heart and tried to solve the riddle of Sofia's disappearance through the means she knew best – good sense and reason – she would surely fail? Those rules no longer applied. Others, more imaginative, less easy to define, were needed.

Tosi, a rational man, saw only a single solution. Bring in the police. Leave this to the Questura. Let them flood the streets with uniforms and the overwhelming power of force and numbers.

Then Camilla Dushku would be dead for certain.

Teresa had come so far down this path already, further than her instincts should have allowed. Now she stood in the open midsection of a freezing-cold vaporetto, braving the wind and rain between Accademia and Rialto, wondering what to do.

She stared through the glass again. It was almost opaque. Either she grasped it now or this nettle would be lost to her, and the fate of Camilla and Sofia abandoned to the ordinary, the dull rote of the slow, mechanical workings of law enforcement.

I don't just want to catch criminals, she thought. I want justice. I want release. These two are different.

The boat was docking at Rialto, on the wrong side of the canal for the markets and the shadowy arcades where Camilla was surely held captive. And, since this was where Jason was headed, perhaps the place Sofia was hiding too.

The rush of faceless people carried her with them as they fought to get off the boat. The rain had eased to nothing more than a gentle drizzle though the Venetians, who, oddly, seemed to hate water with a vengeance, still wandered around beneath an army of umbrellas.

She waited under the awning of a tourist tat store and watched Jason get off, look right and left, in the most amateur of fashions, as if trying to make sure he wasn't being followed.

He walked to the bridge and started to cross it. Towards the market. Towards Il Gobbo.

Sofia was never one to shirk an easy solution. If

she'd met someone during those long, cold nights outside here, someone who'd offer shelter, this would surely be the place she'd stay. One quick journey across the Grand Canal would throw any curious follower off the scent. Then she could scuttle back over the bridge, into the darkness, the nexus of lanes and alleys so tangled even a map might not help a stranger out of the maze.

Why hadn't Teresa realized this earlier? The cold, blunt answer came easily. Because it was in her nature to scan the broad horizon looking for answers. Sometimes this meant you overlooked the ones that lay close by, scraps of paper at your feet.

At the top of the bridge Jason paused and went to the balustrade over the central stretch, staring back towards the Accademia. The canal here was so beautiful, even on a damp, cold February night. To the right the reflections of the lights of the restaurants on the Riva del Vin glistened in the black water. Crowds of carnival figures stood by the edge, captivated by the sight, arms interlinked, silent and happy.

A life was made up of moments, and some of them at least were meant to be like this.

She wandered up, jostled his elbow in a friendly way, and said, 'Fancy meeting you here.'

The young Englishman almost leapt over the stone handrail from shock.

'I'm not that scary, am I?' Teresa asked.

She took the bag from him and started to sort

through the contents. Just as she expected: a stock of food and supplies from the supermarket. Cold chicken and ham. Cheese and water. Something oddly English too. A can of Heinz baked beans.

He didn't say a word.

'It's all right,' she told him. 'You don't need to explain. Sofia can come later. We've more important things to do.'

'I don't know what you're talking about.'

Me neither, she thought. But she told him anyway.

Then she gave the shopping to the carnival couple next to her, a courtly Renaissance prince and his bride, and dragged the young Englishman down towards the arcades.

They were in the square near Il Gobbo. It was seven thirty. The damp dark sky was soaking up the dying sonorous peals of the nearby bells.

The same ones she'd heard when he called her. Or so she thought. Was that all they had? The sound of bells, relayed through a mobile phone? A couple of names, Schütze and L'Arciere, that meant nothing?

She didn't push Jason over Sofia. After she told him about Camilla, it didn't seem necessary.

He was animated, not scared, not quite. He looked at the dark passages around them and said, 'Where do we start?'

She turned to the bar behind them and said simply, 'Here.'

Because this was where it all began. Where it started to go wrong.

They began to work the bars, with no more success than before. The names prompted bewilderment, as did the idea of a mask and costume store that was closed during carnival.

Twenty minutes later they were no nearer to an answer. Ruskin's deadline was almost up.

Jason stopped her after the fourth or fifth place they'd visited.

'We need the police,' he said.

'He'll see them, Jason,' Teresa told him. 'Trust me. I know how these things work. The police will hold us back. Just a little more time.'

'Do we have that? Does Camilla?'

'He's here somewhere. I think I know this man. Or understand him a little anyway. He likes tricks and disguises. But he's rigid, obsessive, fixed in his thinking too. He has rules. If we break those – and from what he said he'd think that the moment he sees a uniform – then he's free to do what he wants.'

'If he harms one hair on her head . . .'

'I know.' She put a hand on his arm. 'If you'd told me about Sofia . . .'

'I couldn't!' he protested.

They were in the piazza in front of the famous parmesan shop. Jason's loud voice was starting to attract attention.

'She told me not to. I promised.'

And a promise is a promise, she thought. Always would be for Jason Cunningham.

His eyes darted away into the alleys running past the market, alongside the canal.

'L'Arciere,' she murmured. 'Schütze. There has to be something.'

'What does L'Arciere mean?' he asked.

'I thought your Italian was better than that.'

'I can talk everyday stuff.'

'It means . . .' She pulled back her arm and mimicked the drawing and release of a bow. 'That.'

He looked at her and said, in English, 'An archer.'

'Yes. He used that name too. It was on one of the passports.'

Jason frowned and at that moment he seemed almost like a schoolchild.

'He used the same name twice? Seems a bit odd.'

'Not the same name. Different languages.'

Jason looked at her as if she were being slow.

Of course it was the same. There was a pattern here and she was supposed to be good at seeing those.

Silvio Di Capua was at his desk.

'Busy right now,' her deputy said. 'Working with those nice people in Venice on your behalf. I think—'

'Shut up, Silvio,' she ordered. 'German dictionary. What does that name I gave you mean? Schütze?'

'Mean?'

'Is it just a surname?'

She waited, knowing all along what he'd say.

'Bowman,' Di Capua came back. 'Rifleman. Archer. Marksman.'

'Fine. Listen to me. He uses variations of the word archer a lot. Let's try different languages. Check for a company in Venice that might have the same name.'

'How long have I got?' he asked, quite calmly in the circumstances.

'I need this now. Pick the main ones. Spanish. Dutch. Greek. I don't know.'

'Greek's a different alphabet,' he pointed out.

'There, you're narrowing it down already. Go into any business or trade directory you can find and see if there's a company anywhere in Venice with a registered name that matches.' Then she remembered what Strozzi had said. 'It may be just the company. Not the one on the shop.'

'You can't be serious,' he muttered.

'Unless you have something better to do . . .'

'Lots,' Silvio Di Capua grunted. 'I'm sorry. If you want this it's going to take a couple of hours.'

'In a couple of hours she'll be dead. Five minutes maybe.'

He didn't say anything. Jason was staring at her. This was all going wrong. What she was demanding was unreasonable, impossible.

The archer.

She thought of Saint-Germain and their unreal conversations on the distant Island of the Dead. There was a third answer, he said. Had to be. It lay in a distant place she never visited, beyond the comfortable, organized world she preferred. Somewhere illogical, irrational.

Teresa Lupo closed her eyes and tried to find a private, silent space inside her, somewhere the dope fumes of the Rialto night didn't intrude, a sanctuary where she couldn't hear the disco music and the slurred, drunken voices chattering over spritz, the rumble of the vaporetti from the Grand Canal, the occasional shout of the gondoliers.

'The only world I know is the one I can see,' she murmured, aware of her inner desperation, aware too that Jason was growing ever more restless beside her.

'What happens if we can't find him?' he asked.

He kills Camilla, she thought. Because I failed him. I didn't pass the test. He kills Camilla because she's one more proxy victim, like Fiorella Gabrielli. And then he's gone.

'There's an answer here,' she muttered, more to herself than him. 'It's just . . . beyond me.'

'It can't be,' Jason Cunningham said abruptly. 'There's no one else, is there? Someone's sending you those stories for a reason. It has to be you. Think about it. Think about what you know.'

What I know.

This is a game. One more riddle with masks. The peals of the Rialto bells down the phone weren't accidental. He was teasing her, taunting her.

There was something he said too.

If you want to know how to find me, ask Sofia. Tell her to give you a sign.

Her head felt fuzzy, disorganized, foreign.

A memory rose in her mind, prompted by the photograph she'd seen only that evening, of Sofia sullen and difficult, like an angry child, at the Lido, on the beach.

Teresa could remember another time, sitting with her in the park near the Colosseum one summer day, Sofia shuffling her fortune-telling cards in the sun.

It was the first thing she did with everyone if she could. A little ritual. A harmless game that meant nothing at all.

A sign.

Teresa didn't know whether to laugh or cry.

Horoscopes. Astrology. Saint-Germain would have been proud. The answer might be something she had always regarded as absurd, a foolish little game.

The painting on Ruskin's door was a centaur bearing a bow.

Di Capua was still on the line.

'Silvio?'

'I'm trying. I'm typing as fast as I can.'

'See if there's somewhere called Sagittario. Or the English, Sagittarius.'

'Any reason why?'

'Because I'm clutching at straws. Because Sagittarius is also known as the Archer. More than anything because I think he may have told me so himself.'

'In that case he's either deeply stupid or astonishingly arrogant. Or both,' Di Capua muttered. She waited. Ten long seconds, no more. Then he said, 'Got it.'

The phone beeped again. She looked. It was an address and a map. Close by. An alley off the Rialto arcades.

'Last known operating premises for an *Impresa Individuale*, a sole proprietor, called Sagittarius,' Di Capua said. 'Formation fifteen years ago. No idea if that's current or not. There's nothing else in that name. Nothing close. If you want—'

'Thank you,' she interrupted.

There was a deep sigh on the line then he said, 'I have to ask. Can I give this to the Questura? They'll scream if I don't.'

'Only if they find out,' she told him. 'No. Not yet.'

'May I know why?'

'Because I need to make sure I'm right. This could just be some trick. What if I turn up with a bunch of cops and he's somewhere else, watching?'

'Point taken. But if I don't hear from you in ten minutes I'm calling them anyway.'

The line went dead.

That's what happens when you let them off the leash, she thought. They get unruly.

The nearby bells struck eight.

'Can we go now?' Jason demanded.

She checked the little map on the phone, and led the way back into the gloom of the arcades.

It was a maze, a warren of narrow, grubby alleys that fed off the main route from the bridge and wound in a tangled network behind the bank of the Riva del Vin. There were no lights here, no people once they passed the handful of bars and restaurants at the edge.

Jason looked twitchy. He was a tall kid, lanky more than muscular, and he kept nervously swishing at his long fair hair.

Not much good in a fight, she thought, and found her mind ranging again to Peroni and the rest of them. What would they be doing if they were here now?

Looking. Imagining. Trying to see in the dark. Checking their weapons.

Some of these lanes were so narrow two people couldn't walk down them side by side. The web map simply placed a large red blob over an area that encompassed at least three alleys, obscuring them all. There were no names, only numbers.

They turned into a short, bleak cul-de-sac littered with rubbish: paper and rotten fruit, abandoned market boxes, plastic bags of refuse. The stench of cats was everywhere.

Jason put a hand on her shoulder and asked, 'What do we do when we get there?'

She tried to smile.

'I'm a pathologist. You're a baker.' She watched

him. 'When I'm sure we call in the cops. They won't be long behind.'

The alley was so dark she could only just make out what lay at the foot. A blind wall at the end, a derelict store, shuttered and dirty, on the left. On the right some kind of commercial storefront with a single glass door and two display windows dimly lit.

Teresa stopped and scanned the brickwork along the sides, remembering what she'd found in Dorsoduro. The glass eye of the camera glittered in the dark like a tiny jewel, set above the shop. She signalled to Jason to stay back then walked ahead.

The front shutter was raised. There was a light behind it. Over the plate glass windows she could just make out a sign: Sagittarius, Costumier.

There was a cough from behind. Jason was getting impatient. She waved at him to stay back. Then she edged towards the door, keeping tight to the side.

One glimpse through the nearest display window was enough.

Teresa turned and walked back to Jason. The camera followed her then reached the edge of its range and stopped. She dodged into a patch of darkness in the doorway of the building by the arcade, took out her phone and called Di Capua.

'Congratulations,' she said. 'Call Paola Boscolo and tell her to send me everyone she's got.'

'Wait there,' Di Capua ordered. 'I'll tell you what they say.'

She could picture him dialling up the Castello Questura as they spoke. That was Silvio. Never do one thing at a time.

'Sorry.'

'Oh please. Don't pull any stupid—'

Teresa Lupo clamped her phone shut and put it away. She knew what she'd seen.

'I think that door's open, Jason.'

'Why would he do that?'

Questions.

'Because . . . he wants me there. He thinks I know where Sofia is and maybe if I find him first . . .' She tried to see the logic, failed. 'Perhaps it'll be easier for him. I don't know. Does it matter?'

'What do you want me to do?'

'Unless he's seen you – which I doubt – he thinks I'm on my own. You work out the best way to use that. Because truthfully I can't.'

She started to move. His hand came to her arm. She looked at him. Perhaps Jason Cunningham was a touch more solid than he appeared.

'Why don't we just wait for the police?' he asked.

'Because we daren't,' she said, then shook him off and strode back to the open door.

It was ajar and she didn't want to think why. Teresa walked straight in, made no effort to hide. She'd only glimpsed Camilla when she peeked through the side window. Now she saw her fully and was chilled by the sight.

She was standing on a plain wooden chair, a noose around her neck, still blindfolded, hands tied behind her back. He'd replaced the gag. Teresa guessed he'd worked the scarlet lipstick over the rag and her cheeks afresh. Her face looked like an open wound.

The heavy hessian rope ran from her bloodless throat tight to an ancient, rusty hook in a ceiling beam. This building was old. A warehouse, perhaps, centuries ago. There had to be so many places like this hidden away in the warren of dead-end alleys that ran off from the Rialto. Somewhere to store things, to hide them. Contraband. People.

Camilla wore the pure white carnival dress she'd seen on the phone, that of a princess maybe. On the back of her head, crooked, askew, was a gaudy silver crown. The girl trembled as she stood there, the rope taut around her neck.

It was impossible she'd been in this position for more than a few minutes. The man put on this act when he saw someone on the camera. The girl was a lure, nothing more. Any longer than that and she would have fallen. Hanged herself.

Teresa reached into her pocket and took out Sofia's kitchen knife, the one she'd found when she decided to enter the top apartment.

Camilla heard her, let go a low, scared whimper.

'It's me,' she said in a loud firm voice. 'Teresa.'

The slender figure in white shook on the chair.

'Stand still,' Teresa told her. 'I'll get you down.

464

This is all going to be fine. The police are on their way.'

She glanced around the room. No one. No sound from anywhere. There were stairs leading off to an upper level. A door at the back with a glass panel. It seemed to run into a dark narrow alleyway. A hidden way out.

He had to have that.

Teresa found a chair near the rear door, pulled it close, stood on it and severed the rope round Camilla's neck. Then she cut the ties around her wrists and the back of the blindfold, loosening the gap enough so that she could drag it off the top of the girl's head, taking the cheap plastic crown with it.

Camilla blinked at the sudden light, looked at her, sobbing, terrified, eyes rolling. The scarlet lipstick smeared against Teresa's cheeks as they embraced. The chairs shook perilously beneath them as she got down, held up her hands, helped the young woman to the floor.

Shaking like a leaf, Camilla cowered in her arms as Teresa looked around the room, wondering, listening.

Glittering gowns and masks. Costumes and the kind of cheap, garish accessories one expected of the theatre – jewellery and maces, swords and lances, medallions and chains and other finery.

And mannequins. An army of dummies dressed as carnival and Commedia dell' Arte characters.

Covered in dust, like long-abandoned corpses. No one came here much to buy. That wasn't the purpose. It was one hiding place among many, a private, insane world where he could retire to dream, to imagine.

Something Falcone had once told her came back. He said that on occasion the insane were marked not by their unpredictability but through some inner, unshakeable logic that was imperceptible to the rest of the world. That the key to understanding them lay in penetrating and adopting their viewpoint, not labelling it, sorting it into some neat, tidy category of illness, assuming that madness meant chaos, a pointless scream in the dark.

These were the most difficult people to apprehend because they were, in so many ways, like everybody else. Rational, cold, determined, yet invisibly attuned to a perspective that few could penetrate.

She was still thinking about that when one of the mannequins, a tall figure, with a cocked head and a black, shiny, leering mask, began to move. He wore the costume of the harlequin, coloured silk diamonds, red and yellow and green, and his gestures were exaggerated and theatrical.

When he stepped out from the shadows at the rear of the store she saw that he carried in his hand a long and gleaming sword, much like the weapon from the night before.

'Good evening,' the harlequin said, and cut through the air with the heavy, glittering blade. 'May I be of assistance?'

He looked strong and accustomed to being in control.

Teresa took one step forward and stood in front of Camilla.

'Sorry,' she said, watching him. 'I lied.'

The mask went to one side. She was reminded of the Plague Doctor and that birdlike pose.

'I don't know where Sofia is. I never have. This game of yours . . .'

He jerked back his head and spat a stream of curses through the cruel black mask.

Then, 'Game? *Game?*'

Camilla was fully behind her now. Teresa had stood up to this man once. She'd do it again if necessary. She glanced at the door.

Jason was there, creeping in, pressed against the glass.

The harlequin flung back his arm and swung his sword through the air. Sharp metal met with the neck of a stiff female mannequin next to him, slashed at the dummy's rich cream dress and high silver wig. The head came off, flew through the air, rattled against the side wall.

He stayed in the same position, blade raised, waiting.

Teresa folded her arms, sighed and said, 'This is all well and good. But I *still* don't know where she is. Honestly. If you only . . .'

Two steps forward, sword flashing. The many-coloured diamonds were a blur in front of her. Then something intervened and it was Jason, screaming, yelling, flailing around. In his hands he held a tall brass ashtray that had stood near the door, brandishing it like a mace.

'Get out,' the young Englishman yelled at them. 'Run.'

He lurched in front of her, fetched the figure in the tight harlequin suit a hard blow to the side of the head.

Camilla dashed through the door. Teresa stayed where she was. The cops had to be here soon. She wanted to see what was behind that leering ebony mask.

The blow had sent the man in the costume of diamonds stumbling back towards the door at the rear. He was clutching at his head. He looked hurt and old at that moment. The mask had slipped just a little and she could see a plaster there. The wound from the night before, she thought. This was not going the way he planned.

Then he reached into an unseen pocket by his waist and took out a small black pistol and started to clamber to his feet, painfully, not with any great ease.

'Time to go now, Jason,' Teresa said, taking his elbow. 'This is someone else's job I—'

She didn't get to finish the sentence. There were loud noises from outside. Men shouting. Boots on stone. Something so familiar she was surprised it took her a moment to place the din. It was the rattle of batons against body armour, the kind of commotion cops created when they wanted to make their presence clear.

Teresa yelled at Jason Cunningham and pushed him quickly towards the front door.

The figure on the floor was half-up, hand on a chair. He looked winded and wasn't moving. Perhaps the blow from Jason had been more serious than it looked.

Uniforms shoving and shouting. She just got to see what was happening before a familiar voice – Paola Boscolo's – began bellowing at her to get out of the way.

I deserve better than that, she thought, and took a last look back.

The harlequin was more animated now, scrambling urgently across the tiles, working his way towards the rear exit, then on his feet again, starting to flee. Two long steps and he was outside and the cops were barely in the place, hunting around with their weapons, scared and alert.

She saw the silk diamonds disappear into a pool of darkness.

'Will you move?' Paola Boscolo yelled.

'There's a way out of the back,' she said, pointing at the gloomy maw that led off from the rear of the store. 'He went out there. I think the alley leads round to the arcades. If you don't get a move on . . .'

A familiar sight. Big, muscular men in blue,

visors down, armour on their chests, pushing everything, everyone out of the way.

'He's armed,' Teresa added as they fought past her.

Not that she needed to mention that really. They had their weapons out already.

Six or eight of them ran ahead with the sturdy young police-woman at their heels. They were yelling at someone out there, ordering him to stop. Not saying the obvious. The threat. *If you don't* . . .

She closed her eyes. He couldn't run so well, it seemed. She wanted to see this man, but alive.

There was a moment approaching, one she hated. It was always wrong, irrational, stupid. Force against force. Brute power against individual unreason.

Once, not so long ago, she had been the one who almost died. Someone else, someone close by was murdered in her place. Yet she still believed, against her own reason, that she had sensed the instant at which another's life had departed. It was the kind of conviction that belonged in fiction, in the fantasies of Arnaud, the Count of Saint-Germain, not in the mind of a rational and analytical woman of science. Back then, though, it had seemed real enough.

There was the violent crack of a single shot echoing off the damp Venetian walls. Then another.

More shouts, from the cops. More warnings.

A third, lone explosion rent the darkness. After

that came a storm of gunfire, too many rounds to count, backed by yells of fear and aggression, the racket that always came with violence and blood.

'Here we go,' she muttered, and waited for the instant she knew from before, the moment she'd experienced when she expected to die in a hut somewhere among the distant ruins of Ostia Antica.

The sudden skip of a heartbeat, the terrifying inability to take a single breath. The sense that something, some spirit, some element of life, had left the world.

That feeling never came for some reason.

The noise from beyond the back door fell to a low murmur of voices.

When the gunfire ended Teresa walked out the back, weaving her way through the uniforms, feeling their armoured vests brush against her. Paola Boscolo and two helmeted officers stood over a broken, awkward shape on the black cobbles near some tall commercial rubbish bins. The diamond patterns of the harlequin suit were just visible in the darkness. The mask was half torn off to reveal a gaping wound to the temple.

'He shot himself,' the policewoman said. 'Dammit.'

Close up Teresa could see blood on the dead man's chest, on his right shoulder, near the stomach.

'He shot himself a lot by the look of things,' she said, trying to keep the edge out of her voice.

One of the uniforms threw up his visor and glared at her.

'It was dark. He fired first. We weren't to know.'

'Certainly sounded that way,' she agreed.

'You're safe, aren't you?' he asked.

'Safe. Yes. And quite . . .' What was the word? 'Ignorant. Likely to remain so, don't you think?'

The cops were starting to get angry, the way officers did when they knew something had gone wrong.

'That's the problem with dead people,' Teresa went on, feeling her temper rise. 'They can be so very uncommunicative.'

Paolo Boscolo's heavy form came in front of her, separating Teresa from the men. There was no politeness or warmth on the policewoman's face.

'Wait for me in front of the shop,' Boscolo ordered. 'I'll need statements from you all.'

Teresa didn't move. She looked around the place, trying to think straight.

'I said . . .' the policewoman repeated.

'Heard you the first time.'

She returned to the store. Camilla was by the doorway in Jason's arms. She looked lost, distraught, someone whose world had been torn apart. She'd come to Venice to find a better, easier life. It wasn't supposed to be like this.

Teresa placed a hand on the young man's arm and said, 'You saved us there. Thank you.'

'Wasn't nothing,' he murmured, holding the girl tightly.

She looked Camilla in the eye and said, 'I want you to go to the hospital with the medics. You need to see that consultant of yours.'

'I'm not hurt!' the girl objected.

'Indulge me,' Teresa pleaded.

A couple of the cops asked what was going on. They weren't close to the action inside. They hadn't seen her arguing with the officers near the corpse so they listened, looked at the Questura card she showed them, then agreed to get an ambulance launch.

After that the three of them waited close by the end of the arcade. Teresa wished again she had a cigarette, considered begging one from one of the cops, thought better of it.

Camilla said, 'Jason told me. I'm glad Sofia's safe. I'm . . .'

She slapped him lightly on the arm, a child's clip, playful almost.

'I am disappointed by your deceit.'

'We're sneaky buggers, the English,' Jason said with a quick grin. 'It's just that most of the time we don't let on.'

Teresa smiled and said, 'I'd like to see her now.'

He stepped back into the shadows. Teresa joined him. Jason Cunningham was smart enough. He didn't need to be told. Before they went he darted forward, kissed Camilla quickly on the cheek and asked, 'You'll be all right?'

'Of course.'

'Good,' he said.

Then Teresa took his arm and the two of them

slunk out of the cul-de-sac, talking nonsense, ignoring the busy, engaged cops there, darting back into the arcades the moment they could.

She didn't ask any questions as they walked through the pitch-black loggia, past Il Gobbo, past the busy bars and the crowds of puzzled, half-drunk carnival-goers. This louche dark face of the city seemed on edge. There were police everywhere. The shots must have echoed through the alleys and piazzas and *calli* of the Rialto. People knew something was wrong.

Jason strode ahead, confident every step of the way, walking so quickly at times it was hard for her to keep up. Hard to concentrate too. She was thinking of so many things. Seeing Sofia finally. Holding her. Calling her mother with the news. Finally managing to achieve something that might heal the fragile breach between them, one that had widened so much over the last few days.

People didn't simply disappear from your life. Sometimes you let them go. They'd done that, both of them, with Sofia, one consciously, the other, Teresa, so absorbed in her work and career that she'd never managed to notice how her aunt, a kind of sister, had slipped into the shadows, struggling to survive. She and her mother had done this with each other too. It would not happen again.

She followed him through a narrow low *soto-portego* and found herself in a tiny *campiello* as black and bleak as any she'd met in the city. Every wall of the cramped square seemed solid dank brick, without windows or decoration save for graffiti and a crooked marble wellhead in the centre. There was only the meanest of light from a lone lamp by the entrance arch.

So quickly she didn't see, he was gone and she found herself alone, cold and shivering in the faint dashes of dying sleety rain chasing into the square from the squally sky.

'Jason,' she called. '*Jason.*'

She waited, hearing her own breath, aware she was lost in a distant backwater beyond the bridge.

Then he stepped out in front of her and in the faint light she could see he was beaming like a schoolkid. Her eyes were adjusting to the darkness. In the right-hand corner there was some kind of alcove so small and black, halfway into the ground, that it was invisible until she found a reason to stare there.

He was holding his right arm. There was blood on it, close to the elbow.

'Did he hurt you?' she asked.

'Not really.'

He still clung to himself, grimacing a little.

'For God's sake, when will you learn to think of yourself before others?'

'When I feel like it,' Jason Cunningham replied. 'I'm sorry I left you there. I wanted to check it was all right.'

He took a few steps towards her.

'Sofia's scared as hell. Got a right to be and she doesn't know the half of it.'

His good arm beckoned her towards the alcove. As they got closer to the far wall she could see there was a door there. Jason pulled on the latch. Beyond, lit by a string of weak bulbs on a line of twisting wire, was a worn stone staircase leading steeply down into the damp Venetian earth. As she looked another door opened at the very end and she could see a face, a distant one.

Cautiously, Teresa began to walk down the passage, heart pumping, mind racing, her footsteps echoing off the uneven brick walls. There was a fragrance rising from whatever lay ahead. As she watched more lights went on there, turning the figure ahead into a silhouette, without a face, any sign or feature she could recognize.

She knew something though. She was approaching the pleasant, welcome aroma of a bakery, of yeast and flour and rising bread. As she got closer to the bottom of the steps she felt the hot breath of some unseen oven begin to wash over her like a kitchen memory from childhood.

The narrow brick artery beneath these unseen buildings in the back of the Rialto seemed to run forever. She heard someone behind, glanced back and saw Jason following her down. Then she was there, stumbling off the last worn step, and the heat hit her like a desert wind. The place was so bright she blinked, felt a little giddy. When she opened her eyes Sofia stood in front of her, arms wide open, dressed in a tight white baker's gown, chest covered in flour, a bleached hat on her head hiding what must have been long blonde curls tucked tightly beneath.

'Where have you been?' Teresa asked, close to tears. 'Where . . . ?'

She'd rehearsed this moment so many times in her head. Practised the speeches, of love and gratitude, admonition, and a resolute determination that things would change.

Every word was now gone. The two women threw their arms around each other, held that close position for a long time.

Teresa felt a great choking sob rise inside her then find some welcome release.

'We're safe? Really?' Sofia whispered in her ear.

The sound of her voice was reward in itself.

'I believe so,' Teresa began. 'I think . . .'

A man walked briskly into view ahead of them. He was dressed like Sofia, in white overalls covered with flour and a baker's hat, and smiling rather foolishly as if embarrassed. When Teresa met his gaze he took off the hat briefly and bowed.

She recognized his face.

'Jerome Aitchison,' Teresa said, astonished, not least because close up, in the flesh, she couldn't for one moment feel afraid.

'The very one,' he said in English. Then, apologetically, 'I mean . . .'

He tried again, this time with a short sentence in Italian. It wasn't very good but she got the drift.

Teresa let go of Sofia. Jason was by her side. He seemed more composed than any of them though he was still clutching at his arm.

'You need that looked at,' she said to him, aware how mundane and inappropriate the words seemed.

'Bleeding all over a bakery,' he answered. 'Dead right I do.' He grinned. 'Good place to hide though. You don't think Signora Rizzolo can make bread as well in that little place of hers, do you? Not when there's so much it goes all over town, into restaurants and places. There's just pastries there. I'm OK with them. But bread . . .'

He let go of his elbow for a moment and held out his hands, waving his fingers.

'There's life in those,' Teresa said and wondered if her head would ever stop spinning.

'Dead right. Jerome here and Sofia needed somewhere to hide when all the trouble started. It was obvious really. People think bread comes out of nowhere. Manna from the skies. No one ever looks inside a bakery. So I put 'em to work. There's a little room at the back where they can stay. Taught 'em how to do a good job too. Brought in the shopping every night. Can't live off bread alone.'

He pulled a loaf off a stacked rack close by and tore it in half.

'Even when it's this good. You try that!'

'Another time,' Teresa said, waving away the crust, her head full of its wonderful scent.

She looked at Aitchison and thought of the photograph she'd found of him in Amsterdam. All the shyness, the awkwardness, the solitary bachelor identity were there, only magnified.

Lights were starting to go on in her head.

'You and Jerome . . .' she began.

Sofia giggled, walked over and cuddled him.

'He's the loveliest man in the world. We're getting married.' Her face fell. 'When we can.'

'And Michael Ruskin?'

Her bright features fell even further.

'Michael promised me we'd be friends again,' Sofia said quietly. 'I told him that was all it could be. Otherwise I wouldn't come back to Venice at all. *I told* him.' She pouted like a spoilt teenager. 'I knew he'd try it on, of course. He was always pushy like that. But he was adamant he didn't have that problem any more.'

'What problem?' Teresa asked.

'His temper.' She stared at the floor and shuffled her feet, shy, ashamed even. 'And the rest. When I met Jerome . . .'

Sofia's eyes widened and Teresa wanted to pinch herself. She'd seen this ingenuous, infuriating look so many times.

'You'd think an old boyfriend would rejoice in your happiness, wouldn't you?' she asked. 'Not turn so foul and scary we had to hide around the Rialto at night just so we could meet . . .'

'Me in that ridiculous costume,' Aitchison added immediately and took her hand. 'That was fun!'

'Not after a while it wasn't,' she went on. 'Michael was so . . . persistent. It got *worse* when I told him about Jerome. Not better at all. I was frightened of him. Of what he might do, to both of us.'

'Ursula's dress?' Teresa asked. 'The one from the painting. The one in your room.'

Sofia shuddered.

'Ugh. That was odd. I came back one day and he'd put it there. Let himself into my apartment without a word. Why? I was supposed to finish it for him or something. Wear it for some special occasion he had planned. Carnival. I don't know. The way he was behaving was so creepy. I knew we needed to get away from him there and then. I wrote you that letter. Jerome and I met up round the corner that night and . . .' She giggled. 'We ran away!'

Teresa remembered the Casino degli Spiriti and the body kneeling there, hands tied tightly in a gesture of prayer. Another victim in the dress of the martyred saint from the Accademia.

'Carpaccio,' she murmured.

'I wish I'd never shown him those pictures,' Sofia said quietly. 'It's as if they unhinged him. Changed him. Not that he needed much of a push, if you ask me. He always had . . .' She twirled a finger by the side of her head. '. . . a loopy side, if I'm honest.'

Saint-Germain's trigger, Teresa thought. The darkness was there to begin with. All it required was a catalyst.

'That painter chap changed me,' Aitchison said brightly. 'We met there. In that little place with the dragons. And the dog.'

They hugged again, all flour and grasping arms. Teresa watched and sighed.

Two peas from the same pod. Fleeing the murderous clutches of the monster who called himself Michael Ruskin, aided by a young and resourceful Englishman who seemed to think it his life's mission to help others.

'Who sent me those stories?' she asked.

All three of them stared at her in silence.

'What stories? We just wanted to stay out of his way for a few days,' Sofia replied, wide-eyed still. 'If he didn't stop being so horrible I thought I might go with you to the police and make him see reason. He was so . . . incensed. Then he made that terrible thing happen. In the piazza. That girl. The man they thought was Jerome.'

'Shocking,' Aitchison said, shaking his head. 'Truly shocking. Do you know that beast Ruskin stole my passport? Someone went round to my digs and talked their way in. Had to be him, not that I could prove it.'

'Well.' Sofia folded her floury arms. 'We couldn't walk out in broad daylight, could we? Even if we wanted to. Jerome was supposed to be dead. It was obvious what they'd think when they found out he wasn't.'

'What?' Teresa asked.

'That all this was my doing,' Aitchison broke in.

'That's what that devil Ruskin wanted. Me in prison and Sofia back. It's outrageous. Ask anyone in Cambridge. It was bad enough with all the nonsense that stupid girl Imogen made up about me.'

Sofia beamed at him and said, very seriously, 'If it weren't for all that nonsense you wouldn't be here.'

'Correct,' Aitchison agreed. 'Nevertheless, I am an innocent injured party, twice over now . . .'

'Ruskin wanted to kill you,' Jason said with a very English bluntness.

They stared at him as if this were somehow unthinkable. The difference in years – he must have been almost three decades younger – seemed to make no difference. They had relied on Jason Cunningham absolutely. Teresa wondered if she could ever win such respect herself.

'Wanted to kill both of you, I reckon,' Jason went on. 'He didn't just make that poor man throw himself off the campanile. He murdered his wife. It's all in the papers. They blamed that on Jerome too. I never told you.'

Sofia's face had gone as white as her baker's gown.

'Why not?' she asked.

'I didn't see the point. Now . . .'

He fell silent.

'Now what?' Sofia asked.

'Now he's the one who's dead,' Jason said.

They seemed like two lost children, holding onto one another for comfort, for protection. Jason caught Teresa's eye. She knew the half-jaundiced expression there and what it was saying. She'd seen the same look on her mother's face. It meant, *you see the problem? Whose is it now?*

The bakery was deep beneath the earth. She took out her phone and knew there couldn't possibly be a signal.

Teresa looked at Sofia and Jerome Aitchison then said, very slowly, very carefully, 'I'm going to go outside now. I'm going to call the police. You have to tell them everything that's happened. Jerome's got nothing to be afraid of. I want you to talk to Chiara too. She's been out of her mind with worry.'

'Oh no,' Sofia said. 'I'm sorry.'

Teresa glanced at Jason, determined to let him know how grateful she was. The young man wasn't even looking at her. He was checking the temperature on the oven.

'Don't worry about that,' she added. 'This could have turned out much . . . worse.'

Jason started pacing the bakery floor, looking concerned.

'Bit of work to be done here before you two knock off,' he said, casting a sly wink in her direction.

Distract them, she thought. Clever.

'Phone.' She held it up to show them.

Then she walked up the narrow worn steps, back towards the tiny deserted *campiello*. A part of her wanted to call Frascati first but that would be wrong. The madness, hers as much as anyone's, was over. She had to do things in the proper order. That meant Paola Boscolo, and it would be a conversation she would relish.

The squalls had moved on. The sky had cleared. She could see stars and a sliver of moon. They reflected in the damp mirrored surface of the uneven brick courtyard, outlining the shape of the battered marble wellhead at its centre.

The sound of an outdoor disco floated over the rooftops, brash, crude rhythms, mood music for an asylum.

As she took the last step and walked out into the little square looking for a signal a small white dog came into view, trotting intently across the black cobblestones before it disappeared into the shadows to her right.

She froze, felt stupid and scared.

A hand fell on her shoulder. When she turned she found herself staring into the dead, cruel features of a shining ebony mask. An arm curved round her neck, sweaty, grubby fingers clambered over her mouth, stifling the scream there before it could be born.

Silk diamonds, green and yellow and red.

'I'll take that,' the man in the harlequin suit snarled through the dead, frozen face as he seized the phone from her shaking fingers.

No bloodstains. No sign of anxiety, let alone any visible wound.

Imagine.

One stray guess as his hand clawed across her mouth.

It was the trick from the piazza, all over again. The body in the alley was someone else. A useful stranger, just like Luisa Cammarota. Camilla was the bait. Some unfortunate stranger was the dummy, the feint that let him watch from the sidelines then follow her all the way to Sofia.

Something cold and metallic touched her face. He took his hand away. The gun was so hard against her cheek it hurt.

'You think you're so damned clever,' the voice behind the mask spat at her. 'Just like she said. Some stupid little bird. You throw down a few crumbs. It follows the trail. Then . . .'

He whipped the weapon viciously at her head and Teresa Lupo found herself tumbling down to the cold black ground, too shocked, too short of breath even to scream, a darkness, close and personal, closing in.

She fell on her hands and knees. The cobblestones bit and grazed her skin beneath the heavy winter clothes as she tumbled sideways. The wall intervened. Her head fetched up hard against the damp crumbling brick.

For a moment she lost consciousness. When she looked up he'd ripped off the ebony mask and his face was in hers. She could feel the heat of his breath, smell the stink of him.

He didn't look like anyone she knew. Fifty or

so. Dark eyes. Sallow skin. Ordinary features twisted with fury. The universal angry, crazy man. No one remarkable at all.

Some dim, half-turning thought told her it was bad she'd seen him. Bad that he didn't care.

His left arm grabbed hers and she was dragged to her feet. They were back at the doorway. The weapon gestured down the steps.

From below, far away, she could make out happy voices over his laboured breathing. Jason's raw Italian as he laughed down there, ordering the two of them to do something to the ovens. Sofia's light musical tones saying something in response. A querulous, edgy reply from the man called Jerome Aitchison.

The harlequin's fingers gripped Teresa's shoulder-length brown hair, held it tight, wrenched her round to look at him. The gun poked towards her eye.

'One word,' he murmured.

He mouthed something she'd heard earlier, screamed down the phone line.

Bang.

Pinning her hard against the wall, he shouted down the staircase, 'Police! This is Inspector Galbani from the Questura. Signora Lupo is with me. You must leave now please. For your own safety. We will transport you. Come.'

His voice was so different, so full of authority and age, that the shift, the skill in his sudden change of character, left her mind reeling. It was as if he was more than one man. Several, all in the same skin.

She wriggled in his arms. The gun came down heavily on her temple and the force and pain brought her to her knees again.

'Please!' he barked. 'There is a launch for you. Signora Bianchi. Signor Aitchison. We need your assistance.'

The man sounded like just about every police inspector she'd ever met. Calm voice, full of authority. Confident. Expectant.

People did what he wanted. Sofia had once, until something, some realization dawned.

She tried to struggle, to scream. The gun dashed down once more. Another savage blow. The darkness pooled in around her. When she came to she was on the ground, face against the wall, too confused to say a thing.

Jason came out first, Sofia and Aitchison close behind. Without warning the harlequin fired and she watched in horror as the young Englishman fell to the ground clutching his stomach, moaning, rolling sideways into the darkness.

The sound he made was so quiet she couldn't help but think he didn't want to cause any trouble.

Teresa was trying to move again at that moment, but it didn't matter. The harlequin was on Sofia already, tearing off her white baker's cap, dragging her hair free, winding his fist into the long, tumbling locks.

It was all so rapid Aitchison had no time to react.

By the time the Englishman was moving towards her the gun was pressed into Sofia's cheek. The look in the eyes of the man in the suit of diamonds stopped him as he reached out to help.

Aitchison stood there, a modest, middle-aged foreigner, hands out, pleading, lost. Teresa got to her feet, felt so dizzy she had to cling to the wall to stay upright. There wasn't a sound from Jason, invisible in the darkness beyond the alcove.

'Shoot me,' he pleaded, taking a step closer. 'Not her. Blame me. I don't care. I don't . . .'

The gun went up. A second shot rose towards the moon.

There were cops nearby, she thought. Someone had to hear.

'Me!' Aitchison yelled, and stood there as the harlequin took a vicious swipe at his head, the barrel colliding with his temple, sending him reeling.

'Tell him,' the man with the gun ordered, racking his hand through her long blonde hair, pulling it so tight she began to whimper. '*Tell him!*'

Sofia clawed away from him, got a little space between them, caught her breath.

'Tell him what?'

'The child! *Our* child.'

Tears started in Sofia's eyes. She didn't want to speak, to acknowledge him.

He put the barrel of the pistol straight against her head and bellowed, 'Say it.'

'Michael! *Michael!*'

There was fury in Sofia's voice and that was a surprise.

'Tell him!'

'Jerome knows!' Then more quietly, 'Of course he does. I told him. He *knows*! So do you. The baby was dead.' Her voice was almost a whisper. 'They told us that. All those years ago. They had no choice. Any more than I did. The doctors insisted—'

'Lies, lies, lies . . .' Ruskin snarled and dragged her round one full circle by her hair.

She was screaming, crying, indignant.

'No,' Sofia cried, stumbling to her knees. 'It's the truth. And—'

He threw her to the cobblestones. She shrieked with pain, then looked up at him, defiant.

'You should have loved me then. I needed that. Not your hatred. Your insanity. *It was not my fault.*'

The gun pointed straight at her head. Teresa was ready to launch herself at this man. Then Jerome Aitchison got in the way, trying to step between the two of them, hand held out, pleading.

'It was a tragedy, man,' Aitchison said. 'An accident. Nothing anyone could change.'

'I can change what I like!'

Crouched on the ground in a heap, not far from the stricken Jason, Sofia leaned back, closed her eyes briefly, turned her face to the night sky. Then she looked into the harlequin's face, with pity, not fear.

'No, Michael,' she said. 'You think you can. But

you're wrong. You were deluded then. You're still deluded now. This has to stop. Believe me. I'm so, so sorry . . .'

Teresa's heart stopped. The grey barrel of the weapon was so close it almost touched Sofia's fore-head.

'And I am *not* afraid of you,' Sofia said simply, staring into his eyes. 'Not any more.'

There was a shout across the *campiello*, a loud voice, full of authority. Words Teresa couldn't understand. A foreign language, unrecognizable.

Not cops. It didn't sound right.

'Too late, too late!' the harlequin bellowed.

A shadow flew out of the darkness. As she watched a shiny ebony cane with a silver handle came down and knocked the pistol out of his hands. The gun scuttered across the black cobble-stones into the gloom. Teresa crossed the alcove and as she did the cane flashed again, more than once, striking the man in the diamond suit, sending him flying to the ground.

She clambered across the cold, wet stones and got to Jason. He was conscious, just, clutching his side, panting. In the scant moonlight his eyes were full of fear. A dark pool of blood was seeping through his fingers.

Teresa put a hand to the young man's face and said, to no one in particular, 'I don't know who the hell you are. But this man's been shot. I need help. An ambulance.'

When she looked back the Plague Doctor's blank

mask was staring towards her. He was still two strides away. The cane remained hard against the harlequin's chest. Not enough to keep a man in check, she thought. Not in itself. There was something more here. Some other form of authority.

'You're a doctor,' he said. 'Have you forgotten?'

'He still needs an ambulance. Call someone. Jerome!'

Aitchison was fumbling at a mobile phone already.

The masked face twisted again, became quizzical and ever more birdlike.

'They will come. He will live,' he said.

A long pause and then he turned to the figure beneath him, asking in a tone of deep disappointment and distaste, 'Are there so many things you don't understand?'

'*Ta gueule*,' the harlequin shouted. 'Shut your mouth!'

She could not begin to guess how these two knew each other.

'Your mouth!' the man on the ground yelled again, and raised a hand, made the sign of a weapon, pulling the trigger, aiming at the white ghostly mask.

'Would you shoot me?' the Plague Doctor asked. 'Here.'

He reached into his cloak and withdrew a small black pistol which he threw to the man in the suit of diamonds.

Ruskin seized the weapon, pointed it up towards

the stars and the reticent moon, directly at the man above him.

'Do it,' the Plague Doctor ordered. 'Go on. Is that how this journey ends?'

'The child was mine!'

'The child was lost! Go on. Do it! If you own the power of life or death, use it on me. Not them.'

Teresa could sense there was something pathetic, tragic between these two men, even if she could not begin to understand its origins.

The figure on the ground hesitated, shrank visibly as she watched.

'This journey is so long . . .' the man in the suit of diamonds said in a voice scarred with self-pity and hatred.

'*Courage*,' the voice behind the mask snapped back. The word sounded more French than English. 'Where did it go?'

'Don't talk to me of courage. Not after all these damned years. You . . .'

There was an incomprehensible howl, a shriek in a language she couldn't follow though it was a scream so full of loathing and despair she found it hard not to be moved, just a little.

Then she saw the weapon turning slowly in the hands of the man crouched on the grimy cobble-stones, rising to his own temple, shakily but with a clear intent.

'Oh no,' she shouted, scrambling quickly across, ignoring the hurt and the bruises, grabbing the gun for herself, tearing it from his fingers.

He was weak, confused, broken. The weapon felt cold and foreign and she realized she could never remember how to check whether the safety catch was on or not.

She kept the little black pistol on him though.

'I want to see you in court,' she said. 'Jerome?'

'Yes?'

A pale, determined face came into view.

'Take off that apron and tie his hands behind his back.'

Aitchison ripped off his bib, got down and wound the ties round the harlequin's wrists. The man didn't protest, didn't struggle. Something here had affected him, and it had to come from the words of the man in the long white mask.

'Where the hell is this ambulance?' she demanded, going back to Jason. The young Englishman's eyes were fading. He was close to losing consciousness.

'Coming, they said,' Aitchison replied.

'Coming,' she repeated.

There was movement from behind. When she looked back she saw the tall figure in the black cloak turning away, as if ready to leave.

'Where do you think you're going?' she demanded.

The beak rotated sideways again. Something had joined him. It sat pale and white and still by his feet. The little volpino.

She held out the gun, not steadily but it was the best she could do.

'Stay there.'

But he was going already. The dog rose noncha-
lantly on its haunches with him and began to trot
steadily towards the exit of the *campiello* as if it
knew the way home.

'I said . . .'

He looked back at her, removed the broad
buckled black hat, bowed quickly, then began to
stride away.

The gun waved and she shouted across the
shadowy *campiello*, 'For God's sake! Please!
Arnaud!'

Her words had no effect.

Jason groaned. As she watched a light seemed
to go out in his eyes.

'Oh no,' she whispered. 'Not now.'

Some memories kicked in, of classes in Rome,
of emergency work in the hospital there in San
Giovanni. Before she knew it she was ripping
Sofia's apron to shreds with her bare hands, going
to work with it on the wounds, doing what she
could. Not thinking about anything but the injured
man in front of her because nothing else mattered.

After a minute or so she bent down and listened
to his breathing. It was shallow and arrhythmic.
But it was there.

Then came a commotion from the alley outside
and two men raced through. They wore paramedic
uniforms and carried a stretcher and medical bags.
Behind was a woman in blue who identified herself
as a police doctor. She talked quickly, knowledgeably, assumed control.

They'd been prepared for injuries, Teresa guessed. Jason was lucky there at least.

She stared at the narrow passage that led back to the arcades of the Rialto. The Plague Doctor would be one more figure in a cloak now, darting through the February shadows.

Sofia was by her side. The medics looked professional, well equipped. They had Jason on a stretcher already, and were getting ready to move.

Sofia looked at her teary-eyed and said, 'This is my fault, isn't it? All of it.'

'Take this,' Teresa said, pulling her phone out of her pocket. 'Call home. Say I'll call too in a while. Chiara needs to hear from you. It's not your fault. Not at all.'

A few minutes later Jason was out of there, rushed to an ambulance launch on the nearest canal. They wouldn't let her go with him. No room, they said. No need. The man they knew as Michael Ruskin was taken in a police boat to the main Questura at Piazzale Roma and the most secure cell the state police of Venice owned.

Teresa had begged a cigarette from one of the police officers by that time. She stood by the wellhead, sucking the smoke into her lungs. It tasted foul and wonderful at the same time.

Paola Boscolo was there. She didn't look mad any more. Nor did she seem keen to start any kind of interview.

After a while this got on Teresa's nerves.

'Don't you even have any questions?' she demanded, close to breaking. 'I have.'

'Tomorrow,' the woman told her. 'Tomorrow will be fine.'

'If he dies . . .'

'He won't,' Boscolo said. 'That's what the doctor hoped anyway. He was lucky you were here. She said you may have saved him.' Paola Boscolo reached over and touched her arm. 'We were all lucky you were here if I'm honest. I'm sorry if it didn't seem that way.'

'Jason . . .'

Teresa couldn't think of anything but the young Englishman, smiling in his subterranean bakery, proud of his secret charges, safe there until they stepped out into the black, icy night.

'He'll be fine,' Paola Boscolo added. 'Believe that. Believing makes a difference. Pray for that. Pray with me if you like. This is Venice. You're never far from God.'

Teresa wanted to scream.

'God seemed a long way from here tonight, don't you think?'

'No, actually,' the young policewoman said straight away. 'I don't.'

Teresa smiled at her as best she could. A friendly gesture. There hadn't been many of those, though this intelligent, unassuming officer had probably deserved them.

'I found this,' Boscolo said, holding out her hand. 'On the well here. It's got your name on it.'

A pause. 'Like the others, I guess. Like the one that disappeared.'

A manila envelope. A few pages inside.

'Yes,' Teresa said, looking at it. 'Just like those.'

One more chapter from Arnaud, the Count of Saint-Germain.

'Thank you,' she said then took the envelope and thrust it into the pocket of her winter jacket.

THE NATURE OF THE BONES

She was roused by the sound of shouting. A coarse Venetian voice. Anger and bewilderment. Teresa Lupo shook herself awake and found she was looking up at a large, red-faced man in overalls who was holding a long Dutch hoe, blade upright.

It was warm already beneath a lagoon sky that was a constant shade of forthright blue.

'This is private land,' he said angrily. 'What are you doing? It's forbidden. The whole of Poveglia is forbidden.'

Teresa struggled to her feet, feeling stiff and a little confused.

'We were brought here last night. It was official. The boat. The jetty . . .'

Arnaud, she thought, suddenly remembering.

His blanket still lay on the ground, but crumpled as if someone had tossed it to one side. The farmer – she assumed this was the man who owned the vines – had a small dinghy tied to a post at the foot of the patch of open space where she'd slept.

'There was someone else,' she insisted. 'He was

ill. He died. I tried to get help. Did you move him?'

The man lowered the hoe and seemed a little less threatening. A small black-and-white spaniel ran to join them from the direction of the jetty and the abandoned hospital.

'There's no one here but you. Fast asleep in my vineyard.'

'That's not possible,' she said, shaking her head. 'I was left with a man. His name was Arnaud, the Count of Saint-Germain. We spoke. For a long time.' About what? It seemed distant, like a past event, dimly remembered. 'He died. Or . . .' Her head felt foggy and she so wanted it to clear. 'I thought so. There was a party on the landing stage by the hospital last night. A group of pathologists from Venice. They thought it . . . appropriate.'

He stared at her.

'I'm sorry,' she told him. 'I had no idea we were coming to a place like this. Trespassing. They left me here. I think they thought it was some kind of joke.'

'A night on Poveglia is a joke?' he asked. 'Let's find your dead friend. The one who can walk.'

They went everywhere, even inside the ruined hospital which had a bleakness about it that depressed her. There was no trace of the Count of Saint-Germain.

'Perhaps your dead friend had a boat of his own,' the farmer proposed. 'He's not here, I assure you. My dog would have sniffed him out by now.'

'I can see that,' Teresa observed, gazing at the shoreline, recalling what Arnaud had said about exercise and swimming in particular. The animal seemed very interested in a small patch of pebbly sand by the jetty, sniffing there constantly. Bobbing away on the water a few hundred metres into the channel was what looked like a cream hat, floating on the lazy lagoon swell.

Teresa Lupo checked her watch. It was just after eight. The symposium was due to meet for its final session at ten in the Aula San Trovaso in Dorsoduro, not far from the San Basilio vaporetto stop. There was still time.

She looked the farmer in the eye.

'I'm very sorry for the inconvenience and disrespect we've shown you, signore. Still, I have another favour to ask, one that will get me off your hands. It's essential I return to Venice immediately. I have an important meeting at the university in Dorsoduro. Things will go terribly wrong if I'm not there.'

'A meeting about what?'

'You wouldn't understand.'

'Try me.'

'About the true nature of the bones reputed to be those of St Mark.' She pointed to the distant city. 'In the basilica. There.'

'I read about that in the paper,' he said. 'You must have lots of spare time on your hands.'

She reached into her bag and handed over her purse.

'Take what you want. If there's not enough I can get more from a machine. After the meeting.'

The farmer scratched his head and looked at the spaniel.

'The taxi thieves would charge you a hundred and fifty or more to come out here.'

'Take it,' she instructed him.

He put a hand to his mouth and thought for a while.

'But I'm a little slower, and you have to put up with me and my dog. We say a hundred and twenty-five. Plus tip.'

Venetians, she thought.

'May we leave?'

He didn't move.

'You don't want to go to the hotel first?' The farmer pointed at her. 'You look as grubby as me.'

She brushed at the front of her shirt, which was once white and was now covered in grass stains and worse, then decided not to look any further.

'I'll go as I am, thank you.'

The Roman pathologist crossed the lagoon in the bows of the little dinghy, her hand on the soft, damp pelt of the farmer's spaniel, her face directly into the briny breeze. It was a journey to remember, one that put her on the same level as the flat, shining water and made her feel, albeit briefly, she was a part of the small, enclosed world that was Venice.

An hour and a half after leaving Poveglia they

docked at a taxi jetty on the broad promenade of Zattere, almost opposite the redbrick Molino Stucky of Giudecca.

She paid the farmer then climbed up the steps to the cobbled pavement gleaming in the warm morning sun. The street was busy with people. Locals going shopping. Tourists walking hand in hand, admiring the lovely view across the channel. A memory rose in her head and she failed to understand why. To the left, just in view, was Palladio's magnificent basilica of Redentore. A place to visit one day.

A few people gave her quizzical looks. Teresa Lupo felt scruffy and tired and mad but none of this mattered because now, finally, she knew just what she wanted to say. Every word had formed in her head as the boat bobbed slowly towards the city. It had been there all along, since childhood perhaps, though she'd always stifled those thoughts. They required, she believed, a catalyst, a trigger. One that turned out to be a man called Arnaud, the Count of Saint-Germain, and a sequence of apparently incomprehensible events that now possessed some semblance of order.

The members of the symposium were on a coffee break when she stormed into the grand lecture room. Immediately the buzz of chatter subsided, to be replaced by a tense and awkward silence.

The Venetian pathologist Alberto Tosi, ostensibly her sponsor, stood there frozen, his cup paused halfway to his mouth.

'How . . . um . . . delightful to see you,' he said.

'Really?' she replied with a smile. She took the coffee from his hand and put it on the table. Several men in dark suits shuffled out of earshot, mumbling inaudibly. 'First question, Alberto. Did you abandon only me in Poveglia last night? Or was there someone else, too? A man, perhaps an observer here. He was called Saint-Germain. Nice-looking fellow. Fifties, or so you'd think. Blue suit. Cream fedora. Fetching smile.'

'We . . . I . . . but . . .'

'Kindly stop babbling. Saint-Germain?'

'Everyone did look for you. I promise.'

'Far?' she wondered.

'Not so far,' he admitted. 'What did you say this man's name was?'

She repeated it and saw immediately that Tosi hadn't a clue what she was talking about.

'I'm sorry. About . . .' He shuffled on his rickety legs, like a teenager caught stealing apples. 'We needed an agreement. No one meant you any harm.'

'Have you voted?'

'We've heard the arguments. We didn't need to. We're of one mind.'

'Have . . . you . . . voted?'

'Not yet. But how many choices do we have? In all honesty?'

'You tell me.'

He laughed and said, 'Why, two, of course!'

She folded her arms, looked him in the eye and

503

declared, 'I want my say, Alberto. I want it now. After you've heard me out, then we vote.'

Teresa Lupo edged a little closer to him, took hold of the old man's tie, and tightened the knot far enough to make him gulp. Then she added, 'You will agree to that, won't you?'

Five minutes later they were back at their seats in the lecture hall, two rows of serious-faced academics, loyal servants of the Church, listening intently, aware they had no alternative.

THE MAN IN THE LINEN SUIT

'Teresa!' Tosi said, beaming. 'How delightful to see you. The journey?'

A few hours on the fast train from Rome with her mother, chatting intermittently but pleasantly. It was nothing. The weather was beautiful, warm and sunny. Venice looked glorious. It was early May. Much had happened in the preceding months.

Now there was time to compose her thoughts, her words.

The old pathologist was on his own when she walked into the meeting room of the Aula San Trovaso. A solitary agnostic among believers.

'Wonderful,' she said. 'How does it stand with the vote?'

Tosi frowned.

'From what I've seen of things so far, if they pick the Pope this way there must be good business in the Vatican for a crooked bookmaker.'

'Closed minds?' she asked.

'With all the certainty of the tomb.'

She laughed.

'What's so funny?' he asked.

'We're supposed to be like that, aren't we? The roles seem to have been reversed.'

She smiled at someone she half-recognized across the room. He was, if memory served correctly, a senior lecturer in forensic pathology at one of the great universities in Spain.

These were intelligent men. Their minds might be set, but that was not the same as fixed.

'Who's the chairman?'

He pointed out a German professor from Frankfurt, a cadaverous individual with long grey hair and half-moon glasses who stood near the podium, examining a paper.

'Bernhardt. I think he's framed the resolution already. We're supposed to vote soon. Planes to catch. Departments to run.' Tosi looked a little sad. 'I'll have to find some other diversion now.'

'I thought you had one,' Teresa told him, and patted the old man's arm.

Tosi blushed. He knew full well what she was talking about.

'Do we have the table booked for afterwards?'

'Of course.'

She'd been looking forward to this for weeks. Sofia and Jerome, Camilla and Jason, Strozzi, Tosi . . . and her mother too. All taking tea and cake on the little wooden jetty of the Pensione Calcina overlooking the Giudecca canal. Once a man called John Ruskin stayed here, his head full of insane dreams about a beautiful doomed saint in a painting in the Accademia, a short walk away by the Grand Canal.

First things first . . .

She walked across and introduced herself to the professor from Frankfurt.

He started to make some small talk.

'Is your mind made up?' she broke in.

He looked a little taken aback by her brusqueness.

'I am of an opinion.'

'May I?' she said, pointing at the paper in his hand. Bernhardt passed it over. There was no surprise there. A simple, straightforward finding of probability so certain that it amounted to a kind of proof.

Teresa Lupo took him to one side and began to speak. These were decent individuals to a man, and every one *was* a man.

Ten minutes later the gathering had assembled in the seats of the lecture room for one last meeting before the vote. She stood at the lectern, looking everyone in the eye before she began.

'Gentlemen,' the Roman pathologist declared, 'I have a counter resolution for you to consider. Before I read it there are some things – important things – I must say. The rudimentary facts of the examinations you have all conducted are clear. The remains in the basilica of San Marco are undoubtedly those of one man, of Greek origin, probably born in North Africa, around the time of the first century AD. This clearly rules out any chance that the preserved head in the possession of the Copts in Alexandria belonged to the same individual who is interred here. Equally we can dismiss any notion that the cadaver of Alexander the Great has been residing in Venice for the last twelve hundred years. The evidence you have assembled suggests that the bones in the Basilica San Marco may indeed be those of the evangelist St Mark.'

In the front row the German professor brightened visibly. Alberto Tosi looked greatly puzzled.

She thought of Arnaud, the Count of Saint-Germain, his lecture on Pascal and Fermat, and the little black book he carried with him everywhere.

'Where we differ,' she went on, 'is in the question of proof, and there you do yourselves a disservice. You should not press science into service to reaffirm your religion any more than I should use it as a prop to support my own atheism. If you extend your questions beyond the verifiable facts and enter the realm of conjecture, you're wandering into the territory of history, which is a place none of us belongs since in this respect it is not a science but an interpretative art.'

Saint-Germain's face, kindly, cunning, rose in her head, though it was nothing more than ink on paper.

'Worse, in so doing, in seeking to replace your doubts with certainty, your questions with answers, you damage, not fortify, your cause. If religion needs proof then what place is there in any of your schemes for faith? What are you but a bunch of doubting Thomases looking for something to prod with your curious fingers? My views are not yours, and that is our mutual prerogative. But if I did believe I'd surely hope I'd have the courage and determination to follow my convictions on their strength alone, without the need of some sample of dusty DNA to bolster them. A talisman to hold up to the world, with a unanimous declaration from a group of highly talented, if decidedly partial, observers who've conspired to get together in this room and declare to all and sundry, "Look, we were right all along".'

They listened, intently she felt.

'As an outsider I would have to ask myself seeing this, "Whom precisely are they hoping to convince? Me? Or themselves?"'

Someone cleared his throat at the back of the room, and she thought she heard a murmured note of appreciation.

'The resolution I propose to you, then, is this.'

She picked up a piece of paper from the desk. It was blank, a prop, nothing more.

'This symposium declares that the bones which reside in the sarcophagus in the Basilica San Marco are those of one man whose identity, unsurprisingly, is incapable of absolute verification after such a great passage of time. If an individual's strength of belief leads him to feel these are the remains of Mark the Apostle then that is, indeed, what they are. Should one think otherwise, a natural scepticism ought to allow for the undeniable truth that we live in a world which remains full of mysteries and conundrums, some of which, thankfully, may never be answered.'

She paused, watching them.

'This is both a question of faith and of doubt, gentlemen, and to what extent one depends upon the other. That is my resolution. Do I have a seconder?'

Tosi's arm shot up immediately, like a soldier's coming to salute.

Twenty minutes later they were outside, walking towards the Pensione Calcina, watching the gentle flow of traffic on the Giudecca canal.

'You spoke so well,' Tosi said.

'Thank you.'

'Such eloquence.'

She wanted to say, *They were not my words. Not entirely.*

'Don't feel bad, Alberto. It wasn't a contest. We didn't lose.'

'Two votes against twenty? That's not losing?'

'No,' she insisted. 'The bones are still the bones. They're unchanged by anything we've said or done.'

'Then why go to all that very articulate trouble?' he asked.

'Because I owed it to someone. And myself too.'

Much had happened over the preceding months, some of it requiring several trips to the city, pleasant visits during which she'd watched winter lift and the light of spring put life back into the streets and piazzas and waterways.

Jerome Aitchison and Sofia became engaged at the end of February, only postponing an immediate wedding because of the near-hysterical pleas of Chiara for a more decorous interval. They waited precisely six weeks before marrying in a civil ceremony in San Marco, surrounded by friends.

By that time it was obvious the wounds had healed between Teresa's mother and her aunt, so quickly and surely it was hard to believe they existed in the first place. A fresh honesty, a new affection was there. And some stability too. Sofia had stayed on to work for the bakery. She'd never looked happier. Jerome – Teresa now thought of him this way, more because of his childlike qualities than his elevation to unclehood – had picked up some part-time lecturing responsibilities at Ca' Foscari, with the promise of further work when his rapidly improving Italian allowed.

Both continued to live in the same crooked palazzo along the waterfront. Like Filippo Strozzi and Camilla, they paid rent to the civil court, not a bank account in the name of an imaginary man called Michael Ruskin.

Strozzi, determined to rely more on making music than masks, had opened a jazz club in San Barnaba. Camilla remained wedded to papier-mâché for the moment but had plans to return to art college since her illness appeared to be in remission.

511

Jason's injuries had required a six-week stay in the hospital near the Fondamenta Nove. Throughout he had occupied a private room overlooking the water, a luxury organized by Alberto Tosi with some deft behind-the-scenes tugging of strings. Teresa always visited him when she came, and usually found Camilla there. The relationship between these two changed visibly over that time. Before, the young woman's reliance on Jason for the transfusions had, perhaps, served to deter any personal interest she might have felt. She'd felt dependent on the young Englishman, and a one-sided need was never a sound basis for love.

Over the weeks she'd visited him in hospital that had changed. They became equals, reliant on one another in equal measure. In late April she and Teresa had pushed him in his wheelchair along the waterfront to the vaporetto stop, then taken the slow boat out to the distant island of Burano. It had been the first warm day of spring. They'd eaten at a small restaurant near the *fermata* at Mazzorbo, a local place that served duck shot by hunters in the nearby marshes. Jason had said little, just smiled. Teresa watched the two of them then took herself off for a walk before catching the boat back to Venice. Words were no longer necessary. In the strange way that human relationships worked, the shared vulnerability that came from Jason's new reliance on Camilla, pushing the wheelchair along the pavement, helping him in and out of bed, dispelled any remaining barriers between them as subtly as the spring rain washing away the winter dirt and grime from the city pavements.

The following evening they all went to Strozzi's little club, a basement close to the Ponte dei Pugni. Sofia and Jerome were man and wife. Jason was walking then, with the aid of a stick, Camilla by his side. And Signora Rizzolo, whose *pasticceria* continued to prosper, arrived on Alberto Tosi's long, proud arm.

Peroni, who'd come with Teresa for that trip, remarked when they got back to the hotel, 'I never believed all that bilge about Venice being romantic. Not until now.'

Then he'd called room service and a bellhop in uniform arrived with champagne and flowers, clearly pre-ordered.

This was not the kind of life she could possibly hope to sustain even if she wished it.

The next afternoon the man charged under the name of Michael Ruskin had been given an indefinite custodial sentence under the mental health laws. The counts of murder – of the Gabriellis and the unfortunate market porter killed in the store then clothed in the costume of a harlequin – remained on the books. The judgement of the prosecutors was that he was not sufficiently sane for them to be pursued. He was sentenced in his absence. Since entering prison Ruskin's health had waned, in ways the doctors failed to understand. He seemed to be suffering from an unidentifiable debilitating disease, one that left him confined to bed, attached, in a very short space of time, to a life-support system.

Two days after the case was heard he died. The cause remained a matter of debate, as was much else about the man. The authorities still had no clear idea of his true identity, only a long and growing list of the false names – masks, as Teresa thought of them – he had used around the world.

From the outset the local police refused to allow her to interview him or see the medical reports, even though she was now back in her position in the Rome Questura, her authority if anything enhanced by what had happened. Venice was Venice. Rome was Rome. Nations apart. The unfortunate administrator Orsini, however, had been demoted to work in a traffic control unit in Ostia. The lesson had not been lost on Teresa Lupo's colleagues.

'Signora Rizzolo is a wonderful woman,' Tosi declared with a sly smile as they approached the outdoor tables of the *pensione*. The remark brought her back to the present. 'It's hard to keep secrets here, isn't it?'

'You've got so many,' she observed. 'It would be rash to expect them all to stay under lock and key.'

Everyone was there, seated at the best table by the water. Sofia looked very beautiful, Jerome deeply adoring.

'More coffee?' Tosi asked as they sat down,

Teresa by Jason and Camilla, Tosi next to Signora Rizzolo. 'The *pasticceria* has some lovely new *dolci*. Jason calls them Eccles cakes. One can hardly believe they're English.'

Sofia and Chiara waved across the table. They were mid-sentence in what appeared to be a long and somewhat risqué story about teenage misbehaviour, one to which Jerome Aitchison listened attentively if a little shocked as they cawed and hooted over the details.

Teresa kissed Camilla and held her, then did the same for Jason. The stick was gone. He looked as fit and healthy and happy as ever.

There was small talk, and the cakes were delicious if unfamiliar.

Her mind drifted. It was hard to associate those cold, bleak winter nights with this glorious afternoon, warm and sunny, not far from the Ponte agli Incurabili, not too distant from the alleys and arcades of the Rialto either. The canal glistened. The black, restless grebes she remembered from February were still there, followed by a line of bobbing chicks.

'Penny for them,' Jason said with a wink.

'A penny for what?'

'For your thoughts. It's an English expression.'

'I feel they're worth rather more than that, actually.'

'Those fools from the First International Symposium on the Genetic Analysis of the Skeletal Remains Attributed to St Mark didn't think so,' Tosi broke in. 'I should have seen what that was all about the moment they came up with such a pompous mouthful.'

'It was a vote about the dead, Alberto,' she said. 'I was contemplating the living for a change. They matter rather more. I was thinking . . . that I'm glad things worked out so well. In the end.'

Most of them anyway.

In a short space of time the afternoon turned more raucous. Teresa was glad in a way that Peroni hadn't been able to come. He would have loved a family gathering like this, would have joined in the jokes and the ridiculous banter easily, in a way she would always find impossible. For them the events of the previous February lay in the past, buried by the pleasure of the present. There was no visible aftermath, no nagging doubts or misgivings. She envied them this facility for setting the dark to one side. She wondered why such a rational feat of practical amnesia was so impossible for her.

After a while bright scarlet glasses of spritz began to emerge. She sipped at one, just a touch. That was enough, though they were all too busy and too engaged to notice. The bittersweet taste, the olive and the slice of orange, all brought back too many memories of those freezing nights near Il Gobbo. A reminder that she could have fallen into that murky and enticing trap too, so easily.

Just after five her phone buzzed. It was a message, a short one, that read, 'I trust you won't forget to visit St Augustine and his little dog one last time. We close at six. On the dot. Those are the rules of the Scuola di San Giorgio degli Schiavoni.'

She found herself unable to breathe for an instant. A mental picture of that dark hall by the bridge in Castello came back sharp and clear, as if from yesterday. And the stiff warden of an indeterminate age, a man who knew all about paintings and little dogs.

'I have to go,' she said, then kissed them all and left for the fast boat to Castello.

The vaporetto was quieter than during carnival, with locals and tourists happily enjoying the warm sun and the wide expansive view of St Mark's Basin. Turner was a winter soul. He had deserted Venice now. In his place the coming summer brought a different palette of colours, bright and sharp and forthright. Those of a native, Tintoretto or Tiziano.

She got off at Arsenale and immediately found the direct route to the little *scuola* by the canal. For a reason she'd never quite fathomed she'd stayed away ever since February, even when there were spare hours on some earlier visits. Something about the paintings, both there and in the Accademia, continued to unsettle her. They were like the city, hard to dislodge from one's thoughts. Like the man who called himself Michael Ruskin too, still half-hidden in the shadows of mystery. Incomplete, indeterminate.

Victor Carpathius Fingebat.

A riddle painted by a curious artist more than five centuries before. A signature of a kind. A boast, even. Some kind of challenge saying: read me, digest me, bring me to life. In her mind's eye she could see the cartellino, the bewildered saint and the little dog as she walked up the freshly swept street towards the modest white Palladian building at its head.

The place seemed busier than she expected when she strode through the green door. Automatically, Teresa turned to her left, where the man would be waiting for her with his dark suit, old fashioned glasses and owlish eyes.

'I've been meaning to give you a piece of my mind . . .' she began, alarmed at the way her right index finger had begun to wag the moment she entered the cool, dark interior. 'I . . .'

A middle-aged woman in a white polo shirt was seated at the little table. She had grey hair tied back in a severe bun and a puzzled, rather stern face.

'The standard donation is three euros,' she said, indicating the box.

A flicker of fury began to rise at the back of Teresa Lupo's head. This was one more trick of his.

'Someone was supposed to meet me here. A man. I expected the warden who usually . . .'

The woman shushed her into silence, her eyes darting to the centre of the hall.

It was packed, Teresa saw, the benches occupied by a rapt party of schoolgirls. English again, judging by the badge on their blazers, which bore the name of a school in Manchester. The children appeared a good couple of years younger than the class in February, little more than twelve or thirteen, too young to be bored by ancient and exotic art. A few had watched the encounter at the entrance. Most had their eyes on a tall, rather shambling middle-aged man in a pale and crumpled linen suit who stood by the painting of St Augustine in his study, waiting for the fuss to end.

The same teacher she'd seen there before. The one about whom the warden had been so rude, calling him, if she recalled correctly, an 'English popinjay'.

His hair seemed darker, brown not the fair to grey colour she recalled. His face was fetching yet unremarkable, the sort one would notice immediately then forget the moment he departed the room.

'May I continue?' he asked very politely.

Teresa sat down rather grumpily on a seat next to the entrance. The woman dangled her fingers across the donations box once more. Teresa passed across some coins and received in return the same kind of antiquated entrance ticket she'd received back in February. Nothing here ever changed, she thought. Except for the price on the ticket, and the person who handed it over.

'*The Golden Legend*,' the man began, 'is a set of stories, as I've said. Myths and fables. One man's dreams about people who may or may not have been real. Lies intended to throw light upon a larger, more reticent truth. As you will have read . . .'

'Sir . . .'

A small girl with a pigtail, seated at the very front, the place where the swots always wanted to be, had her hand up.

'Lucy, isn't it?'

He didn't seem familiar with this class. A local guide, she suspected, brought in for visiting parties.

'That's right,' the girl said primly. 'Are you saying none of them are true?'

He beamed at her and asked, 'None of what?'

'The dragons. And the lions. And the monsters.'

'And the dog,' Teresa added testily. 'Don't forget the dog.'

Lucy gave her a very grown-up basilisk stare as if she'd intruded on some private audience.

'Sorry,' Teresa said, and waved him on.

'I've never seen a dragon,' the man continued. 'Or a monster. But I've seen plenty of lions in my time. And dogs . . . Well. We've all seen dogs.'

'Apart from the dogs, I mean,' the girl said in the persistent and slightly crabby tone of a precocious child. 'And the lions.'

He frowned, thinking.

'That depends.'

'On what?' Lucy persisted.

'On whether you believe the only things that exist are those you can see and touch.' He paused. 'Well? Do you?'

The girl put a finger to her pudgy cheek, thinking. There was a mischievous look on her face. Teresa recognized this kind of child. Serious on the surface, rascally underneath.

'No,' she declared after a while. 'In fact I think the only person who'd believe that would be a . . .'

She waved her hands at her classmates, beckoning, calling for some kind of answer.

'A *prune!*' they chanted in unison, then fell to giggling and nudging each other with their small, sharp elbows.

A light went on in Teresa Lupo's head. She stared at the man standing in front of the Carpaccio canvases. He shrugged his shoulders, eyed her and winked.

A prune. Arnaud's favourite word for someone who'd been a fool.

These children had heard that joke a lot over the last few days too, she guessed. They'd grown to like their guide to the art and history of Venice, to think it fun to throw his own quip back at him. He was a clown, an entertainer. A knowledgeable escort spending a few days a week with any passing group of schoolchildren that cared to hire him. One who must surely have bumped into Sofia on their mutual winding circuit of the city sights.

He smiled at them as they laughed, smiled at

her too, his tanned cheeks suffused with a touch more colour.

She sat in silence, half-listening, looking at the picture of St Augustine, perplexed at his wooden desk, surrounded by the panoply of an organized intellectual life, the little dog, ears pricked and alert, at his feet. His attention caught by something from beyond the bright sunny window, unable to comprehend what it might be.

The rest of the talk was very similar to the one she'd heard in February. It ended on the dot, with the chimes of a nearby church. Six of them. A pretty young teacher joined them close to the end and afterwards led the girls away in a tightly disciplined line. The woman at the door coughed and harrumphed, looking at her watch. Teresa left too and waited outside.

When the man in the linen suit emerged into the golden evening sunlight he looked around him, at the *scuola*, at the beautiful little bridge over the *rio*. He was taller than she had pictured, not the rather dapper middle-aged gentleman who was Arnaud, the Count of Saint-Germain, in her imagination. His suit must once have been natty. Now it was threadbare in parts, as was his hat, which was the floppy, foldable kind one expected of a traveller in the tropics. There were leather patches on the jacket's elbows and the odd stain here and there. His footwear had seen much better days, being battered soft brown sandals worn with pale pink socks. The stick was the same though. Black and shiny, with a silver handle.

'Children,' he said with a shrug. 'Who'd have thought they'd perform the introductions for me? Little devils. Talking of which . . .'

A small white dog was trotting across the bridge towards them, its gait certain and steady, as if the animal was returning from an appointment. It came and sat obediently at his feet.

Teresa bent down. Two serene black eyes returned her gaze. She remembered that far-off night on the Ponte dei Pugni, and Peroni's instructions. A little warily she held out the back of her hand to let the dog sniff it. Then, once accepted, she patted the stiff dry fur on his head.

'You're very privileged,' the man said. 'He can be very picky.'

'Now I see him like this, in the open, in the sunlight . . . He's not a volpino, is he?'

'Very similar in appearance. The volpino's a rare breed. I think this one's some kind of terrier. Several kinds really. Does it matter? He's a loyal and loving companion. Really no trouble at all. May I buy you a spritz?'

Oh yes, she said. Her earlier resolution had disappeared altogether.

They walked round the corner, down an alley, across a tiny *campiello* with stone walls so old they looked like a suntanned giant's peeling skin. She knew where they were going, though she understood too she'd never be able to find the place herself with any great ease.

The Cason dei Sette Morti looked much brighter than it had in February when Tosi had brought her here. Even then it had seemed more welcoming than its fictional counterpart in the story called *Carpaccio's Dog*.

'You made this place sound horrible in that tale you made up about Jerome,' she told him as they walked in.

'I don't want my secrets bandied around in public,' he replied. 'The *baccalà* here's much too good to be shared with the hoi polloi from the cruise ships. Besides, I wasn't entirely sure about Jerome Aitchison when I sent off that little tale. It would have been rash to have dismissed the idea that he'd made off with poor Sofia. Don't assume omniscience on my part. You couldn't be more wrong.'

The same pleasant old bartender was there. He greeted them cheerily and immediately set about heating some milk in the coffee machine then spooning it onto a saucer which he set in front of the little dog. After that, again without being asked, he reached for the Campari bottle, prosecco and olives.

'You're a regular,' Teresa observed.

'A creature of habit,' he agreed. 'You must try the *baccalà*. And the *sarde en saor*. None better.'

The man behind the counter passed over two glasses of the most perfect spritz she'd ever tasted, cold and sweet and bitter, an inexplicable jumble of flavours that she would forever associate with Venice and never attempt to enjoy elsewhere. Then he brought several plates of food before retiring to the tiny patio, just visible behind the bar. There he stretched out on a rickety old sun bed and proceeded to smoke a cigar, eyes closed, clearly not expecting any more custom for the night.

Teresa looked around her at the random collection of books, old amusement machines, photographs, grandfather clocks and the obscure fortune-telling device which still had a sign declaring 'broken' taped over the coin slot. In some odd way it reminded her of the painting she'd just seen, Augustine in his cluttered academic study, hiding from the light of the world, but seeing it from the window nevertheless.

'Alberto Tosi told me this place got its name from some ridiculous old lagoon tale,' she said, half to herself. 'One about ghosts and dead men walking.'

She looked at the man next to her, long and lean in his shabby linen suit.

'Do you believe in ghosts too?'

He tried his spritz and a smear of salt cod on bread, closing his eyes briefly out of pure pleasure. A drop of Campari spilled onto the sleeve of his wrinkled jacket. It wasn't, she saw, alone.

'I'm prepared to believe in anything that's willing to believe in me. What about you?'

She reached forward and lightly pinched his arm, then tried to remove the pink smear of alcohol.

'You don't seem much of a ghost.'

'I was never aware,' he replied archly, 'that I claimed to be one.'

'What do I call you? Arnaud?'

'As good a name as any.'

'What do you have to say to me, Arnaud?' she asked.

He took a deep breath and tried to smile. There was such sadness in him, so deep a sense of resignation, of acceptance, that she could detect straight away the Saint-Germain she'd imagined, reserved, intelligent, charming yet infinitely melancholy too. Only the shell, the mask of outward appearance, stood between the character in the book and the man sipping his drink next to her, on a battered stool in this back-alley bar in the distant reaches of Castello.

'That I'm sorry for the pain,' he said. 'Sorry I couldn't do more to lessen it. I tried to tell you. It's part of my . . . condition that I see some things too well and others not at all. I lack a forensic mind. I am by nature fated to watch, not participate. So I endeavoured to pass on to you what facts I possessed in the hope that someone more astute might know what to do with them. To assemble them into some kind of logical order, one that might bring about a happy conclusion.'

'You could have gone to the police.'

'You did and what good did it do? I knew no more than I told you in those small fictions. They were a collection of facts, of possibilities. Of questions demanding answers.'

'They were infuriating puzzles!'

He hesitated then said, 'There was that aspect to them, I'll admit. I felt from what Sofia told me that you might need to approach the problem a little more . . . loosely than might otherwise have been the case. A touch of the imagination was required. From what I'd learned I wasn't sure you were up to that. Not in your Roman frame of mind.'

'Thank you!'

'Was I wrong?' His eyes darkened. 'Besides, I had my reasons. I don't expect you to accept them, but they were . . . they *are* . . . real enough for me.'

'This man Ruskin . . . Who was he?'

He put down his piece of bread and the remains of a cold sardine.

'I believe you'd label him schizophrenic. A psychopath. Some such convenient term. There are so many to choose from today. Progress, I suppose.'

'And you, Arnaud. What would you call him?'

He looked her directly in the face and said, 'Brother.'

She was lost for words.

'We don't choose who shares our blood, do we?' he went on. 'Nor do we control those who possess it. I didn't him, any more than you could Sofia.'

She tried to laugh.

'Oh please. The insane nonsense in those stories . . .'

He parked his spritz on the counter and gazed at her, a little cross.

'Believe what you wish. He was my brother. As I tried to tell you, sometimes a man, or a woman, is born with a hidden poison inside them. It's not their fault. It's not theirs to master. If they're lucky it never surfaces. When it does . . . then we all pay the cost.'

'The trigger,' she said.

He waved a hand around the cluttered interior of the Cason dei Sette Morti.

'. . . is this. Read Ruskin. Everyone's Venice is different. Where you see antiquity I see squalor. Where another marvels at beauty a second turns away in horror at some gross, naked display of poor taste. Yet it remains a place of wonder for most of us. For him . . .' He seemed unsure of his words. 'What common sense and decency he had departed the moment he set foot here. That painting didn't help.'

He frowned, seeking the right words.

'I think he wanted his own Ursula somehow. An eternal bride. Always virginal. Forever pure. As far as I understand – and be assured, we weren't sufficiently on speaking terms of late to discuss this – he came to feel he was haunted by the ghost of Ruskin and Rose La Touche much as Ruskin was plagued by the insane obsession he had with Carpaccio's Ursula. Possessed twice over, as it were. I should have realized it wasn't a good sign when he took that name. This was years ago. Don't fool yourself that Sofia was alone, the first. That dismal hovel they call the Casino degli Spiriti.' He shuddered. 'Lord knows I had trouble enough with that place in the past . . .'

She recalled Tosi's story, of the murder there when he was a child, the squid with the eyes of a woman.

'If you're talking about what I think, that was more than fifty years ago,' she pointed out.

'Is that all?' The question didn't affect him in the slightest. 'I really should have seen he was up to no good there again.' He picked up the spritz and took a swig, glaring at her for a moment. 'I merely passed on the description in case it proved of some use. Had I known for one instant you intended to break in . . . Good Lord!' That was the one night you shook me off, deliberately I thought. And see what happened! Thank God you weren't so elusive in the Rialto.'

Teresa Lupo blinked, trying to take this in.

'I was trying to lose Alberto Tosi! You mean you followed me around? Everywhere? Beginning to end?'

'From the moment you and your mother stepped off that vaporetto,' he replied. 'I got your picture from the papers and spent many freezing hours meeting every boat that matched with a train or flight from Rome. Of course I wasn't going to leave you entirely alone. Do you think I have no conscience? I was fortunate he'd disappeared from that apartment of his by then. And that I still had a key. He let me use the place a few years before when we were on better terms. He was a very forgetful man sometimes. So many different places to go, I imagine. I've never understood why anyone wants more than a single home. One's too many sometimes.'

Her outrage was growing. She stabbed a finger at him and said, 'You were there? Looking at those cameras? Spying on us all?'

'Only as much as I needed!' he protested. 'I didn't know he had those nasty little things until I got in. And I did turn them off so he couldn't peek himself. Though I suspect he was beyond that by then. It was foolish of me. He might have noticed. I was desperate and I never think straight in such conditions. Do you see my problem? I'm not up to subterfuge, I'm afraid.'

'He was your brother! And you didn't know where he was?'

Arnaud said nothing, simply stared at her.

'Oh, you mean like Sofia,' she replied. 'There you have me.'

'I told you. He was an acquisitive man. He had other places to go. Ones that he never shared with me, for all the obvious reasons. It was never my intention to come back here at all. I never would have, had I not learned Sofia had returned too.

An astonishing decision given the circumstances. Why on earth did she do it?'

The two of them had had that conversation often enough over the past few months. Sofia never really understood the problem. The past was the past. Gone.

'She loves it here. Ruskin assured her what had happened, the baby, the affair . . . they were behind them. Forgotten. She could have the apartment on the cheap and he wouldn't bother her.'

'Ha!' Arnaud shook his head in amazement. 'Cunning on his part, naivety on hers. It was clear to me from the beginning something untoward would happen. His nature was never forgiving at the best. When Aitchison came along, the emergence of a rival, as he saw it, only served to add fuel to the impending blaze. I was pleased she had the good sense to disappear when she did but concerned all the same. He was not a man given to abandoning his obsessions easily.'

'So it became my job to find her?'

Teresa still felt a sense of outrage at the way she'd been used.

'Who else?' he asked. 'Sofia's a talkative woman. She told everyone about her brilliant niece in Rome. Several times over.' He waved an arm around the bar. 'Over *cicchetti* here a few times, believe it or not. All about Jason and Strozzi and Camilla. Jerome too in the end. She felt able to confide in me for some reason. People do. I've no idea why. Your light never found the bushel in any of those conversations, and that's the truth. Where else should I look for assistance than the genius of the Questura? I needed someone who could make an intelligent and dedicated effort to get to the bottom of this riddle.'

He leaned down and fed the dog a morsel of fish.

'I'd have been an idiot not to enlist you in some way.'

'You could have told me something certain! Something . . .' She struggled for the right words. 'Solid. Meaningful.'

'I told you what I knew. Sofia had gone missing by then. Aitchison too. Perhaps that very talented musician in his wheelchair was hiding them. Or the Croatian girl. Or that brave young Englishman. I needed someone with a forensic eye to work things out. To take a look at them and try to comprehend what was going on and how she might be saved. It required a methodical mind, and that kind of thing has always been beyond me. I find it a touch tedious, if I'm honest.'

There was an infuriating expression of offended innocence in his eyes.

'You could have—'

'Could have what?' he interrupted. 'Written you a letter?'

'They were stories!'

'Life's a story, isn't it? Imagine if I'd tried to outline our problem as plain fact. A stranger writes to you to say a man with a mysterious genetic

532

condition is loose somewhere in Venice, possibly with mischief on his mind when it comes to your aunt and her missing boyfriend. He's no idea where but has some stories to tell which you will doubtless find rather far-fetched. You'd have regarded me as a madman and gone back to stumbling round in circles with your pathologist friend.'

'I had to sort your facts from your fantasies,' Teresa complained.

'As did I. That was the point. I couldn't. I'm not very good at that kind of thing, thank you very much.' He frowned, frustrated that he seemed incapable of making his point. 'I have rather more memories in this head than it was built for. I tried to set down what I knew as best I could, in a form calculated to prick your curiosity while passing on the jumble of information I possessed. For the life of me I can't think how else I could have achieved any of this. Can you?'

She was outraged to discover herself lost for an answer.

'Quite,' Arnaud went on. 'It wasn't easy writing those tales, you know. Though I have to say . . .' He preened his shabby collar with pride. 'I do think they're rather good given the time available. And the fact I was almost as much in the dark about details as anyone. Also, I sent that chap Tosi your way, even if I did rather misjudge him. Once I read about that investigation of his it seemed the right thing to do. The papers said you'd worked together before, which was a happy coincidence.'

'Tosi was on my side already. I made sure of that.'

'To the genius of the Questura!' he declared, raising his glass in a toast.

There wasn't the least note of sarcasm in his voice. She doubted the man was capable of it.

'And if I'd not found Ruskin? That night? If I'd failed to work out that . . . hint he left?'

Sagittarius. The knowledge was there all along. The story had prompted its return.

'But you did find him,' he said, a little puzzled.

'Camilla could have died.'

'I doubt that,' Arnaud insisted. 'Unless it suited his purpose somehow. Nothing about him was random or excessive, hard as you may find that to believe. Camilla was your bait. He would have made sure you got to her one way or another. That was what he wanted. To murder some unfortunate porter, place him in the harlequin costume, and fool you all into thinking the dreaded Michael Ruskin was dead. Then follow you to Sofia. Just as he did with Aitchison and that unfortunate pimp in the first place. When it came to devious matters, he had one song to sing usually. I imagine we should all be thankful for that.'

His face fell. He picked at the olive in his glass.

'I regret the porter,' he noted glumly. 'I should have been able to save him. The Gabriellis were gone before I understood how bad matters were turning. But that man will remain on my conscience.'

'If you didn't know . . .'

'Regrets and sorrow are rarely eased by logic in my experience.'

They remained silent for a while. Then his mood lifted abruptly, as if he could shift from dark to light in an instant.

'On a cheerier subject . . . your speech to the symposium! Magnificent. Very moving. If I contributed a little I'm flattered, but all the credit remains yours. Such a forceful and persuasive delivery. Wasted on those fools, sadly . . .'

'You were there too?' she cried.

His bright blue eyes creased with bafflement.

'I don't spend all my time with schoolchildren. Of course I was there. Wouldn't have missed it for all the tea in China. There's a spectators' gallery at the back. Didn't you see? Not hard to wangle your way into academic affairs, you know. Not with my experience. A touch of flattery goes a long way with those people. They ought to get out more.'

'You're a very infuriating man!'

He smiled and made a self-deprecating gesture with his shoulders.

'Sorry.'

'And now?' she asked.

'Now . . .'

For the first time since they'd met he seemed unsure of himself.

Arnaud reached into the pocket of his linen jacket and took out a small glass antique medicine vial with a silver stopper. It was full of a black viscous liquid. He removed the top and held it for her to sniff.

Her heart fell. He seemed so serious, so determined and sincere.

'Very like Calabrian bitter,' she agreed.

'Vecchio Amaro del Capo? This is a little sweeter. As I've already said I feel it's important the cochineal is real, from Lanzarote beetles. Nothing artificial. Though I may well be wrong.'

Then he retrieved a packet of tissues from a plastic bag in his pocket, spat very daintily in one and placed it and the glass bottle back in the bag.

'For you,' he said.

She didn't move.

'Don't you want it?'

'No.'

He seemed amazed.

'Why not?'

'Oh, Arnaud.'

I can get you help, she wanted to say. I can find someone who might get to the bottom of this fantasy. Unwind the tangle of lines that led to Michael Ruskin. This man's brother. Of that she was in no doubt.

But what then? What if he was cured? What would remain of him? How could one remove such a fascinating form of madness without reducing the man to a shell of himself? What if the remedy was worse than the disease?

He was still waiting, holding the bag with the little vial and the tissue.

'You said something once,' she told him. 'Or someone did. In a story I read. You talked about the glorious wonder of doubt.'

'What doubt?' he asked, proffering the bag at her again. 'You live, you die. Think of this conversation twenty, thirty years hence. Will you feel so confident of your position then? You don't have to believe me. Just take it. If this little bottle contains nothing more than cheap aperitif and a lunatic's saliva, where's the harm?'

'And your brother? If you expect me to believe this fairy tale, what did it do for him?'

'I told you. A poison in the blood. We don't blame mankind for cancer. We use our innate intelligence to try to eradicate the disease instead.' He waved the bag like an adult offering a toy to a child. 'Perhaps you can find an answer to that in here too. Don't be so tiresome, please.'

'Tiresome? You're calling *me* tiresome?'

There was no point in arguing. As ever she required facts. That night in the *campiello* in the Rialto came back to her. Words exchanged in an unknown language. The man called Michael Ruskin broken by the loss of a child, turned into a murderous monster. Through what?

Somehow she was sure it was the answer she'd been given – the one put into her own mouth. *Love.*

'Why did it hurt him quite so much?' she asked, hoping to calm things a little. 'Ruskin? Parents lose children all the time. It's devastating but it's a part of us too. Who we are. One tragedy among many. Most of us survive. Cope. We don't react like that, with hatred and violence.'

'If you'd seen what he'd seen. What *I've* seen . . .'

'Please,' she said.

'Hear me out. He'd never fathered a child before. Neither have I. It's part of our mutual condition, I think. Didn't I mention that?'

He took a deep breath and seemed at that instant very old and tired.

'What was it that English poet said? "Any man's death diminishes me, because I am involved in mankind". Some diminish one rather less than others, of course. Either way, after a while there's precious little left to diminish at all. And not much involvement in mankind as a consequence. Enough that he couldn't shoot me that last night. I was touched by that.'

'Yet you . . . ?'

'I lack that poison. Also I am the most careful man you will ever meet. Careful to avoid relations that have consequences. Careful to keep myself to myself.' He held out the bag again. 'Believe it or not but it was a damaged sense of humanity that destroyed him. The false belief he might in some way be like everyone else. That's not possible. We can help, nothing more. If we engage we damage. Ourselves, and others. That's how it is. He knew that but he couldn't stop himself, which is why I still mourn him, but only up to a point. Now . . .'

He was insistent. So Teresa took the bag and

immediately deposited the thing in a tiny rubbish bin beneath the counter.

Arnaud sat there, a little hunched, clutching at the glass of spritz. Not miserable, she thought. Merely resigned.

'It was foolish of me to expect you to understand,' he said eventually. 'Sofia's tales about you were so compelling. So adoring. One creates a picture, an image, that can't possibly be true.'

'I can imagine. I don't want to understand. Perhaps I would have once. Not now. This is your fault.'

'I beg your pardon.'

'In the end it's the mystery that lasts and not the explanation. Is that a good enough excuse?'

'Oh, dear,' he said with a guilty grin. 'You know you're in trouble when people quote your aphorisms back at you. Sacheverell really did write that though.'

'I know. I checked. It's in a book. Just like everything else. You must be an avid reader.'

He raised his glass, toasting her, smiled and said nothing.

'Arnaud. You need to come with me to the Questura. We have to clear up the rest of this mess. Who Michael Ruskin really was. There are so many questions.'

He went rigid with shock.

'Oh no. Oh, definitely not. If I set foot in that place I'd never get out. I thought I'd made my position clear on that. I'm no one's lab specimen.

Nor do I wish to spend my final days wasting away in some prison clinic, surrounded by doctors shaking their heads in bewilderment and placing bets on who gets first crack at the autopsy.'

'There's the issue of his property for one thing,' Teresa said, ignoring the bait. 'His estate.' She paused for a moment, wondering how he might take this. 'From what Paola Boscolo tells me there's quite a lot of money involved. It may be that some will be tied up in legal matters. There'll be plenty left besides.'

'Money?' he cried, aghast. 'You're trying to tempt me with *money*?'

'Someone's got to have it.'

'Find a charity then,' he said, still mortified. 'Do I look as if I'm on my uppers?'

She took in the crumpled, stained suit, the sandals and pink socks, the tropical hat scrunched up on the wooden counter of the bar.

'Yes, frankly. You do. Talking to schoolchildren about paintings and *The Golden Legend* can't pay much.'

'Scarcely a cent! It's fun. I love the young. I still remember when I was a child myself. Don't you?'

'No,' she said. 'At least I try not to. I hated it.'

'I'm sorry about that.'

He reached over and grasped her wrist. She was taken aback for a moment, then she saw what he was doing: checking the time on her watch. It was approaching seven.

'Never carry one of the things myself,' he said, letting go. 'Seems pointless.'

'Please . . . You won't come to any harm. I guarantee it.'

His eyes fell to the floor. The dog was a tight white ball curled up at his feet next to the ebony cane with the silver handle.

'There was a reason I chose that costume, you know. The Plague Doctor. A reason he forced it on the unfortunate Gabrielli too, I imagine. The thing sums up our position in a way. As quacks and frauds, hopeless spectators at a ceaseless banquet in which we can never fully participate. Had you been here a few centuries ago you would have found mountebanks and criminals wearing that long white nose. But decent men among them too. Ones who hoped to help. Who thought they might.'

He seemed briefly amused by some stray thought.

'Not that they'd have seen the fleas, of course. And even if they could, the good men would still be there, wouldn't they? Frittering away their time.'

With a couple of casual flicks he brushed his jacket to get rid of the breadcrumbs and odd lump of fish, the way a bachelor would.

Then he shook her hand briefly, smiled, looked into her face and said, 'It's time I was off. I'm honoured we met, Teresa Lupo. It's a matter of continuing regret it was under such difficult circumstances. I'm relieved Sofia's faith in her niece proved so well-founded. You are an extraordinary woman. It pains me we will never bump into one another again.'

This was happening too quickly.

'Wait, wait,' she said. 'Why not? Where are you going?'

He finished the spritz and stared appreciatively at the glass. Then he picked up the cane and his hat and got his feet, stretching, glancing towards the door.

'Every sane human being has to leave Venice after a while. Otherwise you never escape. I've a mind to go back to Penang. I've missed the asceticism of Islam of late. Or Istanbul. I have to say the Tanzimat period there was one of the more perilous interludes of my life, and Mahmud II a sultan I could never stomach. It takes a special breed of idiot to lose an entire country. Especially one like Greece. I ask you! But it was Constantinople back then, of course, a different place. Today . . .'

'Arnaud! *Arnaud*!'

She was on her feet too, so close to him she could detect an old-fashioned scent, like sandalwood, could see how his skin, neatly shaven, without a single blemish, shone with a wan and weathered vitality. His pale blue eyes were the colour of the spring sky, clear and perceptive, purposeful and direct.

'I'm sorry,' he said. 'I know. You don't want to hear. That's your prerogative, of course.'

He looked down. The dog uncurled itself and sat to attention in the erect, taut pose, ears pricked, eyes bright and expectant, that she recognized so well, from life and the canvas in the *scuola* round the corner.

'I have a favour to ask,' he added.

He reached into his pocket and took out a slender tan strip of leather, one so old the colour had faded to white in parts.

'You only need this on the vaporetto, and that's because of the damned regulations,' he said, waving the lead in front of her. 'On the street he's a perfect lamb. His name is Vittore. I'll leave you to work out the inspiration. I can't possibly take him on my travels. He understands Occitan, Veneto and Italian, in that order. But I'm sure you can bring him round. He's perfectly house-trained, aren't you?'

The dog was staring at him affectionately, tail wagging, a little bemused by this conversation.

'A saucer of warm milk, preferably from a coffee machine, is advisable around six thirty. Otherwise he feels unloved. His diet apart from that is very routine. Dry food, plenty of water. On no account let him eat brassica however much he pesters. The results . . .'

'Arnaud!' She took his arm and for some inexplicable reason felt her eyes begin to well with tears. 'I can't possibly take your dog.'

'He can't come where I'm going. Besides, strictly speaking he's not *my* dog. He was a stray. A rescue.

I took him in for company when I came back. He was decent enough to accept me.'

She watched as he bent down and patted the little animal twice on the head, looked into those bright black eyes, then got up, stifling a cough.

'He's about six years old, I think. That gives him another eight or so if you're fortunate.'

'Please don't do this . . .'

'There's a wisdom about dogs,' he went on, ignoring her. 'They're not like us, trying to brush mortality aside in the hope it might simply disappear. For a dog the idea of death is nothing more than a ridiculous fleeting nightmare. He lives in the full knowledge his existence will never come to an end. So every day begins afresh, every moment has some unforeseen promise in it.'

He reached over and threw some money on the counter.

'We can learn from this. We should. Some more than others.'

Arnaud, the Count of Saint-Germain – he would always bear that name – turned and stared at her, into her. At that moment he was the man from those strange stories, no one else, and Teresa had no idea what to do, to say or feel.

'We watch them grow, from puppy to prime to feeble old age. All in such a short space of time, for us anyway. A man or woman with feelings, witnessing this passage, remembers they're just like us. On the same journey. Merely one that happens to be a little shorter, with fewer opportunities perhaps, though full of all the same excitements and uncertainties, terrors and joys. The wisdom of dogs is to remind us of our own arrogance and stupidity in believing tomorrow may somehow prove more precious than today.'

His eyes never left her.

'I envy them that sometimes, which is deeply foolish, but more than anything I'm grateful for such a simple, innocent truth. It's been a source of comfort over the years. I tried to give the man you think of as Michael Ruskin a dog once but he never understood. Some people don't. I pity them.'

He placed the leash on the counter.

'Besides,' he added, suddenly brighter, 'Sofia once told me that lucky man of yours – Peroni? – adores animals as much as anyone, so I know he's going to a loving home.'

A smile returned. He seemed distracted, lost in his own private world.

'I tried to tell you a little of this in that very first story. In my own way. Somewhat cryptically, I imagine. Those were my words about dogs, not Sofia's. I knew all along it would probably come to this . . .' He pushed the lead towards her. 'What other ending could there be? But don't hate me for trying.'

'No,' she whispered, unable to think, to move.

'Vittore.' He crouched down, taking the animal's small head in his hands. 'She's yours now. Take good care of her.'

With that he picked up his hat, doffed it once, said a brief good-bye then walked briskly through the door of the little bar, out into the soft, warm evening.

The place was silent, deserted. There was no sign of the barman. Nothing but this little animal at her feet, staring up at her, expectant, as if on tenterhooks.

Teresa Lupo sat down, looked around her, at the machines and the books, the abandoned and broken contraptions and devices that men and women placed around themselves seeking amusement, enlightenment, some sense or reason for the passing days.

Settled at the wooden counter, the dog a white triangle beneath her, she stared out of the dusty windows, transfixed by the radiant light there, remembering the painting from the *scuola*, an image very like this.

The cartellino, she thought.

The imperfect, the unfinished. A cryptic scrawl by a long-dead genius, a question mark for eternity, passed on to successive generations to puzzle over and hope to unravel.

She reached down and touched the dog, smiling, saying his name . . .

Vittore.

It was carefully chosen, like all the words used by the man who liked to pretend he was someone, something else. Or, in his own terms, *was* him. *Is* him.

Tenses.

They matter.

The resolution she had proposed in the Aula San Trovaso could encompass many similar predicaments if she wished to be generous.

Victor Carpathius Fingebat.

She knocked back the rest of the spritz, closed her eyes and started to laugh. It was all so stupidly obvious, even a child should have seen it. And perhaps they did, only to forget later when adulthood came upon them.

The dog and the cartellino were saying the same thing, making an identical heartfelt call to the stiff, introverted man at the window, imprisoned by his books and machines and knowledge.

Teresa Lupo gazed into the gentle sunlight streaming through the dusty panes of the Cason dei Sette Morti and heard the words in her head, spoken in the calm and rational – perhaps *super-rational* – tones of the man she would always think of as Arnaud, the Count of Saint-Germain.

What next, the dog said in its master's voice.

What next?

AUTHOR'S NOTE

The Carpaccio paintings mentioned here can be viewed in the locations in the book, the delightful Scuola di San Giorgio degli Schiavoni in Castello and Room XX of the Accademia. Further information on the man known as the Count of Saint-Germain may also be found in the books referenced in the relevant chapters, from Pushkin to *Historical Mysteries*, the obscure memoir of Andrew Lang published in 1905.

Since this is a work of fiction I have taken severe liberties with some aspects of Venetian history and geography. The Casino degli Spiriti seen here is entirely imaginary, and nowhere near the building of the same name which is part of the Palazzo Contarini dal Zaffo in Cannaregio. The scratched outline of the murderous Turk holding a bleeding heart may in real life be found on the right-hand side of the main door of the Scuola Grande di San Marco, now the entrance to the hospital of Giovanni e Paolo. I'm grateful to Alberto Toso Fei's *Venetian Legends and Ghost Stories* for this and other information. Research photos taken during the writing of this book, and many other titles, can be found at davidhewson.com.

D.H., Venice, December 2009 to September 2010